"This book deserves INFINITY STARS."
—BRIE

"Twists and turns that left me dropping my jaw
and literally pontificating out loud."
—CORINNE

"Completely unpredictable...*No one is as they seem.*"
—KIANNA

"I devoured the book in under 48 hours!!"
—MADELEINE

"This book is a rollercoaster...
My jaw was consistently on the floor."
—KATELYN

"This book had me completely glued to my Kindle.
If I wasn't reading it, I was thinking about it."
—STEVIE

"A gripping read...[Karp]'s officially made it
onto my favorite authors list!"
—JULIE

"Wow! Wow! Wow!...Such a wild ride—five big stars!"
—LIKESTOTRAVEL

"A rollercoaster of emotion,
mystery, and rich storytelling that keeps you hooked...
This one is a must-read!"
—BRITTNEY

"An emotional, compelling read that stayed
with me long after I finished."
—ANGELA

PRAISE FOR MARSHALL KARP

"Marshall Karp is a genius storyteller!"
—HANK PHILLIPPI RYAN, *USA TODAY* BESTSELLING AUTHOR

"Marshall Karp knows how to keep a story running
full speed, full time."
—MICHAEL CONNELLY, #1 *NEW YORK TIMES* BESTSELLING AUTHOR

"Brings to mind Robert B. Parker, Janet Evanovich, Dean Koontz,
Stuart Woods, and a lot of other fast-paced authors."
—JANET MASLIN, *THE NEW YORK TIMES BOOK REVIEW*

"Marshall Karp is up there with Carl Hiaasen
and Donald Westlake and Janet Evanovich—smart, fast-paced,
clever, and really, really funny."
—JOSEPH FINDER, *NEW YORK TIMES* BESTSELLING AUTHOR

"Rousing…Shocking plot twists, clever dialogue,
and dead-on characterizations keep the pages turning.
Readers will agree that his happy welding of police procedural
and sly humor is the best yet in the series."
—PUBLISHERS WEEKLY (STARRED REVIEW) ON *NYPD RED 7*

"*NYPD Red 7: The Murder Sorority* is one of the most
engaging thrillers of the year. James Patterson could not have passed
down the torch to a more suited author than Karp."
—KASHIF HUSSAIN, BEST THRILLER BOOKS

"Totally original, a sheer roller-coaster ride, packed
with waves of humor and a dynamic duo in Lomax and Biggs.
Karp shows a master's touch in his debut."
—DAVID BALDACCI, #1 *NEW YORK TIMES* BESTSELLING AUTHOR, ON *THE RABBIT FACTORY*

"Smart, funny, and intuitive, Lomax and Biggs glide through the overlit shoals of Los Angeles like sharks through ginger ale."
—DONALD WESTLAKE ON *FLIPPING OUT*

"Marshall Karp could well be the Carl Hiaasen of Los Angeles—only I think he's even funnier. *The Rabbit Factory* will touch your funny bone and your heart."
—JAMES PATTERSON, #1 *NEW YORK TIMES* BESTSELLING AUTHOR

"Marshall Karp needs a blurb from me like Uma needs a facelift. This guy is the real deal, and *Bloodthirsty* is a first-class, fast, funny, and fabulous read by a terrific writer."
—JOHN LESCROART, *NEW YORK TIMES* BESTSELLING AUTHOR

"Blending the gritty realism of a Joseph Wambaugh police procedural with the sardonic humor of Janet Evanovich, Karp delivers a treat that's not only laugh-out-loud funny but also remarkably suspenseful."
—PUBLISHERS WEEKLY ON *FLIPPING OUT*

"Better than mostly anything on the market… *The Rabbit Factory* is, quite simply, stunning."
—CHRIS HIGH, *TANGLED WEB* AND *SHOTS MAGAZINE*

"Wickedly funny…this quirky, off-kilter novel also has a really big heart…[and] an emotional core that will make readers care about these tough but vulnerable crime fighters and keep them hoping for a sequel."
—BOOKREPORTER.COM ON *THE RABBIT FACTORY*

DON'T TELL ME
HOW TO DIE

BOOKS BY MARSHALL KARP

THE NYPD RED SERIES
NYPD Red 7: The Murder Sorority

COAUTHORED WITH JAMES PATTERSON
NYPD Red 6
Red Alert (a.k.a. *NYPD Red 5*)
NYPD Red 4
NYPD Red 3
NYPD Red 2
NYPD Red

THE LOMAX AND BIGGS MYSTERIES
Terminal
Cut, Paste, Kill
Flipping Out
Bloodthirsty
The Rabbit Factory

DANNY CORCORAN AND THE BALTIC AVENUE GROUP
Snowstorm in August

STANDALONE NOVELS
Kill Me if You Can (with James Patterson)

NEW YORK TIMES BESTSELLING AUTHOR OF NYPD RED 7

MARSHALL KARP

DON'T TELL ME HOW TO DIE

BLACK STONE PUBLISHING

Printed in the United States of America

First edition: 2025
ISBN 979-8-8748-2439-6
Fiction / Thrillers / Domestic

Blackstone Publishing
31 Mistletoe Rd.
Ashland, OR 97520

www.BlackstonePublishing.com

For Sean, Ed, Tom, and Dennis.
Thanks, guys.

PROLOGUE
THE ANGEL OF DEATH

ONE

At six feet eight, 360 pounds, Irv Hollingsworth was not only the biggest TV weatherman in Heartstone, New York; his larger-than-life personality and his flair for showmanship had made him the most popular in the county.

Which is why instead of reporting from a warm, dry studio that watershed June morning, Big Irv, dressed in bright yellow waist-high waders and a matching XXXXL slicker, was broadcasting live from Magic Pond during a torrential downpour.

"I'm here at Heartstone Medical Center," he said, letting the rain lash his face for effect. "The hospital has been operating on auxiliary power for the last twelve hours. And I do mean operating. I spoke to the chief surgeon, Dr. Alex Dunn, and he told Channel Six that despite this nor'easter, it's business as usual inside.

"But outside is a whole different story." The camera panned to take in the rest of the medical center's campus. Big Irv slogged across the muddy grounds to the swollen edges of Magic Pond, which had crested far beyond its banks.

"Normally, this is where hospital workers and locals would be sitting around enjoying their morning coffee," he said, stopping at a partially submerged bench, its seat lost beneath the murky waters. "But as you can see, Magic Pond has—"

And then, as if the media gods had come down to help the big man claim his place in broadcasting history, she appeared on camera. A woman. Floating face down on the surface of the pond.

For a second, maybe two, the only sound that could be heard was the white noise of the rain hammering on the water. Then Big Irv regained his composure and heralded her arrival with two words. Probably not the same two that most people would choose, but Irv was a TV pro. He knew what would resonate.

"Good Lord," he said in a reverent hush.

Within seconds, the internet's lust for the bizarre kicked into high gear, and the video of the hulking man in a yellow rain slicker gently guiding the sad remains of a woman in a lavender sweat suit to shore spread like a virus on steroids.

Within minutes, Big Irv, a local celebrity here in Heartstone, would be seen by millions of people around the world. I'm the mayor of Heartstone, and I'll bet that the mayor of Helsinki saw the poignant footage before I did. It's the curse of social media. Death and bad weather course through the ether with the speed of light.

As Irv's star was rising, mine was rapidly sinking. Thirty hours of relentless rain had left my town with roads that were submerged, trash pickups that were suspended, power lines that were down, and emergency services that were stretched to the limit.

My inbox was also flooded. The emails were split between my being woefully unprepared or deplorably unresponsive. Either way, I expected the front page of the *Heartstone Crier* to be a photo montage of downed trees, mud-caked basements, and disabled cars in three feet of water. The headline might not say "This Mess Is All Mayor Dunn's Fault," but society needs a scapegoat, and I was the obvious front-runner.

And then came the coup de grâce. Chief Vanderbergen called.

"Minna Schultz is dead," he said. "Her body was found floating in Magic Pond."

Immediately, my instincts as a former prosecutor for the DA's office kicked in. "Foul play?" I asked.

"The ME isn't here yet," the chief said.

"But *you* are," I said. "What's your take?"

"There's no obvious signs of trauma, but let's face it, the woman had enemies."

Enemies was an understatement. Minna Schultz had destroyed a lot of people's lives over the years. Most of them would probably show up at her wake just to make sure she was really dead.

"Of course we can't rule out suicide," the chief added.

"Absolutely," I said, although I doubted it. Anyone who ever met Minna would know that she wouldn't have the common decency to whack herself.

"One more thing, Mayor Dunn. The Channel Six weather guy discovered the body while he was on the air. The video has gone viral."

"Shit," I muttered. "So we're talking media frenzy."

"Yes, ma'am."

"I'll be there as soon as I can," I said, ending the call.

"Madam Mayor," a familiar voice said.

I looked up, and there she was, standing in my doorway, a dripping-wet pink umbrella in one hand, the tools of her ugly trade in the other.

The Angel of Death.

She was blond, in her early thirties, and still holding on to her kick-ass high school cheerleader body and flawless skin. Her name was Rachel Horton, and like the six other phlebotomists who had come before her, her job was to draw my blood three times a year to make sure I hadn't contracted the same fatal disease that killed my mother.

It had been a medical ritual for me and my sister Lizzie for over a quarter of a century. But this was the first time one of those smiling bloodsuckers ever showed up in my office unannounced.

"Rachel," I said. "Whatever it is, I have no time for you."

She flashed me a perfect smile and held up her blue soft-sided medical tote bag. "I only need a minute, Mayor Dunn," she said, as perky as a Girl Scout delivering a box of Thin Mints. "Dr. Byrne needs some more blood."

"What did he do with the blood I gave him last week?"

"He said the lab screwed up," Rachel said, capping off the ominous news with yet another sunny smile that was so genuine I realized I'd misjudged her. Rachel was not the Grim Reaper. She was more like one of those lovable yellow Minions, gullible enough to believe that the lab actually bungled a routine blood test.

The lab screwed up. I've been married to a surgeon long enough to know medical malarkey when I hear it. It's a classic doctor ploy. Rather than tell you straight up that your first set of test results looks suspicious, they give you the healthcare equivalent of "the dog ate my homework."

But I knew the truth. My white blood cells were amassing the troops and were hell-bent on killing me just like they killed my mother.

"Make it fast," I said, sitting back down at my desk.

"You'll feel a little prick," the sweet young thing said to me with a straight face, which never fails to make me wonder if she gets the sexual innuendo. She stuck the needle in my vein, and I closed my eyes.

It was a Thursday. I would have to wait till Monday before my hematologist made it official, but when you have a fatal disease hanging over your head for twenty-six years, you learn to arrive at your own medical conclusions before your doctor has the clinical proof and the balls to tell you what you already figured out.

I was dying.

"What's so funny?" Rachel asked.

I hadn't realized I was grinning, but I had to admit that my entire morning was rife with macabre humor. I was only a few weeks past my forty-third birthday, and I suddenly realized that I was going to be spending my forty-fourth with Minna Schultz. In hell.

Yeah, hell.

I'm a fairly popular mayor and a rather well-liked human being. On paper I look like a shoo-in to be ushered through the Pearly Gates and into the Kingdom of Heaven by St. Peter himself. That's just because I've been able to hide the truth from the rest of world.

But I can't hide from God, so I had no doubt that when my time was up, I was destined to spend eternity burning in hell for my sins.

TWO

Rachel removed the needle, put a piece of gauze over the vein, and taped it to my arm. "There you go," she said. "You survived another one."

Survived, I thought. Interesting choice of terms.

She zipped up her bag and gave me a cheery "Have a good one."

I wasn't having a good one when you got here, and I'm certainly not going to have one now, I thought, but I opted for, "You too. Close the door on your way out."

Minna Schultz would have to wait. I went to my laptop and typed into the Google search bar: *How often do labs screw up blood tests*. Google, always trying to stay one step ahead of me, immediately gave me some options to finish my question: *in cats, in dogs, in criminal cases, in early pregnancy.*

"This is not a good day to test me, Google," I said, banging out the words *in humans* on my keyboard.

I got ninety-six million results. I scanned the first few till I found an encouraging number. Labs make twelve million mistakes a year.

Yes, but out of how many, I thought, trying to decide if twelve million was a life raft. I was about to explore Google's credibility quotient by typing in *How many dogs a year actually do eat homework*, when my cell phone rang.

I looked at the caller ID and burst out laughing.

It said JIFFY ESCORT SERVICE.

My husband, Alex, the absolute love of my life, knows how to make me laugh. One of his favorite pranks is to sneak into my phone and change his name in my contacts. Today his timing was off. I stifled the laugh and answered the phone.

"I heard," I said, throwing on my coat. "I'm on my way."

"I'm at the pond," he said. "How are you holding up?"

How was I holding up? I wanted to take him in my arms and say, "You run the damn hospital. Can you find out if some klutz in the lab spilled their Red Bull all over my last blood test, or am I a dead woman walking?"

But nothing sours Alex faster than a whiny patient having an "I know I'm going to die" episode. I let it go.

"It's going to take us at least a week to get back to normal," I said, "but I managed to get the County Environmental Commission to send two generator trucks, so I have the equipment I need to keep our little shitstorm from overflowing into the Hudson River."

"Great. You can play that up when you run for reelection."

Reelection. More dark humor. God was working overtime today.

"What's going on at the pond?" I asked.

"A few dozen people braved the storm in the beginning, but the rain is finally starting to let up, and the crowd behind the yellow tape is starting to build."

"Tell Chief Vanderbergen to take pictures. They're all suspects."

"I doubt it. I saw the body. No sign of trauma. I don't think we're looking at a homicide, Maggie."

"Suicide?" I said.

"Not my call," he said. "That's for the medical examiner to decide."

"Alex . . ."

"What?"

"How are *you* holding up?"

He let out a long exhale. "Minna Schultz has been a roadblock to everything we're trying to do here at the hospital. That's over now, but I would feel a whole lot better if we beat her in court. This . . . this just leaves a stain on the whole project."

"If she did commit suicide, that would be her motive," I said. "She knew she couldn't win, so rather than lose publicly, she decided to piss all over your victory on her way out."

"You sound like a lawyer."

"A lawyer in desperate need of a hug," I said. "I'll be there in ten. Love you."

"What an incredible coincidence," he said. "I love me too."

It was a tired old line, but it always made me smile.

I hung up, looked down, and it caught my eye. The gauze bandage that Rachel had taped to my arm.

I peeled it off and tossed it. But I couldn't ignore it. It was a graphic reminder that I had been getting ready for this day for more than half my life.

The first time I found out I was a candidate for an early grave, I was seventeen. You'd think it would have destroyed me. Just the opposite. It was the perfect excuse to break away from my poster-child-for-teenage-excellence image. I was still president of my class, snagging straight As, going to church on Sundays, and rocking the SATs with a 1500, but once Dr. Byrne told me I had the markers for a fatal inflammatory blood disease, I developed an instant case of the fuck-its.

Sex, drugs, alcohol, rule-breaking, risk-taking? Fuck it. If I was going to die young, I was going to live life as hard as I can.

Of course, I couldn't compete with my best friend, Misty Sinclair, a one-woman wrecking ball who'd call me and say, "Let's crank shit up to eleven and break off the knob." But I ran a pretty strong second. Because, hey . . . what the hell did I have to lose?

And then I met Alex Dunn, and suddenly I had an anchor in the insanity of my life. Three years later, when I gave birth to Kevin and Katie, my Mommy genes kicked in, and I found a purpose beyond the adrenaline rush of survival.

Dying young was no longer all about me. It was about them. What would happen to them if I died?

The more I ruminated about it, the more obsessed I became with their lives after my death. It was not a random obsession. My shrink confirmed what I already knew. It was PTSD.

When my mother died, I watched in horror as women circled my grieving father like hammerheads on a feeding frenzy. And when the wrong woman stepped in to take my mother's place, the consequences were devastating.

I refused to let the same thing happen to Alex and my kids. I know it sounds insane, but the idea I'd buried in the darkest recesses of my brain became a priority as soon as the Angel of Death with her little pink umbrella showed up at my door.

I was going to spend my last remaining days on earth searching for the next Mrs. Dunn. I might not find her, but I would die trying.

PART ONE
WOMEN WITH CASSEROLES

CHAPTER 1

TWENTY-SIX YEARS BEFORE THE FUNERAL

I've had twenty-six years to contemplate the fact that a ripe old age might not be in the cards for me. But my mother was caught completely by surprise. She thought she still had half her life ahead of her when the doctor blindsided her with the diagnosis—hemophagocytic lymphohistiocytosis. They call it HLH because it's impossible to pronounce. It's also impossible to cure. But they don't tell you that.

"There are new advances in chemotherapy every day," Dr. Byrne told her. "They may not be the wonder drug we're hoping for, Kate, but they can slow down the spread. They can buy you time."

Time. That was the magic word. Time to impart more of her life skills to her teenage daughters, time to allow her husband to come to grips with his impending loss, time to savor the familiar warmth of her countless friends.

She knew that the ravages of chemotherapy could steal the very time it was supposed to deliver. But her doctor was optimistic, her 24/7-support group was deep and unwavering, and she knew that everyone at St. Cecilia's parish would be praying for a miracle.

"I've decided to go ahead with the chemo," she told us at dinner that snowy December night. Six months later, she told us how much she regretted that decision.

I remember that day vividly. It was the start of the summer between my junior and senior year in high school, and I was in the kitchen of our family restaurant cracking lobster claws for the lunch special.

It was a mindless job, which gave me the opportunity to use my brain to focus on something much more important—coming up with a killer essay for my college applications. Would it be better, I mused, to write about something global like the technology revolution, or should I stick to the tried and true—a personal challenge I've overcome, and how it shaped my—

"Yo, Maggie, what the hell are you doing?"

I looked up. It was my sister Lizzie.

"What does it look like I'm doing?" I said. "I'm prepping for Chef Tommy."

"Sure you are. I'm tempted to tell Grandpa Mike to change the blackboard from creamy lobster bisque to extra crunchy, but I don't want to spend the whole day giving the Heimlich maneuver to people who are choking on soup."

She reached down into the bowl of lobster meat I'd been filling and started picking out the shells I'd been absentmindedly tossing in.

"Sorry. I was deep in thought."

"You daydreaming about Van again?" Lizzie asked.

"No. My *Vantasies* are strictly a bedtime thing. I was trying to work out an idea for a college essay."

"Well, you better work fast. Applications are due by December thirty-first, and—oh my God—it's June twenty-fourth already. You're running out of time!"

Lizzie is my Irish twin, born 314 days after me. She's also my fiercest competitor, my biggest pain in the ass, and my dearest friend. I love her beyond words, which is appropriate since I hardly ever come right out and say it. She, in turn, expresses her affection for me by busting my chops on a regular basis.

She clutched her throat with both hands and began to gag. "I can feel the pressure building. If only you had been elected president of next year's senior class. Oh, wait—you were," she said, relaxing the choke hold. "Problem solved."

"You know how many class presidents apply to college?" I said, picking out the last of the rogue shells. "I'm not that unique."

"You could be if you wrote about how you miraculously managed to get elected despite living your entire life in your younger sister's shadow."

I was working on a comeback line when we both heard the throaty growl of the Harley Electra Glide as it barreled up Pine Street.

"Here comes Dad," I said.

"Sucking the serenity right out of the neighborhood," Lizzie added.

Dad's motorcycle roared into the parking lot and stopped at the reserved space next to the kitchen door.

Chef Tommy banged a metal spoon on an empty soup pot three times, and everyone in the kitchen—me and Lizzie included—yelled out in unison, "God bless Black Monday."

It's the standard homage whenever my father arrives at the restaurant—kind of like playing "Hail to the Chief" for the president. There's a long story behind that ritual, and it gets recounted every year at the Thanksgiving feast for our employees and their families.

The back door swung open, and Finn McCormick charged into the room. He's a big man, six feet four, barrel-chested, with a full head of thick hair that shook loose when he removed his helmet. He peeled off his leather jacket and yelled, "What's cooking?" to the kitchen crew.

It's a far cry from his past life with his preppy haircut, conservative suits, and monthly commuter ticket to his job as a stockbroker on Wall Street. That's the life that ended eleven years ago when the market crashed.

"Good news, girls," he said, spreading his arms wide. "You are done. Get out of here."

"Are we fired?" Lizzie said. "Or did Child Protective Services finally catch up with you?"

That got a belly laugh. "You wish," he said. "But alas, it's only a brief reprieve. Your mom wants me to give you the rest of the day off and send you home."

"Is she okay?" I said.

"Hard to say. What woman in her right mind wants to spend the day with her teenage daughters?" He flashed us a wide grin. "Just kidding. She seemed downright chipper all morning. Oh yeah—she's fixing lunch, so she told me to tell you not to eat here."

"Don't eat at McCormick's," Lizzie said. "Good advice."

Another big laugh from my father. Which of course was Lizzie's mission in life. Early on she had decided she wanted to be a doctor, and ever since she read about the healing powers of laughter she became the family stand-up comic commando, bombarding us with one-liners every time any of us had so much as a sniffle.

My mother, of course, had a lot more than a sniffle.

"Dad, are you sure she's okay?" I asked again.

"She looks better than she's looked in months," he said. "Besides, you know your mom. If she wasn't okay, she wouldn't want you guys around."

"That's great news, Dad," Lizzie said. Then she turned to me. "Especially for you, Lobster Girl."

"What do you mean especially for me?"

"*How My Mother Beat a Rare Blood Disease*," she said. "It's got all the makings of a great college essay."

CHAPTER 2

Lizzie got her driver's license when she turned sixteen in March, and the four-year-old Acura Integra that had been all mine for ten months now belonged to both of us. We can barely share a bathroom, so we politicked for another car. But our parents' logic, which basically boiled down to "you go to the same school—just work it out," prevailed.

"I'm driving," Lizzie said when we got to the parking lot.

"Fine," I said. "But that means I'm in charge of the radio."

"Oh God, you're going to play that annoying shitkicker music, aren't you?"

"I won't know till I'm on the road. Make a decision," I said, jangling the keys in front of her.

"This is why we each should have our own car," she said, snapping the keys out of my hand.

She got behind the wheel, and I started rifling through the CDs.

I pulled out a Garth Brooks album, popped it into the CD player, and turned up the volume.

The pub is only three miles from our house, but it was enough time to make her sit through four annoying shitkicker songs.

There was a lime-green Honda Civic hatchback with a mashed right rear fender parked in front of our house.

"Nurse Demmick is here," I said as Lizzie pulled into the driveway.

Marjorie Demmick is the school nurse at Heartstone High, a friend of my mother's from church, and one of a small platoon of women who have been there for her during her illness.

We were just getting out of the car when Marjorie, who always looks like she's in a hurry, bustled out of the front door of the house.

She's short, plump, with beautiful ivory skin, and a head full of tight red ringlets. "Hello, girls," she called out in a squeaky voice that would be adorable for a character in an animated movie, but is extremely grating in real life. "Enjoying your summer vacation?"

"We are indentured servants at an Irish pub," Lizzie said. "Can't wait till September. How's Mom?"

"Well, I just spent some time with her, and this is the best I've seen her in months. She even put on some makeup today. I couldn't stop telling her how beautiful she looked. And now she's puttering around the kitchen like . . . like . . . like . . ." She pursed her lips and looked up at the sky, grasping for an analogy.

"Julia Child? Martha Stewart? Betty Crocker?" Lizzie ventured.

"Oh, that's so funny," Marjorie squealed. "You girls are so smart."

"But you think she's doing well," I said.

"Oh yes. Look, I'm only a school nurse, but I think her treatment is working. And I'll bet now that you two are here, she is going to get even better."

Nurse Demmick was like a walking, breathing Hallmark card. I've never seen her anything but upbeat and positive.

We thanked her for stopping in, said goodbye, and opened the front door. The intoxicating aroma hit me immediately.

"In the kitchen," my mother called out in a singsong voice. "I hope you're hungry."

The kitchen smelled like the inside of a Cinnabon. Mom was just taking a pan out of the oven. She set it down and turned around.

Nurse Demmick was right. My mother looked beautiful. She was wearing a flowery pink summer dress, her strawberry blond hair was tied back in a ponytail, and her face, which had been drawn and tired for months, had a rosy glow. I didn't know if it was from the makeup or the medical treatment, but I didn't care. I hadn't seen my mother looking this good in a long time.

Lizzie inhaled the sweet fragrance that had hit us when we walked in and would seduce passersby on the street if we left the windows open. "Cinnamon swirl raisin bread," she said. "What's the occasion?"

My mother, who has never been the type to pull any punches, smiled. "I'm vertical—an occasion definitely worth celebrating. When was the last time we had a mother-daughters picnic?"

If she had asked that question when we were seven and eight years old, the answer probably would have been last weekend. But once we became teenagers, picnics at the park were replaced by volleyball team practice, homework, babysitting, and talking incessantly with other girls about boys.

"Everything is packed and ready to go," she said, pointing to an ancient handwoven picnic basket that was sitting on the countertop. "All I need is ten minutes to make the Monkey Paws. Then we're going to Magic Pond."

"I'm driving," Lizzie said.

"*I'm* driving," my mother corrected. "We're taking the Mustang."

The 1996 red Mustang GT convertible was my father's gift to my mother on her fortieth birthday the year before. It had less than two thousand miles on it when she got sick and couldn't leave the house. Dad started it every week and would drive Mom to her doctor appointments in it, but Lizzie and I had never been behind the wheel. It was *Mom's Wheels.*

"Chop, chop," Mom said. "Wash up, so we can get this show on the road."

"I've got the bathroom first," Lizzie said, bolting toward the stairs.

"You look fantastic," I said to my mother, giving her a gentle hug.

"You should have seen me when I was your age. Boys were dropping like flies."

She turned back to the oven, popped the golden-brown loaf out of the pan, and expertly drew a knife across the center. Steam lofted up from the fresh-baked bread.

"Perfect," she said. "I've had a wonderful morning, and it's going to be a glorious afternoon."

And it was.

Until the four words.

CHAPTER 3

During my mother's illness, my father had lovingly washed and waxed the Mustang, so when Mom backed it out of the garage for the first time in months, the bright red car gleamed in the afternoon sun like one of those vintage fire engines that roll up Waterfront Avenue every Fourth of July.

The top was down, the shiny black boot snapped snugly in place, and with her mixtape already queued up in the cassette player, Mom made it clear that she was not only behind the wheel; she was also in charge of the music.

While Mom was packing the picnic basket, Lizzie and I had tried to guess what the first song on the tape would be.

"Slam dunk," Lizzie said. "'Love Will Keep Us Together.' The Captain and Tennille. It's Mom's go-to song."

"Too predictable," I said. "That first song is not going to be about the music. I know Mom. We're on our way to Magic Pond for the first time since we went ice-skating in December just before she got sick. She's going to want to come up with something that's totally about the moment."

"Spare me the logic," Lizzie said, "and cough up a song title."

"'Teddy Bear's Picnic.'"

"From when we were in *kindergarten*?" Lizzie said, like it was the dumbest idea in the world. But then she shrugged because, on second thought, it was just the kind of crazy sentimental thing my mother might do.

Lizzie and I played Rock-Paper-Scissors to see who would ride shotgun. I won. She climbed in back, and I settled into the soft leather bucket seat up front.

Mom pulled the Mustang onto the street, and the moment we'd been waiting for arrived. She tapped a button on the cassette player, and the warm whiskey voice of a Texas shitkicker erupted from the speaker.

Lizzie clapped both hands to her cheeks, looked up at the sky, and yelled, "Oh my God." Not because it was the country music she hated but because the choice was so inspired. She leaned over and kissed Mom on the back of the neck.

And as we drove down Crystal Avenue on that glorious summer afternoon, the four of us—Lizzie, me, Mom, and Willie Nelson—sang about the joys of being on the road again.

Ten minutes later we arrived at Magic Pond, found a quiet shady spot to spread our blanket, and walked over to the water's edge.

The pond is large by city standards, a two-acre freshwater ecosystem where birds, frogs, plants, bugs, and people coexist in quiet harmony. I inhaled deeply, and a sense of serenity washed over me as I studied the reflections in the water—the trees, the clouds, and of course, the seven-story hospital complex that loomed above it all.

Magic Pond is not part of a city park. It is the centerpiece of Heartstone Medical Center. The story of how that came to be is a hodgepodge of fact, fiction, and folklore.

This is what I know to be true. In 1872 Elias Majek, a young brickmaker from Germany, immigrated to America and settled in the Hudson Valley, where the soil was rich in clay deposits.

His timing was perfect. As immigrants teemed into New York City by the hundreds of thousands, the demand for bricks to raise the metropolis to new heights skyrocketed. And by the dawn of the twentieth century, Elias and Eleanor Majek were the wealthiest couple in the county, living in a forty-two-room mansion looking out at lush gardens, abundant fruit orchards, and their magnificent freshwater pond.

In 1912, at the age of seventy, Elias sold the brickyard and celebrated his retirement by taking Eleanor on a long-overdue vacation. They sailed across the Atlantic aboard the luxurious ocean liner *Mauretania*. It was a far cry from the passage he had made forty years earlier, when he came to America in the steerage compartment of an ancient steamer out of Hamburg.

They spent the next month touring Europe in grand style, but Elias was saving the best for last. He had a special surprise planned for their trip back to New York, and on April 10, 1912, the happy couple arrived in Southampton on the southern coast of England for the maiden voyage of the world's largest ocean liner, White Star's queen of the seas—*Titanic*.

Five days later Elias perished in the frigid waters of the North Atlantic when the unsinkable ship hit an immovable iceberg.

Eleanor was one of 705 passengers rescued from their lifeboats by the RMS *Carpathia*. A year later she contracted tuberculosis. It's at this point that the story of the Majek legacy becomes shrouded in mystery.

It's been said that Eleanor's doctor gave her less than six months to live. She spent much of that time sitting by the pond, reading, drawing, or writing in her diary. But instead of dying, her health improved, and she survived for another nine years.

When she died in 1923, she bequeathed her property to the people of Heartstone with the stipulation that her home be converted into a hospital. She also requested in her will that the pond not be reconfigured or altered in any way in order to preserve its magical restorative powers.

Over the decades the hospital doubled and tripled in size, and then doubled again. And Majek Pond became Magic Pond as generations of people trekked to its banks to pray for speedy recoveries, healthy babies, or medical miracles.

And now my mother, my sister, and I stood on the shore, ready to entrust our most fervent desires to God, Jesus, and the ghost of Eleanor Majek.

Mom unsnapped the brass clasp on the cracked leather change purse that had belonged to her mother. She plucked three pennies from the pouch and gave one to each of us. One by one we closed our eyes and tossed the coins into the water.

"Now let's eat, drink, and be silly," my mother said.

We sprawled out on the blanket; Mom opened the picnic basket and passed out the Monkey Paws. It's the name Grandpa Mike gave to Grandma Caroline's peanut butter, honey, and banana sandwiches on fresh-baked cinnamon swirl raisin bread.

I was starved and attacked the gooey, chewy treat. Lizzie began wolfing hers down as well. Mom poured three cups of strawberry lemonade from a Thermos and nibbled at her sandwich.

"I have a surprise," she said. "You know all those pictures I have in shoeboxes that I've been threatening to sort through one of these years?"

I stopped eating as she reached into the picnic basket and pulled out a thick photo album bound in bright green fabric. *The McCormick Family* had been carefully inked on the cover in Mom's perfect Catholic schoolgirl handwriting.

"Ta-da!" she said, setting it down on the blanket.

Lizzie opened it to the first page, and there were four black-and-white shots of Mom, Dad, and the Harley Electra Glide, each one taken in a different location.

"These are from 1979," Mom said. "Your father and I went to the biker rally in Sturgis, South Dakota. It was our last big road trip—thirty-five hundred miles—and I was pregnant with Maggie at the time. I don't know what I was thinking."

"Sounds like the poor kid got bounced around a little," Lizzie said.

"More than a little. It was almost all interstate, but I had to make a lot of pee stops, and some of those side roads were bumpy as washboards."

Lizzie drummed on the side of her head with both fists and smirked at me. "Well, that explains a lot," she said.

Mom turned the page, and there was an artfully arranged cluster of pictures of me as a baby.

"Oh, there's the little darling now," Lizzie said.

I put my hand over the pictures. "Stop," I said. "What's going on?"

They both stared at me.

"What are you talking about?" Lizzie said.

I ignored her, closed the album, and slid it to the side. "Mom . . . what's going on?"

She kept staring at me, stone-faced.

"Maggie, what the hell are you doing?" Lizzie said. "Mom's finally having a good day, and you're ruining it."

"I'm sorry. I'm not used to Mom having good days lately, and I'm trying to ask her if it's real."

"I don't get it," Lizzie said.

"She got sick in December, and she kept getting sicker, and then she wakes up one day in June, and like Cinderella, she's all dressed, and her hair is done, and we drive to Magic Pond for a picnic, and now all of a sudden there's a family photo album, which has been on her bucket list for years, and I just want to know what's going on. Is this real, or does the Mustang turn into a pumpkin at midnight?"

Lizzie didn't say a word. She was wrestling with my logic, and I could see in her eyes that my questions were starting to make sense.

She turned to my mother for answers.

Mom just looked at us. Well, she didn't exactly look. She kind of squared off, sizing us up, like we were about to get in the ring and go fifteen rounds.

And then she said them.

Four simple words that she uttered only once. Yet of all the hundreds of millions of words I have heard before or since, those are the four that will forever be burned into my soul.

I have written them in the margins of countless notebooks, screamed them into caves and canyons so I could hear their taunting echoes, traced them onto frosty car windows and steamy shower doors, and ached as I watched them trickle down into trails of tears.

Four words.

How strong are you?

CHAPTER 4

Life is filled with defining moments—those pivotal points in time where your entire world can change in a heartbeat.

By the age of seventeen I'd had a few, but none that I couldn't handle. It's not just that I was lucky or blessed, which admittedly I was, it's more that when things don't go my way, I have this unique ability to turn them around.

My father calls it Irish grit. Mom said it was a gift. Lizzie has a different take. She says, "The only reason everything works out exactly the way Maggie wants is because she's an obsessively compulsive micromanaging control freak."

Harsh. But not without merit.

This time was different. I knew from the look in my mother's eyes that this would not be something I could fix. I didn't know exactly what she'd say next, but I knew that this picnic in the park would not have a happy ending.

How strong was I?

"Very," I lied, my mouth dry, my breathing shallow.

"And I'm stronger than Maggie," Lizzie said. "Ask anybody."

Mom smiled. She'd always been so proud of Lizzie's bravado. She took a deep breath. "It's not working," she said.

"What?" Lizzie said. "What's not working?"

"The transfusions, the new chemo, the brilliant doctors . . . hundreds of people praying for me . . . nothing is working."

"Don't give up," Lizzie said. "It's only been a few months. The next round of transfusions is going to do it."

"There is no next round. This past one was a Hail Mary. It didn't work, and there's nothing left to try. Dr. Byrne had a long talk with me yesterday. I'm out of options . . . and I'm almost out of time."

"I don't understand. You seem so healthy," Lizzie said, her fists clenched, her body taut, determined to reverse Mom's news with irrefutable logic. "You're baking bread. You're driving the car. You look fantastic."

"It's all smoke and mirrors. Dr. Byrne put together some kind of concoction with vitamin B-12, antioxidants, and God knows what else, and Marjorie Demmick came over this morning, gave me a shot in the ass, touched up the outside with a little blush, added some pink lipstick, and presto change-o, I look like a million bucks. But Maggie was on the right track. The Mustang won't turn into a pumpkin, but by tomorrow morning I'll look like two cents."

I felt the tears welling up. "Why would you do this?" I said. "This whole . . . charade? Why did you get our hopes up?"

"I made a big mistake." She reached across the blanket and put one hand on my knee, the other on Lizzie's arm. "I never should have put myself through all those medical procedures hoping for a miracle. I should have spent these past six months with you. I can't get any of that precious time back, so I asked Dr. Byrne if there was anything he could do to give me one more joyful day with my daughters. This was supposed to be it, but you caught me. I am so, so sorry. I wasn't trying to get your hopes up. I was trying to give you one last final happy memory."

"Dad came into the restaurant all excited this morning," I said. "He was going on like you'd turned the corner. He really thinks you're getting better, doesn't he?"

Mom nodded. "Your father is the world's worst poker player. If I told him the truth, you'd have read it in his face, and I wanted one last sunny afternoon with you before you found out. I'll tell him tonight. The big man is going to crumble. He's going to need you to help him get through this." She shook her head. "No, it's more than that. You're all going to need to help each other."

Lizzie got to her feet. "But first I need a group hug."

We helped Mom get up, and the three of us embraced for a solid minute. No tears, just silence, each of us wrestling with her own thoughts.

"I'm writing you each a letter," my mother said when we finally let go. She lowered herself to the blanket, and Lizzie and I dropped down next to her. "I started writing them back in February. You know what they say—'hope for the best, but plan for the worst.'

"I'm glad I started when I did, because I didn't realize how much I have to tell you. I'd been planning to spread it out over the next forty or fifty years, but now the best I can do is a crash course. I tried to think about all the important advice a mother can give her daughters. Things you can't learn in books. Or worse yet, there are dozens of books on the subject, every one of them with their own point of view, and I wanted to make sure you had the wit and wisdom of Kate McCormick before you made any life-altering decisions."

"I hate to break it to you, Mom," Lizzie said, "but if your letter to Maggie has any good advice on the virtues of remaining a virgin till her wedding night, you're too late."

That broke the ice. Mom howled in laughter. I poked Lizzie in the arm, but I didn't care. I was pretty sure my mother had already figured it out. And I was also confident that she hadn't shared her suspicions with my overprotective father.

I have no idea how many times the three of us have been to Magic Pond together, but the next two hours were the best ever. First, we went through the photo album, and page by page, with Mom giving us a hilarious running narrative, we watched ourselves grow up.

And then we talked. No subject was off-limits. Thinking back, I realize that we asked my mother a lot of questions about her past—her childhood, her achievements in school, and of course, everything she could possibly tell us about her relationship with my dad from the first day she met him.

Her questions to us focused on the future. She asked about our plans, our dreams, and so many of the other parts of our lives she knew she wouldn't be here to watch unfold. To this day, I wish we could relive that moment, and give Mom better answers. Lizzie knew she wanted to become a doctor, and eventually she did. But all I could tell my dying mother at the age of seventeen was that the University of Pennsylvania was my first-choice college.

I never got the chance to tell her that I married a wonderful man; had two beautiful, intelligent, healthy children; found a challenging career that brought me joy and would make her proud; and that my life was purposeful, productive, and relevant.

But there are times, especially when I'm alone in my private little attic hideaway rereading her handwritten eighteen-page letter to the teenage me, that I feel she is up there with me, and she not only knows what I've accomplished but she also knows I couldn't have done it without her inspiration.

At about three o'clock that afternoon, Mom started to fade. The magic elixir Nurse Demmick had given her was starting to wear off.

"You're looking tired," I said. "Why don't we pack up and go. We can talk more later. Dad's going to bring home dinner."

"Okay, but let's stay five more minutes," Mom said. "There's one more thing on my mind, and I can't talk about it at home."

"Lay it on us," Lizzie said.

And then my mother dropped the second bomb.

CHAPTER 5

"This is about your father," my mother said. A smile bloomed on her face at the mere mention of him. "He's only forty-three years old, and that man is tough as nails. He's going to live at least another forty-three years—probably more.

"But . . ." she said, and then paused, choosing her words carefully. "But he's not going to want to spend all that time alone."

"Don't worry, Mom," Lizzie said. "Maggie and I will be there for him. We promise." She turned to me for confirmation.

"I don't think that's what she's saying, Liz." I looked at my mother. "You know we'll be there for him, but that's not what you're talking about. Right?"

"Right. Let me try it again. Lizzie, your father will grieve when I'm gone. You all will," she added quickly. "I know how difficult it will be, but when the initial pain lifts, and I promise you it will, you and Maggie will move forward in the very same direction you were headed—college, a career, marriage, a family . . ."

We nodded, still not sure where this was going.

"It won't be the same for your father," she said. "Years ago, he and I charted a course from our twenties all the way into old age. We had plans; we had dreams. Nothing exotic. Just the simple things most married couples think about—retirement, a house on a lake, travel. But when I die, a lot of those dreams will die with me, and with the path to his future gone, I'm afraid he'll be rudderless . . . lost at sea."

Lizzie looked lost herself. I knew Mom had something important to say, but she was treading so lightly that it was hard to connect the dots.

"I spoke to Father Connelly," she said. "The church has support groups to help people get through their loss. There's one specifically for teens."

"We'll be okay, Mom," Lizzie said. "Maggie and I have each other."

"That's your choice, but tonight when I talk to your father, I'm going to ask him to please go to some of the meetings for widows and widowers. Father Connelly told me it's the best way for him to cope with his loss. I know he will miss me something fierce, but eventually I know he'll come out on the other side and be ready to find a life partner to share the second half of his life."

"*A life partner?*" Lizzie said. "You mean a *stepmother.*"

We were no longer treading lightly.

"No. You're not five years old. You don't need another mother to take my place, but your father will need another woman to make him feel whole again, and I want you to promise me that you'll support him, maybe even help him choose the right person."

"Eww," Lizzie said. "You want us to find Dad a girlfriend?"

My mother laughed. "Trust me, sweetie, the girlfriends will find him. I know you think of him as Daddy, but in the grown-up world, Finn McCormick is a successful, funny, lovable, sweet hunk of a man. He goes to church, volunteers for school functions, and he's the magnet that draws people into the restaurant. I guarantee you that once he is single, women will flock to him like stray cats to an overturned milk truck. The problem is, he's not going to know how to handle it."

"Mom, women flirt with him all the time," I said. "They see the wedding ring, but they have a couple of glasses of wine, and they get all playful. Don't worry. Dad knows how to handle them."

"He won't once I'm not there to come home to. And they won't be *playful.* They will know that he's lonely and vulnerable, and let me tell you, some of these women are predators. I know. I've seen it firsthand."

"You've seen women hitting on Dad?" I said.

"No, nothing like that. Forget it." She waved me off.

"No. I'm not forgetting anything. What did you see?"

Mom sat there organizing her thoughts. Finally, she said, "Did you know Bernadette Brennan? She used to come into the restaurant all the time."

"Yes!" Lizzie said. "Didn't she die?"

Mom nodded and crossed herself. "Last year just before Thanksgiving. I went to her wake. I never told anyone this story before, but I was standing on the receiving line, and Rita Walsh was in front of me. She was wearing a flower print dress with a Queen Anne neckline, which struck me as a little bit out of season for November and maybe not the most delicate choice for a wake. But, hey, she works in the women's clothing department at Macy's, so who am I to tell her how to dress?

"Anyway, when she gets up to the front of the line, she kind of sidles up to Leon Brennan—that was Bernadette's husband—and she flashes him more than a little bit of cleavage. And the poor man—his wife is dead, but he isn't, and he can't help it. He takes a good look. And then Rita starts in with, 'Oh, Leon, I'm so sorry about Bernie. She was so wonderful. After this is all over, I'm stopping by, and I'm bringing you a nice, hot home-cooked dinner.' And then he said something, and I couldn't hear him, but Rita gives him a little laugh and strokes his hand, and says, 'Oh, Leon.'

"Can you imagine? Right there in the funeral home with Bernadette laid out in a box, not even in the ground yet, and that . . . that tramp is coming on to the poor dead woman's husband. It was none of my business, so I forgot all about it until four o'clock this morning when I woke up with my mind racing.

"I always knew that recovering from this disease was a long shot, but I kept telling myself I could beat it. Now that I know I can't, I woke up thinking about your father standing there at the wake, shaking people's hands, thanking them for coming, and there's Rita Walsh flashing her tits and offering to come over with a pan of baked ziti."

"That's not going to happen," Lizzie said. "Mrs. DiMarco told me that Rita and Mr. Brennan are getting married."

"Married?" Mom said. "That's insane. The woman is practically the same age as his daughter."

"The daughter is four years younger," Lizzie said. "Mrs. DiMarco told me. Then she said Rita's a gold-digging bitch, and she feels terrible for her friend Bernadette, and she wishes she could talk some sense into Mr. Brennan's head, but she doesn't think he'll listen. Then she asked me what I would do."

"What did you say?"

"What I said to her was I don't know. But what I said to myself is I wonder if Mrs. DiMarco, who is divorced, feels sorry for her dead friend, or does she feel sorry for herself because she has the hots for Mr. Brennan, and Rita beat her to the punch."

Mom leaned over and hugged Lizzie. "Child, you are wise beyond your years."

"I guess we know why you couldn't talk about this at home," I said.

"Oh God, please don't tell your father about this. I realize it's a terrible burden to put on you girls, but if I can't be around, I'll die happier knowing the two of you will be there to love him, and watch over him, and . . . and . . ."

Lizzie finished the sentence for her. "Keep the bitches from digging their claws into him."

The words hit my mother like a gut punch. But they were exactly what she needed to hear. I could see the tension visibly drain from her body. A smile crossed her lips, and her eyes welled up. "Thank you," she said.

It was a moment I will never forget. Twenty-six years later, I would relive it. Only this time, I would be the woman who was dying, and the thought that I would be leaving the man I loved to the mercy of a calculating band of ziti-baking, husband-hungry predators would make my imminent death all that more difficult to accept.

CHAPTER 6

"You didn't tell me we were having company for dinner," Mom said as Dad came through the door with Victor, one of our busboys, both their arms laden with food.

"Don't worry. He's not staying," my father said. "It's just the four of us, but I didn't know what you were in the mood for, so I brought some of everything. Meat loaf, baked salmon, pork chops, colcannon, mac and cheese . . . a whole bunch of veggies that I'm sure nobody will eat, plus Chef Tommy made your favorite—an orange pound cake, and I've got a quart of vanilla ice cream. I wound up with so much damn food that I couldn't get it all on the bike, so Victor followed me in his car. Thanks, kiddo. I'll see you tomorrow."

Victor nodded shyly, gave Mom a quick hug, and hurried out the door.

"Finn, are you nuts? There's enough food here to feed a village," my mother said.

"Hey, lady," he said, wrapping his arms gently around her. "If you don't like it, call Pizza Hut. Girls, get the food on the table, while I kiss your mother and tell her how beautiful she looks."

Dinner was bittersweet. It had been a long time since we'd done this as a family, and Dad was overjoyed. "So . . . tell me all about your outing to Magic Pond," he said.

Mom, cheery and upbeat as ever, launched into all the fun stuff—the ride in the Mustang, the picnic, the photo album, and of course, the ritual tossing of the coins into the pond and hoping for medical magic.

"Well, you better go back there often," Dad said, "because clearly Eleanor Majek's magic is working."

Lizzie and I put on our best game faces, knowing what was to come.

Years later, the two of us named it *The Last Supper*, because there was enough food to feed Jesus and all twelve apostles, and because it was the last time the four of us ever sat down at the table together.

After dessert, Lizzie and I said we were going out, and we'd be home around ten.

"No drinking and driving," came the knee-jerk Dad reaction.

"Chill out, Dad," I said. "We're just connecting with some old friends. We're not going to drink."

"And Maggie can barely drive," Lizzie said, laughing as we went out the door.

Technically, we had told the truth. We weren't going to drink. But we had said nothing about smoking a little weed. We'd also left out the fact that our old friends had been born in the middle of the eighteenth century. Caleb and Birdie Heartstone, who founded our fair city, were currently residing in the cemetery that bore their name.

I drove there, parked the car, and we walked along a path till we got to Caleb and Birdie's mausoleum, our favorite spot to toke up.

I lit a joint, and we passed it back and forth, not saying a word, just leaning back against the stone crypt, looking up at the darkening summer sky, and quietly self-medicating our anxieties away.

Lizzie finally broke the silence. "You high yet?"

I never know how I'm going to react to weed. I guess it's the luck of the draw, depending on what my friend Johnny Rollo is dealing that day.

"Definitely getting there," I said. "But it's not the kind of high where I'm flying and everything gets trippy. It's more just this soft, mellow glow washing over me."

"That's the little ganja faeries massaging the cannabis receptors in your brain," Lizzie said. "I read it in a medical book."

"Don't make me laugh," I said. "I'm dealing with serious thoughts here."

"Like what?"

"Like how ironic it is that this afternoon Mom tells us she's going to die, and right after dinner we head straight for the graveyard."

"That's not irony, Mags. It's more like we don't have a lot of choices. We can't exactly smoke dope at home. This is the go-to place for kids to get stoned or hook up. Did you and Van used to get it on back here?"

"Just quickies and BJs, but it's way too creepy here to have great sex and then curl up naked together and go to sleep. Van had his dad's fishing cabin for that."

"You think Van is having sex now?"

"No. I think he's the only marine in South Korea who is remaining celibate so he can come back home in three years and marry his high school girlfriend. I may be a romantic, but I'm not an idiot. Van is nineteen years old, for God's sake. I read in *Marie Claire* that men hit their sexual peak at nineteen. Women don't get there till around thirty-five."

"So, what you're saying is that right now the guy you're being faithful to is on the other side of the world banging some middle-aged Korean woman."

"You're an idiot," I said. "But you're a funny idiot."

"Have you cried yet?" Lizzie said.

"No. I've cried a lot since Mom got sick, but not since . . ." I paused, thinking back to that afternoon. "I got weak in the knees as soon as she said those words. *How strong are you?* I mean, I knew what was coming next."

"Me too. I haven't cried yet either. I keep thinking about Dad. Dating! What did Mom say . . . 'Women will flock to him like stray cats to an overturned milk truck'? It's funny—Mrs. DiMarco said the same thing about Mr. Brennan, except she said, 'Honey, those hags were bringing him food, baking him cookies . . . they were all over him like flies on cow flop.'"

"You think Dad is going to remarry?" I said.

"Probably. It's what men do. Women not so much, or not so fast, but men . . . Do you want to hear something really disgusting?"

"Sure."

"Do you know Beverly Reidy? Brown hair, glasses, kind of a science nerd, but I like her. I sit with her at lunch sometimes. Her mother died last year, and guess who her father started banging pretty soon after the funeral?"

"I give up."

"The mother's *sister*. Beverly's aunt. Beverly came home early from school one day because she was sick. The father's bedroom door was shut, but she could hear the two of them in there banging their brains out. She ran out of the house and came back a half hour later. The dad and the aunt were in the kitchen having coffee and looking all normal and shit, but now every time Beverly sees the two of them together, she says her skin crawls. She's at the point that she wants them both out of her life."

"You're right," I said. "That's disgusting. I hope you're not planning on sharing that with Mom."

"You're an idiot," she said. "And you're not even a funny idiot."

I smiled. I love my sister. Even her trash talk makes me happy.

We lit up a second joint and sat there painting scenarios and conjuring up what-ifs. We made a list of women who might go after our father once he was single, and we split them into four groups—gold-digging predators, horny bitches, clueless losers, and Mrs. Doubtfire, who could come to work for us as a housekeeper, but she could never replace our mother, because underneath the wig, the makeup, and the padding was a penis.

We were that stoned.

We drove home hoping to slip quietly into the house and go directly to our rooms, but Dad was sitting on the porch steps.

Lizzie and I got out of the car, and he stood up. The radiant, joyful, smiling life force we'd had dinner with was gone. He stood there, head lowered, shoulders slumped, heartbroken.

He let out a long, low, stifled wail and spread his arms wide. Lizzie and I ran to that familiar safe space, burying our faces in his chest, hugging him, clinging to one another, and the three of us stood there sobbing, bracing ourselves for the loss of the woman we loved most in the world.

CHAPTER 7

Mom still had a few good days left in her. One by one, she reached out to her closest friends, and one by one, they came to the house for brief farewell visits. That first weekend she chatted with them in the garden, but with each new day her rapid downhill slide was clearly visible, and by midweek she was relegated to welcoming her visitors from her bed.

Even so, she insisted that life at 811 Crystal Avenue remain as close to normal as possible. She forced Dad to go to work. He half-heartedly went in for the busy times, but most nights after the dinner rush, Grandpa Mike and the rest of the crew at McCormick's held down the fort till closing.

Lizzie and I alternated shifts. One of us would go into work, while the other would sit at home with Mom. Dr. Byrne came by every day, and when Mom finally became too weak to do the simplest things for herself, a hospice nurse came in to help.

On July 3, 1997, I knew it was the beginning of the end. It was my turn to stay with her, so Lizzie and Dad reluctantly went to handle the heavy Fourth of July weekend crowd at the restaurant.

Mom slept most of the day. About 6:00 p.m. she woke up looking a little better than she had in days.

"Call Dad," she said. "Tell him to come home. And bring Lizzie."

"What's wrong?" I said.

"Nothing. I've been thinking about something, and I finally feel good enough to try it."

Fifteen minutes later my father pulled into the driveway on his Harley, my sister right behind him in the Acura.

"What's wrong?" he said, sitting on the edge of the bed and taking Mom's hand.

"Nothing. I feel almost human, and there's something I want to do."

"Name it."

"I want to take one last ride."

"Please don't say *last* ride. But sure, let's go for one *more* ride. I'll pull the Mustang out of the garage."

"No," Mom said. "I want to go on the bike. Like the old days."

"Honey, are you sure you're in any condition to ride around on a motorcycle?"

Mom smiled. "The only thing I'm sure of, Finn, is that I want *one more ride*. And it's now or never."

He smiled back, but I could see his blue eyes glistening with tears as he stood up and lifted her out of bed.

He carried her to the living room, and Lizzie and I helped her dress for the adventure.

"I don't think I can handle leathers and a helmet," she said. "See if you can find me a cardigan and some kind of kerchief to cover what's left of my hair."

Five minutes later, wearing a pink nightgown, a gray sweater, and a red, white, and blue bandanna tied up in a headscarf, she was ready.

Dad wanted to carry her, but she wanted to get to the bike on her own two feet.

"Okay," Dad said, "but you are definitely not sitting behind me holding on for dear life. You're sitting in front, and I'm behind you, making sure you don't fly off."

"Ooh, I love it when you get all macho biker boy with me," she said.

He kissed her and helped her onto the Harley. Then he got on, his beefy body shielding her, his arms keeping her safe.

Helmets are mandatory in New York, and I picked his up from the driveway and tried to hand it to him.

"Not this time, kiddo," he said. "Now you and Lizzie get in the car and follow us."

"Where are you going?" I said.

"That's up to your mom. Where to, love?"

"Finn, my good man, I'd like to go back to a place we haven't been to in eighteen years."

"And where might that be, my lady?"

Mom turned, and I could see a small twinkle in her eyes, a mischievous smile on her face.

"1979."

CHAPTER 8

Dad rolled on the throttle, and the Harley roared to life.

He pulled out of the driveway, not at rocket speed, but with the measured grace and style of Morgan Freeman driving Miss Daisy to the market in her 1949 Hudson Commodore Custom Eight.

Mom sat up tall in the saddle, gazing out at the road ahead, then slowly turning her head to take in the homes on either side.

"Oh my God, she looks so regal," Lizzie said as we followed them in the Acura. "Like the queen of bloody England."

Evening was beginning to streak the sky with color. Some of our neighbors were out—having drinks on their porch, watering their lawns, playing ball in the street. They'd probably ignore a passing motorcycle, but when one is trundling along at fifteen miles an hour, and the biker chick in the driver's seat is wearing a pink nightgown, people stop what they're doing. They look. They smile. They wave.

And Mom, like the queen of bloody England, waved back. *Noblesse oblige.*

A mile from the house, Dad came to a roundabout, pulled the bike into the right lane, and turned onto Throop Avenue.

There was only one stop along Throop worth visiting: Heartstone High School.

Dad drove onto the campus and stopped at the edge of the

four-hundred-meter oval track. It was a quiet Sunday summer evening, but there were still at least a dozen people out there jogging.

"Hallowed ground," Lizzie said, gazing at the painted white lines and the rich brown cinder track.

Hallowed indeed. It's where my parents met.

We'd heard the story a thousand times. They were teenagers. Heartstone High had their annual track-and-field meet against six other schools in the county, and one of the biggest events of the afternoon was the women's sixteen-hundred-meter relay race.

The first runner for Heartstone stumbled out of the starting block, and the Hawks were dead last after the first lap. The second girl picked up some distance, and then the third did the same, but by the time the anchor got the baton, the Heartstone fans knew it would take a miracle to win.

Coach Williams had that miracle in her back pocket—Mary Katherine Donahue, a freshman in a field of juniors and seniors. Nobody knew the girl back then, but today her name is in the record books—one of the fastest runners ever to burn up a high school track in the state of New York. She had started that last leg a daunting twelve meters behind the leader, but she broke the tape half a step in front of the pack.

The Hawks fans went wild. One of them, a burly sophomore, climbed out of the stands, made his way down to the field, and waited for the school's newest rock star to come over to the sidelines.

"You were amazing," he said, extending a hand. "I'm Finn McCormick."

The poor girl was exhausted, dripping with sweat, her thick red hair twisted in a damp, limp knot behind her. "Mary Katherine Donahue," she said. "Call me Kate."

They've been inseparable ever since. And now they'd returned to the scene of that first handshake.

"Uh-oh," Lizzie said.

There was a large green-and-white sign at the edge of the field spelling out the regulations for anyone using the facilities. *No tobacco, alcohol, or other controlled substances allowed. No food or beverages allowed. No bicycles, skateboards, rollerblades, or strollers allowed.*

Dad guided the bike up to the sign.

"If you want to get technical," I said, "it doesn't say anything about middle-aged couples on Harleys."

Even if it had, I'm sure my father wouldn't have cared. He pulled the bike onto the track.

"Wait a minute," I yelled. I turned to my sister. "If they're gonna do this right, they're gonna need a soundtrack."

I grabbed the box of CDs, dumped them all on the floor, and scrambled through them till I found the one I needed.

I stuck the disc in the player and hit the play button. Trumpets blared, and the very same inspirational music that lifted Rocky Balboa as he ran up those steps in Philadelphia filled the air and spilled out onto the field.

Dad pumped one fist high in the air, gripped the throttle with the other hand, and revved the engine.

I expected him to putt-putt around the field at about the same speed as he went through town. But I was wrong. The song echoing across the field was called "Gonna Fly Now." And that's exactly what Dad did.

He flew. Gunned it. Chunks of heavily rolled, carefully tended stone and cinder flew in all directions as the Electra Glide barreled down the track.

Later that day I cornered him and asked what he was thinking when he went tear-assing around the oval like that.

"It wasn't my idea," he said. "I thought she'd be happy with that first little cruise through town, but when we got to the track, she said to me, 'You better haul ass around this track, Finn McCormick. I want my last ride to be on a real motorcycle, not a goddamn parade float. I want to feel the wind in my face, and my heart pounding in my chest. I want to feel *alive*.' So, I kicked it."

Boy, did he kick it. I don't know exactly how many laps they took around that track, but every time they whizzed past us, I got a brief glimpse of intense joy on my mother's face that I hadn't seen in months.

And then the cops showed up.

CHAPTER 9

A Heartstone PD patrol car rolled onto the field and pulled across the running track.

"This just in, folks," Lizzie said, holding an imaginary microphone to her mouth. "The cops have finally caught up with the bizarre biker gang who have been terrorizing the neighborhood. They're setting up a roadblock now."

Two uniformed police officers stepped out of the car, and as Dad sped around the track for the umpteenth time, they flagged him down.

He skidded to a stop.

Lizzie killed the music. "Quick, Magpie," she said. "Bail out before they spot you. I don't care if I get busted, but it will look bad for the president of the senior class to be caught playing DJ while her parents destroy school property."

"Thanks for the offer," I said, "but right now I'm not the president of anything. I'm the daughter of that crazy Irishman, and if they throw him in jail, they can lock me up too."

The two cops walked over to the bike. One was blond and in her midtwenties. I'd never seen her before. But I recognized the older one. Kip Montgomery had known my parents since high school. And when Kip, his wife, and their three kids came into the restaurant for dinner, Dad would always send over dessert on the house.

I was about thirty yards away, but it looked like he gave both Mom and Dad a friendly small-town police officer hello. Then Dad got off the bike, and he and Kip walked off to talk in private. Dad did most of the talking. Finally, Kip took out his radio.

"This is serious, folks," Lizzie said. "Officer Montgomery is calling for backup."

"Shut up," I said. "Dad's coming."

My father ambled over; a grin spread across his face. "Get back in the car and hang tight," he said.

"Excuse me, sir," Lizzie said, thrusting the fantasy microphone in his face. "Elizabeth McCormick, *Heartstone Crier*. Can you tell our viewers what the bleep is going on?"

Dad belly-laughed. "Don't worry, kiddos. It's all good."

He walked back to Mom, and the two of them powwowed. Then he scanned the gathering crowd of gawkers, spotted a trio of twelve-year-old boys on bicycles, and signaled them to come over.

The kids responded with a classic "*Who us, mister?*" look on their faces. But he beckoned again, and they decided to find out what he wanted. Pretty soon their heads were nodding vigorously. Dad reached into his pocket, dug some cash out of his wallet, handed it to them, and they raced off.

"Ma'am," the inquiring reporter said. "Can you tell our audience what the hell that was all about?"

"It's Dad," I said. "Don't ask."

Five minutes later, two motorcycle cops and two more squad cars joined the group. Dad revved up the Harley, rolled over to us, and said, "Follow me."

"Where are we going?" I said.

"That's up to your mother," he said. "But wherever it is, we've got ourselves a police escort."

The turret lights on all three cop cars went on, flashing red and blue against the graying sky. And with the biker cops clearing the traffic along the way, the motorcade moved out smartly.

First stop on the journey was St. Cecilia's, where my parents got married. The three kids on bicycles must have been the advance team, because by the time we pulled up to the church Father Connelly was standing outside, along with two of the younger priests, and some of the staff from the rectory. There were hugs, kisses, and blessings, and then off we went again.

The convoy proceeded along High Street at a leisurely pace—about twenty miles an hour. Mom, who'd had her thrill ride for the day, didn't complain.

"Next stop, Main Street," Lizzie said.

She was wrong. The procession hung a left on MacDougal, a two-lane thoroughfare that skirts the business district and is peppered with gas stations, fast-food outlets, chain drugstores, car dealerships, and not much else.

"What the hell is here?" Lizzie said.

I had no idea. And then one of the motorcycle cops stopped traffic, and the entourage crossed the road and turned into a strip mall.

"Holy shit," I said, looking at the Chinese restaurant nestled between a Staples and the Sew Rite fabric store. "Dragon Heart."

Lizzie gave me a blank stare.

"It's where Mom and Dad were having dinner when her water broke, and she went into labor with me. They never got to finish dinner, so Mr. and Mrs. Lum delivered it to the hospital the day after I was born."

A white-haired Chinese couple was outside waiting for us. Mrs. Lum had a silver tray with an assortment of appetizers on it. Dad popped a dumpling in his mouth. Mom took a mini egg roll, thanked the Lums profusely, and held on to it. I was sure she'd pass it to Dad as soon as we were out of sight.

"Next stop has *got* to be Main Street," Lizzie said.

It was. And from the reception we got, our three young town criers had done their job well. It was as if all of Heartstone had dropped what they were doing so they could make way for the lady in the pink nightgown. Cars pulled over and honked their horns as we rode by. People shouted from windows, and almost everyone at the outdoor cafés that lined the block stood up and gave us a standing ovation.

We drove past the firehouse, where a dozen firefighters hooted and saluted as their electronic message board flashed *HFD loves Kate Mc-Cormick.*

And then we turned onto Pine Street, where the sidewalk in front of McCormick's was packed with customers, waiters, and kitchen staff. In the middle of them all was Grandpa Mike, arms high, a flag in each hand—one red, white, and blue; the other green, white, and orange.

Loud pipes howled as twenty of Dad's biker buddies roared out of the parking lot to join the celebration, and the caravan, which had started out with a single motorcycle and a chase car and was now a joyous mob, wended its way to Crystal Avenue, where the whole neighborhood was there to welcome us home.

Someone set off a string of firecrackers, which may have been for Mom, or it might just have been some kid getting a jump on the Fourth of July. People who knew our family well called out her name, pumped their fists in the air, and many of them—big, strapping men included—dabbed at their eyes.

Our police escort stopped just past our house, and the cops got out of their cars and off their bikes as Dad pulled into the driveway.

He lifted Mom off the Harley and turned her to the crowd. She looked exhausted, but exhilarated. She waved, threw kisses, said thank you over and over, and finally, Dad carried her inside the house and upstairs to her bed.

She kissed us all, told us she loved us, went to sleep, and never woke up.

CHAPTER 10

My mother had done her research on the downside of dying at home. A week before she passed, she sat down with the three of us and gave us our marching orders.

"Rule number one," she said with the same sense of urgency she'd had when we were kids, and she taught us about stranger danger. "Once I'm gone, do *not*—repeat, do not—call 911. A lot of people do, thinking that the cops will help them transport the body. But what happens is that the first ones to arrive are the paramedics. They're on a mission—save lives. So even though I'm dead as a mackerel, they will start pounding on my chest and cracking my ribs . . ."

"The hell they will," Dad said, jumping in.

"Let me finish. Pounding my chest and cracking my ribs, which will quickly escalate into a fistfight with my husband. *That's* when the cops will show up."

Dad acquiesced. "So, you want us to call the funeral home first."

"No. First call Dr. Byrne. He and I discussed this. The law says you need a physician to sign off on the cause of death. He'll come right over and fill out the paperwork. Otherwise, the state of New York will ship me off to the morgue for an autopsy to figure out what killed me. Whatever you do, please do not let them cut me up."

"What if we get an offer from a medical school willing to pay big bucks for a fresh cadaver?" Lizzie said, her face completely deadpan.

Mom clapped her hands and shrieked with laughter. "Oh God, I am so going to miss this shit."

"How do you think I feel?" Lizzie said. "I'm losing my best audience. Maggie barely *understands* most of my cryptic banter."

I was jealous of my sister's innate ability to deal with death so matter-of-factly, but I loved her for how effortlessly she could keep Mom smiling during those final days.

My mother and I were a lot alike. We needed to be in charge. So, while she still had the strength, she dragged Dad to Kehoe's Funeral Home to pick out her casket, her dress, the flowers, the Mass card, and whatever else Mr. Kehoe had on his extensive, expensive checklist.

Mary Katherine Donahue McCormick passed peacefully at 3:27 a.m. on July 4, 1997. My father was holding her hand when she took her final breath, but he didn't leave her side to wake me or my sister until seven. His excuse: "The next few days won't be easy on any of us. I figured you'd need your sleep."

Dr. Byrne was a man of his word. He came immediately, filled out the death certificate, and stayed until Mom was on her way to Kehoe's. No autopsy—the top box on her checklist.

Grandpa Mike arrived after eight o'clock Mass, and his eyes teary, his voice shaky, he announced, "I put a sign in the window and hung the bunting over the front door. Then I poured Kate her last drink, set it on the bar, and locked up. Just like I did with Grandma."

It was only the second time since he opened the place on St. Patrick's Day 1965 that the lights at McCormick's had gone dark.

News of Mom's passing spread quickly, and by 2:30 p.m. the first hot home-cooked meal made its way into our kitchen—chicken divan, delivered by a neighbor, Josie Henson, early forties, three kids, recently divorced.

Lizzie and I had been told what to expect. "You may get a few who bring flowers, or wine, or pastry," Mom said. "But the ones on the prowl will come with Corningware, Pyrex baking dishes, or dutch ovens—anything they have to come back for a few days later.

"I can hear them now," she said. "'Just stopping in to pick up my dish, Finn. How are you holding up? Let me know if there's anything I can do for you.' It won't matter what he says. They'll keep coming back."

She was right. They came in droves. It didn't matter that Dad owned a restaurant. They just kept showing up with food as if the poor man didn't know where his next meal was coming from.

Grandpa Mike called them "women with casseroles." But, of course, he was from back in the day, when a girl might get lucky with some baked tuna, noodles, and mushroom soup topped with crumbled potato chips. But the vultures of the late nineties had ramped up their culinary skills.

Some of the meals bordered on gourmet, like Isla Cantor's Moroccan couscous with tender chunks of lamb, topped with golden raisins and slivers of almonds; or Nikki Conklin's buttery quiche laced with goat cheese, arugula, and prosciutto; and my favorite, Jill Sawyer's lobster mac 'n' cheese, which Lizzie and I polished off in one sitting.

It was a competition with Dad as first prize, and by the end of the week Lizzie and I calculated that there were between eight and twelve contenders. It was impossible to get an exact count because some of them were so subtle we couldn't tell if they were in play or just good-hearted friends.

We trusted none of them. So, when Andrea Tursi showed up, her Dow Chemical boobs cascading over the top of a scoop-neck sweater, we watched her make a beeline to the kitchen, check out the competition, and swap the name tag on whatever crap she brought with Deborah Roelandt's signature chicken and dumplings. Then she headed straight for the golden ticket—my father.

"She's exactly the kind of calculating bitch Mom told us to keep an eye on," Lizzie said, putting the name tags back where they belonged.

Each night, we would transfer all the entries to Tupperware, wash all the dishes, and return them the next morning. We were pretty sure most of the women knew what we were up to. We didn't care. We were on a mission. We dubbed ourselves the Casserole Patrol.

The wake was a two-day affair that snarled traffic along Brandywine Avenue for a quarter of a mile on either side of the funeral home. I knew Mom was popular, but as Lizzie put it, this was more than people paying their respects. This was Wake-a-Palooza.

The lines snaked around the block. My father wore the brand-new black suit and tie Mom bought for him. Pinned to his lapel was her tiny gold claddagh ring, a symbol of their love, loyalty, and friendship. For hours on end the three of us stood dutifully next to the casket as more than five hundred people filed in to clasp our hands, hug us, and softly speak words of sympathy and condolence.

The funeral Mass was at St. Cecilia's on a warm summer Friday morning. Any number of people would gladly have been honored to eulogize my mother. But she made it clear that she only wanted her husband and her two daughters.

Dad went first. The man has the soul of a poet and is blessed with the Celtic gift for storytelling. For twenty minutes, working without notes, he mesmerized the room as he recounted the tale of their romance from the day they met on a high school running track to their final night on the back of a Harley.

He was brilliant—the quintessential loving, grieving husband—and my first thought as he stepped down was how proud Mom would be.

Then Lizzie put it all in perspective for me. "We're doomed," she said. "After that tribute, every single woman in the whole damn church is going to want to scoop him up."

Lizzie was next. She introduced herself as Mom's favorite *bad daughter*, and in her own devilishly sweet way, she put the F-U-N in funeral.

And then it was my turn.

I still have a vivid image of sunlight streaming through the stained glass as I stepped up to the pulpit to deliver my eulogy. I looked down at the sea of black dresses, somber faces, and anxious eyes, and I wanted to run. Then I looked down at the white casket with a spray of red roses, and I heard my mother saying, "Breathe. Repeat if necessary."

I breathed. And the words flowed.

"My mother's favorite place in the entire world is less than a mile from here. You all know it: Magic Pond. She loved to remind her daughters that she's been taking us there since before we were born. I remember as a little girl tossing stones into the water, and wondering why some go straight to the bottom while others hit just right, and their ripples travel across the surface, transferring energy as they go.

"That same thought crossed my mind this week as hundreds of you came to the wake, and again this morning as I look out across this sanctuary, and I see her family, her friends, her neighbors, her restaurant family—both staff and customers—her book club, her garden club, her biker buddies, her three high school teammates from that historic five-thousand-meter relay, her coach, the ladies of the Christmas committee, our mayor, our school bus driver from Heartstone Elementary, doctors and nurses who cared for her during her illness, and at least a hundred people I hardly know, but whose lives were touched by my mother.

"Some people can live a hundred years and barely have an impact on the world. But the life force that was Kate McCormick for forty-one short years on this earth still lives on in this room. We are the many ripples she left behind."

I'd written everything down on index cards before I spoke, and I still had two cards left to read. But as I gazed out at the crowd, at the women with tissues to their eyes, and men with heads bowed, I knew I had said just enough.

I stepped down and walked to the front pew. Dad stood and hugged me. Lizzie squeezed my hand. As soon as the three of us settled back in our seats, the choir director stood, and forty-eight men and women in magenta robes rose as one.

The crowd was probably anticipating one of Father Connelly's go-to hymns, like "Alleluia! Sing to Jesus" or "Amazing Grace," but he was merely officiating. Mom was running the show.

The organ came to life—not a somber chord, but a driving gospel rock beat. The choir began swaying, clapping, and oohing. Two of the singers thumped tambourines, and for the next five minutes, that requiem became a joy fest as the choir, and eventually every man, woman, and child in that church, stood and sang "Ain't No Mountain High Enough."

No dirges for Kate McCormick. This was her love song to my father. This was the send-off she wanted, and she'd planned every inch of it.

The only thing she knew she couldn't control was the parade of women who would come by to comfort my father as soon as she was in the ground.

CHAPTER 11

"Lions don't hunt," Lizzie said to me one afternoon about three weeks after the funeral.

It was the lull between lunch and happy hour, and we were sitting in a booth at the rear of the restaurant, giving in to our midday sugar cravings—Lizzie with a slice of pecan pie, me with a dish of rice pudding.

"Sorry," I said. "I was debating whether or not I should go back to the kitchen and add some whipped cream to my sins. What did you say about lying?"

"Not lying. Lions. The kings of the jungle. The male of the species. I said they don't hunt."

"How do they eat?"

"Mama brings home the bacon," Lizzie said. "The females do 90 percent of the hunting. Usually, they go after gazelles or antelope or zebra—something they can take down on their own. The only time the males help out is if the prey is too big for the lioness to handle on her own, like a giraffe or an elephant. The rest of the time, old Leo just sits around on his fat ass waiting for the little woman to bring home dinner."

Like a lot of teenage girls in the nineties, I was tuned into the feminist movement—especially the part about equal pay for equal work. But at sixteen Lizzie was obsessed with girl power, and more than a little angry at men for, as she put it, *keeping women down since the beginning of time.*

"I love you, Elizabeth," I said, "but can we go through one afternoon without getting into gender politics."

"I'm not talking politics. I'm talking about lions. I saw it on one of those Animal Kingdom shows last night, and I couldn't fall asleep. I kept thinking about Dad."

"And you think Dad is a fat-ass lazy lion?"

"No, Maggie." She popped a forkful of pie into her mouth and made me wait for the kicker. "Dad is a gazelle."

I inhaled sharply and forgot to let it out. My mind raced, and I knew where she was going. Worse yet, I knew she was right.

"Breathe," Lizzie said, quoting one of our mother's favorite mantras. "Repeat if necessary."

I breathed.

"You're back there in the kitchen," she said. "I'm up front day after day watching the lionesses stalk him. And they're not bringing casseroles. They're wearing push-up bras, painting their nails, and dabbing their pulse points with Eau d' Gold Digger."

"Mom warned us this would happen," I said, scraping the last of the rice pudding from the sides of the bowl. "But she didn't exactly tell us what to do when it did. I don't know how we're supposed to keep every single woman in Heartstone from—"

"They're not even all *single*," Lizzie said. "A couple of them are married but looking for an upgrade. And then there's Mrs. Umansky."

"Oh my God. She's like seventy years old."

"Right. But she's sure her daughter Velma can bring Dad the same happiness he had with Mom. And I'm not making that up. She said it to my face."

"How is Dad handling all this?"

"Watch one of those nature films, Maggie. The gazelle doesn't figure it out until the lioness has pounced and is ripping his throat out. Dad is basically clueless. He just keeps thanking them for their concern, and when they leave, he tells me how kind and caring everybody has been. It's getting harder to watch. I'm thinking about asking him if I can work in the kitchen and wash dishes."

"Pardon me, ladies, but what are a couple of nice young girls like you doing in a dump like this?"

I looked up. It was Dad, a meat loaf sandwich in one hand, a bottle of Bud in the other. I slid over, and he sat down.

"You look intense," he said. "What are you two talking about?"

"Lizzie was telling me about a documentary she saw last night."

"Bullshit. You're talking about me."

"Don't flatter yourself, old man," Lizzie said.

"Hey, I'm not a total idiot. I'm sorry. I haven't meant to ignore you, but I'm . . ."

"Dad, you haven't been ignoring us," I said.

"Of course I have. I promised your mother I'd be there for you, and I've been living in my own world."

"It's called grieving," I said. "You're entitled."

"I know, but I haven't paid much attention to the two of you."

"News flash," Lizzie said. "Teenage girls don't thrive on parental attention. Keep up the good work."

He chomped down on the meat loaf sandwich and took a swig of his beer. Lizzie finished the last of her pie. I decided to go for broke.

"You know they're hitting on you, don't you?" I said.

"What?"

"All these women who are cooking for you, stopping by to check on you, calling to see if you need anything—some of them have an ulterior motive."

"*All* of them have an ulterior motive," Lizzie said, jumping on the runaway train.

"Like what?" He didn't need us to answer. He was right. He wasn't a *total* idiot. "Oh, Jesus, I don't know what you girls are reading in those women's magazines, but you're way off base. First of all, I'm not looking for a girlfriend. Second of all, these women are your mother's friends. They're not trying to poach her husband. And third of all—"

"Finn." It was Grandpa Mike at the bar. "Telephone."

"Tell them I'm busy."

"I tried that, but it's Alice Bodine, and she says she just has one *teensy-weensy little question.* Something about the corn pudding soufflé she's baking for you."

"Baking," Lizzie said. "That's completely different from poaching."

"It's not what you're thinking," he said, standing up. "And even if it was, I'm not remotely interested."

Lizzie waited for him to walk over to the bar, pick up the phone, and deal with Alice's teensy-weensy little question.

"*I'm not remotely interested,*" she repeated. "Isn't that what the gazelle said when the lioness said, 'I'd love to bring you back to my place for dinner'?"

CHAPTER 12

I decided to take a break from fixating on my father's love life and obsess about my own. I hadn't heard from my boyfriend since before my mother died, and I ached to have him hold me and comfort me.

Van was the only boy I'd ever loved, the only boy I'd ever slept with, and now, at a time when I needed him more than ever, he was seven thousand miles away.

I'd met him a year ago. It was the summer before my junior year, and my overprotective father, who couldn't help noticing that his two daughters were—and I quote—"blossoming," decided to have us work at the restaurant. His logic was simple: (a) he could keep an eye on us, and (b) he could keep us away from "those damn horny teenage boys."

It might have worked. Except for the fire.

About two months before Lizzie and I started our summer jobs at the restaurant, there was a kitchen fire. It could have been a total disaster, but the McCormicks have a knack for turning lemons into lemonade. So, Dad and Grandpa Mike decided to roll the dice, take over the empty dress shop next door, build a bigger, better kitchen, and double the size of the place.

Van had a summer job working for our contractor. I worked the day shift as a waitress. And for two months, while half the restaurant was operational and the other half was under construction, I spent as much time as possible bringing coffee, sandwiches, and cold drinks to the half where there were no customers.

I was sixteen. Most of the boys in my class were still going through that gangly teenage growth spurt. Van was seventeen, and he was definitely not a boy. He was six feet tall with a mop of thick blond hair, deep blue eyes, a strong jaw, and the magnificent hard, muscular body of a man. He was totally out of my league.

But that didn't stop me. I knew it wouldn't be easy. Not with my hawkeyed father always hovering about. But for all his paternal vigilance about "boys, who only have one thing on their minds, Maggie," he seemed completely unfazed by my regular visits to the construction site. It didn't hurt that I told him I might want to become an architect, and I was learning a lot from Nick Ridley, the crew boss.

The hard part was getting through to Van. He hardly noticed me. I don't think he was shy. I think it was probably because he was too intimidated to start flirting with Finn McCormick's daughter while he was on the job. But little by little, I worked my untested girlish charm, and by mid-July we were talking regularly. Actually, I did most of the talking. Van was the strong, silent type, but that gave him a special quality that most boys—most men, in fact—don't have. He was a great listener.

Van was about to go into his senior year, and his plan was to join the Marines right after graduation. My plan was for him to be the one to take my virginity before the summer was over.

Our first date wasn't really a date. He'd told me during the week that he and his friends were going to spend Saturday at Waterfront Park Beach. I said, "Small world. I'm going there too. Maybe I'll run into you."

It was a total lie, but I had no trouble recruiting a few of my girlfriends to help me turn it into a reality. And—surprise, surprise—we ran into Van at the beach. It didn't hurt that we cruised the parking lots till I spotted his motorcycle.

I was a young girl, but I filled out my bikini like a grown woman, and I caught more than a few dads—who were there with their families—checking me out.

For the next four hours, Van and I did that dance teenagers do when they know they have the hots for one another, but they don't have enough experience to leave the party and hop into bed.

We walked on the beach and talked. We rubbed suntan lotion on each other's back. I straddled his shoulders, and we played chicken fight in the water with our friends. We won the first two rounds, but on the third one, we got bowled over, and we both went in the drink.

I came up coughing and sputtering and grabbed on to him to steady myself. "Are you okay?" he asked, putting his arms around me.

I pulled myself against him, felt the bulge in his board shorts, and I pulled closer still.

"Almost," I said, my lips drifting closer to his. He leaned in, and we kissed. "Mmmmm . . . feeling better already. Except I think I'm getting too much sun. Irish girls don't tan; we burn."

"Dutch boys have the same problem. We should both get off the beach." He smiled. "You want to go hang out someplace shady?"

"What'd you have in mind?"

He pretended to think about it, but it was obvious he'd already worked it out in his head. "You any good at ping-pong?"

"I can beat your sorry ass with one hand tied behind my back."

"You're on," he said. "I have a ping-pong table in my basement."

"I don't know," I said. "I'm kind of grungy from lying on the beach all day. I'd hate to make a lousy first impression on your parents."

"My parents aren't home. We have a cabin in the Adirondacks. They're up there for the weekend. We can blast the music as loud as we want."

"I don't have wheels," I said. "I drove here with Tiffany."

"I've got my bike and an extra helmet."

"I don't know," I said, making him work for it. "What do you think my father would say if he saw me riding around on a Honda?"

"It's not a Honda *lawn mower*. It's a V65 Magna—one of the fastest production motorcycles on the planet. I let your father borrow it last week. He came back with a shit-eating grin on his face, which from a Harley guy is a rave."

I shrugged. "In that case . . ."

If I had any second thoughts, I got over them as soon as I got on the back of his bike and wrapped my arms around his chest. We'd spent the whole afternoon ogling one another half naked. I was ready for the other half.

I knew what I was going to do, and I made a mental note of the date: August 8, 1996—the day I was going to lose my virginity.

CHAPTER 13

"This is me," Van said, slowing the bike and turning onto a quiet tree-lined block.

As soon as I looked up and saw the street sign, my sixteen-year-old brain took it as a clear-cut omen that I had made the right decision. *I can't think of a more perfect name for the place where I had my first sexual experience than Harmony Road*, I thought, composing my diary entry in advance.

The two-story clapboard house was painted a warm gray with white trim. A bluestone walkway lined with marigolds wound from the sidewalk through green grass to an arched oak front door.

The inside was just as charming, and under other circumstances I'd have told him how pretty I thought it was. But I wasn't there for a house tour.

"I lied," I said as soon as he closed the door. I moved closer, reached up, and put my arms around his neck. "I'm lousy at ping-pong."

He smiled, and I wondered if he had any idea how incredibly sexy he was. "Are you saying you brought me here under false pretenses?" he said, blue eyes scolding playfully.

"Totally," I said.

"Well, in that case, I'm glad my parents aren't home. They'd be upset if they found that their only son was smitten by a wily, conniving—"

"Smitten?"

"Big time. Can't you tell?" he said, wrapping me up in his arms.

We were done talking. He lowered his face toward mine, and I lifted myself on my toes to meet him. I'd kissed boys before, but they always seemed to be racing through it, their lips pressing hard, their tongues working fast, hell-bent on rounding first base so they could run their hands under my bra and get to second.

Not Van. His lips were soft, and the kiss was long, slow, and gentle. He held me in his arms, his hands never roaming.

When the kiss was finally over, I put my lips to his left ear. "I've never done it," I whispered. "But I'm ready."

He didn't say a word. He just took me by the hand, and we went upstairs to his bedroom.

Over the years I've heard other women talk about their first sexual experience. For some it was painful—not just physically but emotionally. The most common regret is "He stuck it in, finished in a hurry, and then he only called me when he wanted to bang me again."

It was different for me. I wasn't coerced. I was totally willing. In fact, once I met Van, I *wanted* him to be the one. The first time was, as you'd expect, awkward. He wasn't a virgin, but the way he fumbled with the condom bespoke his amateur status. Foreplay consisted of him saying, "Are you sure you want to do this?"

"I'm sure," I whispered, and he got right to it.

It didn't last long. It took him less than two minutes. It would take me another three years before I had my first orgasm. But I'd done my research, so it came as no surprise. What did surprise me was the rush I felt as he called out my name and erupted inside me. When it was over, I waited for the shroud of Catholic guilt to envelop me. It never came. Instead, I was overcome with joy at how easily I could make him that happy.

I'd read about the so-called power women have over men, but I'd never really experienced it. This beautiful, caring, desirable man wanted my body—reveled in it—and I got to call the shots.

Today I'm the mother of twins who are almost the same age as I was then, and I shudder to I think that at this very moment, they may be thinking about their own leap into adulthood.

Sex was better the second time, even better the next, and as the year progressed, Van and I grew bolder, more adventurous, and by the end of my junior year I had no doubt that we were trying things neither of our parents had dreamed of.

And then Van graduated and enlisted in the Marines. I tried to convince him to at least apply to a few schools, but college didn't interest him. His father and his two uncles were Marines, and the Corps was in his DNA.

He left for Parris Island in July 1996, and a year later, when my mother died, he was stationed in Seoul, South Korea.

Mobile phones had not yet gone mainstream, so I wrote to him at least three times a week. Van wasn't much of a writer, so his letters were uninspired recaps of his life in the military, and over the course of a year they had dwindled from weekly to sporadic to hardly ever.

And then he called. It was a Monday morning, and I was in the shower when the phone rang.

Lizzie banged on the bathroom door. "Dry yourself off, Juliet. Romeo is calling from Korea."

My mind did cartwheels. It was August 8, a year to the day since Van and I first had sex. He was calling for our anniversary.

I threw on a robe and ran for the phone, deliriously happy.

"Hello," I said.

"Hey, Maggie."

"I can't believe you remembered."

"It's hard to forget," he said. "I mean, I got your letter saying your mom died. I just didn't write back, because . . . well, you know how it is with me and writing letters. Anyway, I'm really sorry. And tell your dad that too. And Lizzie."

"Thanks. How are you?"

"I'm okay, but I have some bad news. That's why I'm calling."

It wasn't about our anniversary. I should have known that guys don't pay attention to things like that. "What's the bad news?"

"I got married."

My knees buckled. "I don't understand what you just said."

"I got married. Yesterday. Her name is Sujin. I don't love her like I love you, but I got her pregnant, and I had to do the right thing. I'm sorry, Maggie. I'm really, really—"

I dropped the phone, lowered myself to the floor, buried my head in my hands, and cried my broken teenage heart out.

CHAPTER 14

Lizzie scooped me off the floor and practically carried me to my bedroom.

"He dumped you, right?" she said, not waiting for me to regain my composure.

"Worse," I said and sobbed out the news.

"Boys suck," she said. "Men suck. Anything with a penis sucks."

"Except Dad and Grandpa Mike," I said.

"Yeah, but they probably sucked when they were Van's age," she said, wrapping her arms around me. "Don't worry, sweetie. I got you. Just tell me what you need."

"Matches. I'm going to burn every letter he ever sent me."

"Screw the letters. You'll feel better if you burn a joint and put yourself into a drug-induced state of self-pity."

"Mmmmm, sounds good. You got one?"

"Me? Honey, you're my weed dealer. I'm just the innocent little sister you corrupt. Call Johnny. He's always selling."

"I can't call. He changes his cell phone number every couple of months."

"So go over to his place. Get stoned. I'll tell Dad you're not coming into work today. All I have to do is say, 'Maggie has lady problems,' and he'll wave his hands in front of his face and say, 'Spare me the details.'"

"Thanks."

"And don't worry," Lizzie said. "You'll be okay. There are plenty of other guys out there."

"I thought you said anything with a penis sucks."

"Oh, I'm not going back on that, but if we're going to preserve the species, some have got to suck less than others. It's just that it's impossible to tell the good ones from the bad ones."

Johnny Rollo was the perfect case in point. He was foul-mouthed, quick to throw hands, and no stranger to the Heartstone Police Department. But there were times when he could be the sweetest, most caring guy on earth.

I remember saying that to Lizzie once, and her response was, "Yeah. Just like Michael Corleone before he had his brother Fredo whacked."

Johnny lived in the old Marian Motel, a run-down, two-story stretch of connected rooms that dodged the wrecking ball in the late eighties and was reborn as the Marian Arms, an apartment complex where people paid their rent by the week.

Johnny supposedly lived there with his mother, although in the few times I'd been there to score weed, I'd never seen her. I remember asking him once where she was.

"She's on sabbatical," he said, his eyes serious, his voice earnest. "She's a visiting professor at Crack University."

I never asked again.

Johnny was not a morning person, so I waited till noon before I drove over. I parked, locked my car, went upstairs to unit 209, put my ear to the door, and instinctively jumped back when I heard the gunfire.

And then I remembered who I was dealing with. Johnny spent a good chunk of his time playing video games. I banged on the door.

"Nobody home," the voice yelled from inside.

"Johnny, it's Maggie McCormick," I yelled back.

The shooting stopped. A few seconds later the dead bolt on the inside snapped back hard, and the door opened. Johnny stood there, shirtless, a cigarette dangling from his mouth, a pair of ratty jeans sagging down around his hips, exposing about six inches of red tartan boxers.

"Christ, girl," he said. "You look like shit. Come on in."

I stepped in. The entire unit was bedroom, living room, and kitchen all crammed into a single dark, claustrophobic space. A glass bong sat on the coffee table. The inside was crusted with brown-green grunge and looked like it hadn't been cleaned in months—if ever. The whole place reeked of marijuana and ripe teenage-boy stink.

"Sorry to bother you," I said.

"No bother. I was just saving the planet from alien invaders," he said, dead-bolting the door and pointing at the pixelated creatures frozen on the television set. He picked up the controller, and the screen went to black. "Either you've got some real serious hay fever, or you been bawling your eyes out."

"My boyfriend dumped me."

"That sucks. You want a Pop-Tart? I got strawberry and chocolate."

"Thanks, but you got anything stronger?" I pointed at the bong. "Maybe something we can put in there instead of in the toaster?"

He dropped his cigarette into an empty beer can. "Sorry, babe. All I've got left is the primo shit."

"Fine. I'll take it. How much?"

"Girl, after what you've been through, I'm happy to give it to you on the house. The problem is, you can't handle what I've got. This shit is wheelchair weed. A couple of hits, and you won't be able to walk."

"I don't care. I can handle it. Please."

"No, man. I can't be responsible for—" He stopped. "Unless . . ."

"Unless what?"

"Maybe we can shotgun one," he said. "But just one."

I gave him a blank stare.

"What are you—like in middle school? Shotgunning is a way to get double the pleasure from a single bag of weed. I'll fire up the bong, inhale, and then I'll pass that hit over to you."

"How?"

He opened a drawer in the coffee table and pulled out an empty toilet paper roll. "With this remarkable high-tech device recommended by stoners everywhere. Allow me to demonstrate."

The bong was loaded and ready to go. He lit it, inhaled deeply, held it in his lungs for about ten seconds, put the toilet paper roll to his mouth, and then gestured for me to put my mouth around the other end.

As soon as I was in position, he exhaled, and I sucked hard on the cardboard tube. He wasn't kidding. This was not the marijuana I was used to. I felt it immediately. Or maybe I just wanted to feel it immediately. It didn't matter. "Oh my God," I moaned.

"Pretty good, huh? That's the THC fucking with your brain's happy campus. But don't worry. You're not getting the full blast. I am. You're only getting secondhand smoke, so you won't get totally trashed."

He took another hit and exhaled through the tube. I inhaled deeply and got more than I bargained for. I gagged, started coughing, and finally spit out the piece of cardboard that I'd sucked in.

"This is nasty," I said, my fingers on the soft, soggy end of the toilet paper roll. "How many people have had their grody wet lips wrapped around this thing?"

He shrugged. "Three, four, I don't know."

"Do you have anything cleaner?"

"Jesus, you're high-maintenance." He tossed the cardboard roll onto the floor. "Your only other choice is direct contact," he said, tapping his mouth. "Your call, sweetheart."

He took another deep hit on the bong, leaned in, pulled me close, and stopped just short of my lips.

I didn't hesitate. I put my lips to his and drew in the smoke. Euphoria.

"I don't do this with my guy friends, you know," he said, grinning.

"I don't care. Just shut up and do it again."

He did. Then again. And again, only this time I wasn't satisfied with the weed.

I put a hand on his bare chest and slid my fingertips over one nipple. It was much darker, much hairier than Van's. And it was hard.

"Did I do that, or was it the weed?" I said.

"Do what?"

I stroked one nipple, then the other. "Did I get these two guys to stand at attention?"

He laughed in my face. "Jesus F. Christ, McCormick, that is so lame."

"What?" I said.

"You. Coming on to me like one of those cheeseballs from *The Young and The Restless*."

"I don't know what you're talking ab—"

He grabbed my elbows and jerked me to my feet. "Let me save you the trouble, kid."

He backed me against the wall and pressed hard against me.

The suddenness and the raw sexuality of it all petrified me and completely turned me on at the same time. My entire body quivered.

His jeans and boxers were already low on his hips. I didn't think. I dug my fingers inside his beltline and pulled them to his ankles, pushed him back down onto the sofa.

I could see in his eyes that this turnabout was the last thing he expected from the cheeseball with the lame soap opera dialogue. I straddled him, lifted my hips, and like Van before him, and every man since, he moaned as he entered me and felt the welcoming warm wetness engulf him.

He cupped my breasts, and every pleasure receptor in my body began firing. The rage inside me turned to pure sexual energy. I'd learned a lot over the past year, and I knew just how to move to drive him to the edge.

"Whoa, whoa, whoa," he yelled, trying to pull out. "I don't need no kids."

"I'm on the pill," I said, gyrating out of control.

That's all it took. His hands gripped my hips, and he thrust upward hard. Once. Twice. A third time. He made it to nine before he exploded, and I pressed my head to his chest as that feeling of joy and the sense of power of what I could do for yet another man swept over me.

Johnny wasn't the cuddling type. He rolled me off him, and the two of us lay there breathing heavily. I stared at the water-stained ceiling, the gray-brown paint peeling from the walls, and the lone cloudy window, a strip of flypaper speckled with God-knows-how-many victims, dangling from the head jamb.

And then—just like that—I started laughing. Hard.

"What's so funny?" he said.

"This, dude," I said, my hand sweeping across the dismal space. "Us."

He sat up. "News flash, babe. There is no us. Never will be. You got what you came for. Johnny Rollo, at your cervix. One and done."

He rolled off the sofa and pulled up his pants. "You hungry?" he said.

"Starving," I said. "What have you got besides Pop-Tarts?"

"Beer."

"Sounds like a party," I said. "And while you're at it, I'd like a bag of that killer weed to go."

"You're out of luck. That was the last of it. I'll have more tomorrow. If you want some, track me down at the Pits after midnight."

Track me down. If anybody else said that to me, I'd think, what an asshole. But in Johnny's case, it was part of his charm.

I smiled to myself, knowing that as soon as I got home, my sister would ask how I'm doing, and I'd be ready with the perfect answer.

"Much better," I would say. "I hopped on the bus to Bad Boy Town and revenge-fucked the mayor."

CHAPTER 15

When you're only seventeen, and your plan for the evening is to score some weed from your dealer at midnight, it helps to have a father who puts in a fourteen-hour day, comes home at eleven, showers, and is out like a light by eleven fifteen.

I left the house at eleven thirty and drove to the Pits, a huge abandoned rock quarry about five miles out of the jurisdiction of the Heartstone Police Department.

The line to get into the parking area moved slowly, and as I got closer to the front, I could see why. Johnny Rollo was directing traffic. Some cars got waved through. But some stopped, the driver's window would go down, Johnny would reach in, and in seconds his hand would come back, and the deal would be done.

Business was brisk.

He gave me a noncommittal head toss when I rolled down my window. "Welcome to my world," he said. "Glad to see you made it."

He tossed a bag of weed on my front seat, and I pulled some money out of my wallet.

"You're in luck," he said, pushing my hand away. "We're giving away free samples to every honor student who rolls in. So far, you're the only one."

I knew better than to argue. "Thanks," I said. "I knew all that studying would pay off one of these days."

"Park over there by that Jeep," he said, pointing. "Stay in your car, lights out till it starts."

"When's that?"

"You're an honor student. You'll figure it out."

He smiled. He needed dental work, but that only added to his earthy sexiness.

"See you later?" I asked.

"Probably not. It's my busy season. But there's a lot of assholes around here, and they get ass-holier as the night goes on. If anyone gives you a hard time, call me. My cell number is in the bag."

He stepped away from the car and waved me on. I pulled up next to the Jeep and turned off my lights.

Dozens of cars were parked nearby, and I could make out the shapes of the passengers, lit only by the glow of whatever it was they were smoking.

Outside my window, the world was deathly quiet. But the thoughts inside my head were clanging like a runaway pinball machine. My dead mother. My despondent father. My college applications. Sex with Johnny Rollo. "There is no us," he'd said. "Never will be," he'd said. "One and done," he'd said. Then why did he give me his phone number? Why did he give me free weed? Why did he say, "If anyone gives you a hard time—?"

The silence was suddenly shattered by the aggressive sound of Metallica exploding through the cavernous space. Then the night lit up as hundreds of cars circling the quarry's upper rim turned on their headlights.

My honor student brain figured it out immediately. Party time. I got out of the car.

"Maggie!" a voice called out.

I turned around. "Misty," I said, happy to see a familiar face.

Misty Sinclair and her family lived at 822 Crystal Avenue, across the street and half a block away from my house. They'd moved to Heartstone when Misty and I were both in fourth grade, and the two of us tried to be friends at first. But we had nothing in common.

I loved school. Misty got by, but she'd much rather have fun, and by the time we were in seventh grade we'd completely drifted apart. I was focused on academics, sports, and extracurricular activities, while Misty was more into music, hanging out with her friends, and—somewhere around the age of eleven—boys.

"I haven't seen you since your mom's funeral," she said. "How are you doing?"

Normally, I'd have said, *Pretty good, looking at colleges. How about you?* But nothing about my life felt normal. "Not so great," I said. "I've spent the summer washing dishes, I'm worried about my depressed, widowed father, and I just found out that my boyfriend got married because he got some girl in Korea pregnant."

"Van got . . . ? Oh, you poor thing. No wonder you went and jumped on Johnny Rollo."

She'd blindsided me. "I . . . I didn't . . . who told you that?"

"Nobody told me. Johnny's the biggest weed dealer in the entire school, and he's not half bad-looking. He bangs any girl he wants, and then he tells her to meet him someplace public so everyone can see the latest notch on his bedpost. I got to go to a basketball game."

"You slept with him too?"

"Welcome to the club, girl. This your first time here?"

I nodded.

"Why don't I help you lose your rock quarry virginity. We'll get some beers and dance our brains out. This place totally rocks, and the sheriff usually gives us about an hour before he sends out the troops to chase our asses out of here."

She was right. About everything. We drank some beer, danced our brains out, and had fun—a lot of fun. The cops showed up an hour later.

"Time to blow this pop stand," she said. "Can you give me a ride? I came here with Tracey and Melissa, but you live right down the street from me, and besides, you're a lot more fun."

We got in my car, cackling like a couple of drunken schoolgirls.

"We're on a roll," Misty said. "Let's not quit now."

She opened her bag, pulled out a pint of vodka, unscrewed the cap, lifted the bottle in the air, and offered up a toast.

"Girl power!" she bellowed—two words that had started as the Spice

Girls catchphrase and had swept the globe to become the official feminist battle cry of our era. She took a swallow and passed the bottle to me.

"I hate to sound like the class nerd," I said, "but here's to our senior year and getting into the college of our choice." I tipped the vodka to my lips and took a swig. "Mine is Penn. What's yours?"

"I'm not going to college," she said, downing another drink.

"Oh, come on," I said. "I know you hate sitting in a classroom, but college is so much more than that. You'll have a blast."

"Maggie, I'm not applying to college. My family doesn't have the money. I'm not even sure I'll finish high school, and if I do, it won't be at Heartstone."

"That's crazy. You're drunk."

"No, I'm broke. My father doesn't have a nickel to send me to college."

I handed her the bottle and tried to clear my head. I knew her father. Arnold Sinclair owned a busy dry-cleaning store, and as far as I could tell, he was well-liked and well-off. The Sinclairs lived in a nice house, they bought Misty a car when she turned sixteen, and they went on a skiing vacation to Aspen over Christmas. There was no way they could be broke.

"I don't understand," I said.

"You know the new fifteen-story apartment complex on Crosby Avenue?" Misty said. "It's called the Commodore. Last winter my father signed a lease to open up a dry-cleaning store in that building."

"I heard that."

"It's expensive. Our original store does pretty well, but it costs a lot to open a second store with all new equipment in a lah-dee-dah building like the Commodore. He sank a shitload of money into it—a lot more than he expected. Once he got started, he couldn't pull the plug, and he wound up having to borrow from the bank, but he was sure it would pay off. He was going to open the new place in September, but it all went to hell. In July he went out of business."

How did I not know that? I thought. And then I realized that my mother had always been the one to let us know if someone in the neighborhood got divorced, had a knee replacement, or won a hundred dollars on a scratch-off ticket.

"What happened?" I asked.

"Minna Schultz happened. Do you know her?"

"No."

"She's a real estate agent and a total cunt. When the Commodore was ready to start selling apartments, she went to one of the owners and tried to get an exclusive listing. He wouldn't give it to her. So, she went to the guy's partner and tried to get it from him. She thought she could play one owner against the other, but it backfired, and they gave the listing to another real estate agent."

"Serves her right," I said, trying to be supportive.

"Yeah, but then the bitch went totally ballistic. She decided to totally trash the Commodore and make it impossible for them to sell anything."

"How is that possible?" I said. "The place is beautiful. It's in a great neighborhood."

"But it's got a dry-cleaning store as part of the complex."

"That only makes it more attractive."

"Not when Minna launches a campaign to say that the cleaning solvents my father uses are toxic."

"Are they?"

"They're the same chemicals all dry cleaners use, but that didn't stop her. She printed up flyers—thousands of them. They were everywhere—in mailboxes, stuck under windshield wipers, she even had them taped to the swings and the jungle gym in the park."

"What'd they say?"

"There was a skull and crossbones on the top. On the bottom was a chart from the EPA showing how one tablespoon of dry-cleaning fluid can contaminate two Olympic-size swimming pools, and a gallon can pollute an entire reservoir. In the middle was a big box that said Sinclair Dry Cleaners is poisoning the air and the water at the Commodore, and that buying an apartment there would be like signing a death warrant for your family.

"The building tried to save its own ass by running an ad campaign to say that they are safe, but my father's reputation was ruined. He never opened the new store, and he owes the bank a fortune that he can't pay, so they sued for anything they could get. They now own the original store, and they're going to auction it off to recoup some of their losses. Meantime my father is wiped out."

"What are you going to do?"

"My father has the perfect solution—booze. He drinks all day and all night. My mother can't stand it anymore. She's taking me and my brother Charlie to live with my grandparents in Colorado. She's going to tell my father tonight. That's why I came to the Pits. I didn't want to be there when it happened. The poor man is going to go to pieces."

I slowed down as I came to the edge of town and stopped at a red light on Main Street. We were less than a mile from home. She handed me the bottle, I put it to my mouth, tilted it up, and drained it dry.

I heard the siren and turned around. A cop car was coming up on us fast, its red and blue turret lights spinning. I shoved the empty bottle under the driver's seat and managed to eke out two words.

"Oh, shit."

CHAPTER 16

The cop slowed down just enough to eyeball the intersection for on-coming traffic, ran the red light, and raced on.

I slumped in my seat. "Oh my God, my father was asleep when I left the house. He'd kill me if I got a DWI."

"My father was sitting in the living room, watching TV, and drinking himself to death," Misty said. "I had to go all Ferris Bueller on him to sneak out. I put some pillows under my covers, climbed out the window, and met Melissa four blocks from my house."

More sirens. I turned around as two more cop cars came barreling toward us.

But they whizzed right past. "One local, one state," I said. "I wonder what's going on?"

"And they may wonder what a couple of teenage girls are doing riding around at two in the morning. If they stop us, we're definitely spending the night in jail. Maybe you should park the car, and we can walk home."

"Fantastic idea," I said. "But I'm too drunk to walk." The light turned green. "But you can get out. I won't be mad. I swear."

"Maggie, you are the single worst person I could be driving around with," Misty said. "But you're still the best thing that's happened to me all day. I'm not going anywhere, asshole. Just drive super careful and try to stay awake."

I put the AC on max and pointed the vents in my face. I shook my head as clear as I could get it, and I moved forward at just below the speed limit. We both kept our eyes peeled for cops, but Main Street was deserted, and three-quarters of a mile later, we got to Crystal Avenue.

I made the final left turn of the long ride and breathed a sigh of relief. "Home sweet ho—"

Three blocks away, the street in front of my house was filled with emergency vehicles, their red, white, and blue flashers lighting up the night.

"Just park it anywhere and get out before the cops see us," Misty said.

I pulled to the nearest curb, hopped it, and knocked over a garbage can. I didn't care. I killed the engine. We jumped out of the car and started running, or whatever it is you call the forward motion of two drunks on a mission.

Up and down Crystal Avenue, lights were on, and people were coming out of their houses. The police had cordoned off the road, so Misty and I cut over to the sidewalk, only to run into a cluster of cops.

"Hold on there, ladies," a female cop said, stretching her arms out and blocking our path. She was local, but I didn't know her. Her name tag said Pemberton. "Get back there behind the barricades."

"We don't live behind the barricades," I shouted. I pointed at my house less than fifty feet away. "I live at 811. She lives across the street—822."

Officer Pemberton, who had been treating us like we were just a couple of nuisances who had interrupted her gabfest with the other cops, turned and pointed at Misty. "You—822," she said. "What's your name?"

Misty said her name, but the vodka had taken its toll, and it came out Mishty Shinclair.

"Misty Sinclair?" the cop said, articulating every syllable.

"Yes, ma'am."

Pemberton turned to me. "And you?"

"Maggie McCormick. I live right over—"

Pemberton cut me off. "Stay right here—both of you," she said, pulling out her radio. "Lieutenant, I've got the girl from eight-two-two."

"Hold her," the voice crackled back.

"Officer Pemberton," I said, an angry drunk trying to sound sober and respectful. "Can you please tell us what's going on? Is anybody hurt? I want to go home."

"You will," she said. "Just wait."

Misty grabbed my hand. "Maggie, did you hear what she said? What did she mean about 'the girl from eight-two-two'? Why is she talking about my house and not yours?"

"I don't know," I said, squeezing her hand tighter.

"Detectives, she's over here," Pemberton called, pointing at Misty.

A man and a woman, both wearing a badge on a chain around their necks, walked up to us. "Misty Sinclair?" the woman said.

Misty nodded. "What's going on?" she said.

"I'm Detective Singleton, and this is Detective Kirk. We need to talk to you." She looked at me. "Alone."

"She's my friend," Misty said. "Can't she come?"

"She's going to wait right here for you with the officer. We won't be long." The detective put her arm on Misty's shoulder and walked her behind the knot of uniformed cops on the sidewalk.

I was exhausted. "Can I at least sit down?" I asked my new babysitter. I didn't wait for an answer. I dropped down on the curb, put my chin in my hands, and stared at the people on the other side of the barricade—men in shorts and T-shirts, women in robes, one holding a baby in her arms.

And then I saw him. His back was to me, but the bright green 2XL McCormick's T-shirt was all I needed.

I jumped up and screamed, "Daaaaaaad!"

He was standing with two cops, and he had his arm around my sister. He wheeled around, looking left, looking right. I screamed again.

"Maggie," he bellowed, spotting me. He came running. Lizzie was right behind him.

I bolted for the barricade, but Pemberton grabbed my arm.

"That's my daughter," he yelled. "Let her go."

Officer Pemberton wasn't taking orders from civilians. She tightened her grip.

The cops who had been with my father caught up with him. One of them was Dad's old classmate, Kip Montgomery. He held up both hands. "It's okay, Monica. I know her. I'll take her from here."

"The detectives want to talk to her." Pemberton shot back.

"Tell them she's with me."

Pemberton let go. I scrambled under the barricade and threw myself into my father's arms.

"Maggie, are you okay? I thought you were upstairs sleeping. Jesus H. Christ, you smell like a goddam distillery. Where the hell were you?"

"I had a bad day, okay?" I snapped, pulling away from him. "After you went to sleep, I snuck out and went to the quarry. I had a few drinks. Same thing you and Mom did when you were seventeen. What's going on here? I was with Misty, but the detectives took her away."

"Misty's okay?" my father said.

"Stupid drunk," I said, "but yeah."

"Thank God. We were . . . we were worried. I'm glad she's safe."

"Please tell me what's going on," I said, my eyes tearing up.

"It was late. I was watching TV, and I hear *bang-bang*," Dad said. "Two gunshots coming from outside. No question."

"Oh my God," I said. Lizzie put a hand on my shoulder, and I pulled her close to me.

"I called nine-one-one, and I slipped onto the porch to see if anyone was wandering the street with a gun. Ten seconds later, there were two more shots, only this time I could see the muzzle flashes in the second-floor bedroom window of Arnie Sinclair's house."

I put my hands to my mouth. In my head, I could hear Officer Pemberton on her radio. *I've got the girl from eight-two-two.*

"I ran back inside, grabbed my gun, and just as I came out, there were two more shots. The lights were on in Arnie's house, so I ran across the street. I tried the front door, and it was unlocked, so I pushed it open, and yelled out, 'Arnie, Lois, it's Finn. Are you okay?' And Arnie yells back from upstairs, 'Go away, Finn.'

"I figured some maniac must have broken in, and I think maybe I can scare him off, so I yell, 'I called 911. Help is coming.' But Arnie screams, 'It's too late for help. Don't come up. Go away.' And then I can hear the sirens. They get closer and closer.

"And then . . ." His big chest was heaving as he spoke. "And then . . . Arnie yells, 'God forgive me,' and bang—one more shotgun blast. I called upstairs to Arnie, but there's no answer. I start to put the pieces together in my head, and I backed out to the street. Thirty seconds later the cops got there."

"Mr. Sinclair shot himself?" I said, half deduction, half question.

My father looked at the two cops at his side.

"As far as we can make out, Mr. Sinclair took his own life," Officer Montgomery said.

"What about Mrs. Sinclair and Charlie?" I asked. I was trembling, and Lizzie held me tight.

"I'm sorry to tell you this Maggie," Officer Montgomery said, "but they were both shot. They're gone."

"Oh my God," I said. "If Misty had been home . . ."

"She's a very lucky girl," my father said. "I didn't go in there, but Kip did. Arnie's body was on the floor in Misty's room. The pillows that were under her sheets were blown apart."

I collapsed into his arms, buried my head in his chest, and sobbed.

And then I heard the piercing wail cutting through the night as the two detectives finally broke the news to Misty.

CHAPTER 17

I woke up the next morning to the sound of Misty puking her guts out in my bathroom.

I cracked my eyes open just wide enough to see the time. Ten fifteen. I closed them again and rubbed my head. It didn't help. At seventeen I wasn't a very experienced drinker, and this was my first full-blown, I-swear-to-God-I'll-never-do-this-again hangover.

I let out a long, low moan, and the wreckage of the past forty-eight hours flooded back. Dumped over the phone by my boyfriend in Korea, meaningless retaliatory sex with my drug dealer, sneaking off to the midnight rave, the drunken drive home, and the unimaginable, unforgettable scene on Crystal Avenue. And then finally, holding Misty in my arms, while she railed at her dead father, "Why Charlie, Daddy? Why Charlie?"

My father had offered her the guest room, but she was too petrified to sleep alone, so we spent the night huddled together in my bed.

"Maggie . . ."

I opened my eyes again. She was standing in the doorway wearing my green bathrobe.

"How you doing?" I asked lamely.

She shook her head.

I desperately needed a hot shower and clean clothes, but she shucked the robe, grabbed her jeans and shirt off the floor and put them on, so I decided to do the same.

The smell of fresh-brewed dark roast hit us as soon as we got to the top of the stairs. "Coffee will help," I said.

"Good morning," my father said. If it were any other day, we'd have gotten a textbook parental lecture on the perils of drinking and driving. But not today. He looked at Misty. "I spoke to your grand-father."

She stared at him, confused. "How . . . ?"

"The local cops called the Colorado state police, who tracked down your grandparents, broke the news to them, and gave them my number. Your grandfather called here a few hours ago. I told him you were okay, so we decided to let you sleep."

"Thanks. Did he say when they're coming?"

"They're not. Your grandmother is not healthy enough to make the trip, and your grandfather won't leave her alone."

Disbelief spread across her face. "They're not . . . but . . . how am I supposed to do this on my own? I don't know how to plan a funeral."

My father put his hand on Misty's shoulder. "It's okay. That's not your responsibility. Your grandparents will take care of everything. They're flying your mother and brother to Colorado."

"What about my father?"

I could see the strain on my father's face. He was the messenger, and I had the feeling he didn't agree with the message. "They decided to let the county take care of him."

"The county?"

"Misty, they just lost their daughter and their grandson. That's who they want. And you, of course. They're sending you a ticket. Once you've settled in with them, they'll find a broker here to sell the house and ship whatever you—"

"*Settled in*? Are they crazy? Do they think I'm moving to the middle-of-nowhere, Colorado? I hardly even know them. No way. I'm staying here."

My father looked at me, then back at Misty. "Fine. We have an extra room, and if it's okay with your grandparents you can stay with us for as long as you—"

"No, no, no, Mr. McCormick. I love you guys for taking me in, but I didn't mean stay *here*. I couldn't possibly walk out that front door every day without looking across the street and seeing my house, and the cop cars, and the ambulances, and the detectives telling me that my entire family was dead. I meant I'm staying in Heartstone. This is where I go to school. This is where my life is . . . what's left of it. I'm not leaving."

"I'm afraid that's not going to be your decision to make. You're a minor. The courts are going to want to make sure you're placed somewhere safe in a home with responsible adults."

"That's okay," Misty said. "I have a responsible adult who will take me."

"Who?" I said.

"Her name is Savannah Jeffries. She's twenty-eight years old. She works for an insurance company. She's married to an electrician, they have two kids, and they live in East Willow, which is still in our school district."

"That's fantastic. It would be so good if you could stay in Heartstone," I said. "Who is she anyway?"

"She's my . . . she's my sister."

I looked at her cautiously, wondering if she'd gone off the deep end. "Misty," I said, "I didn't know you had a sister."

"Neither did I," she said. "I only met her three weeks ago."

"Why don't you sit down at the table," my father said. "Do you want some breakfast?"

"No thanks," Misty said. "But some more coffee would be good."

He refilled her cup, and the three of us sat down. "So how did you find out you had a sister?" he asked.

"One night my parents were fighting," Misty said. "He yelled at her a lot after he lost the store—always about money. Charlie's new sneakers were too expensive, or she was running the air conditioner too much, but that night he was screaming because she got her hair done, and didn't she know they couldn't afford shit like that anymore?

"Most of the time she just let him blow off steam, but I think she was sick of being blamed for everything, and she started yelling back. 'Maybe if you'd kept your dick in your pants, you could have saved a quarter of a million dollars on child support, and I could afford to get a decent haircut.' He came right back at her and said, 'You leave Savannah out of it.'

"I was in my bedroom, so they didn't think I could hear, but they were so loud. I just froze hoping to hear more, but they dropped their voices. It didn't matter. Any idiot could put two and two together. The next day they were out of the house, so I went to his office. He had three file cabinets, and he was obsessive about keeping records. I had to go back seven years, but I found it—canceled checks made out to Alicia Barbieri—child support for her daughter Savannah. They went back every year for as far as he kept records."

"But you said her name was Savannah Jeffries," my father said.

"That's her married name. I found Alicia Barbieri in the phone book; called and told her I was a friend of Savannah's from high school. She gave me Savannah's new name and phone number. I didn't call right away, but once my mother decided to move to Colorado, I didn't know where to turn, so I went to her house. As soon as she opened the door, she knew who I was. She told me that my dad got her mom pregnant when they were seniors in high school, and she never had a relationship with my father, but he sent a check every month till she was twenty-one, so she knew all about me and Charlie and my mom. She's so nice, and you wouldn't believe how much she looks like me."

"And she agreed to take you in?" my father said.

"She didn't even hesitate. I told her I was still hoping to convince my mother to stay in Heartstone, but Savannah said that even if we did, she still wanted me in her life. We're sisters."

Two days later Savannah arrived, and the police escorted the two of us to the Sinclair house, which was still sealed off in yellow crime scene tape. Misty, who could barely look at the outside, didn't have the stomach to go with us.

An hour later, with all her worldly possessions loaded into the back of Savannah's minivan, Misty and I walked to her car.

"Maggie," she said solemnly.

I braced myself for a teary goodbye, but that wasn't Misty's style.

"I spoke to a lawyer," she said.

"Who?" I said. "About what?"

"Toby Cullen's mother. I told her how Minna Schultz put my father out of business. It's because of her that my family is dead. I want her to go to jail."

I was still five years away from starting law school, but I had no doubt what Mrs. Cullen would say.

"Was she helpful?" I ventured.

Misty responded with a sneer. "No. First, she gave me some bullshit about freedom of speech, and then she said if my father sued Minna for defamation of character, he might have had a case, but he was the one who pulled the trigger. He's the murderer. Not her."

"Minna Schultz is a terrible person," I said. "But sometimes bad people get away with doing horrible things."

"Not this time," Misty said. "I could deal with her killing my father. Maybe even my mother. But my brother . . . that kid—he was . . ."

She stopped, her face etched with rage and grief. I put my hand on her shoulder, but she shrugged it off. Vitriol thrives without compassion.

"Charlie was ten times smarter than me. He had a real life ahead of him. Better than mine. Much better than my father's. Minna Schultz stole that life, Maggie." She dropped her voice to a menacing whisper. "And if the justice system won't settle the score, then I will."

"Misty . . . please," I said. "Anytime you want to vent, call me. But do me a favor. Don't repeat what you just said to me to anyone else."

"Or . . . *what* . . . Maggie?" she said, spitting out the words.

"I'm not sure, but if you start threatening Minna, she can sue you for—"

"Bullshit!" she shot back. "Minna Fucking Schultz can't do anything to me that's worse than what she's already done. You were there, Maggie. You were there that night my life was destroyed forever. Don't tell me not to talk about it. Don't tell me to sweep it under the rug. I will tell anybody and everybody who will listen—one day, I'm going to make that bitch pay."

Twenty-six years later, those words would come back to haunt her.

CHAPTER 18

To be honest, I was relieved when Misty moved out. We hadn't been close before that night at the Pits, and with September right around the corner I needed to get my head wrapped around school. I was the senior class president—I had colleges to visit, essays to write, and of course, I was still worried about my father.

Mom had warned us what to expect. "Oh, he'll put up a good front," she said. "Finn McCormick, macho, macho man. But don't let him fool you into thinking he's okay. He'll be as empty on the inside as I would be if he had died."

She was right. On the surface he seemed to be doing well, but Lizzie and I lived with him. We could tell he wasn't sleeping well or eating right. We could see that the Harley sat idle in the garage. We knew he spent hours alone in his bedroom turning the pages of the photo album Mom had left behind.

Grandpa Mike knew it too, and Lizzie got him to open up about it one Sunday after dinner when the three of us were cleaning up. "Sure, your father puts on the happy face and holds out the glad hand at the bar, but he's as transparent as a ten-dollar toupee. He can't fool me. I went through the same thing when your grandmother, God rest her soul, passed. But he ain't about to let anybody see the pain he's going through. He is one stubborn Irishman."

"I hate to break it to you, old man," Lizzie said, "but that's redundant."

Grandpa laughed. "Don't worry, girls. Your father will be okay. It's just going to take time for him to come out on the other side. It'll take time for the whole lot of us. Remember—we *all* lost her."

He was right, but not 100 percent. Mom had told us that afternoon at Magic Pond why Dad would have a tougher time dealing with her loss than we would. "When I die," she said, "I won't be there to watch you walk that glorious path you're each headed down. You'll miss me, but the path will still be there, and you *will* walk it. Your father and I planned a future together. When I die, the road ahead dies with me. He'll be lost. He'll need help. He just won't ask for it."

Those words were still burning in my brain when I went to the Heartstone Library during the second week of school. Beth Webster, the head librarian, saw me, asked me to step into her office, and closed the door.

Beth was one of those pretty, wholesome, girl-next-door types who seemed to have transitioned effortlessly into her midforties. Her hair was blond and bobbed, her smile warm and infectious, and her energy boundless. She loved books and people, although it's hard to say in which order.

"Maggie," she said, giving me a wraparound hug. "How are you and Lizzie doing?"

I shrugged. "We're back in school. That helps."

"And your father?"

"If you ask him, he's fine. Holding up well. The unsinkable Finn McCormick. But in the opinion of this amateur teenage shrink, I don't think he's really dealt with it yet."

"Oh my," she said, putting her hands to her chest. She eased herself into her desk chair. "I can't begin to tell you how much I relate to that. It's exactly what I went through when . . ."

She froze. Her eyes opened wide, and she beamed—the classic look of someone who's just had an epiphany. She sprang out of her chair. "I've got just the thing for him," she said. "Wait right here."

She opened the door, marched out of her office, and headed for the stacks. A woman on a mission. Three minutes later she was back with a book.

"It's called *I'm Fine. Don't Worry. Next Question*," she said. "I think it could do your father a world of good. Please give it to him for me."

"He's not exactly a big reader, Beth. And if he ever were looking for a good book, the last place he would go would be the self-help section."

"It's not a self-help book. It's more of a memoir, and it's hilarious. The author talks about all the crazy things he did to put on a perfect game face so the world would think he was okay after his wife died, even though he was miserable."

"Sounds like my father."

"Good," she said. "Just tell him I said . . . never mind."

She sat down at her desk, slid a piece of library stationery from a tray, and began writing furiously. There was a reason why the other librarians called her "Beth, the Energizer Bunny." When she was done, she put the note in an envelope, sealed it, tucked it in the book, and handed it to me.

"Now give it to him. You don't have to say a thing. It's all in the note."

I thanked her, spent the next two hours in the library, and went home. At seven my father showed up with a shopping bag full of food, and the three of us went through the motions of a family dinner with the usual *how's-school-fine-how's-work* questions.

After dinner I gave him the book. He opened the note.

Dear Mr. McCormick,

Like so many others, I knew and loved Kate. What a wonderful woman, and what a terrible loss. I know from personal experience that nothing can get you through the grief, but there are ways to get around it. This book helped me. I hope it can help you. I couldn't find a card for you in our files, so I used Kate's. I'm sure this is a book she would want you to read.

Sincerely,
Beth Webster

"Really, Maggie?" he said. "So now the local librarian is trying to fix me?"

"She didn't say that, Dad. She said it's a book Mom would want you to read."

"What does she mean, 'This book helped me'?"

"Her husband was killed in a plane crash two years ago."

"Oh, Christ, yes. I remember. Mom and I went to the wake."

"So, then you'll read the book. She said it's really funny."

"I'll get around to it," he said, setting it down on the coffee table. "Just as soon as I'm in the mood for a good laugh."

CHAPTER 19

I told Lizzie about the book Beth had sent.

"He's never going to read it," she said. "Take it back to the library, stop trying to fix everything and everybody, and get back to your life. Rumor has it that school started last week."

"Started?" I said. "More like it exploded. Whoever said senior year was easy wasn't taking two AP courses, trying to get into an Ivy League college, or serving as president of the senior class."

"Or banging Stephen DeMille," she said, a smirk on her face.

"Allegedly."

"Well, that proves it, Counselor. Your failure to deny is a blatant confirmation," she said. "Hey, I think it's great. Stephen is smart, he's pretty decent looking, and his mother's not a crack whore. You've really upped your game since Johnny Rollo."

I laughed. "Johnny Boy set the bar low. Stephen is passable, but I don't know if I'll ever find anyone as incredible as Van."

Lizzie put her infamous imaginary microphone up to her mouth. "Will poor Maggie McCormick settle for humdrum sex, or will the stalwart Irish lass take on every swinging dick at Heartstone High until she recaptures the magnificent orgasms of her youth? Let's ask her." She shoved the fake mic in my face.

The truth was, she wasn't that far off the mark. In addition to my heavy academic workload, my responsibilities as class president, and the looming deadline for college applications, I was obsessed with one other thing. Sex. I loved it, and I wanted more.

"So, who's next?" Lizzie asked.

"You're an idiot," I said.

"I'm just a hardworking reporter trying to get some answers. Do you have anything I can share with our viewers?"

"Yeah. Tell them you have to kiss a lot of frogs before you find your prince."

"Sounds like this serial frog kisser has her next victim lined up. Can you tell us who it is?"

"If I tell you, will you leave me alone?"

"Probably not, but I won't tell a soul." She tossed the invisible mic over her shoulder. "Okay, now it's just between us sisters."

"Rico Montero," I said.

"*Ay caramba!* You're going ethnic."

"He's Mexican. He thinks I'm ethnic."

"Well, I hope this one works out for you."

It didn't. Thirty years after the women's liberation movement took root in the industrialized nations of the Western world, Rico either hadn't heard of it or he flat-out rejected the concept. He was a throwback to the days when women were expected to be barefoot, pregnant, and in the kitchen. Not exactly my life's goals, but the sex was good, so we were still a couple on the morning of the senior class Halloween breakfast.

It's an annual tradition at Heartstone. The seniors dress up for Halloween, eat a pancake breakfast at the cafeteria, and take a group photo for the yearbook. The theme that year was come as a person you admire.

I was in awe of Sandra Day O'Connor, the first woman appointed to the Supreme Court, so I wore a long black robe and a lace collar, and I carried a gavel.

But it was Misty Sinclair who rocked the room. She showed up in a pair of crotch-hugging, ass-grabbing red satin hot pants, a matching V-neck with five inches of cleavage spilling over the top, and a pair of red-sequined fuck-me shoes. And just to make sure nobody mistook

her for Mother Teresa or Mary Magdalene, she had a pair of horns pro-
truding from her teased hair, a kinky little fur-trimmed pitchfork, and
a pointy red devil's tail.

Boys drooled, girls trashed-talked her, and at least half a dozen faculty members dropped by unexpectedly—all male.

I sat next to her. Our fleeting friendship had never gone to the next
level once she moved in with her sister, but I still rooted for her. "I totally love your outfit," I said. "You look scandalous."

"Thanks. I was trying to look like hell, but scandalous sounds
equally hot."

"How's it going with Savannah?"

"Not great. I mean I love her to death, and the kids are fantastic,
but I've got to get away from her husband."

"What's wrong with him?"

"He can't walk past me without getting a hard-on. He pawed me
once when Savannah was out shopping, and I shoved him off. He's
good-looking, great bod, but I'll be damned if I'm going to wreck the
marriage of the only person I've got left in my life. I'm moving to Los
Angeles right after graduation. I'm thinking about taking acting lessons."

After breakfast was over, I was expected to speak. Normally it's a
nonevent where the class president makes a few announcements, asks
for volunteers for various committees, and ends with a variation on "the
first three years have been great, but this one is going to be the best ever."

I had a better idea. "My father owns a pub," I said, stepping up
to the podium. "And he'd like to make a donation to the class of '98."

I had a slide projector set up, and I flashed a picture of a
fifteen-and-a-half-gallon stainless steel beer keg on the screen.

The kids cheered, and half a dozen of Rico's friends who were all
at the same table started chanting, "Boss Lady. Boss Lady. Boss Lady."

I cringed. I knew it wasn't a compliment. I knew they called me Boss
Lady behind my back, and they called Rico Boss Lady's Bitch to his face.

"Before you get too excited about that keg," I said, "I should tell
you that since we're all underage, it's empty."

I got the expected chorus of boos.

"But we're going to fill it up," I said. "Then we're going to seal it. And then . . ." I went to the next slide—the same keg, with the words *Heartstone High School Class of 1998 Time Capsule* on it. "We're not going to open it again until our twenty-fifth reunion, at which point my father will give us as many kegs as we need—all full."

I'm not sure if they liked the idea of a class time capsule or the promise of free beer twenty-five years down the road, but they all whooped their approval, with Rico's buddies pounding the table and catcalling their Boss Lady mantra.

Duff Logan jumped up on his chair. Duff, the undisputed class clown, was a master at working the teenage funny bone, and his legion of fans quieted down to give him center stage. "I say we put Principal Drucker in the time capsule," he yelled, "and see if he's any less of an asshole when we let him out in twenty-five years."

The room went nuts. I know a good exit line when I hear one, so I pumped my fist, shot them a V-for-Victory sign, and stepped away from the podium.

"Maggie!" It was Rico storming toward me. "I can't take this shit."

"What shit?" I said.

"You always running the show. My friends say you treat me like I'm your goddam dumb Mexican pool boy."

"Rico, your friends have no idea how I treat you."

"I don't care. It looks bad. If we're going to stay together, you've got to resign from this stupid president job."

"I have a better idea," I said.

"Yeah, what?"

"We're done," I said, banging my gavel on one of the cafeteria tables. "*Terminado.*"

"*Puta*," he bellowed. His friends turned, and he gave me the finger. "*Vete a la mierda*," he added, more for their benefit than for mine.

I smiled as he walked away, feeling very Sandra Day O'Connor about my decision.

I hated to admit it, but I couldn't wait to share the news with my bogus newscaster sister. Most days the two of us would get home from school about the same time. But one of the waitresses had asked for the night off to take her kids trick-or-treating, so Lizzie agreed to work the dinner shift.

By the time she got home it was almost ten, and I was dying to tell her that I was shopping around for my next frog to kiss, and ask what she thought about Duff Logan, who wasn't particularly good-looking, but he was funny as hell.

"You'll never guess what happened at the Halloween breakfast," I said.

"Tell me later," she said. "I've got something more important to discuss."

"Well, if your shit's *more important*, then by all means—"

"How about this?" she said, a smug little grin on her face. "I'll tell you what it is, and you decide if your news is more important than mine."

"Fine," I said. "What is it?"

"Dad's got a girlfriend."

CHAPTER 20

I followed Lizzie into her bedroom and closed the door. "It was inevitable," I said. "A bunch of them have been coming to the restaurant almost every night and circling him like flies on shit. Which one is it?"

"None of the usual suspects. This one's a dark horse. Her name is Connie Gilchrist."

I shrugged. "Never heard of her."

"Me either. Dotty said she moved into town about a month ago. She's renting a house over on Oriole Drive."

Dotty Briggs was one part night manager, one part den mother, one part hawk. Not much happened at McCormick's—or in Heartstone, for that matter—without Dotty digging up all the dirt.

"What else did Dotty tell you?"

"Connie is about forty, honey-blond hair, pretty smile, nice body—"

"I don't care what she looks like," I said. "I want to know how someone shows up in town, and a month later she's got her hooks into our father."

"Her *hooks*? That sounds a little harsh. You don't know anything about her."

"Fine," I said, sitting down on the bed. "Tell me what you heard."

Lizzie turned on a lamp and killed the overhead light. "Okay," she said, lowering her voice. "It was a dark and stormy night . . ."

"Damn it, Lizzie, does everything have to be a joke with you?"

"It's not a joke. I'm trying to paint a picture here."

"Sorry. It just sounds like the opening of a 1940s movie. Go on."

"Anyway, Dotty said one night about three weeks ago it was pouring like crazy. The place was practically dead—almost as many staff as customers—and this Connie walks in. She's definitely not a barfly looking for someone to pay for her drinks. She's classy—nice clothes, perfect makeup, even though it's raining. She sits down at the bar and orders two Manhattans. Dad makes them and offers to bring them over to a table. She says no thanks. She met her husband at a bar. They were both drinking Manhattans."

"So, where's the husband in all this?" I asked.

"Dead. He died a year and a half ago. Apparently, this little ritual with two drinks is her way of celebrating their life together."

"That's perfect! The grieving widow meets the grieving widower."

"Relax. That's what Dotty thought at first. Her antenna went up, but she said all they did was talk. Connie drank half of one drink, half of the other, and left after about an hour."

"And I'll bet she came back the next night," I said.

"You'd bet wrong, sister. She hasn't been back since."

"You just said Dad's got girlfriend."

"Did I say that? Oh yeah . . . maybe that's because you always think what's on your mind is more important than what's on mine, so I might have beefed up the facts a little to get your attention."

"Well, now you've got it. What happened?"

"Dotty couldn't listen to every word, but mostly they talked about what it's like to lose a spouse, and before Connie left, she gave Dad the name of a bereavement group she was going to."

"Dad hates the idea of support groups."

"Apparently, he's come around. Dotty's pretty sure Dad has been meeting her there a couple of times a week. She spotted a pamphlet on his desk—*Comforting You in Your Time of Loss.*"

"*Comforting*? That sounds like code for having sex."

"Oh, for God's sake, Maggie, do you really think Dad has been walking around in a funk because he wants to get laid? He's lonely. His marriage to Mom was about companionship, about getting on a Harley and driving wherever the road took them. All these women who have been throwing themselves at him are scaring him away. Connie might be the first one who really understands what he's going through. So, she convinced him to go to a support group—isn't that what Mom wanted?"

"Alone—not with a date! I don't trust this woman. She could be another predator like Rita Walsh, trying to get inside Leon Brennan's pants before his wife was even in the ground."

"You know what your problem is?" Lizzie said. "You have sex on the brain."

"And you have your head in the clouds. So, Connie got him to go to a few meetings. How do you know he's not going back to her place afterward and banging her?"

The overhead light snapped on. "Why don't you ask him?"

It was my father.

"Not that my sex life is any of your business, but before you start turning speculation into rumors that quickly become gospel, let me go on record. I'm not banging anybody."

"Dad, I'm sorry," I said.

"You should be. Your mother and I discussed three things about sex before she died. First, she gave me her blessing to have sex whenever I was ready. Second, she gave me a list of warning signs to look out for, so I don't confuse a hot meal and a hot body with a genuine down-to-earth woman."

I expected him to go on, but he stopped. He just stood there staring at me, his arms folded across his chest.

I couldn't deal with the silence. "What was the third thing?" I asked.

"She said, 'Finn, if I were you, I wouldn't ask Maggie about her sex life. The less you know, the better off you'll be.'"

I closed my eyes and buried my head in my hands.

"So then, you've been going to these bereavement meetings," I heard Lizzie say.

"I have. Not the ones at St. Cecilia's. I know too many people there.

I've been going two or three times a week, sometimes at United Methodist, sometimes the Episcopal church over on Greenwood."

I put my hands down and opened my eyes. "Are they helping?"

"I don't know. Maybe. They say that time heals all wounds, but they also say that misery loves company, and it helps to know that other people are going through the same emotions that I'm going through. Some of us go out for coffee or drinks after the meeting, so that helps a little too."

"Well, I guess that's a good thing," I said. "It gives you a chance to meet people you can hang out with—maybe go to a movie or dinner or something."

He smiled. "Let me explain something to you, sweetheart," he said. "I have a dozen friends who keep inviting me to go bowling, play poker, take in a ball game—the list goes on. I don't have any trouble finding someone to do things with. But when your mother died . . ."

He paused and swallowed hard. "When your mother died," he said, tears welling up in his eyes, "I lost the only person in the world I could do nothing with."

He opened his arms, and Lizzie and I both fell into them. "Don't worry, girls. We'll get through this—the three of us."

He hugged us both, told us he loved us, let go, and left the room. Lizzie looked at me, gave me a half shrug, and followed him out the door.

I dropped back down on the bed, and in that moment, as my own eyes filled with tears, I knew that I had never loved him more—or loved myself less.

CHAPTER 21

A week later Dad invited Lizzie and me to join him and Connie for Sunday brunch at the Lakeview Lodge, a sprawling complex with a few dozen log cabins set on a lake about five miles out of Heartstone.

As soon as I met her, I could understand what my father saw in her. Like my mother, Connie was a people person, the kind of woman who seems comfortable in her own skin and can interact with almost anybody.

Introductions could have been awkward, but she made it effortless, taking each of us by the hand, telling us how many wonderful stories she had heard about Mom, and then extending her sympathies for our loss. Having been consoled by hundreds of people since my mother's death, I know a hollow condolence when I hear one, but Connie's was heartfelt and sincere. First impressions count a lot, and she was off to a great start.

Unlike most grownups confronted with teenagers, she didn't fall into the "So how's school?" trap. She'd done her homework, and with the skill of a professional interviewer she soon had me talking about my role as class president, and then, knowing that Lizzie's goal was to become a doctor, she told us about her grandmother, who in 1928 was the only female physician in a county of more than fifty thousand people.

"She practiced medicine until she turned eighty," Connie said. "She died at the age of ninety-two. I wish you could have met her. She was quite an inspiration."

"So, what did she inspire you to do?" Lizzie asked.

"Nothing quite as noble as save lives, but she did teach me to follow my heart. My passion is painting. I studied art at Hunter College." She held out her hands, and we could see flecks of color embedded inside the rims of several fingernails. "And as you can see, I'm still at it."

"I've seen her work," Dad said. "She's good."

"If only everyone were as generous as your father," Connie said. "I'm not exactly a starving artist, but I still have to supplement my income by giving private lessons, or if I get lucky, picking up substitute teaching jobs."

I didn't care how she earned a living. I was more interested in my father's comment. Unless Connie was bringing her paintings to the support group meetings, Dad had seen them up close and personal. I filed that away.

"So did you move here to teach?" Lizzie asked.

"No, I came here to paint. My late husband was a yacht broker. It's like a real estate broker; only instead of selling homes he sold ridiculously expensive boats. I've always loved the Hudson Valley, but we lived in Miami, where there's lot of sun, lots of water, and lots of people with money who want to cruise around on it. After he died, I knew I didn't want to stay in Florida, but it took me over a year to settle the estate, sell the house, get rid of the furniture, pack up, and get on the road."

"How'd you decide on Heartstone?" Lizzie said.

"That was a no-brainer. Back when I was in college, I would drive up here from New York City. I love painting Americana, and Heartstone is a treasure trove of barns, farms, Federal houses—even this lodge is a throwback to kinder, gentler, simpler times. And unlike Florida, you've got four seasons. I got here in late September, and I can't tell you how many tubes of red, yellow, orange, and gold I've gone through. I just finished a painting of the pond across from the hospital. It's so serene. It gives a girl a chance to drop the word *idyllic* when she goes out to brunch. I can't wait to paint it when its freezes over."

"Magic Pond," my father said. "It was Kate's favorite place."

"Well, in that case, I really hope I do it justice."

"I'm sorry about your husband," Lizzie said. "How did he die?"

"Lizzie!" Dad snapped.

"Finn, that's okay," Connie said. "My grandmother would have asked the same exact question."

Lizzie isn't easily stroked, but being compared to a trailblazing feminist physician totally captivated her. Her eyes warmed, and she got that sheepish, aw-shucks look that happens whenever she gets a compliment she can't handle.

"Steve was seventeen years older than I am," Connie said. "He was out on the ocean with a prospective buyer, and he had a heart attack. The client had no idea how to pilot the boat and could barely figure out the radio. By the time the Coast Guard got there, it was too late. It was quite a shock. One morning he went to work, and that afternoon two detectives showed up at my studio to inform me that I was a widow. Your father and I have been discussing the pros and cons of sudden death versus a long protracted illness."

"And where'd you net out?" Lizzie said.

"They both suck something fierce," Connie said.

My father stared at this new woman in his life, and his eyes crinkled, the corners of his mouth turned up, and the apples of his cheeks puffed out. It was a look I knew well—so much more intimate than a mere smile. It was the same special way that he gazed at my mother when she said or did something that made him proud. He was beaming.

But I don't think he was reacting to what Connie said. I think he was thrilled to watch his almost-girlfriend and his youngest daughter forge a bond.

He didn't say a word, but I decided that I knew what he was thinking.

One down, one to go.

CHAPTER 22

"What did you think of Connie?" Lizzie asked me after brunch.

I shrugged off the question. "She's okay."

"She's *okay*? Way to heap on the accolades, Margaret."

"Hey . . . can I help it if I wasn't blown away the way you were?"

"I wasn't *blown away*. I liked her. Dad likes her. Hell, *Mom* would've liked her."

"I doubt it. Mom was big on table manners. Did you see the way the woman wolfed down that omelet?"

"So she was hungry; she ate fast. Is that your issue, or just one of your typical pungent observations?"

"What do you want me to say? I just met her. It would be one thing if she was Connie Gilchrist, artist, husband died, new in town. But no— she's Connie Gilchrist, total stranger, who might or might not become a permanent fixture in my life. Give me time. Let's just see where their relationship is going."

Wherever it was going, it moved along at a pretty rapid clip. That night at dinner Dad made it obvious that they were a lot more than bereavement buddies.

"What are you two doing on Friday?" he asked.

"Sleeping in," Lizzie said. "It's Veterans Day. No school."

"I know," he said. "That's why I picked it. As long as you

have the day off, I need you to come in to the restaurant and help set up."

"Set up what?" I said.

"An art show. Connie's got a lot of really great paintings, but she's new in town. Nobody knows her. This is the perfect way to get her name around, give her some exposure."

"Cool," Lizzie said.

"Cool if we were a museum," I said. "But people kind of come to our place for food. How are we supposed to sell paintings? And what would you like with your meat loaf, Mrs. DiBenedetto? Baked, mashed, still life, or landscape?"

"For God's sake, Maggie, we're not selling the damn things," my father said. "If people want to buy one, they can talk to Connie. She'll be there. We're just hanging them on the wall. Lots of restaurants do it. It'll class up the joint a little."

"I would have thought that an Irish pub with half a dozen Harleys parked outside, and a white-haired Gaelic grandpa behind the bar with a full repertoire of dirty limericks would be classy enough, but maybe I was wrong," I said.

Dad laughed. "That's the spirit," he said, as if my teenage snark were a form of enthusiastic approval.

On Friday at 10:00 a.m., Lizzie, Dad, and I helped Connie set up. Apparently, there's an art to nailing a bunch of hooks in the wall and hanging pictures of Americana alongside Guinness signs and black-and-white photos of old-world rugby teams. We spent hours hanging, unhanging, and rehanging all twenty-two masterpieces until the artist finally gave us her blessing.

"Finn," she gushed, "you have the best daughters."

"Oh, they're keepers," he said. "It's going to be a great night."

It wasn't. Connie had been wearing jeans and a work shirt when she left at 1:30 p.m. She had plenty of time to get dressed for the event, but when the dinner crowd started strolling in at five, she still wasn't back. By 5:15 p.m., my father was nervous, and by 5:45 he was frantic.

"It's not like her to be late," he said, as if the two of them had a long history together, rooted in her unflagging punctuality.

It was a little after six when the cop car, its turret lights flashing, pulled up, and Officer Kip Montgomery escorted Connie into the restaurant.

"Sorry I'm late," she said. "I had car trouble."

Officer Montgomery smiled at my father. "That's one way to put it, but my official report is going to say that your lady friend here lost control of her vehicle, fishtailed across Foley Road, hopped the sidewalk, and took out three garbage cans."

Dad put his arms on Connie's shoulders. "Oh my God, are you all right?"

"A little shell-shocked, but I think my Volvo wagon may be down for the count."

"Rear suspension ripped right out of the frame," Montgomery said.

"Jesus, she's lucky to be alive," Dad said. "Kip, a million thanks. Next time you're here with Nancy and the kids, dinner is on me."

Montgomery held up a hand. "Just doing my job, Finn. But I'll let you treat the kids to dessert." He tapped two fingers to the brim of his hat. "Ms. Gilchrist. Good luck with your show."

"I bet you could use a drink," Dad said to his lady friend as soon as the cop was gone.

"I could use a hug first."

He obliged, stepped back, and looked her over. She was wearing an A-line blush pink cocktail dress, silver strappy heels, and her honey-blond hair was short with curled layers. A pair of pink-sapphire-and-diamond teardrop earrings set off her hazel eyes.

"Your car may be a wreck," he said, "but you look fantastic."

He walked her to the bar, and I grabbed Lizzie. "That bitch is wearing Mom's earrings!" I whisper-screamed.

"Relax. Dad lent them to her."

"Why didn't you tell me?"

"I don't know. Maybe because they're *Mom's* earrings."

"Technically they're ours."

"I wasn't at the reading of the will, but technically I think they're Dad's."

"How can you be so cavalier about this?" I said. "Can't you see this was exactly what Mom was talking about?"

"Maggie, the earrings are gathering dust. Dad lent them to Connie for one night. Stop obsessing over her and take a look at him. The man's happy."

I turned to the bar. Dad, one hand hoisting a beer, the other resting casually on Connie's arm, was more jubilant than I'd seen him in months. I hated him for it.

He caught me staring at him, put down his beer, held both hands in front of his face, and wiggled all ten fingers at me—a throwback to the days when my idea of a good time was a ride on his shoulders and a game of Chutes and Ladders where he let me win.

I couldn't stand it. I left the restaurant. Daddy's little girl needed booze, weed, and a night of uncomplicated, meaningless sex.

CHAPTER 23

My plan had been for Duff Logan to be the next notch on my sexual conquest belt. When we were sophomores, he tailed me like a puppy dog, so I figured he'd jump all over me when I finally gave him the chance. Turned out I was wrong. Duff was gay. The only reason he followed me around was because he had the hots for Van.

The pickings were slim at Heartstone High, so I went back to the devil I knew: Johnny Rollo.

The sex was good, the weed was free, plus I liked Johnny. Under all his macho street-kid bullshit there was a certain sad sweetness about him. He also had some life skills that I was lacking.

That night after I bolted from the art show, we did the deed, hit the bong, and I told him how much I hated Connie.

"I know you don't want to hear this, but she's probably not as bad as you think," he said. "Your problem is that you have daddy issues. You'd hate any woman who went near your old man."

"Not true! This one's devious. Spend some time with her and you'll see."

"Good idea. Maybe I'll run into her at one of those fancy art galleries I hang out at."

"Or maybe," I said, "you can come to Thanksgiving dinner with me and see for yourself. She'll be there."

"No way."

"Please. Our Thanksgiving dinners are legendary. We have them at the restaurant after the last turn. It's not just my family. A lot of the staff are there, and the food is incredible."

"I don't know. I was going to meet my mom for a turkey sandwich and a crack pipe, but hell, she won't even notice if I don't show up. I'll do it if you just promise me one thing."

"Anything," I said, ready to get down on my knees and pull down his pants.

"Promise me you'll stop ragging about this Connie chick. I'll be there, but if you even mention her name once, the deal is off."

"I promise," I said.

Thanksgiving was less than two weeks away, and I decided that the best way to keep my mind off Connie was to throw myself into my latest project—the senior class time capsule. Kids kept asking me what could and what couldn't go in. There were no rules, so I made them up as I went along.

And then one night it hit me. The time capsule was the answer I had been looking for. I sat down at my desk and wrote a letter to my future self.

I poured my heart out about my plans for the future and waxed on about how I had my heart set on going to Penn—the one school I knew could help me realize my dreams. I wrote till two in the morning, put it away for a day, and then rewrote it the next night, and polished it the night after that.

And when I was finally finished, I printed out a copy, and I shared it with Lizzie.

"Why are you letting me read this now?" she said. "I thought it's supposed to be sealed in that beer keg and not be opened for twenty-five years."

"I lied. It's not really going into the time capsule," I said. "It's the essay for my application to Penn. It lets me show them that I'm a leader in my class, I'm thinking about my future, and I'm passionate about getting into their school."

"That's brilliant," she said. "Admissions people like it when a kid is gung ho. I bet they eat this shit up. What are you doing for the other schools you're applying to?"

I held up six more copies of the letter—all identical. The only thing I did was change the name of the school I was dying to get into.

"You're a genius," Lizzie said. "Any one of these places would be lucky to have you."

The Saturday morning before Thanksgiving, Lizzie and I were working at the restaurant. Dad was supposed to be there by eleven, but we didn't hear him roll up until twelve thirty. The two of us walked out into the parking lot to bust his chops about being an hour and a half late.

His bike pulled in, and he took off his helmet. Right behind him came Mom's Mustang, sparkling clean, top down, Connie Gilchrist behind the wheel with her scarf, her kerchief, and her oversized sunglasses, looking like a poor man's Audrey Hepburn in *Roman Holiday*.

"Dad! That's Mom's car," I said.

"Connie's Volvo is totally shot. The guys at the shop told her it would be cheaper to buy a good used car than to pay to have a twelve-year-old Volvo welded together."

"So you sold her Mom's Mustang?"

"No. I lent it to her till she can buy something on her own."

"It's been a week since she totaled her old one. How long does it take?"

"Not that it's any of your business, but cars cost money. Her husband may have sold yachts to rich people, but he wasn't any good with his own finances. He left her with a lot more debt than assets. I told her she could use the Mustang till she gets back on her feet."

"I thought one of us was going to get it."

"A teenage girl doesn't need a flashy car. It's an asshole magnet. Right now, you and Lizzie are sharing the Acura. When the time comes that you need two cars, I'll find a good, solid, age-appropriate used one. Now drop the subject. She's coming."

Connie had parked the convertible and was walking toward us, smiling and waving. She gave me a hug, then Lizzie, then grabbed my father by the hand, and they walked through the kitchen door of the restaurant together.

"I don't believe it," I said. "First Mom's earrings, and now her Mustang?"

"I think we've been over this before," Lizzie said. "Mom's not using them."

"That's not the point. The point is those things all belong to us."

"No, Maggie, the point is that live women wear dead women's earrings, they drive dead women's cars, and they shack up with dead women's husbands. Deal with it." She walked through the kitchen door, leaving me standing there alone in the parking lot.

I lowered myself to the ground and buried my head in my hands. Nothing made sense. Connie Gilchrist was slowly destroying our family. Not only was she ransacking my mother's treasures; she was driving a wedge between me and my sister.

Genghis Connie.

CHAPTER 24

Thanksgiving is the biggest day of the year at McCormick's. We serve a five-course, prix fixe, good old-fashioned traditional American Turkey Day dinner, but Grandpa Mike and Dad love to shake things up by offering some of their signature Irish classics, like colcannon instead of green bean casserole, or Bailey's Irish Cream mudslide cake in addition to pumpkin pie.

There are three seatings—noon, two thirty, and five o'clock—and we are always booked solid at least a month in advance. Then at seven thirty, when the last of our customers waddles out in a food coma, we lock the front door, and about a hundred of us—cooks, waitresses, bartenders, busboys, dishwashers, and their families—have our own Thanksgiving feast.

Johnny Rollo couldn't believe it. "You're feeding all these people for free?" he said.

"They work hard all year. This is one of the things my mother and father do to . . ."

Out of nowhere, the wave of sadness flooded over me, and my voice caught. I tried to fight it. "It's what they do to show their . . ." Again the words stuck in my throat, and this time tears spilled onto my cheeks.

"I get it," Johnny said, putting his arm around me and walking me to a quiet corner of the room. "You miss your mom. It's okay. Cry it out."

I pressed my face to his chest and sobbed into the soft warm fabric of the sweater I had just given him so he'd feel dressed for the occasion.

"I knew I shouldn't have worn my good cashmere," he said.

That stopped the flood, and I started laughing. "It's not cashmere," I said. "It's acrylic."

"And there's the difference between you and me," he said. "You can only afford acrylic, so you buy acrylic."

"And what would you have done?"

"Stolen the cashmere."

I laughed again, wiped away the tears, and I kissed him. I knew in my heart that there was no future for the two of us, but in 1997 and again decades later when I needed him the most, Johnny Rollo—cold-blooded, hard-hearted, self-proclaimed in-it-for-himself bad boy Johnny Rollo—was there for me. And I loved him for it.

The kitchen doors opened, and a platoon of servers, led by my grandfather, my father, and Chef Tommy Hogan marched platters and trays and tureens and bowls and baskets of food onto a thirty-foot groaning board that had been stretched out down the center of the room.

Only when it was nearly filled to overflowing and ready to collapse under its own weight did Grandpa Mike step behind the bar, clang the brass bell that is usually reserved to acknowledge extremely generous tippers, and called out to the crowd, "Soup's on."

The tables had been pushed together so that we could have two long rows of banquet-style seating. Johnny and I filled our plates and sat across from my father, who had Lizzie on his right and Connie on his left.

We ate, we drank, we talked, we laughed, and somewhere around nine o'clock the chanting started. Chef Tommy was sitting ten chairs away from us at the far end of our table. He stood up, and ladle in one hand, frying pan in the other, he banged them together and got the group's attention.

"God bless Black Monday," he sang out.

Those in the know chanted back. "God bless Black Monday."

Then Rubén the line cook stood up, raised his arms in the air, and yelled, "*Dios bendiga el lunes negro.*"

The Hispanic contingent among us echoed it back in unison.

Then it was back to the English chorus. "God bless Black Monday."

Then in Spanish, then in English, then in Spanish, then in English, until everyone in the room joined in, including Connie and Johnny, who had no idea what it all meant.

Finally, my father stood up, and the group broke into applause.

"I want to thank you all for coming," he said, "and if this is your first rodeo, let me tell you what this tumult is all about.

"The year was 1987, and back then I wasn't the handsome and dashing, overconfident innkeeper that you see standing before you now."

Groans, laughter, and applause from the crowd. Dad ate it up. He was in his element now.

"I was, I'm sad to tell you, a stockbroker. A pencil-pushing, number-crunching, short-haired, suit-and-tie-from-Brooks-Brothers, riding-the-Metro-North-to-New-York-City-every-day, midlevel-Wall-Street asshole."

He waited for the laugh to subside. "And I worked at Lehman Brothers. Did I mention it was 1987? Anyway, on October nineteenth of that fateful year, the stock market tanked. It was a Monday. Black Monday. On Tuesday morning I was fired, and on Wednesday, I woke up with a god-awful hangover, got on the Harley, and rode over to my first and only job interview, and I handed the owner of the business my résumé. Tell 'em what it said, Pop."

Grandpa Mike stood up. "First of all, it was the most unprofessional résumé I ever saw. It was handwritten. In pencil. It said, 'Finn McCormick, MBA, Hofstra University, 1979. Seeks challenging opportunity in the hospitality industry. Irish pub preferred.'"

Another round of laughter, and Dad picked up the story. "So, there I was, practically begging my old man for a job, and he says to me, 'I can't afford you.' I say would you rather see me on the unemployment line? And he says, 'Save me a spot. We're in the red. We'll never make it through the winter. I figure I'll close up shop right after New Year's.'

"Now I've got an MBA. It wasn't hard to figure out why an old Irishman couldn't make any money running a pub. When he opened this joint on St. Patrick's Day thirty years ago, he put a sign in the window. *There's a bunch of so-called Irish pubs here in Heartstone. This is the only one worth a damn. Come on in. First drink is on Mike.*

"And come they did—the O'Learys, the O'Sheas, and all the other O-apostrophes who were longing for a taste of the old sod. But twenty years later they'd rather sit at home nights and watch *Jeopardy!* and *Wheel of Fortune*. And nobody came to take their place. It was 1987, and Mc-Cormick's was stuck somewhere in the first half of the twentieth century.

"So, I said, I'll buy the place from you. And he said, you can have the whole kit and caboodle for ten bucks. I said, ten bucks? For this loser? So we haggled, and I wound up getting it for a dollar."

He looked out at the room. "Now who was here in 1987 when we were a few months from pulling the plug?"

Hands went up.

"And who busted their asses working extra hours without asking for an extra nickel?"

The hands stayed high.

"And who started sharing in the profits when there finally was a profit?"

Same hands.

"McCormick's is a family business," my father said. "But a lot of people not named McCormick are part of this family. So now you know why we celebrate Thanksgiving together. And why we say, 'God bless Black Monday.'"

The room cheered.

"One more thing. This is the first year Kate isn't running around the room, giving hugs, kissing the kids, and packing doggie bags for you all to take home. But she's still with us." He raised his glass. "To Kate."

Everyone drank. And someone, probably Lizzie, hit play on the sound system and the room filled with the Dubliners singing "Whiskey in the Jar." Grandpa Mike grabbed Dotty Briggs and twirled her onto the makeshift dance floor. The party was just getting started.

I walked Johnny over to our quiet little corner of the room. "What did you think?" I said.

"You're a lucky girl, Maggie," he said. "You've got a great family."

"No, I mean about Connie."

"What do you know about her?" he asked.

I told him the little she had told us.

"I think she left something out," he said. "Something big. You'd never pick up on it, but me coming from where I come from, she couldn't hide it from me."

"What do you mean you coming from where you come from?" I said.

"Maggie, my father did a six-year bid at Sing Sing. Then he did five more in Dannemora, not to mention county jail three or four times."

I nodded. I'd known that.

"Over the years, at least half a dozen of his prison buddies would swing by to keep my mother *company* . . . if you catch my drift. A couple Black, a couple white, but they all had one thing in common. No matter how long they'd been out, they couldn't shake their mess hall eating habits. Did you see how Connie grabbed Felipe's hand when he reached across her plate to get the salt?"

"Yeah, I caught that. She said he startled her."

"He didn't startle her. She was guarding her food. Did you see how fast she ate? She inhaled it before I even got my hands on the mashed potatoes. She's conditioned."

I gave him a blank stare. "Conditioned to what?"

"*Institutional dining*," he said. "That move she made on Felipe was a classic jailhouse tell."

He paused to see if I made sense of the words. And then he left no room for doubt.

"Trust me, Maggie," he said. "That woman did prison time."

CHAPTER 25

I stood there, the sounds of fiddles, pipes, tin whistles, banjos, and bodhran drums in my ears, mixed with the cacophony of handclapping, foot stomping, well-lubricated revelers, and I was sure I'd heard Johnny wrong.

"*Prison?*" I said.

"I know," he said. "She's pretty slick, but I was eyeing her at dinner. She hunches over when she eats, and she uses her elbows and arms to block her plate." He mimicked the action.

"So?"

"So, Felipe is lucky she didn't stab him with a fork. Protecting your food is a big thing when you're locked up. So is eating fast. Some chow lines give you six minutes to hoover it all down before they rotate. You do that three meals a day for a couple of years, and it's a hard habit to shake."

"You think she was in for *years?*"

"I can't put a clock on it, but you don't just pick up table manners like those after a bad day in traffic court."

"I told Lizzie she had bad table manners! I spotted it when we went to brunch with her and my dad. I thought she was just kind of—I don't know—low rent. But prison? Holy shit, Johnny, we have to tell my father."

"First of all, sweetheart, there is no *we*. Second of all, what are you going to say? The guy who sells me weed is up on his prison lore, and he thinks this chick you've been banging is an ex-con?"

"You're right. My father is already pissed at me because I haven't been jumping up and down about how fantastic she is, so I'd better be a thousand percent positive. Do you think she has anything in her purse, like parole papers? That would prove it."

"Her purse? No way. Her house, maybe, but not her purse."

"Then you've got to help me break in and get it," I said.

His head snapped back. "You want me to break into her house? Jesus, Maggie—are you out of your mind? You know the cops have a hard-on for me. You trying to get me arrested?"

"Oh God, Johnny, I'm sorry. I don't want you to get in any trouble. I just thought . . ."

He broke into a big wide smile. "Hahhhh! I'm just busting your chops. Breaking and entering is the highlight of my résumé. When do you want to do it?"

"She's already got my mother's car and her jewelry, so the sooner the better."

We didn't have to wait long. On Saturday morning the happy couple took the train into New York City to do some Christmas shopping. An hour later Johnny and I parked three blocks away from Connie's house on Oriole Lane.

"How do we get in?" I asked.

"The front door," Johnny said. "I checked it out yesterday. It's a slam lock. I could teach a three-year-old to open one."

"Teach me."

"First you need the right equipment." He pulled a piece of plastic from his jacket pocket. It was about the size and shape of a candy cane.

"Where'd you get that?"

"Sears. They have a burglary tools department."

"Johnny, this isn't funny."

"Relax. I cut it out of a milk jug." He put his thumb against his index finger. "You just slide it between the jamb and the door," he said, slipping the plastic between his two fingers. "Then you drag it down, yank it out, and the hook on the cane trips the lock."

He went through the motions. It wasn't the most convincing

demonstration, because I couldn't tell if the plastic had actually parted his fingers, or if he just popped them open on his own. But I had to trust him. He was as close to a criminal genius as I was going to get.

It worked. We walked up to the front door of Connie's house, and he opened it as quickly as if he'd used a key.

"You're welcome," he said once we were inside.

The house was woody—cedar on the outside, pine on the inside. The main living space was about twenty-four by twenty-four with a towering ceiling and lots of glass, so light filled the room. There was a stone fireplace at one end and a full kitchen on the other. Several doors led to what was probably the bathroom and bedrooms, and a wide, thick mahogany staircase with open risers led up to a loft.

"Nice digs," Johnny said.

I walked upstairs to her studio space in the loft. There was a work in progress on the easel and a few canvasses propped up against a wooden trunk. I figured those were the rejects she decided weren't worthy of hanging on the walls of her new boyfriend's pub.

"I'm going to cruise around and see if I can find anything interesting," Johnny said.

"And I'll see if I can find anything incriminating." I went downstairs and found her bedroom. The bed was made, the tops of her dresser and night table were neat and orderly, and there wasn't a stitch of clothing or a pair of shoes lying around.

I opened her closet. Everything was meticulously organized. Sweaters, blouses, skirts, pants, and in one small section, several hangers with men's clothes—my father's. Disgusted, I shut the door.

There was a second, smaller bedroom, and that's where I found the desk. It was white metal and probably cost less than a hundred bucks at Staples, or ten at a garage sale. The base was a pair of double file-drawer pedestals, and there was a pencil drawer in the center. I tugged at each drawer. Locked.

"Johnny," I yelled. "I got something."

"I'm in the bathroom," he yelled back. "I'm taking a leak."

Two minutes later he showed up with a pair of silver candlesticks in his hand. "It looks like you're taking more than a leak," I said.

"They were buried in the back of a closet," he said. "She'll never even know they're gone, and I can get fifty bucks easy for them."

"Put them back," I said, "and help me open these drawers."

He set the candlesticks down and studied the locks.

"Can you get them open without scratching the paint?" I said.

"Probably." He dropped to the floor, slid under the desk, and came up ten seconds later with a key in his hand. "Make that definitely. It was taped to the underside of the middle drawer. She's not exactly a master criminal."

I unlocked the two file drawers on the left. Empty. Then I tried the pencil drawer. Pencils. Finally, I unlocked the right side and slid open the top drawer. There was a stack of papers in there.

"Take them out one at a time and keep them in order, so you can put them back the way you found them," Johnny said.

I went through them slowly—receipts, bills, a copy of the support group pamphlet my father had been reading, a catalog from Blick art supplies, and underneath it all, a manila folder about an inch thick.

I opened it, and my stomach wrenched.

"Oh my God," I said.

"What is it?" Johnny asked.

It was a page out of a newspaper, folded several times, so that what jumped out at me was a black-and-white photograph of a beautiful young woman in her midtwenties.

The camera had caught her just as she threw her head back, spread her arms, and looked up at the sky. Her long, thick hair was captured in midtoss, her smile unfettered by fear or doubt, her eyes radiating with joy and the love of life.

"You know her?" Johnny asked.

"It's my mother," I said, my voice barely above a whisper. "This is her obituary in the *Heartstone Gazette*."

I unfolded it. Several sections were highlighted. I began reading.

"Kate McCormick, co-owner with her husband, Finn, of the popular bar and restaurant McCormick's . . . two daughters, Margaret, seventeen, and Elizabeth, sixteen . . . The McCormicks have a long history of generosity to the community . . ."

"There's more newspaper clippings under here," Johnny said.

There were four more, all obituaries, all for women in their forties and early fifties who died over the summer, all highlighted.

"How many men is she stalking?" I said.

"Look closer," Johnny said. "These four have a little *X* at the bottom. Your mom's obituary has an asterisk. Your father's the target."

"This whole thing has been a scam," I said. "As soon as my mother died women have been coming on strong—practically throwing themselves at my father. He's managed to keep them at bay. But Connie walked into the bar one night and ordered two drinks—one for her, and one in memory of her dead husband. My father wasn't ready to date. If a woman said, 'Let's go to a movie and dinner, and see where it goes from there,' he'd have run the other way. But Connie sucked him in with her sad-and-lonely-widow bullshit, and then she brought him to her bereavement group, and held his hand . . . and . . ."

"And one thing led to another," Johnny said. "Your Dad's a man, Maggie. Cut him some slack. You can't hold this against him."

"I won't," I said. "He was vulnerable. She preyed on him."

"I take back what I said about her not being a master criminal," Johnny said. "This bitch knows what she's doing."

"But now *I* know what she's doing," I said. "And I'm going to stop her."

"How?"

I shook my head. I had no idea. I gazed back down at the picture of the beautiful young woman so full of life and promise, and silently asked her to show me the way.

CHAPTER 26

Johnny and I put the desk back exactly the way we found it, then left the house as easily as we came in.

"I'm leaving town for a couple of days," he said when he dropped me off at home.

"Where you going?"

"Here and there," he said, which was his polite way of letting me know that even though I knew he sold drugs, his business was none of my business.

"It's my busy season." He grinned. "A lot of my customers are looking forward to a green Christmas, and I don't want to disappoint them."

He must have seen the look of abandonment in my eyes because he quickly added, "You'll be fine. If you need me, you've got my number."

He drove off, and for the first time since Connie Gilchrist entered our lives, I felt totally alone.

I thought about telling Lizzie, but how do you start? *So I asked my drug dealer to help me break into Dad's girlfriend's house this afternoon.* No, Lizzie was the wrong one to tell. I thought about talking to Officer Montgomery, but Johnny explained that you can't commit a felony and then ask the cops to help you out, because you suddenly discover you're in kind of a jam. I needed more proof. I needed information.

But it was 1997, and it would be four more years before Google was invented. So I did what high school students in search of answers had been doing for generations. I went to the library.

Beth Webster was in her office. "Maggie," she said, bubbling over as if I were exactly the person she'd been waiting for all day. "How is your senior year going?"

"Good," I said.

"I'm going to miss you when you go off to college. Can you believe Christmas is just around the corner? To what do I owe the pleasure?"

"How do I get some background information on someone?"

"Well, that's why God made encyclopedias, microfiche, and librarians. What can I help you find?"

"Um . . . this person isn't famous, so she's not going to be in an encyclopedia. I met her, and I want to know how I can find out more about her."

"She might be in LexisNexis."

"That's great. What section is that in?"

"It's right here in my office. LexisNexis is a computer service that provides legal and business research. They have a vast database. It's pricey, but the library has a subscription."

"How much would it cost me?"

"Oh, it's free to members, but it takes a little experience before you get the hang of navigating your way through it. Just tell me who you're looking into, and I'll see what I can find."

"Her name is Connie . . . or maybe it's Constance . . . Gilchrist."

"Oh . . ." Beth said, tilting her head the way people do when they've heard what you said, but they don't quite believe you said it. "She's your father's . . . artist friend. I went to her opening at the restaurant last Friday night. I didn't see you there."

"I had to leave early," I lied. "What did you think?"

"It was a lovely show."

"No, I mean personally—what did you think of her?"

Beth knew it wasn't a casual question. She answered cautiously. "I only spoke to her briefly, but she seems charming."

"Yes, she does *seem* charming."

"You sound like you think otherwise."

"I'm just a girl looking out after her father. Do you think this LexisNexis would know anything about her?"

"It would help if I had some more input beside her name. What can you tell me?"

"She's from Miami. Her husband, Steve, was a yacht broker. He died a year ago of a heart attack. She studied art at Hunter College, and her grandmother was a famous doctor back in the 1920s, but I don't know her name."

"That's a start," Beth said. "I'll see what I can find."

"Do you want me to come back Monday, or do you need more time?" I asked.

"Honey, it's a computer. Just pull up a chair near the staff help desk and give me twenty minutes."

Twenty minutes passed. Then another twenty. And then one of the other librarians came out with a message that Beth needed just a little while longer.

Finally, an hour and fifteen minutes into the wait, Beth came out, looking very serious. "You are one incredibly insightful young woman," she said.

"You found something?" I asked.

"*Something*? Sweetheart, I hit the jackpot," she said, waving the computer printout she had in her hand. "Connie Gilchrist may indeed be charming, but according to some very reliable sources, she was arrested for grand larceny in three different states."

CHAPTER 27

"Grand larceny?" I said, loud enough for several admonishing heads to snap in my direction. But when they saw that I was already face-to-face with the chief enforcer of library decorum, they smugly went back to what they were doing.

Beth put a finger to her lips and guided me over to a table in a far corner.

"Did she stick up a bank?" I asked, dropping my decibel level dramatically.

Beth smiled. "No, that would be armed robbery. Larceny simply means she was charged with taking someone's property without permission. Grand larceny means that the property was worth more than X dollars. The amount varies from state to state."

"And she did it in three different states?"

"Georgia, Texas, and Maryland."

I was dumbfounded. "I thought she lived in Florida."

"That's debatable. I didn't find a record of her in Florida. At least not yet, but I'd kept you waiting so long that I decided I had more than enough to tear myself away and confirm that your instincts were spot-on."

"Did she go to jail?" I asked, and the image of Connie hunched over her Thanksgiving dinner flashed in my mind.

"Not the first time. But in 1985 she was sentenced to three years in prison in Texas. She did eighteen months and was released. In 1989, she was sentenced to five to seven years in Maryland. She did four and a half and was released a year ago."

"What did she steal?"

"Money and things she could sell for money," Beth said. "But what's interesting is whom she stole it from."

"Who?"

"Her husband."

"What?" I said, my whisper getting louder and harsher. I caught myself and adjusted the volume. "She robbed him three times? Why did he take her back?"

"Nobody took her back. She didn't rob one husband three times. She robbed three different husbands."

I held up three fingers and waved them frantically at Beth. It was the closest I could get to a shout.

Beth stifled a laugh and nodded her head violently. We were silently screaming in the library and getting away with it.

"She said her husband who died was a yacht broker in Florida," I said softly. "I assumed his last name was Gilchrist, but maybe it wasn't. Were any of her husbands named Steve?"

Beth shook her head.

"Did any of them sell boats?"

"Nope. And they're all still very much alive."

I stared at Beth, trying to put the puzzle pieces together. "So she just lied about everything?"

"Not quite. LexisNexis did verify that her maiden name is Connie Gilchrist, and she did graduate from Hunter College with an MFA in studio art."

"What did they say about her husbands?"

Beth's eyes lowered. "This is going to be painful, so try to stay calm. Each one of them had been a widower before she married them, and according to the court records, she married them less than six months after she met them. In one case, they were married in two months."

I sat back in my chair, tipped my head up to the ceiling, and closed my eyes. That had been my mother's worst nightmare, and now it was my reality. By the time I sat up straight and opened my eyes, Beth was flipping through the pages of the computer printout. She found what she was looking for and read it to me.

"Husband number one was David Lowry from Athens, Georgia. Mr. Lowry is an architect. Number two was Dr. Henry Tanner, an orthodontist from Dallas. The third one was Malcolm Griffin, who owns a car dealership in Baltimore."

She refolded the document and handed it to me. "The sordid details are all in here."

"Thank you," I said.

"All I did is what I do every day for a lot of people. I helped you research a project. The question is, what are you going to do with the information?"

"I . . . I haven't thought about it. What do you think I should do?"

"Tell your father and let him take it from there."

"He'll be pissed that I mucked about in his private life, and he'll be even more pissed that I dragged you into it."

"Maybe so, but considering what you dug up out of the muck, I would think he'd forgive you. As for my involvement, just don't mention my name. If he asks, you did it all on your own. I know how to keep a secret."

"I don't know what to do."

She took the computer printout back and wrote something on the last page. "That's my home phone number," she said. "If you can think of any way that I can help you, call me there or here."

"It would help if you could bring my mother back," I said. "She'd know what to do."

Beth rested her hand on mine. "Your mother was an incredible woman—strong, smart, and extremely brave. I know that you have a lot of her in you. I'm sure you'll figure out what to do."

"Thank you."

"One last thing, Maggie. Just in case you don't want to wade through the entire report, you should know that all three of the men divorced Connie."

"Can you blame them?"

She smiled. "That's not quite what I was getting at. My point is that the sooner you talk to your father the better, because legally Connie Gilchrist is free to remarry."

"The fuck she will!" I bellowed.

A chorus of shushes reverbed through the library.

Beth stood and held up her hands to everyone in the room in a gesture that both apologized for my outburst and at the same time let the shushers know that she had it under control.

Then she leaned over, took one more quick look at the computer printout of Connie's crimes, and whispered in my ear, "The fuck she will."

CHAPTER 28

My mother and I were sitting on a blanket on the grass at Magic Pond. I was about eight years old, which would mean my sister was seven, but for some unexplainable reason, Lizzie wasn't with us. It was a bright, sunny summer day.

The red Mustang came out of nowhere, barreling down the road, hopping the sidewalk, and tearing up the lawn as it headed toward us.

Connie was behind the wheel. She came to a stop just at the edge of our blanket.

Mom jumped up, and I scrambled to my feet and hid behind her. "That's my car," she yelled.

"It was," Connie said. "And now it's mine."

"I want my car," Mom said. "And my husband. Give them back."

"Never," Connie screamed. "I'm keeping them both."

I waited for my mother to do something, but she didn't move. And then I realized she *couldn't* move.

"Maggie," she said. "Don't let that woman take Daddy."

I tried to stop Connie, but I could barely move either. It was that familiar sensation when I'm trying to run, but I can't cover any ground. Panic set in, and at some point I knew I was dreaming. I knew I wasn't eight years old, and I knew it was impossible for my mother to meet Connie, but I couldn't fight my way out of the dream.

And then it ended. Actually, there was no ending. The dream had no conclusion. No finale. I just woke up, and it was over.

After I had talked to Beth in the library, I had walked to Magic Pond and sat there trying to figure out what to do. Beth's best advice was to tell my father. But I dreaded how he might react. What if I showed him Connie's prison record, and he said something crazy like, *"I knew that. She told me all about it, and I'm okay with it. She's reformed now, and I love her. Why the hell did you have to get the goddam librarian involved?"*

Later that evening my father had called me and said that he and Connie were wiped out from shopping and had decided to spend the night in the city. As soon as I hung up, I wondered if he'd been telling the truth, or if there were quickie marriage chapels in New York like there were in Vegas.

Lizzie went out with friends, came back at eleven, and went to bed. I spent the night at home alone, writing in my journal and watching TV. The last thing I did before I fell asleep at midnight was reread the LexisNexis printout.

And then my mother came to me in that dream.

Now it was daylight, Sunday morning, and I laid in bed, wide-awake and half smiling because I'd been able to spend some time with her. And it was just the two of us, and we had been at our favorite place in the world.

But I'd disappointed her. She couldn't stop Connie from taking away my father, and I couldn't help. "I'm sorry, Mom," I said softly.

I stared at the ceiling, and it came to me. "On second thought," I said, "I'm not *that* sorry. Why did you ask the eight-year-old me to stop Connie? Why didn't you ask the seventeen-year-old me?"

I heard the answer as clear as if my mother were standing in the room beside me. *"I did ask the seventeen-year-old you. Remember our last picnic at the pond, when I told you I was dying? I told you what happened to Bernadette Brennan's husband when she died. I said I know it's a terrible burden, but I'll die happier knowing you'll be there to love your father, watch over him, and keep the predators from digging their claws into him."*

"Oh yeah," I said, smiling up at the ghost of my mother. "You did ask me, didn't you?"

She hadn't asked Beth. Or Johnny Rollo. Or Grandpa Mike. And she certainly couldn't count on my father to take care of himself. So she asked her two daughters.

And we'd both said yes. But Lizzie had fallen for Connie's lies. She'd been duped just like my father had.

That left me.

"Maggie," I could hear my mother say. *"Don't let that woman take Daddy."*

Only this time I wasn't dreaming.

CHAPTER 29

I showered, dressed, and turned on ESPN. It was week fourteen of the football season, and both New York teams were on TV. The Jets were playing Buffalo at one o'clock, and the Giants were playing Tampa Bay at four. McCormick's, with its state-of-the-art thirty-two-inch SONY TV sets, would be wall-to-wall with hungry, thirsty, rowdy fans, so I knew my father would take an early-morning train back to Heartstone.

He called from the bar at eleven. "You and Lizzie okay?"

"Another boring night in suburbia," I said. "How was the big city?"

"Crowded and expensive, but we had a good time. I'll be working late. I should be home around ten. Call me if you need me."

My plan was to confront his jailbird girlfriend. I doubted if I'd need him.

"You bet," I said. "Love you, Dad."

"Love you too."

He hung up without saying, "Oh, by the way, I bought Connie this incredible engagement ring at Tiffany's," so I knew two things. There was still time to put an end to their relationship, and nobody else was going to be able to do it but me.

I waited till two o'clock before I drove over to Connie's house. I rang the doorbell, and I heard her yell from inside. "I'll be right there."

She must have been upstairs in the loft working, because it took a while for her to get to the door, and when she opened it, she was wearing a paint-stained Hunter College sweatshirt.

"Maggie," she said, surprised to see me. "Come in, come in."

I stepped inside; she closed the door, led me into the living room, and pointed me to the sofa.

"Sit down. Make yourself comfortable," she said.

"I'll stand. This won't take long."

"Suit yourself," she said. "To what do I owe the pleasure?"

"This is not a social call. It's business."

"Oh my. You sound serious. What can I do for you?"

"I want you to stay away from my father."

"Oh, sweetheart, I know how difficult it's been for you to lose your mother. And I'm sure it's confusing for you to see your father with another woman. But can't you see how happy he is?"

"Is he as happy as Mr. Lowry was?" I said.

She didn't blink.

"Or Dr. Tanner?"

She stood there, stone-faced.

"Or how about victim number three, Malcolm Griffin?"

"Well, well, well," she said, dropping the deadpan expression. "If it isn't Nancy Drew, girl detective. I wondered who had been snooping around my house, rifling through my things. Take a tip from a professional, missy. Next time tell your boyfriend to put the toilet seat back down. Did you find what you were looking for?"

"You know I did. And you heard what I said. Stay away from my father."

She rolled her eyes. "Oh, please. Your father's a grown man. He makes his own decisions."

"You're right. He does. But he hasn't been making informed decisions. What do you think he'll say when he finds out you did prison time for stealing from your ex-husbands?"

"That was the old me. I paid my debt, and I got my life straightened out. And what happened? I moved to small-town America, I met a nice guy, and his daughter and her hoodlum boyfriend broke into my house. You're the one who committed the crime here. Not me. So get your facts straight."

"You want the facts?" I said. "You moved to small-town America, you tracked the obituaries in the local paper, you targeted my widowed father, then you walked into his bar one night and suckered him in with a sob story about a dead husband who never existed. And I'll bet your pioneering grandmother, Marie Curie, doesn't exist either, but you sure conned my sister into buying your bullshit.

"If you want to report me to the cops for breaking into your house, be my guest. I'll be happy to sit on the witness stand sobbing my heart out to the jury that I would do it all over again, because that's what a loving daughter does to protect her father from a predator.

"As for my hoodlum boyfriend, he may not be smart enough to put down the toilet seat, but he knows a lot about the life you live. Here's what he told me: 'Sometimes you win, sometimes you lose, and sometimes you get lucky and someone gives you the chance to cut your losses before the cops show up.' I'm that someone, and I'm giving you twenty-four hours to tell my father you're done with him. Dump him, shit on him, break his heart—I don't care. Just end it, or I will expose you for the bottom-feeding phony that you are."

I had her, and she knew it. But I could tell by her scowling eyes and sneering lips that she wouldn't go gently.

"Fine," she said. "I'll leave him alone. Although somehow I doubt that he's your biological father."

"What the hell are you talking about?" I said.

She looked at me with sheer contempt. "I know Finn McCormick," she said. "He's a good man, a gentle soul. He couldn't possibly have fathered a piece of shit like you. My best guess—you're the product of some lowlife dirtbag who fucked your worthless tramp of a mother. I hope she rots in hell."

Tears rolled down my cheeks. I knew I'd won. I knew my threats had scared her off. But the price of victory was more pain than I could bear.

CHAPTER 30

The next few days were torture as I watched my father get more and more agitated. But he didn't say a word about what was bothering him. Lizzie didn't notice, and I, of course, didn't ask.

Three days after my showdown with Connie, the two of us came home from school, and he was sitting in the living room with a pitiful look on his face that I couldn't ignore.

"Dad, are you all right?" I said.

He gave me a perfunctory head nod.

"No, you're not," Lizzie said. "What's the matter? Is it Grandpa?"

"Connie's gone," he said, choking out the words.

"Gone where?" Lizzie asked.

He shook his head. "I don't know. I hadn't heard from her since we got back from the city on Sunday, so this afternoon I went over to her house. The Mustang's not in the driveway. I have a key, so I went inside. It's empty."

"What do you mean empty?" I said.

"Her clothes, her things, her suitcases, her art supplies—all gone. The only things that are there are the landlord's crap furniture and a few of my . . ." He stopped himself. Why tell your teenage daughters about the clothes you have hanging in your new girlfriend's closet? Some details are better left unsaid.

"Did she leave a note?" Lizzie asked.

He shook his head.

Lizzie pressed on. "Did you call the cops?"

"And say what? I met this woman two months ago. And now she's gone."

"She's not gone," Lizzie insisted. "She's missing."

"Excuse me," I said, "but I don't think people who go missing pack up all their shit. Connie is a free spirit. It sounds like she just took off."

"Why would she do that?" Lizzie said.

"That's what I keep asking myself," Dad said. "We were planning a little ski trip after Christmas."

"Maybe somebody kidnapped her," Lizzie said, picking up the phone. "I think we should call the cops."

"Don't!" I yelled. "Nobody kidnapped her. She left on her own, and she's not coming back. Now hang up the phone and sit down."

Dead silence. Lizzie did as she was told, and they both sat there gaping at me.

"I hate to be the one to tell you, but Connie Gilchrist was not the person she said she was." I took a deep breath and dropped my voice. "She's an ex-convict."

"That's insane," my father said. "Where did you hear a cockamamie story like that?"

I held up my hand. "Don't move." I went upstairs to my room and came back with the LexisNexis report. "It's all in here. Connie is a predator, Dad. She preys on grieving widowers and then bleeds them dry. There are three that we know of."

I handed my father the printout. "You read it," he said, passing it to Lizzie. "I don't think I can."

For the next fifteen minutes she read it out loud, word by unbelievable word. By the time she was finished, the three of us were drained.

"Where did you get that?" my father asked.

"They have this legal research database in the library. I didn't know how to use it. Beth Webster helped me."

He winced. "Oh, Jesus. How many other people know about this?"

"Just Beth, and she promised not to say a word to anyone."

"I can't believe I fell for her bullshit," Lizzie said.

"I fell for it too," my father said. "And those men—she took them for a lot of money."

"And you were next," I said.

He put a hand to his face and rubbed his forehead. "I guess I was," he said, "but . . . why did she leave before she got her hands on my money?"

"She got the car," Lizzie said.

"She didn't move here for a car. I don't understand why she decided to walk away in the middle of the scam."

"I went to see her on Sunday," I said. "I told her what I knew, and I said I'd keep it a secret if she backed off. I thought she'd just let the relationship go cold. But I guess she panicked and left town. I had no idea she'd take Mom's car."

"Call the cops," Lizzie said. "How hard could it be to find a red Mustang convertible?"

"And what happens if they catch her?" I said. "Dad, do you really want her back? Do you want the story in the paper?"

"Of course I don't, but if God forbid she plows into a school bus, it sure as hell better be on record that I reported the car missing. Plus she's a career criminal driving a stolen vehicle. She's not going to keep it long. If we're lucky, the cops will find it in a parking lot at JFK."

"Even if they do," I said, "I doubt if they'll find Mom's jewelry."

It was a gut punch, and my father reeled. "Jesus . . . don't tell me."

"I just checked Mom's jewelry box when I went upstairs to get the report. The good stuff is gone. Did you lend her anything besides the earrings?"

"No, but she had the run of the house," he said, sinking into his chair. "I feel like such an idiot."

"Don't," I said. "She's a professional. She's done it to other men, and she'll do it again."

"You dodged a bullet, Dad," Lizzie said. "And I hate to admit it, but Maggie was right."

I gave her a sisterly smile. "Aren't I always?"

"Don't gloat, kiddo," my father said. "You saved my ass, but I don't appreciate the fact that you mucked around in my private life."

"Sorry, but we promised Mom we'd take care of you," I said.

He smiled. "So you're blaming this all on your poor dead mother? Did she say how long you're supposed to watch over me?"

"Until you get your head screwed on straight," I said.

"Sounds like you've got a lifetime job ahead of you," he said.

"So are we calling the cops or not?" Lizzie said.

"I'll go down to the station," Dad said. "I'll report it so we have an insurance claim, but I'll talk to someone at the top of the food chain and ask him to keep it under wraps, so it's not the main topic of conversation at the beauty parlor tomorrow morning."

"What about her paintings?" Lizzie said. "They're still hanging at the bar."

"Two of them sold," my father said. "I'll give Connie the benefit of the doubt, and if I don't hear from her in a week, I'll donate the other twenty to St. Cecilia's for their rummage sale."

He didn't hear from her in a week. In fact, we didn't hear from her in decades.

Until that day, twenty-five years later, when Connie Gilchrist resurfaced to haunt us one last time.

PART TWO
MY TURN TO DIE

CHAPTER 31

THE DAY OF THE FUNERAL

"Slide the wide end of the tie through the front loop to create the base of the knot," the reassuring voice on the YouTube video said.

Kevin Dunn did as instructed. Like most teenage boys, he sucked at tying a tie, but like any other challenge Kevin faced in life, he was determined to figure it out on his own.

If you ask for help, he said silently to his image in the mirror, *the tie wins*.

"Now pull the narrow end of the tie until the knot is tight at your neck," the voice continued. "Pinch the knot to create a dimple, adjust your shirt collar, and slide the narrow end of the tie through the loop at the back of the wide end."

For the fifth time that morning Kevin did exactly that.

"If the tip of your tie is resting just at the top of your beltline, you've got the perfect length, and you are looking sharp."

Moment of truth. He stepped back and looked in the mirror.

"Yes!" he said, pumping a fist in the air. "Dunn nails it in five! A personal best."

He went to the window and scanned the street. There were three news vans and maybe twenty or thirty neighbors standing outside waiting for the family to come out.

There was a bang on his bedroom door. "Yo, Kev!"

"I'm busy," he called out. Not that that would stop her. Kevin was the good child. His twin sister always did what she wanted.

The door opened, and Katie Dunn stepped inside. Black dress, black scarf, black nails, black lipstick, red sneakers. The girl never missed an opportunity to make a statement.

She stood in the doorway and giggled. A classic Katie tell. She was stoned.

"What do you call a kid whose parents both die?" she asked.

"An orphan," he said, indulging her.

"What do call him if only *one* parent dies?"

"I give up."

"Horphan. Half an orphan. That's what we are. I made it up." She unleashed another round of giggles.

"Really, Katie?" Kevin said. "Today of all days? Why would you get high?"

"Weed is medicinal. It helps people cope with their grief."

"The whole town is going to be looking at us," Kevin said. "You think the reporters will be stupid enough to think you're *coping*? They're just going to say that Mayor Dunn's idiot daughter was crunked out of her gourd. Where did you get the weed?"

"Dad's office. That's where they keep it. It's legal, in case you hadn't heard."

She lifted Kevin's jacket from the back of his desk chair and produced a little baggie from the folds of her scarf.

"I rolled one for later," she said, tucking it into one of his pockets. She tossed him the jacket.

"So now I'm the one who's holding," he said, putting it on.

"Right. If we get caught, we'll both make the front page."

Kevin stepped in front of the mirror. Black jacket, charcoal-gray pants, deep-purple shirt, black tie with pencil-thin gray stripes—exactly like the picture he'd found on Google images.

"You look totally handsome," Katie burbled.

He couldn't remember the last time she'd said anything remotely nice to him. Further proof that she was totally wasted.

But he knew he looked good. That was his biggest problem.

Not yet sixteen, he was already six feet tall—two inches shorter than their father. He'd also inherited their father's strong jawline, expressive hazel eyes, and engaging smile, but while Alex Dunn used his good looks to charm his way through life, Kevin was uncomfortable with the fact that female heads turned when he walked into a classroom. Faculty included.

Of all the skills Kevin Dunn had yet to master, the most intimidating was how to deal with women.

He turned away from the mirror and went to the window.

"Chill out," Katie said. "They'll get here when they get here."

She plopped down on his bed. "Guess what else I found in Dad's office?"

"I don't care."

"Dad wrote a eulogy for Mom," she said.

"Jesus . . . Katie."

"It was just sitting there in his computer, so I read it."

"How did you get into Dad's . . ."

"Oh, Kevin, don't be an idiot. I figured out his password three years ago. It's I-Love-Katie-Best."

Kevin ignored the dig and went straight for the trespass violation. "You've been looking at Dad's private stuff for *three years?*"

"Not the work stuff. Just things about the family. 'Specially emails between him and Mom. I like to keep tabs on what they know about stuff we do."

"*We?*" Kevin snapped. "Yeah, they would really freak out if they knew I brought two books back late to the library last month. You're the one who gets stupid drunk with your lacrosse team—Oh, shit. Here they come."

Katie tottered to the window as the procession pulled up. Two motorcycle cops, Chief Vanderbergen's SUV, two long black Cadillac limos from Kehoe's Funeral Home, a fire truck festooned with flowers, a Heartstone ambulance draped with black bunting, and, bringing up the rear, at least twenty more bikes—all Harleys—Grandpa Finn's crew.

The crowd on the street had doubled. Almost every one of them—friends, neighbors, reporters—were recording the moment for posterity.

"Cool," Katie said.

"Not cool," Kevin, shaking his head. "We can't even die like normal people."

"We're not normal, bro. We're Heartstone royalty. Maybe by the time you're my age, you'll finally understand that."

Kevin gave her the finger. They were twins, but Katie never missed an opportunity to rub in the fact that she squeezed through the birth canal seven minutes sooner than he did. And she'd been pushing him around ever since.

She pressed her face to the window. "You know, you're right, Kev. It's not that cool. If I were running the show, I'd definitely have had a marching band, lots of balloons, and a clown car."

Kevin couldn't help himself. He laughed. And then, staring down at the somber motorcade, the laugh caught in his throat and turned to sobs.

The sound that came out of him started as a low moan, built into a mournful cry, and crescendoed into a heart-rending wail.

"It's not fair!" he screamed in a hoarse whisper. "It's not fair!"

Katie reached for him, and he let his heaving body fall into her arms.

"I didn't know I was gonna cry," he said. "I'm sorry. I'm sorry."

"It's okay, bro." Katie said, rocking him gently. "This will fix you up."

She retrieved the joint from his jacket pocket and lit it.

Kevin took a long, slow pull, coughed twice, exhaled, puffed again, and passed it back to his sister.

"You feeling better now?" Katie asked.

Kevin nodded, a sweet smile on his face.

"I hope so," she said, "because our entire reserve supply of recreational drugs is about to go up in smoke."

He laughed. "Sorry. I feel like such a pussy for crying like a baby."

"You are a pussy," she said, inhaling and ashing the joint like a pro. "Always have been."

He laughed again. "One dead possum, and I'm branded for life."

There was a knock at the door.

"Shit," Kevin whispered.

"Chill out, bro." Katie said. "What are they going to do? Tell us we can't go to the funeral?" She turned to the door. "Who is it?"

"It's your aunt. The one with the keen sense of smell. Can I come in? We don't have to talk. I'm happy to just inhale."

Aunt Lizzie was one of the cool ones. "Come in," Katie yelled.

Their mom's sister pushed the door open and quickly closed it behind her. "Oh, good," she said. "You all got the memo. Wear black. We'll fit right in with this whole funeral thing." She took in Katie's red sneakers. "Nice touch with the kicks."

Katie responded with a hair toss. "Fashionistas do not cave to grief."

"I've been sent to inform you that we're leaving for the funeral home in fifteen minutes."

"Can't wait," Katie said.

Lizzie sat down on the bed. "What are you guys doing? I mean, besides the obvious."

"Just calming our nerves," Katie said, passing the joint to her aunt. "And reminiscing about our youth."

"I hate to break it to you, kids," Lizzie said. She inhaled deeply and exhaled slowly. "But this is your youth."

"We were thinking about ten years ago," Katie said. "The dead possum in the attic."

Lizzie gave them a blank stare. "What dead possum?"

Kevin's head jerked up. "Are you serious? Mom never told you her famous roadkill-in-the-attic story? Katie and I were like five and a half when it happened."

Lizzie shook her head. "Your mom never told me anything that would make her look like she was guilty of bad parenting. And dead marsupials and small children sound like they have the makings of a serious maternal failing."

She took a second puff and passed the joint to Kevin. "Tell all."

He took a short hit and gave it to his sister. "It was a hot, hot summer day," he said. "Me and Mom and Katie came back from a picnic at Magic Pond."

"Monkey Paws and strawberry lemonade?" Lizzie said.

"Is there anything else?" Kevin said. "It's like part of our heritage."

Lizzie responded with a thumbs-up. "So far she's sounding like a Gold Star Mommy."

"Anyway, we pull into the garage, and the whole place smells like the Land of a Million Farts, so I say, 'Who cut the cheese?' And then Mom turns around, and she says . . ."

They had choreographed their routine years ago. Kevin gestured to his twin.

"It's not cheese, my little chickadees," Katie croaked in her scariest wicked-old-witch voice. "There's something dead overhead. Which one of you is brave enough to go up to the attic and check it out?"

"This is where the dead possum comes in," Lizzie said.

"Almost," Katie said. "So I say, 'Me, me, me. I want to go up there.' But my wuss brother is too chicken."

"I wasn't chicken. I hated the smell."

"So Mom says, 'Let's all go upstairs and see who makes it back alive.'"

"Creepy in some circles," Lizzie said. "But if you know anything about how your mom and I were raised, that still qualifies as perfectly normal parenting."

"Anyway, I go up first," Katie said, "and there it is, all bloated and rotting in the heat, with hundreds of black flies feeding on his carcass."

"Dead possum," Lizzie said.

"Roadkill in the attic. Totally gross," Katie said. "Guess what happened next?"

"You realize, of course, that I'm a doctor," Lizzie said. "Stifling hot attic, no ventilation, nervous five-year-old boy who just stuffed himself with peanut butter, honey, and banana sandwiches on cinnamon swirl raisin bread, and washed it down with pink lemonade. I'm going to go with little Kevin barfed his brains out."

"All over little Katie. Big, thick, slimy brown chunks," Katie said.

"In my defense," Kevin said, "she was holding up that fuzzy, germ-infested ball of death. What was I supposed to do?"

"Did your mother at least clean you up?" Lizzie said.

"I took a twenty-minute shower. Mom washed my hair twice before I calmed down and twice more before I decided I no longer smelled like vomit and dead possum."

"Quick doctor question—any emotional scars or PTSD as a result of your horrifying childhood incident?"

Katie shook her head. "No. We're just regular fucked-up teenagers whose parents are both local luminaries."

"*Were*! Not are," Kevin said. "They *were* local luminaries. We're down to our last luminary."

"Thank you, Brother Buzzkill," Katie said. "We're out of weed, and you just harshed my mellow."

"Bite me, Katie!"

"Hey!" Lizzie snapped before Katie could counter. "Did I mention that I was a doctor?"

Silence.

"I can write a scrip for this shit." She pulled a baggie out of her purse and tossed it to Katie. "Here you go, kid. Roll us one for the road."

CHAPTER 32

"I met this really hot guy," Lizzie said.

We were having lunch at the White Dog Café on Sansom Street in the heart of the University of Pennsylvania campus. High school was long behind us. I was in my final year at Penn Law, and Lizzie was in her second year at Penn Medical.

"He asked me out," she said.

A lot of guys asked Lizzie out. She was tall and slender with the body of a ballerina, the winsome face of an Irish farm girl, and the wicked sense of humor of a leprechaun.

"Did you tell him you prefer girls?" I said.

"Mags, he's a fourth-year med student. I was trying to impress him, so I broke the news in Latin. *Ergo sum lesbian.*"

I laughed.

"He wants to meet you," she said.

"Me? How does he even know who I am?"

"As soon as I turned him down, he said, 'Are there any more at home like you—only straighter?' I showed him your picture. He's interested."

"I'm not. The subject is closed."

"Don't be an idiot. You have a few relationships go south, and—"

"Not a few. *Six* since I showed up here in Philadelphia seven years ago," I said. "Six is not a few."

"So now what? Are you going to give up men and come over to the dark side?"

"No. I'm going to give up looking for love in all the wrong places, lock myself up in the law library, and study my ass off till I pass the bar. A law degree will take care of me in my old age, which is more than I can say about any of the men I've picked."

"Bingo," she said, pointing a finger at me. "You just defined the problem. Did you hear what you said? '*The men I've picked*.'"

I gave her a blank look. "What are you talking about?"

"Maybe you're not bad at relationships, Maggie. Maybe you just suck at picking the right guy."

"And so I should let my gay sister who—correct me if I'm wrong—never dated a man in her life—pick Mr. Right for me."

"Trust me," Lizzie said. "This guy's worth it. And he's not just *Mister* Right. Next year this time he'll be *Doctor* Right."

"Not interested."

"I'm telling you: Alex is drop-dead gorgeous."

"Then I'm sure *Alex* won't have any trouble finding a date."

"That's the problem. He attracts them in droves. But you know the type of women who come on strong to guys like Alex. Spoiled, privileged, shallow debutantes who didn't go to college to pursue a career or achieve financial independence. They're trolling for a husband, and a handsome med student with a great future ahead of him will make Daddy and Mommy very happy."

"Sounds like Alex has bared his soul to you."

"We went out for drinks last week. We talked. I like him a lot."

"I hope you two will be very happy together," I said.

"Would you at least check out what he looks like?"

"Fine," I said, pointing at her flip phone. "Show me his damn picture."

"I'll do better than that," she said, looking over my shoulder and waving her hand. I thought she was signaling for our waiter. But she wasn't.

A man stepped up to our table. He was, I thought at first glance, genetically blessed by the gods. Haunting blue eyes, a granite jaw, a confident smile that showed perfect white teeth, broad shoulders, strong masculine hands—I was still taking inventory when he spoke.

"Hi, I'm Alex Dunn," he said, his voice warm and captivating. "You, of course, are Maggie."

I nodded, unable to take my eyes off him.

"And from the look on your face," he said, "I'm pretty sure I know what you're thinking."

He couldn't possibly know what I was thinking. I barely knew. But the dampness between my legs was a clue. I wanted to tear his clothes off and jump his bones. I'd never been so gobsmacked by the physical presence of another human being in my life.

"And what am I thinking?" I asked as casually as I could.

"You're incredibly uncomfortable, and you'd probably like to throttle the hell out of your sister."

I looked at Lizzie. She knew what I was thinking. I definitely wasn't going to throttle her. I was going to award her the game ball, name our firstborn daughter after her, and apologize for ever doubting her.

"My work here is done," she said, standing up and flashing me a victory smile. "You guys are on your own."

Mission accomplished, she picked up her bag and left the restaurant.

Alex didn't move. He was still standing tableside. I looked up. About six feet two. Thick chestnut-brown hair. Soft, upturned lips.

"She talks about you a lot," he said. "Showed me your picture. But she didn't say you'd be here. She sandbagged me."

"Welcome to my world," I said. "She said you asked her out."

He laughed. "*Asked her out?* Not exactly. I'm just getting over a relationship. Third one in three years. I started to wonder what I'm doing wrong, and I thought it might help if I had a woman's point of view, so I had drinks with Lizzie. I picked her because she's gay. She's safe."

"She's a meddler," I said. "People like us are never safe around meddlers."

"Apparently. Do you mind if I sit down?"

I scanned the restaurant. At least half a dozen college girls were staring at Alex over their sandwiches, their Diet Cokes, and their coffee cups. *Did I mind if he sat down?* If I did, I bet he wouldn't have made it out the door before one or more of them pounced.

"Have a seat," I said, crossing the words "lock myself up in the law library" off my mental things-to-do list.

He sat, and I could almost feel the other women whose eyes were glued to the tableau let out a collective *lucky bitch.*

I looked at my watch. 12:47 p.m. on a Friday afternoon—the start of my first date with Alex Dunn. It didn't end until 7:15 a.m. Monday morning.

CHAPTER 33

I hadn't been in the market for a new boyfriend, so when we high-tailed it out of the White Dog Café that Friday afternoon and headed for Alex's apartment, all I was hoping for was a torrid night with the best-damn-looking guy I'd ever been with.

He did not disappoint. And then came Saturday morning. I'd had more than my share of awkward goodbyes—throwing my clothes on in a hurry and doing the walk of shame in front of neighbors, and occasionally, the same doorman who'd seen me go upstairs the night before.

This was different. It was 11:00 a.m. We were in bed, still naked, enjoying a late-morning breakfast of Friday night's leftover Chinese food.

"Lizzie told me about your mother," he said. "I'm sorry for your loss."

"Thanks. Did she tell you about the crazy lady who almost took my father for all he was worth?"

"No. She said there was some family drama after your mother died, but that it was your story to tell."

So I told him the tale of Connie Gilchrist, leaving out, of course, the part where Johnny Rollo and I broke into her house.

"Wow," he said. "If I was your father, I'd have sworn off women for the rest of my life."

"And how long do you think it would take before the next dumpster fire in high heels and a push-up bra came along to change your mind?"

"Good point. As you can see, I'm susceptible to beautiful and intelligent women."

"All men are, and my father is no exception. So Lizzie and I orchestrated a meet and greet between him and the librarian, Beth Webster."

"And are they dating?"

"Not anymore. They got married two years ago. I love her, Lizzie loves her, and I know my mother would approve of our choice. So," I said, "your turn."

"What do you want to know?"

"I don't know . . . start at the beginning."

"Okay. It was September 11, 1978, and I was left in a Dillon's grocery store shopping basket at fire station 6 on North Plum Street in Hutchinson, Kansas."

He wasn't smiling. He wasn't kidding. "Oh my God," I said. "You were abandoned?"

"I like to think I was rescued. Whoever left me there couldn't take care of me, but they loved me enough to leave me someplace safe."

"Did you ever find out who your birth mother was?"

He shook his head. "Not a clue. It might have been some local schoolgirl, but I was found on a Monday. The Kansas State Fair was on the previous weekend, so it's possible that I could have been left by any one of the thousands of exhibitors or carneys who were passing through Hutch at the time. The note in the basket said, 'This is Alex. Please find a real mother and father to love him.'

"I'd been well fed and taken care of, and the hospital pegged me at four weeks old when I was found. That's a long time to hold on to a baby you know you can't raise, so I'm sure it wasn't an easy decision for her to give me up."

"Who became your parents?"

"I was lucky. I could have gone into the foster system and bounced around for years. But the fire chief and his wife . . . I'm sorry, this is kind of a bummer topic for a first date."

"This stopped being a first date about an hour after you sat down at my table at the White Dog," I said.

He smiled, and I marveled at the power he had over me just by moving a few facial muscles.

"Yeah, you're right," he said. "I don't usually let women do the kind of things you did to me on the first time out. I've studied anatomy, but clearly you are my superior in that department."

"And we still have two days left to the weekend," I said, munching suggestively on a cold spare rib. "Now tell me about the fire chief and his wife."

"My mom and dad," he said. "Nancy and Kevin Dunn. It was 1978. Their only child—a son, Dylan—had been killed in Vietnam six years earlier. They were in their early fifties at the time. They weren't thinking about more children, but then along comes this newborn in a basket from Dillon's supermarket—it didn't matter that it was spelled different from their son Dylan. My mom—she wasn't my mom yet—she decided it was a sign. She told my dad they had to adopt me. And he just said, 'If that's what you want.'"

"Just like that?" I said.

"That was my dad. He was the easiest guy in the world. He's gone now, but he always let my mother call the shots. Never argued, never complained. So they adopted me. The doctors did the math, and the official court papers say I'm Alex Dillon Dunn, born in Hutchinson, Kansas, on August 11, 1978. It may not be a hundred percent accurate, but it's been blessed by the powers that be in the Sunflower State, so that's my story."

"And are you going back to Kansas when you finish med school?"

"Probably not. Mom is pushing eighty; she's got some moderately progressive cognitive impairment, but last year she moved into an assisted-living facility, and she seems to be happy there. I grew up in the Midwest, but I've become kind of fond of the East Coast, so I think I'll stay here. Not in Philly. I'm definitely not a big-city kid. Anyway, I've still got two years of medical school before I have to think about where I'm going to do my residency."

I had already thought about it. Heartstone Medical Center. But I didn't tell Alex. Not on the first date.

CHAPTER 34

Falling in love was different the second time around. I was sixteen when I willingly and happily gave my heart, my soul, and my virginity to Van. I spent hours scrawling his name and mine in countless notebooks, but I never once thought to ask him what his goals were after the Marines.

At twenty-four my perspective had changed. I had a life plan. There were boxes to be checked, and Alex checked off every one of them, including a few I didn't even know I should have.

He was heart-stoppingly handsome, fun to be with, definitely up to my performance standards in the bedroom, had a promising future ahead of him, and maybe best of all, he was a lot like his father—a true partner, but content to let me steer the ship.

Falling in love with Van had been like getting hit by a Mack truck. With Alex it was like walking into a car showroom and shopping for the perfect ride. He was the Rolls-Royce of boyfriends. I wasn't about to let him go.

We were married a month after he finished med school. Six years later we were the perfect doctor-lawyer couple living in a beautiful Tudor-style house in Heartstone, less than a mile away from my father and Beth. Alex was a thoracic surgeon at Heartstone Medical Center, and I was an assistant district attorney with the county.

Lizzie had been right. Not just about Alex but about me. *The only reason everything works out exactly the way Maggie wants is because she's an obsessively compulsive micromanaging control freak.*

I got pregnant, as planned, a few months before my twenty-seventh birthday. I wanted two children—a boy and a girl—and even though some things are beyond my micromanaging skills, the gods were kind enough to put them both in my belly at the same time. They were due on New Year's Eve, but their cribs, car seats, tandem stroller, and everything else on my extensive list had been ready since Halloween.

My career with the prosecutor's office was going well, and not wanting to lose momentum, I decided to work right up until the holidays before taking my maternity leave.

It was the Saturday before Christmas, and I was the on-call prosecutor when Detective Nate Coniglio called me.

I liked Nate. He was the kid brother of a girl in my high school class. He was eleven, and I was seventeen, and I thought he was adorable. Then his sister told me he had a massive crush on me, which only made me think he was even more adorable.

"Maggie," he said, "I've got a fatal accident on East Shore Road. Looks like the driver had a heart attack, hopped the embankment, and luckily for the passenger, the car hit an outcropping of rocks; otherwise, it would have wound up at the bottom of Greenwood Lake."

"And you're calling me because . . . ?"

"We found half a kilo of cocaine in the trunk."

"Did you have probable cause?"

"Didn't need it. Trunk popped open on impact. It was right there in plain sight. We ID'd the driver as Sammy Womack—a skel from the city with a long narco history."

"Never had the pleasure," I said. "What's the story on the passenger?"

"Him you know. Did a few bids in county. He's under arrest. He had four eight balls in his pocket, but I think we can charge him with the weight in the trunk. Name's Johnny Rollo. I was hoping to get a statement, but he lawyered up."

"I'll be right there," I said.

I slammed the phone down and headed for the car fuming. I was pissed at Johnny Rollo. I hadn't heard from him in years, and I was pretty sure I knew why. I'd come a long way since the two of us shotgunned weed and broke into houses. He hadn't, and knowing him, he was embarrassed to run into me.

"Well, you're going to run into me now, asshole," I yelled at the windshield as I drove toward the lake. "Typical of you to wait till I'm eight-plus months pregnant before you need my help."

Who was I kidding? He hadn't asked for help. He knew I was an ADA, but he'd lawyered up, making it impossible for me to talk to him in private. "Asshole," I repeated, just in case the windshield hadn't heard me the first time.

Nate Coniglio met me at the scene. "Maggie, I need a little time before I can fill you in. I've got a four-hundred-pound dead drug dealer wedged behind the wheel of his Escalade. I'm working out the logistics of getting the fat bastard to the morgue."

"Hey," I said, patting my fifty-inch waistline. "On behalf of fat bastards everywhere, show a little respect."

He laughed.

"I'm freezing, and the heater in my Volvo is blowing hot and cold," I said. "You got a place where I can keep warm?"

He pointed to a cluster of vehicles, all with the engines running. "That's mine over there—the black Ford. Give me about ten minutes," he said and hurried off to deal with the late Sammy Womack.

I headed for Coniglio's car until he was out of sight, then turned toward the blue and white SUV with the county PD shield on the side. I could make out a man in the back seat. A young, uniformed cop was standing outside the front door.

"Hey, Andy," I said. "Did the EMTs finish patching up our perp?"

"Oh, hi, Mrs. Dunn," the cop said. "Yeah, I think they're getting ready to leave."

"Do me a big favor. Grab them before they go and get a statement from them. Anything Rollo might have said while they were working on him is admissible in court. Can you handle that?"

Could he handle that? I'd just asked him to take part in a drug bust investigation. His eyes went wide. "I'm all over it."

He took off. I opened the driver's-side door, slid behind the wheel, turned around, and looked at Johnny on the other side of the metal divider. There were butterfly bandages over his right eye and a contusion on his cheek.

"What the hell are you doing here?" he said.

"The question is: What are *you* doing here? You were a nickel-and-dime pot dealer. Now you're holding half a key of coke. Why did you decide to go all Scarface on us? Can't get enough jail time selling weed?"

"That coke's not mine. It's Sammy's."

"And you just happen to be going along for a ride with a guy who has twenty thousand dollars' worth of uncut blow stashed in the trunk of his Cadillac? How did that unfortunate circumstance come about?"

"I fronted Sammy the money."

"So it *is* your coke."

"Technically, no. It's Sammy's. But it's my investment."

"Who are you—Warren Buffet? What do you know about investing?"

"Hey, it's a good ROI," he said, "unless your asshole business partner drops dead at the wheel, and the goddamn OnStar lady sends Five-Oh. I swear to God, Maggie—that shit was all Sammy's."

"What about the four bags they found in your pocket?"

"All right, so maybe I took a little off the top before Sammy started cutting it. One of my best customers has a bachelor party coming up. It was going to be a one-and-done deal."

"You got the *done* part right. They nail you for this, and you're looking at ten years upstate."

"Thank you for your legal expertise, Counselor, but I already lawyered up, which means your ass is in trouble if you get caught talking to me."

"And if I don't talk to you, your state-appointed, overworked, underpaid lawyer will give you minutes of their precious time, then give you the good news—my office will let you plead out. And if you take it, I'll see you in seven and a half years instead of ten."

I looked out the window. Coniglio and the cop I'd recruited to talk to EMS were still busy. "We don't have much time to work this out," I said, "so listen to me, and listen good."

CHAPTER 35

"Docket number five-two-zero-two." Bailiff Ben Hudson's deep baritone voice resonated through the courtroom.

Judge Horace Vanderbergen was behind the bench. He had known me since I was ten. Our families went to the same church, his kids went to school with me and Lizzie, and he and his wife, Fredda, had been Friday-night regulars at our restaurant for years.

That doesn't mean that he cut me an ounce of slack when I appeared before him. In fact, there were times when I thought he'd been tougher on me than he had to be just to assert his impartiality.

But that Christmas Eve morning, with the judge nearing retirement and me on the cusp of motherhood, I'm pretty sure he glanced at me with a faint smile and a warm paternal eye.

The bailiff went on. "John Rollo, charged with criminal possession of a controlled substance in the seventh degree."

As I'd expected, the judge snapped his head toward the bailiff, then looked down and rifled through the papers in front of him.

A solid minute passed before he looked up again. He smiled at me, and this time there was nothing faint about it. "Good morning, Mrs. Dunn," he said. "I didn't expect to see you here."

"Nor did I, Your Honor. Hopefully this is my last hurrah before . . ." I patted my belly. Judge Vanderbergen appreciated brevity.

"Mrs. Dunn," he said, "possession in the *seventh*? The people are charging Mr. Rollo with a *misdemeanor*?"

"Yes, Your Honor."

"Approach, please." His voice was stern, the smile gone.

Johnny's freebie lawyer, Will Tucker, looked at me across the aisle. He was young, green, and visibly nervous. In the grand scheme of things that was better than old, jaded, and callous. I could tell by the look in his eyes that he wasn't sure whether the judge wanted me to approach the bench or both of us.

I hand-gestured, and Will followed me.

"Maggie," Judge Vanderbergen said, his mic turned off, "the defendant has a history of dealing—"

"Your Honor," young Will piped up, "my client's prior—"

"Zip it!" the judge barked.

Tucker shut up fast.

The judge went on. "They had half a kilo of uncut cocaine in the trunk, and the only thing the people are looking for is a slap on the wrist?"

"Your Honor, if I may . . ." Tucker said.

"Go ahead, Mr. Tucker."

"The police found a small fraction of that amount on Mr. Rollo's person, which he has admitted was for personal use. He has a bad drug habit. The real culprit here is Samuel Womack. I'm sure the prosecutor would have liked to come down hard on Mr. Womack, but the wrath of God beat her to the punch."

"Some might say that's one dealer down, one to go, Mr. Tucker," the judge said. He turned to me. "God can't smite them all, Mrs. Dunn. Why aren't the people stepping up to the plate? Wouldn't you at least like to take this to a grand jury?"

"Your Honor, if we were confident we could secure an indictment, we would go forward, but the coke we found on the defendant was separate from what was found in the trunk, and without the ability to link the two, we don't feel we'd be able to meet the threshold of a higher charge."

Vanderbergen frowned. He wasn't buying it. "Counselor, the man was booked Saturday afternoon. It's Monday morning. The people are entitled to more than a day and a half to make a case."

"I realize that, Your Honor, but in that short period of time Mr. Rollo provided us with information that will assist us in ongoing narcotic investigations. He also admitted that he has a substantial narcotic addiction, and he is willing to plead guilty today if Your Honor would remand him to inpatient drug treatment at a substance-abuse community residence."

The judge rubbed his chin. He was wavering.

"Your Honor, my client is desperate to get clean," Tucker said. "And I strongly believe that this is one of those cases where rehabilitation would be more effective than incarceration."

"I will take it under consideration, Mr. Tucker, but for now I am inclined to give the people a few more days to—"

I felt the pop and let out a yelp as the water gushed out of me and splashed to the floor.

"Maggie!" It was the court stenographer.

"Mrs. Dunn, are you all right?" the judge asked.

"Yes, Your Honor," I said meekly. "A little embarrassed."

"Nonsense," he said, peering over the bench at the puddle beneath my feet. "There's nothing embarrassing about going into labor. However, my thought to give you more time to formulate a convincing argument for the grand jury seems academic at this point. Step back, please. Mr. Tucker, help counsel to her seat."

Tucker, his shoes and pants cuffs wet, did as he was told.

"Mr. Rollo," the judge said.

Johnny stood. "Yes, Your Honor."

"Do you understand that you have been charged with a misdemeanor seventh-degree possession of a controlled substance with a recommendation of drug treatment in exchange for a guilty plea today?"

"Yes, Your Honor."

"How do you plead?"

"Guilty, Your Honor," Johnny said.

"The court accepts the guilty plea, and you are sentenced to six months of inpatient drug treatment. I want you back here in ninety days with a status report . . . and it better be glowing."

"Yes, Judge, it will be."

"And Mr. Rollo, I hope you understand that you just got the best Christmas gift ever. Don't squander it."

He banged his gavel. "Bailiff, get an ambulance. And get someone from maintenance up here with a mop."

CHAPTER 36

That day I brought three new lives into the world. Mary Katherine, named after my mother; Kevin William, named after Alex's father; and Johnny Lee Rollo, a twenty-nine-year-old battle-scarred drug dealer most people were ready to give up on, lock up, and forget.

But I'm too bullheaded to give up. I believed in Johnny, Judge Vanderbergen believed in me, and somewhere along the way Johnny finally wound up believing in himself.

He stopped using, he stopped dealing, and he started recovering.

Three months after his arraignment he was back in court, and the report from the rehab was every bit as glowing as the judge had demanded. Afterward, the two of us stood on the courthouse steps while his drug counselor waited in the transport van.

"Congratulations," I said. "You've come a long way in ninety days. I don't think I've ever seen you looking this healthy."

"Healthy? Is that code for fat? I put on like ten pounds."

"It's not code for anything. And trust me, Johnny, those ten pounds look damn good on you."

"Sorry, babe, you're too late," he said, a lovable bad-boy grin on his face. "You had your shot, but at this point in my life I can't get involved with a married woman who's nursing twins."

I put both hands to my heart and feigned a pout. "I'm crushed."

"But I still wanted to get something nice for the kids. The problem is, I'm on a short leash, so I couldn't exactly go shopping in any of your finer establishments, so I did the best I could."

He produced a brown paper bag from under his jacket. "This is from the baby gift department at 7-Eleven," he said. "The twins aren't ready for it yet, but one of these days when they grow into it, tell them it's from their Uncle Johnny."

He handed me the bag. I started to tear up as soon as I looked inside.

"Oh, Jesus, girl," he said, "don't get all gooned up on me now."

"I am so proud of you," I said.

"I couldn't have done it without you, Maggie," he said. "I owe you. Big time."

"You don't owe me anything."

"Didn't you see *The Godfather*? When an Italian says he owes you, don't tell him different."

"Fine. You can pay me back tomorrow."

"You name it. What do you want?"

"Ninety-one days."

"Oh, crap, don't tell me you fell for that one-day-at-a-time trick too."

"I didn't realize it was a trick."

"Are you kidding me? It's a total con game. I've been drinking beer and smoking dope since I was nine years old. It took me twenty years to figure out I was an addict, but the docs at the rehab knew it as soon as I stumbled through the front door. But did they tell me to quit drinking and drugging forever? Hell no. They know they can't get a junkie to quit doping for the rest of his life. Instead, they asked me if I can lay off just for today. I say yeah. I can do anything for a day. So I give that shit up for twenty-four hours, and what do you think they say to me the next day?"

"Wild guess," I said. "Can you lay off just for today?"

"Exactly! Is that a scam or what? The bastards have snookered me ninety days in a row. And worse yet, I'm buying it, so when a newbie shows up, I tell him that the program is working for me, and another convert gets suckered in. I'm telling you, Maggie, this one-day-at-a-time shit is the ultimate Ponzi scheme."

"I'll have the DA's office look into it immediately," I said.

The driver of the van tooted the horn.

"That's Gus," Johnny said. "He's been driving that druggie buggy for twenty-six years, and the poor dumb bastard is still high on life and bubbling over with gratitude. That's what happens to guys who keep drinking the Kool-Aid." A wide grin spread across his face. "I gotta go."

Johnny Rollo had been my drug dealer, my lover, my partner in crime, and my most trusted confidant. I wanted to hug him and hold him and tell him that I, too, was bubbling over with gratitude. But I was an assistant district attorney who had convicted him of a crime, and we were standing on the courthouse steps. I extended my arm, and we shook hands.

"Thank you, Counselor," he said. "For everything."

He turned, and I stood there as he climbed into the van and drove off. Then I opened the paper bag and took another look at the baby gifts.

Two boxes of Pop-Tarts. One chocolate; one strawberry.

CHAPTER 37

If you want to send an Irish family into joyful overdrive, give birth to a set of twins on the night before Christmas. For the next two days, well-wishers flooded the family room at the hospital to celebrate. It was loud, it was jubilant, and because visitors are welcome from seven in the morning to nine at night, it was nonstop.

That all changed when I got home, and I got to set the rules. Not only was I trying to get my kids and my own life on a schedule but I needed some respite from the hubbub, so I could spend some quality one-on-one time with my immediate family. For the next few weeks, visitations would be by invitation only.

When the twins were five days old, Grandpa Mike came to the house with a tin of Barry's loose-leaf tea that he has shipped directly from Ireland, along with some scones he baked himself, and a jar of Folláin Irish rhubarb and ginger jam.

He set out a little spread at the kitchen table, brewed the tea, and poured three cups. Grandma Kate might not be here in person, but she would definitely be here in spirit.

"*Slàinte*," he said, raising his mug.

I tapped my mug to his. "*Slàinte Mhaith*," I said. "So tell me, old man, how does it feel to be called *Great*-Grandpa Mike?" I asked him.

Instead of exploding with his usual folksy brand of joy and Irish humor, he looked at me pensively and mulled over the question. Finally, he said. "God's honest truth, Maggie . . . I'm afraid to blink."

His answer caught me by surprise. "I'm not sure I understand."

"I was born in 1933 in a wee village in County Donegal. I blinked, and I had a wife, a son, and I owned a bar in America. I blinked again, and my Kate was gone, my son was a widower, one of my little grand-daughters was a doctor, and the other was a hotshot lawyer making babies of her own. And suddenly, it's the twenty-first century, another Christ-mas has rolled around, and I'm a seventy-four-year-old great-grandfather. Like I said, darling, I'm afraid to blink. So think twice before you do."

I smiled and thanked him for his wise words.

"Not so much wisdom as experience," he said.

"With a dash of poetry," I added.

"Well, that comes natural when you're born in Donegal."

We spent a glorious hour together, and after he left, I thought about my own tendency to race through life. The ten years since my high school graduation had flown by. When did I marry a surgeon, pop out two kids, and become a hotshot lawyer? Had I paid attention to the moments, or had I been too busy with tomorrow to focus on today?

I sat down at my desk, opened a Word document on my laptop, and started typing.

New Year's Resolutions for someone who has broken every New Year's Resolution she ever made:
- *Don't blink.*
- *That's all. Just don't blink.*

But of course I did. No matter how noble my intentions, time re-fused to slow down, and my life moved on at the pace of a runaway train. The next dozen years became a blur of kids' birthday parties, school projects, dual tonsillectomies, summer vacations, picnics at Magic Pond, and a dead possum in the attic. My career was filled with glorious triumphs, painful defeats, and the politics of working in a male-dominated system.

Maybe if I had kept a journal, those years leading up to my fortieth birthday would have stayed in sharper focus. But in truth, I was just another working suburban mom. My life was interesting, but hardly worth documenting.

With a few exceptions.

It was a lazy Sunday summer afternoon when my cell phone rang. The caller ID had a 206 area code. It wasn't one I recognized. I answered cautiously. "Hello?"

The voice on the other end was equally hesitant. "Maggie . . . it's Misty."

The two of us had emailed in the first few months after she moved to LA, but we hadn't been in touch in years.

"Misty," I said, genuinely ecstatic to hear from her. "How are you?"

My enthusiasm reopened the door. "Funny you should ask," she said, sounding like her old self. "For starters, middle age is breathing down my neck. Also, I left my husband, I have a new job, and I moved to New York City."

"I am so sorry about your marriage, but you moved to New York? I can't believe it. Deets, girl. I need deets. Tell me everything."

"No way, bitch," she said, laughing. "It's going to take us many hours and multiple bottles of wine to catch up, and we are not going to do it over the fucking phone."

"Oh my God," I said. "I can't believe how much I missed your foul mouth. I'll take the train into the city Saturday, and we'll have lunch."

"No. We'll have dinner, get shit-faced, and you'll spend the night at my apartment. You missed too many episodes of the Misty Sinclair Soap Opera to catch up over a lousy lunch. Deal?"

"Deal."

We met in the back room of a tiny French restaurant tucked away on East Eighty-Second Street. I hadn't seen Misty in sixteen years, and she looked better than she had when she left Heartstone. "You look incredible," I said.

"Look who's talking," she said. "You look fantastic."

"As long as I hide the stretch marks."

We'd never been great friends growing up, but that night on Crystal Avenue surrounded by police and emergency vehicles had created a bond that neither of us could forget, and within minutes, we were yakking like two boozy schoolgirls driving down that winding mountain road on our way home from a midnight rave at the Pits.

She'd been right. It took her hours to catch me up. The short version: Four years of waiting tables, lots of acting lessons, and a few acting jobs that didn't last very long or take her very far.

"And then I met Ross," she said. "He was a set decorator, and he offered me a job as his assistant, which in show business translates to a lot of late-night sessions without any clothes on, but it was great. He taught me the craft—how to turn each set into the perfect environment for the characters who inhabit them. The furniture, the lamps, the curtains, the art on the walls, the sculptures in the garden—I loved it. I decided to hell with acting. I wanted to be in production—on the other side of the camera. Six months after I met Ross we got married. Turns out he was not only a brilliant decorator; he was also a serial wife beater.

"I gave it a few years, but I'm not cut out to be a battered wife, so one night when he was passed out in a drunken stupor, I went all Lorena Bobbitt on him. I cut off his dick and ran for the hills."

"Oh my God, you didn't."

"Well, not in real life, but I did put it in a script I've been working on." She laughed. "I finally ditched him, found a school in Seattle that would accept me, and got a degree in interior design. I got a job with a great firm that specializes in designing commercial space, and I just moved to their New York office. How about you?"

"Married to a doctor, we have six-year-old twins—a boy and a girl—and I'm an assistant DA for the county."

"Jesus, Maggie . . . that sounds like what you'd say if you were a contestant on a game show. Go deep, girl."

I dug deep. Deeper than I'd gone with anyone but my sister. My hopes, my dreams, my fears, my resentments—I let it all out, and she listened with a passion. No judgment. Just empathy. I had no idea how much I had missed her, needed her, trusted her.

After dinner we went back to her apartment, and we talked into the night. Somewhere around 3:00 a.m., when we finally went to sleep, I realized that Misty Sinclair was the best friend I never knew I had, and I was overjoyed to have her back in my life.

CHAPTER 38

"I was adopted," Alex informed me one evening at dinner.

"I believe you may have mentioned that the first time we slept together," I said. "The Dillon's basket, the fire station on North Plum Street, the note from your birth mother—riveting story, although my fascination may have waned after hearing it a few hundred times."

"Ah yes, but I've been adopted *again*. Dr. Theobald took me to lunch today."

"Oh my God, that's incredible." Alex was a surgical resident at Heartstone Medical. Theobald was a world-renowned surgeon. Every few years he would take some young doc under his wing, and their career would take off. "So does that mean you have a mentor?"

"Not just any mentor. Justin is one of the most respected—"

"*Justin?*"

"I know . . . it sounds weird. The man is a rock star, but I kept calling him Dr. Theobald at lunch, and he finally said, 'For Pete's sake, man, call me Justin.'"

"He actually said, 'For Pete's sake'?"

"He and his wife, Lydia, are devout churchgoers. I think Pete's sake is about as blasphemous as they get."

"Well, Jesus H. Christ, man," I said. "This is great goddam news. I can't wait to meet those fuckers."

Alex's face lit up in a smile, and he leaned across the table and kissed me. "This is why I love you, Maggie McCormick-Dunn."

"And would you like to know why I love you?" I said, kissing him back. "Because nothing makes me happier than someone who *gets* me. And you, Alex Dillon Dunn, really, really, really get me."

Alex flourished under Justin Theobald's tutelage, and as the years went by, the older man went from teacher to father figure to trusted friend.

And then one night, Alex, who had never been much of a drinker, came home reeking of alcohol. I didn't have to ask him why. The words tumbled out of him in a flurry of sobs.

"Justin is giving up surgery. He's been diagnosed with Parkinson's. He's only fifty-two years old, Maggie. Everything he's worked for—a brilliant career—over."

"Over?" I said, trying to make sense of the news. "But his whole world revolves around his work. What will he do?"

Alex shook his head. "You know Justin—he's a man of faith. He's decided that his affliction is a sign from God that he was meant to be doing something else with his life. Something with a purpose. Something for the greater good."

"Like what?"

"I have no idea."

But the board members at Heartstone Medical had an idea. They'd been looking for a new CEO, and as soon as they heard Dr. Theobald was available, they decided that their search was over. It was a wise decision. Justin was not only a natural-born leader; he was a visionary. Six months after he took the reins, we were having Sunday dinner with him and Lydia when he decided to share his dream with us.

"I want to build a Level I trauma center at Heartstone," he said.

We were stunned.

Lydia smiled. "The two of you look like you need another glass of wine."

"Or a defibrillator," Alex said. "Keep talking, Justin."

"Look, I know it's a bold plan for a hospital our size, but I've done some feasibility studies. We already have the perfect location—the acreage on the south side of the campus. It's a beautiful spot overlooking the pond.

"We'll need to secure a two-hundred-million-dollar revenue bond to finance construction, but I believe we can do it. And if we do, we can offer our patients a higher level of care and better clinical outcomes, attract more of the best and brightest doctors, and turn Heartstone Medical into one of the premiere health organizations in the state of New York. What do you think, Alex?"

"Without trying to sound like a suck-up, I'd say it's brilliant."

"I should have known better than to ask my favorite suck-up," Theobald said. "Maggie, what do you think? You never pull any punches."

"Since brilliant is off the table, I'm going with inspired." I paused. "However . . ."

"Aha! You smell a problem. Don't hold back," Justin said, egging me on. "Poke a hole in it now so I can find a fix before I present it to the board."

"The Crocker Street Development Group," I said. "They're planning to build an eighty-eight-unit townhouse complex across the road from our campus, and guess what their big selling point is."

Lydia held up her hand. "A spectacular view of Magic Pond," she said. "One of their investors is a member at our club. They haven't even broken ground, and she's already offered me 'charter member ground floor pricing' starting at one point three million. She must have said the words 'spectacular view of Magic Pond' five times in two minutes. Tacky, to say the least."

"What's her name?" I asked.

"Minna Schultz. Do you know her?"

If the Theobalds were a little less genteel, I might have said, *"She's the heartless bitch who destroyed Arnold Sinclair's business and ultimately drove him to murder his wife and son, then take his own life. You're damn right I know her. I'd like to rip her black heart out and shove it up her ass. The only problem is, I'll have to fight off my best friend, Misty, to see who gets first crack."*

But some things are best left unsaid.

"I've heard of her," I said. Then I turned to Justin. "Please don't shoot the messenger. You asked me to poke holes. Minna Schultz will not stand idly by and let the hospital block her view."

"Well then, it will be my job to inform her that it's not her view. It's ours."

CHAPTER 39

Step by step Justin moved the project forward. First creating a business plan, then getting the hospital planning board and our wealthiest constituents behind him, and finally securing a promise from a New York City bank to float the $200 million bond.

And then he announced the news to the press. Within hours Minna Schultz tweeted that the new trauma center would not only destroy acres of Heartstone's green space but it would also poison the pond.

Dr. Theobald calmly responded by explaining that he was working with one of the country's leading aquatic engineering firms, planned to dredge the pond, remove the six to eight feet of muck and sediment that had accumulated over the past hundred years, and then restore the natural bottom, leaving cleaner water and a healthier ecosystem.

Minna didn't let up. She brought in experts of her own, all of whom branded the new trauma center as a toxic environmental threat.

Theobald tried to reason with her, which of course was futile. He tried negotiating, and when that failed, he held a town hall forum where he had hoped public opinion might help change her mind.

Alex and I were there that night. Minna was geared for battle, armed with *conclusive evidence* that dredging Magic Pond would not give it new life, but would destroy it. And when she was done attacking the vision, she went after the visionary.

Microphone in hand, Minna harangued Justin viciously, calling him a washed-up quack who was trying to cling to a failed medical career by running a multimillion-dollar hospital business without having a shred of business training.

Even by Schultz's standards the attack was ugly and evil and inflammatory. I could see the sweat on Justin's face as she lashed into him. His hand tremors were more pronounced. Finally, fists clenched, he stood up to respond, clutched his chest, and fell forward. Half a dozen doctors raced to his side to help. One gave him CPR. But he was dead before he hit the floor.

Minna Schultz had claimed another victim.

Justin Theobald was only fifty-five. There were no successors on the horizon. The board asked Alex to step in. They said it was temporary, but none of the candidates measured up to either Theobald or Alex. A month later the board came back to Alex. They promised he wouldn't have to give up surgery, but for the first few years his medical practice would have to take a back seat.

He wavered. And then they told him he was the only person who could pick up the standard and help realize his mentor's dream.

That was the knockout punch, and Alex became the new CEO of Heartstone Medical.

The following morning Minna Schultz announced that she was running for mayor of Heartstone. It was a brilliant move. The current mayor was retiring after two terms, and the field was wide open. If Minna won, the new trauma center would most likely lose its funding.

Money people don't part with their money unless all the regulatory approvals are in place. As mayor, Minna would wreak havoc with the town planning board, the health department, the DEC, and every other governmental agency she could infiltrate. Backers don't like political resistance, and they would bow out.

Alex and his team spent the weekend at an off-campus conference center brainstorming for ideas that would stop Minna.

That Sunday evening, he came home drained, but with a gleam in his eyes.

"You figured it out, didn't you?" I said.

"I think we did," he said. "We're putting up our own candidate for mayor. We'll hire a seasoned campaign manager, put together a strong marketing team, staff it with field workers to get out the vote, and fund it like it's a statewide election instead of a mayoral race in a town of fifteen thousand people. We can do it, Maggie. We can win."

"You bet we can win," I said. "The kids and I volunteer to lick envelopes. Who's the candidate?"

"You."

"Very funny. Who's the candidate?"

"I'm serious, Maggie. The five of us made a list of possible candidates in private, and then we compared lists. You were at the top of every one."

"You want me to run for mayor? That's insane."

"No. Minna running for mayor is insane. You running might be more of a Hail Mary, but it also might be a brilliant strategy. You were born and raised here. Everyone knows you. They know your family. You already work for the people as a prosecutor. You're photogenic. You're a great speaker. You don't have any skeletons in your—"

"Stop, stop, stop," I said. "Being able to smile for a camera, speak to a crowd, and having a recognizable last name aren't exactly good reasons for me to run for mayor."

"I wasn't telling you why I thought you should *run*. I was telling you why I thought you could *win*. And if you win, Heartstone wins. This trauma center will mean more jobs, a shot in the arm for the local economy, and dramatically better health care for our community."

"Maybe so, but I'm an officer of the court, and it's going to look like I'm in cahoots with my husband, who is CEO of the hospital. You back my candidacy, I win, and Heartstone Med has the mayor in their back pocket."

Alex laughed. "First of all, anyone who knows you would know you've never been in anybody's back pocket. Second of all, who cares what it *looks* like? All I know is that if Minna Schultz wins, Justin's dream is moribund, and our town loses the opportunity of a lifetime."

"And that greedy bitch will make millions selling views of something she doesn't even own," I said, taking the bait.

"It sounds like you're running," he said, reeling me in.

I ran. I ran the only way I know how—with all my heart and body and soul and with every ounce in my being.

And on that rainy evening in November, an hour and a half after the polls closed, with every television in McCormick's Bar turned to Hudson Valley News, the final results scrolled across the screen.

Minna Schultz: 2,109
Maggie McCormick-Dunn: 7,781

Eight weeks later, on January first, with my friends and family filling the first six rows of the community center, and my eighty-nine-year-old grandfather holding the Bible given to him by his grandfather, I was sworn in as the first female mayor of Heartstone, New York.

After the swearing-in ceremony, Grandpa Mike took me aside. "I wish your grandmother and your mom were here to see this. I know they'd be as proud of you as I am. Probably more. How do you feel, girl?"

"God's honest truth, Grandpa . . . I'm still in shock. One minute I was prosecuting criminals, and the next minute I'm running a town. I'm not sure how it all happened."

"Well, I have a theory, lass," he said.

"Lay it on me, old man."

His blue eyes danced, and he gave me a broad smile. "You must have blinked."

CHAPTER 40

The first five months of my administration turned out to be a nonstop series of blinks. They flew by in a blur.

But that second Thursday in June is etched in stone. It started with the storm of the century. And then came the devastating one-two punch.

First, Rachel Horton hit me with a left jab. "Dr. Byrne needs some more blood."

The chief followed up with a right cross. "Minna Schultz is dead. Her body was found this morning floating in Magic Pond."

Driving to the crime scene I kept thinking about that day a lifetime ago when Misty, still raw from the loss of her parents and her brother, told me that Minna's role in their deaths would not go unpunished.

"One day, I'm going to make that bitch pay," she'd sworn.

"Don't go around repeating that to the rest of the world," I told her. "Or one day it's going to come back and bite you in the ass.'"

But Misty was too angry to keep quiet. She vented her rage to anyone and everyone who would listen. And today, I thought as I parked my car at Magic Pond, is the day I had warned her about.

My sister Lizzie, who only had to walk from the hospital, was already there when I arrived. "This has got to be the biggest crowd Minna ever drew," she said. "So far, I've counted fourteen cop cars—local, state, and sheriff's department, plus EMS, the ME, and a dive team from the county."

"And a pack of bloodthirsty jackals," I said, pointing at the cluster of reporters, news vans, and camera crews.

"You know what they say, Maggie—give the people what they want, and they will come."

"Mayor Dunn! Dr. McCormick!" It was the chief. He waved us through the perimeter and led us behind a privacy screen that had been set up to block the macabre scene from public view. Maureen Jessup, the medical examiner, was kneeling beside the body.

"Maureen," I said, "I need—"

"I'm not done yet, Maggie," she said without looking up. "I need a little time."

"I know, I know. Just give me some good news I can feed to the public."

Maureen lifted her head and looked to me. "You want good news? Tell them she's dead. That ought to make a lot of people happy." She turned back to her work.

I looked at Lizzie. "Do you see those vultures over my shoulder? If I don't tell them something, they'll make up their own shit."

"Ignore them, Mags," she said. "This isn't your first media circus. You've done this a hundred times."

"As a prosecutor. This is my first one as mayor."

"You want me to help you lose your virginity?" she said. "Get out there with a bullhorn and tell them what they want to hear."

"Which is what?"

"I don't know," Lizzie said. "How about something like this: 'The bloated and bludgeoned cadaver of my biggest political rival was just pulled from the very same body of water that had been at the core of our venomous conflict. So lock up your womenfolk and children and grab your pitchforks and torches. There's a homicidal maniac on the loose.'"

"Thanks," I said. "You're no help."

"Maggie, in a town like Heartstone, where three people getting food poisoning at the firehouse potluck dinner is front-page news, that's exactly what they're hoping for."

"I know, but I need to give them something reassuring."

"Okay, let's try this: 'Beloved philanthropist Minna Schultz died peacefully of natural causes in her sleep last night. The medical examiner is completely clueless as to how her pruned and puckery ass wound up floating in Magic Pond.'"

I didn't crack a smile, but Maureen laughed out loud. She stood up. "You two are annoying the crap out of me. If I give you something with a positive spin, will you take your sister act on the road so I can focus on my work here?"

"Yes!" I said. "Absolutely!"

"Here it is: There are no obvious signs of external trauma or defensive wounds."

"So, you're leaning toward suicide?"

"Come on, Maggie. How long have we been working together? I am not leaning toward anything. You asked for some good news, and the best I can give you is that nothing is jumping out at me that suggests homicide. But that can all change once I've got her on the table and I've spent some quality time with her up close and personal."

I knew that was as good as I was going to get. I looked up at the chief.

He gave me a nod. "We can work with that."

For a small-town cop, Chief Vanderbergen was remarkably media savvy. "This is a lot like a car wreck on the highway," he said. "Everybody slows down because carnage is fascinating—as long as it's not your own. But as soon as a cop gives them a 'nothing-to-see-here-folks' wave, they lose interest and get on with their journey.

"The press will play Minna's death for all it's worth, but for now you can take some of the steam out of their rhetoric, just by saying something insipid, but reassuring."

"Like what?" I asked.

He flipped open a pad and read from it. "We are closely examining the circumstances surrounding Ms. Schultz's death, and we do not believe there is any threat to the community, nor are the police looking for anyone at this time."

"Perfect," I said, taking the pad out of his hand.

I read the statement exactly as he'd written it, and then segued into what was really important—the storm that had been pelting us for the past thirty hours. My message was simple: it's over, we weathered it, and we'll be coming out of it even stronger. Classic political bullshit, but it seemed to do the trick.

"Nicely done, Mayor Dunn." Lizzie said. "Always a pleasure to watch you work your magic, but now I've got to get back to my boring day job healing the sick and comforting the dying."

"Don't go," I said. "Something happened. Rachel came to my house early this morning."

She gave me a blank stare. "Rachel . . . Rachel . . ."

"From Dr. Byrne's office."

"Well, well, well. I guess that's one of the perks of being mayor. Your phlebotomist makes house calls. I still have to show up at his office."

"I *did* go to his office. Last week. But something is wrong, so she showed up this morning and took it again."

"And?" she said.

"*And*? And what do you think? Twenty-five years, and I've never had to do a retest. Doesn't that tell you something?"

"No. Not really." She paused and then let out a long sigh. "Oh, Jesus, Maggie. Have you already written the script? What did Rachel say?"

"She said that the lab screwed up. What is that supposed to mean?"

"I'm going to go out on a limb here, Maggie, but maybe the lab screwed up. It happens all the time. Do you remember Covid? Do you know how that got started? Somebody in a lab in China screwed up."

"That's never been proven."

"Fine. You want more examples? Go to the memorial wall on the Lab Safety Institute's website. Death by explosion is an occupational hazard. Doctors and technicians handle deadly viruses all the time. And sometimes they mishandle them." She put her cell phone to her ear. "Honey, I'm not coming home tonight. I dropped the damn monkey pox beaker, and . . ." She ended the scenario with a coughing fit.

"I don't know why you don't take this seriously," I said.

"Because labs are not robots, Maggie. They're full of human beings who make mistakes because they woke up with a hangover, or their kid didn't get into college, or their wife ran away with the FedEx driver."

"Can you check with the lab and see what went wrong?"

"Absolutely not! I'm a doctor. I can't walk into the lab and say, 'Who the hell screwed up this time?' Especially since you're not my patient." She gave me a hug. "You'll get the results next week. Don't worry. You'll be fine."

She headed up the path toward the hospital.

"That's the best you can do after four years of medical school?" I called out after her. "'You'll be fine'? I want a second opinion."

She stopped and turned. "Okay! You'll be crazy! Crazy and fine! It'll make a great bumper sticker when you run for reelection."

CHAPTER 41

"Hey, Mom," Kevin said, when I entered the kitchen the next morning. "Some guy is trashing you and Dad on social media."

"That's nice," I said. "I hope he spelled our names right."

"Sorry, Mom," Kevin said, putting on his most adorable sad face. "No names. It just says, 'The blatantly suspicious drowning of former mayoral candidate Minna Schultz was the culmination of a heavily funded, well-executed corporate and political plot to silence her tenacious environmental efforts.'"

"Well, that sucks," Alex said, joining the fun. "It's too vague. This town is full of corporate and political villains. How are people supposed to know the Dunns done did the deed?"

Katie slammed her hands on the table and jumped up. "You people sicken me! That poor woman gave her life so that the privileged among us could forever have a spectacular view of Magic Pond. I'm done being a Dunn. I'm changing my last name!"

"To what, you ungrateful child?" Alex snapped.

"Schultz!" She tossed her hair defiantly and stormed out of the room.

"Aaaaaaaaand scene!" Kevin called out.

Katie pranced back into the room, throwing kisses and taking bows, while the rest of us applauded.

And that was that.

Within minutes, my kids were off to school, my husband was back in Alex World, and I was in the car on the way to work. But that impromptu little tableau had touched a nerve. When the four of us were actually under the same roof and in the same room together, we were the happiest family in the world.

I should have been overwhelmed with gratitude. But one ugly thought kept getting in the way. *Who would take my place when I was gone?*

Fortunately, the aftermath of the death of my political rival kept me so busy that I had no time to pay attention to my demons.

At 4:00 p.m., the chief came to my office with an update on the investigation.

"Good afternoon, Madam Mayor," he said, lowering himself into the barely comfortable government-issue side chair across from my desk.

He was in great shape for a forty-five-year-old man. Tall, lean, no sign of middle-age paunch, a full head of closely cropped silver-gray hair, a neatly trimmed beard, and an affable smile. According to Lizzie, who knows everything about everybody, he was "happily divorced after twenty years of marriage, but not dating, and not really looking."

"Good afternoon, Chief," I said. "You're smiling."

"It's my way of throwing people off. It's a little trick my dad taught me years ago."

"And how is Judge Vanderbergen these days?"

"He's doing his best to navigate retirement. He spent the winter driving my mom nuts. Now that spring is here, he'll go up to the cabin and annoy the hell out of the fish. Mom loves to tell everyone that they have something between them that does wonders for their marriage." He paused. "Two hundred miles of New York State Thruway."

I laughed. "Send your parents my best. So . . . what have you got?"

"Minna Schultz's lungs contained pond water."

"So she was alive when she went in," I said.

"That's correct. The ME has concluded that the cause of death was consistent with drowning. She also did a quick tox that showed traces of clonazepam in Minna's system. Not enough to kill her, but it's common for people who are hell-bent on drowning to pop pills so they lose consciousness once they hit the drink. Otherwise, their survival instincts would kick in and they'd fight to stay alive.

"We searched her house and found a bottle of Klonopin. The prescribing doc was Ezra Perkins. I swung by his office, and he told me he's been treating her for depression and anxiety for years. She went into a tailspin when she lost the election and the townhouse project went south. I got a statement from Dr. Perkins, took it to the ME, and she said we have no proof that Minna took the pills on her own."

"Were there any signs of a struggle? Any defensive wounds? Any indication that someone forced her to take the pills?" I asked.

"None. Not on her person or in her house, but . . ."

I groaned. Nothing good ever follows the word *but*.

"The ME waved it off. She said, 'Someone could have slipped them in her Chardonnay,' which, by the way, along with a couple of peanut butter and jelly sandwiches on English muffins, were the only contents they found in her stomach."

"Peanut butter, jelly, and white wine?" I said.

"Clearly Minna marched to the beat of her own drum," he said.

"Damn her!" I said. "She spent the better part of a year accusing my husband of environmental genocide. You would think she'd have at least dashed off a quick suicide note condemning her oppressors. She wasn't the type to skulk off quietly."

"No suicide note, but we found this." He removed some papers from his pocket. "They're drafts of an apology letter. They were on her laptop, written a week before her body was found. I printed them out."

"Who was she apologizing to?"

"Misty Sinclair."

My stomach knotted. "Misty?"

"Minna Schultz hosed, cheated, screwed over, and downright made a lot of people miserable, but I can't think of anyone who she owed an amend to more than Misty. Here's her first attempt," he said, handing me a sheet of paper. "Look at the time stamp on it."

"June first at 9:22 p.m.," I said. "That's the same day she had the final showdown with Alex at the hospital."

I read it.

Dear Misty. whan I saw you in town over the MemrialDay weekend I was totally oerwhelmed. I know I shouldnt have run off but I needed time to think. I know you blame me forwhat your father did but

"It's riddled with typos," I said. "She must have been totally drunk."

"And at a loss for words. Her second stab was time-stamped three minutes after the first. She ran out of steam even faster on this one." He handed me a sheet of paper that was almost blank.

Dear Mistyy—first and foremost I am a envvironmentalitst

"And here's the last one. It was written the following morning at 5:49," he said, handing it to me.

Dear Misty, 25 years ago when I campaigned against the use of toxic solvents by your father in his dry cleaning business, I had no idea that my strong stance would lead to such a tragic outcome. You were too young and too raw back then for me to explain to you that my protests were out of my heartfelt concern for the health and welfare of our community and not the vindictive business attack for which I was accused.

Then when I saw you in town over this past holiday weekend all the pain that I have tried to bury since that night came flooding back to the surface, and I was too overwhelmed to talk to you. So I ran. I'm sorry for that, and I'm deeply sorry for your loss. And while I know you can never forgive me, I want you to know that I did not put a gun in your father's hand, and that simple truth has helped me sleep these past 25 years. You deserve so much more

than this simple note, but maybe it will serve to open a door, and
that one day we will find a way to heal together.

Sincerely yours,
Minna Schultz

"Wow," I said. "A little defensive, but it reads like a genuine apology. And no typos. It's like she woke up sober the morning after and spilled her guts out. Do you know if she ever sent this to Misty?"

"It's not in her sent email, and I plan to contact Ms. Sinclair and find out. But what's important here is not whether she sent this letter but that she wrote it. It attests to the fact that Minna Schultz was filled with guilt and remorse just before her death."

"And do you think that it will convince the ME to call it suicide?"

"Not by itself. But add that to the fact that Minna's shrink corroborated that she was clinically depressed, her assistant said she'd been moody and despondent, and Dr. Dunn can recount her meltdown on June first and her vow to get even if it's the last thing she did."

"Excellent police work, Chief," I said. "Thank you."

His lips parted and turned upward.

"You're smiling again," I said.

He shrugged. "No promises, but the ME told me off the record that she's leaning toward calling it a suicide. I think showing her this letter to Misty Sinclair is going to clinch the deal."

The smile got broader. It wasn't the little trick his father taught him to throw people off. It was the real deal. A victory smile.

Twenty-four hours later, the medical examiner signed Minna's death certificate. *Cause of death: Drowning. Manner of death: Suicide.*

Two days after that, my doctor told me I had four to six months to live.

CHAPTER 42

The banner was stretched across the entire length of the bar. There was a sparkly silver-and-green shamrock on one end, the flag of Ireland on the other, and in the center, in big bold Celtic lettering, it read:

The Party of 9/10ths of the Century
Happy 90th Birthday, Mike

It was Saturday, the tenth of June, and McCormick's was celebrating Grandpa Mike's Big Nine-Oh. The food was on the house—mountains of sandwiches and salads, platters of fruit and cheese, and baskets of sweets were laid out on the groaning board like a grand old Irish picnic. Drinks were at 1930s prices, and just in case you didn't have exact change, there were bowls of nickels on the bar.

Gifts were encouraged. Grandpa posted a list two weeks earlier—clothes (men's or women's, any size), toys (new or in good condition), and cash (crisp or crinkled)—all of which would go to St. Cecilia's. In bright red at the bottom of the list he'd scrawled, *If you bring anything for Mike you'll be thrown out on your arse.* The whole town was invited, and by late afternoon the place was packed to the gills, and the gift table was piled to the rafters.

At 6:00 p.m., Misty showed up, all smiles. We had reconnected when my kids were born, and at this point, we were part of the fabric of each other's lives. But with both of us working crazy hours and living sixty miles apart, too much of our daily contact was by phone, text, or email. That was about to change.

"I have *awesome* news," she said, as soon as we found a semiquiet booth in the back.

"You finally stopped overusing the word *awesome*," I said. "Oh no, wait. That can't be it."

"There are two other words I also haven't stopped using," she said. "One is a verb; the other is a pronoun. You want to hear them?"

"I'll pass. Just tell me the awesome news."

"I just got a call from my broker. They accepted my offer. I'm moving into the house on Old Carriage Road."

"Oh my God," I said, leaning across the table and squeezing her hand. "That actually is awesome."

When the hospital started interviewing interior design firms for the trauma center, Misty was in charge of her company's pitch. They got the win, and Misty, knowing she'd be project managing the job for the next year and a half, decided to keep her apartment in New York and buy a second home in Heartstone.

"And now that I'm about to become a taxpayer in your fair city," she said, "I've got question for you, Madam Mayor. Why did your chief of police call me?"

"The chief called you?"

"Don't play dumb, Maggie. He called and asked if I'd had contact with Minna Schultz recently. I told him I'd been house hunting in Heartstone over Memorial Day weekend. My broker and I were coming out of a place on Cromwell Road just as Minna was heading in. She saw me and ran for the hills. He asked if I'd heard from her since then, and I said no. What's going on?"

"She committed suicide."

"I know. But why did he call *me*?"

"I have no idea. It was a suspicious death. The cops were investigating. They called a lot of people."

"Suspicious, like maybe someone murdered her?"

I shrugged.

"Did he think *I* killed her?"

"Of course not."

"You know that for a fact?"

"Absolutely."

"It's amazing how you can have *no idea* what he wanted, and then in the very next breath you *absolutely know for a fact* what he didn't want."

"Isn't it great? It's one of the superpowers you develop as a politician."

"So what you're saying is you know, but you can't tell me," she said.

"Yes. And even if I could tell you, you wouldn't want to know."

"Excuse me, ladies," Alex said, sliding into the booth next to me. "I have a small problem to discuss with you. I just heard that Misty bought a house in town."

"Why is that a problem?" I said. "All you have to do is lift your finger, and your project manager will come running."

"It's great for the hospital," Alex said. "But I barely have any time with my wife as it is. With Misty in town, she's going to occupy a big chunk of the little time I get with you."

"I see your point," I said. "You should have married someone less popular."

The brass bell behind the bar clanged, and my father stood in the middle of the room, one hand on Grandpa Mike's arm, a microphone in the other. Everyone settled down, and Alex and I worked our way through the throng to get closer to the guest of honor.

"Thank you all for coming," Dad said. "Is this the finest old coot ever to get behind the stick?"

Cheers from the crowd.

"Pop, what year did you leave County Donegal?"

Grandpa leaned into the microphone. "1950. Right after the war. I was all of seventeen."

"And tell us all what you miss most about the good old days in Ireland."

Grandpa smiled. "Rosie Banaghan. I can still picture her. Porcelain skin, silver combs in her red hair, smelled like mountain heather."

"And she was your boyhood sweetheart?"

"Heck, no. She was me teacher at St. Mura's, and I was head over arse in love with her. Sadly, I was ten, and she was twenty-four. But now," he said, playing to the crowd, "I'm ninety, she'd be a hundred and four . . . there'd be a lot less tongue waggin'."

The packed house exploded with joy.

"Truth be told," the old man said, his brogue getting thicker as he worked the room, "there'd be a lot less of anything waggin'."

It took close to a minute before my dad could get control of the revelers. "Settle down, folks," he said into the mic. "You're only encouraging him."

Dad put his arm around Grandpa Mike's shoulder, and the throng quieted. "Pop, I know you said you didn't want a gift, and it might have worked on these guys, but since when has your family ever paid attention to you? After ninety trips around the sun, we had to get you a little something."

He waved at Lizzie, who was behind the bar. The lights dimmed, and all the TV monitors came alive.

The sweet sound of a tin whistle filled the air, and a single word blossomed onto the screens: *Donegal*. A few beats later, a second image faded up below it: *1933*.

The film began with archival shots of the old sod. Some in black and white, some in sepia, a few in the washed-out colors of the era.

People awwwed and sighed and muttered undecipherable tributes under their breath. Not everyone in the bar was Irish, but every one of them—the Cappadonnas, the Speros, the leather-jacketed bikers—was either grinning or holding a hand to their mouths to keep from crying.

Grandpa Mike just stood there mesmerized, his son's arm still around his shoulder.

And then the music burst into the rollicking sound of the Pogues singing "Whiskey in the Jar." The screen erupted with the words *Donegal 2023* and suddenly everything was in vibrant color.

For the next ninety seconds the video transported us all to the place Michael Francis McCormick would always call home.

People started clapping, dancing, and singing along, as Grandpa shouted out the names of every church, road, and castle that flashed across the screen. And then a wide shot. A drone camera flew across the bog, swooped over emerald-green pastures hugged by ancient stone walls, and finally settled on a white stucco building with the name Biddy's O'Barnes proudly emblazoned across its face.

"Jesus, Mary, and Joseph," Grandpa yelled. "It's Biddy's! Best pint in Donegal."

At least a hundred locals stood outside the pub, and as the camera zeroed in on the mass of smiling faces, they all raised their mugs and sang out, "Happy Birthday, Michael!"

The Pogues hit their last "whack fall the daddy-o; there's whiskey in the jar," and the video came to a colossal close.

Everyone rose to their feet, and joyful pandemonium swept the room.

"*They* seemed to like it, Pop," my father said. "But what did you think?"

Grandpa Mike leaned into the microphone. "Blew me away, son. Made me wish I was there."

"Well, in that case, I've got good news and bad news," my dad said.

"I'll take the good news."

"You *are* going there, and all those folks you saw at Biddy's O'Barnes are waiting to toast you. You're leaving tomorrow," my father said, handing him an Aer Lingus flight envelope.

The old man was stunned.

"Are you ready for the bad news?" my father asked. He didn't wait for an answer. "I'm going with you."

Grandpa Mike, wiping away tears, hugged my father, and all hell broke loose.

The trip had been a well-kept secret. Only Lizzie, Alex, and I knew, along with Chef Tommy and Dotty Briggs, who would run the place while my father and grandfather spent ten days on the windswept shores of County Donegal.

And there was one more surprise waiting for him. Lizzie was flying to London for a medical conference tomorrow. But when the mayor of the county designated Wednesday, June 14, as Michael McCormick Appreciation Day, Lizzie decided to fly to Ireland to join him. My father had asked me to be there too, but my life was too hectic for me to leave Heartstone.

I stood there, Alex, Katie, and Kevin at my side, my own eyes tearing up, my heart filled with joy for what I had, but aching for my mother, and I thought how blessed I was.

Thirty-six hours later, it would all turn to shit, and my sister, my father, and my grandfather—three pillars of strength who had been there for me my entire life—would be three thousand miles away when I needed them most.

CHAPTER 43

I woke up Monday morning in a sweat. I'd had a sex dream, and my mind was doing its best to hold on to the details before they slipped away.

The dream camera was overhead, and I could see the teenage me in the back seat of my mother's red Mustang, screaming, "Yes, yes, yes!" and clawing at the man on top of me.

I've had sex in a lot of places, but never in my mother's car. So I had no idea who the guy was.

It didn't matter. Whoever he was, he hadn't gotten me off in the dream, and I needed a man to finish the job.

I put one hand between my legs and reached across the bed for Alex with the other.

He wasn't there.

I looked at the clock. 6:42 a.m. He was probably downstairs making my tea.

I closed my eyes and started without him. Nothing aggressive. Just enough stimulation to feed the desire in the pit of my stomach.

A minute later he came bounding into the bedroom. He set my mug of tea on the night table and kissed me on the forehead.

"Forget the foreplay and take off those pants," I said.

"I can't, babe. A bus overturned on I-eighty-four. Two dead and about forty injured. The state cops are diverting a dozen of them to us. It's all hands on deck, and I'm captain of the ship."

Another kiss on the forehead, and he was gone.

I pulled my hand from under the covers, sat up, and swung my legs to the floor. The images of my dream were getting fuzzier and fuzzier, but the desire was still there. My real man was gone, but I still had my old reliable Mr. Plastic Fantastic in my dresser drawer. As long as I had fresh batteries, he never left me hanging.

I picked up my mug, tilted it toward my mouth, and took a few swallows. "Thanks for the tea, Alex," I said into the ether. "At least you're good for something in the morning."

My cell rang, and I jumped like I'd just been caught trash-talking my husband.

I recognized the number, and the dark cloud that had hovered over me all weekend settled onto my shoulders. I answered.

"Maggie, it's Noah Byrne. Sorry to call so early, but I wanted to get to you before the Monday-morning rush."

Dr. Byrne had been my mother's doctor, and for over twenty years he'd been Lizzie's and mine. He's from the School of Doctors Don't Call with Good News. Three times a year his nurse calls me and says, "Your lab results were fine." A call from Byrne himself could only mean that something was not fine.

"What is it, Noah?"

"Can you come in this morning?" he said.

Bad news, if it's not *that* bad, can be conveyed over the phone. Really horrible news is always delivered face-to-face, an outstretched doctor's hand to hold, a box of tissues on his desk.

"That sounds ominous," I said.

"Don't project, Maggie. We'll talk when you get here. My first patient is at eight. Do you think you can be here before then?"

A half hour later I was in his office. And despite the fact that he'd said, "Don't project," I had. And I'd been right.

"The lab here in the hospital gave me the results of your blood test last week," he said. "I didn't like what I saw, but I didn't want to alarm you, so I had Rachel draw a second round and sent them to the Kensington Lab in St. Louis. They're top of the line. They emailed me the results last night. They're not good, Maggie."

He slid a three-page printout of my blood test across the desk and started to take me through it line by line.

"No," I said, halfway through the first page. I turned the printout over. "Plain English, please."

"You have the same condition your mother had."

"How much time do I have?"

"Whoa, Maggie. Slow down. We can fight this."

"That's what you told my mother." As soon as the words came out of my mouth, I regretted saying them. "I'm sorry, Noah. You did everything you could."

"I wish I could have done more, but you have a better shot than she did. The medical landscape has changed. Chemotherapy has come a long way since your mother's day."

"For breast cancer, yes. Every year a million people march to raise money for a cure. But nobody gives a shit about some unpronounceable blood disease they never heard of. The truth is that zero strides have been made since 1997. And I know that for a fact because I've consulted another doctor."

"Who?"

"Dr. Google. According to him, 'familial HLH is fatal with a survival rate of two to six months. Chemo can temporarily control the disease, but symptoms inevitably return.'"

"So that buys you time, and then we look for other options. There's a clinical trial for a new drug that—"

"Do you ever buy lottery tickets?" I said, cutting him off.

"What do you mean?"

"Lottery tickets, Noah. You know—Mega Millions or Powerball."

"Not often, but when the jackpot is some outrageous amount, I'll do a ten-dollar quick pick."

"And once you have the ticket in your pocket, do you think about what you're going to do with it when you win that outrageous amount of money?"

He smiled. "Virginia and I are doing very well financially. We could win half a billion dollars, and it wouldn't change our lives that much."

"So why buy the lottery ticket?"

"Because on the remote chance that we did win, we would open a foundation and give the money to those in need. Maggie, we seem to have gotten away from the matter at hand. Why are we even talking about this?"

"Because I've been playing the blood test lottery for over twenty years, and unlike most people, I'm hoping my numbers *won't* be drawn. But just like you, Virginia, and everyone else, I've dreamt of what I would do if I were unlucky enough to hit the hemophagocytic lymphohistiocytosis jackpot."

"And what is that?"

"I will *not* go through what my mother went through. The chemo drained her dry and left her in a state of constant fatigue. I watched it, and I don't want my children to watch it happen to me. And I definitely don't want to be part of a clinical trial for a new wonder drug and hope that (a) it really does work and (b) I'm not part of the 50 percent who are popping sugar pills.

"Mom's biggest regret was that she wasted the last few remaining months of her life looking for medical miracles. I'm doing what she wished she had done. I accept that I have a fatal disease, and I want to live my life out enjoying my husband, my kids, my friends, and my family, and if I'm lucky, doing something for the people of Heartstone that I can be remembered for."

"Fair enough," he said.

"You're not going to try to talk me out of it?"

"No. You're not the first patient to opt out of treatment because they feel the downside far outweighs the possible good it could do. I respect your decision, and I admire your ability to accept the diagnosis with such grace. Clearly you are Kate McCormick's daughter."

"Thank you," I said. "That's the nicest thing you've said to me all morning."

He smiled. "Would you like me to go with you when you tell Alex?"

"No. He's got a lot on his plate, and this morning he added a busload of crash victims. I'll tell him when the time is right, so I'm invoking our doctor-patient confidentiality agreement."

"I *will* try to talk you out of *this* one. Keeping this kind of news from your husband is a slippery slope. I can keep your records confidential for now, so Alex can't access them, but eventually you're going to tell him, and he's going to ask you, me, or both of us how long you've known about this. The longer you wait, the more hurt and angry he'll be."

"I know that. But I also know that if I tell him immediately, he will be just as devastated. You know Alex as a coolheaded physician and a rock-solid hospital CEO, but he has abandonment issues. It may have something to do with the fact that his birth mother left him at a fire station.

"He totally lost his bearings when Justin Theobald died. If I tell him I'm dying, he'll be useless to the hospital, to the kids, and to me. I'll go from wife, lover, and life partner to patient. *Terminal* patient. Once he knows he's going to lose me, the two of us as a couple will never be the same." I picked up the blood test printout and waved it at him. "For now, Noah, this is just between you, me, and HIPAA."

Byrne is an old hand at this game. Once I played the HIPAA card, he knew it was over.

"I don't agree with your decision," he said. "But I'll honor it."

I left his office, got behind the wheel of my car, stared out at the gray-blue early-morning sky, and let the news wash over me.

I'd often wondered what I'd do or how I'd feel if this day ever came to pass.

I'll probably get drunk, I thought. Or stoned. Or both.

But now that the moment was here, I had no desire for a drink or a joint.

I only wanted one thing. A man to hold me, his arms wrapped tightly around me, my tears on his warm, strong shoulders.

My husband wasn't available. But I knew someone who was.

I took out my phone and dialed his number.

He picked up on the first ring.

"Hello, Van," I said.

CHAPTER 44

Ninety minutes later I was in my office, where I approved the purchase of a brush hog to the everlasting gratitude of the Parks Department, argued about street-cleaning regulations, hosted a luncheon for the downtown business alliance, and generally put out the fires, big and small, consequential and not, that flare up constantly.

Except for the fact that I'd just been given a death sentence cocktail and followed it up with an adultery chaser, it was a perfectly normal, boring, hectic day in the life of a small-town mayor.

I picked up some Thai food on the way home, had dinner with my kids, and because there's a no-electronics-at-the-dinner-table rule, we had a fun twenty minutes, with the conversation ranging from Kevin announcing that he wanted to give up the violin to Katie telling me about the *totally dope* movie she saw where one of the bad guys puts the other in a woodchipper.

"*Fargo*," I said. "It came out when I was a teenager. I loved it."

"Awesome," she said, either amazed by the fact that we both could possibly like the same movie, or that her mother was actually once a teenager.

After dinner Alex called to give me an update on the condition of the twelve bus passengers who were admitted to Heartstone General.

"Stable," he said. "Every one of them."

"I know. The kids and I saw you on TV," I said. "Also, did you know that the governor sent out a tweet thanking you and the staff for your quick response and your dedication to public service?"

"Public service?" He laughed. "Typical political puffery. We're a hospital. It's what we do. Look, honey, I've gotta go. It's been a media circus here all day, and as usual I'll be the last clown out."

"Do you have any clue when you'll be home?"

"My best guess? About a quarter after never."

"Spoken like the devoted public servant I know and love."

"Love you back, Mags. Kiss the kids."

He hung up.

The kids were nowhere to be kissed. They had dutifully cleared the table and disappeared into their netherworlds, not to reemerge again till morning.

I had the whole night and the whole house to myself. I was finally able to do what I had desperately needed to do all day. Have a long heart-to-heart talk with my mother.

I went to the garage, yanked the cord on the attic stairs, and my army of stalwart orange sentinels tumbled out, a few of them hitting me on the head and shoulders on their way down.

Ping-pong balls. Seven of them.

"Good evening, ladies," I said as they clattered to the concrete floor below.

They were my early-warning system. If anyone had so much as tugged on that attic door since my last visit, the shock and awe of my little plastic warriors would have rained down upon them. And knowing my family, I guarantee they would have shrugged it off and not bothered to put them back. Bottom line: I might not be able to identify the intruder, but at least I'd know I'd been breached.

I lowered the stairs all the way and quickly began scooping up the troops. One, two, three, four, five, six . . . six . . . six . . .

I was one ball short. I flipped on my cell phone light and ran the beam across the floor. Oil stains, ancient paint spatter, thick clumps of dirt-caked leaves, gauzy spiderwebs rich with their latest prey. But ball number seven was nowhere to be found.

I dropped to my hands and knees, sweeping the light across the floor, slower this time, and wondered why I'd decided I needed seven balls to stand guard when one, or two, or at most three would have easily done the trick.

Because you're the champion of overkill, the voice inside my head said. *Because when you have something to hide, paranoia trumps logic. Because you don't trust anybody, even your own—*

A splotch of orange peeked out from under the stark white freezer. I zeroed in on it with the light. A big black bold STIGA logo confirmed its identity.

"Gotcha," I said, plucking the rogue ball out of its sanctuary and shoving it into the bag with the others.

I stood up and exhaled. I don't even know why I bother worrying. My house has two attics. The one over the bedrooms on the second floor is where we store the stuff we have to get to during the year, like Christmas lights, Halloween decorations, luggage, and Alex's fifty-quart lobster pot. It's easy to access. Just open a door and walk up a flight of stairs.

The one over the garage is no-man's-land, an inconvenient storehouse for all the junk we no longer need but can't seem to part with. At least that's what Alex thinks, which is why he hasn't been there since we bought the house. As for the twins, after the dead-possum incident I don't think they'd venture up that ladder if Apple opened a store up there and was giving out free iPhones.

I tucked the Ziploc bag full of ping-pong balls under my arm, climbed the stairs, turned on the light, and with my head down low, I navigated my way through a makeshift path till I encountered an oversized plastic rocking horse. His paint was peeling, and the four heavy-duty springs that attached to his tubular metal stand were tinged with rust.

I moved him out of the way and sat down on the floor. We all have secrets. Mine are up here preserved in a cardboard carton marked Aunt Rosie's Good China.

It's my burn box. It's filled with all the things I want incinerated after I'm gone, and there's only one person in the world I trust to do that without opening the box or looking at the contents—my sister Lizzie.

You may wonder why I haven't destroyed the whole lot of it myself. I can't. I won't. They're part of my history. Sweet or painful, they make up the fabric of my life. And there are times in my life when I have to reconnect with them.

Today was one of those times. I opened the burn box.

Yes, I had asked Lizzie to destroy it once I'm gone, but in truth there were no smoking guns in there. Just things I didn't want shared with the world. Like love letters I'd received from Van after he joined the Marines, plus some I'd written but never sent after I found out he was married.

Every poem I had ever written was in a manila envelope marked *God Awful Teenage Girl Poetry*. And, of course, there were diaries, seven of them in all, one for each of my teenage years.

I picked up the volume marked seventeen and started flipping through it. An hour flew by, and I realized I wasn't flipping. I was reliving the year that my mother died, one painful diary entry at a time. I put it down and fished out another item of major significance that was stashed in my burn box. It was meant to be burned, but only a little at a time. A bag of loose joints.

I lit one, drew the smoke into my mouth and sucked in more fresh air as I inhaled. It was just another one of the little tricks Johnny Rollo had taught me to increase the potency of the hit.

And then I pulled out a second box. My legacy box. The private stuff I wanted to be kept and judiciously passed on. Reports and essays I'd written that dated back to middle school; awards I'd won; *Dunn Gets It Done* buttons, bumper stickers, and other souvenirs from my campaign for mayor; and, of course, the real purpose of my trip up to the Possum Graveyard, reminders of my mother—gifts she'd given me, the eighteen-page letter she'd written, and silly things she'd saved from her mother.

I picked up the framed photo of her when she was nine months pregnant with me. "Hey, Mom," I said. "I'm dying."

I took another hit on the joint, and another, and sat staring at the picture until the THC slowly opened up a channel of communication between us.

"Any advice from an old pro?" I said.

"You did the right thing turning down treatment," she said. "I wish I had."

"I'm worried about what will happen to the kids when I'm gone," I said.

"I know. For me, the hardest part about dying was not knowing who would step in and be there for you and Lizzie."

"We got lucky," I said. "Beth is one of a kind."

"Yes, but the world is littered with Connies."

She was right. When my mother died, my father was a bighearted, blue-collar, knock-around barkeep, and plenty of women swooped down on him. Alex, with his movie-star magnetism and his seven-figure earning potential, would attract even more. The hospital was a hotbed of nurses, doctors, technicians, and patients, all looking for husbands. Most of them were looking for the perfect happily-ever-after guy. But I knew that there's always a handful looking for the take-him-for-all-he's-worth guy. And if she destroyed his life and his kids along the way, that's their problem, not hers.

I finished the last of the joint and stretched out on the attic floor, my brain in a cannabis haze. I folded my arms across my chest and stared up at the rafters. Only they weren't rafters anymore. They were the walnut ceiling panels at Kehoe's Funeral Home, and I was in a box, Alex and the kids dressed in black at my side.

And then they came. The perfumed piranhas in pretty print dresses, circling, moving in, angling for the best position, their noses twitching at the scent of money—

I bolted upright. "Get out, you fucking bitches!" I screamed. "Keep your fucking claws off my fucking family!"

The sobs came in waves. "My family . . . my family . . . my family . . ." I whimpered.

My family. My shy, supersensitive son, who would be lost without a strong mom to help him navigate the adolescent minefield. My sensational maverick daughter, who will go off the rails without somebody she respects to rein her in. My broken-at-birth husband, who will crumble if he is abandoned yet again.

I closed my eyes, and my ears homed in on the hum of the attic fan.
I breathed in the sound, and soon it went from monotone to musical.
And in my head I sang along with it.

"Ain't no mountain high enough. Ain't no valley low enough." My
mother's love song to my father.

When I opened my eyes, I was staring down at her picture. She
looked so beautiful in her pink floral maternity dress, her eyes already
glowing with the joy of motherhood, her hands gently cradling the me
that was to be, safe inside her belly.

"Thanks, Mom," I whispered, kissing her gently. I neatly packed
and resealed the box and made my way downstairs, a woman empow-
ered. A woman on a mission.

Find the next Mrs. Dunn.

CHAPTER 45

I woke up Tuesday morning feeling painfully alone. Alex spent the night at the hospital. Lizzie was out of the country. And while the late-night séance in the attic with my mother helped give me clarity, the conversation was admittedly lopsided.

I needed to talk to another living human being. But who? Father Connelly came to mind. I remember how grateful my mother was to have him administer the sacraments, but I needed more than someone to anoint me with oil and tell me that the love of Jesus could help me make sense of my suffering.

Then there was Misty. I could almost picture her eyes welling up as I told her she was going to lose the person who had been like a sister to her. And then I imagined the meltdown that would follow when I told her I decided not to pursue standard medical protocol. I wasn't ready to put her through that kind of pain.

There were only two people I trusted to give me the love and compassion I needed without judging me for my decision to forgo treatment. One was in London. I called the other one.

"Hey, Johnny. It's Maggie. I wanted to see if I could catch you before you left for work."

"You should have called me seven and a half hours ago. I'm just at the end of my shift."

The background noise was deafening. "I can barely hear you," I said.

"I'm in competition with a forty-ton cement mixer," he shouted. "We're on a continuous pour. The trucks have been delivering concrete around the clock for three weeks. This week I caught the night shift."

The first job Johnny landed when he got out of the halfway house had been carrying ninety-four-pound bags of cement for a construction company. A year later he'd learned to read blueprints, get the perfect water-to-mix ratio, and use all the tools of the trade. Now he was a foreman supervising the trucks with the giant rotating barrels and telling them where and when to pour their concrete.

"Can we talk when your shift's over?" I yelled into the phone.

"Better than that," he said. "Let's do breakfast. Corky's. Eight thirty."

An hour later Johnny and I were sitting across from each other in the same diner, in the same booth we'd been coming to since high school. We spoke at least once a week, but we hadn't been able to connect in person for two months.

"First things first," I said. "Let me see pictures."

He leaned over and swiped his phone until he got to a picture of his wife, Marisol—a tall, classically beautiful woman with radiant black hair and creamy caramel skin—and his three daughters, ages four, six, and eight, each wearing a pastel-colored Easter dress with a matching bonnet. Behind them, with his paws wrapped around the girls, was a giant, fluffy white Easter bunny.

"Just when I thought they couldn't get any more gorgeous," I squealed. "What mall did you take that in, and how come you're not in the picture?"

"No mall," he said, and swiped again.

It was almost the same picture, only this time the bunny was holding his head in his hands. It was Johnny.

A wave of joy surged through my body. "I am so, so proud of you," I said.

"And I am so, so grateful to you."

"You did the heavy lifting, Johnny."

He laughed. "Any idiot can carry a couple of million pounds of concrete. You're the one who gave me the shot. So, what's up? You need any help running your little kingdom, Mayor Dunn?"

I told him. No foreplay. No punches pulled.

He sat there. Stunned. Speechless. And then he did something I'd never seen him do, even when his life was about to go down the toilet.

He cried. His lips turned down and quivered, and he fought to hold it together. Finally, the tears spilled over, and he sat there silently shaking his head, as if by denying the reality of what I said he could make it go away.

I reached into my purse and pulled out a tissue, but he waved it away—his macho way of communicating that Kleenex was for sissies. Then he took his sleeve and wiped it across his face, adding a big, wet, loud manly snort, just in case anyone in the diner had seen him having a moment.

I stood up. He looked up at me, his eyes wet, and then he slowly shifted his weight, slid out of the booth, and wrapped his arms around me.

"Is there anything I can do?" he asked.

"You're doing it," I said, hugging him back.

"No, I mean like do you need a kidney or something?"

I knew he was joking, but if I had said yes, he'd have dragged me to the hospital and told Alex to take one of his kidneys before I changed my mind.

"The only thing I need is a friend," I said, "and you're probably the best one I ever had."

He held me tight, rested his head on my shoulder, and sobbed unabashedly.

CHAPTER 46

Nobody gets to choose how they come into this world, but some of us are lucky enough to have a say in how we go out. Now that I knew the clock was ticking, I wanted to exit on my own terms.

I've seen people document their final days by sharing their journey on social media, garnering thousands of likes, retweets, and sad-faced emojis on their way out. That's not my style.

I'd become a public figure, but I had no desire to be in the limelight surrounded by hundreds of well-wishers. I wanted to die in the dignified quiet and comfort of my home, with a small circle of close friends and family watching me set sail.

But I knew I'd need a rock-solid support group along the way. Telling Johnny had been cathartic. For the next few days, he was my lifeline, helping me wrestle with questions like, "I want to leave each of my kids a letter like my mother left me and Lizzie. How honest can I be?"

His answer was brilliant. "Pretend you're making your closing argument to a jury. Only tell them the things that will get you the verdict you're looking for."

The most burning question over the next few days was how to break the news to Lizzie. Johnny had the simple solution for that one too.

Her flight arrived at JFK at 1:40 p.m. Thursday afternoon. That morning, at Johnny's suggestion, I called her car service, canceled the pickup, and was waiting for her at Terminal 5 when she cleared customs.

"What are you doing here?" she said, giving me a quick sister-hug and handing me one of her bags.

"Today is National Welcome Your Sister Back to America Day," I said.

"Never heard of it."

"I'm a powerful mayor. I decreed it. But don't think it's because I love hanging with you. I just couldn't wait to hear every single thing I missed out on by not being with Grandpa and Dad in Donegal."

The ride home was joyful, and I couldn't help thinking back to our last picnic at Magic Pond with Mom. These would be the few hours of calm before the bomb dropped.

"So, tell me the best thing that happened on the trip," I said as we headed north on I-678.

"I met this real hot orthopedic surgeon at the medical conference. Her name is Olivia. She's from Toronto. She'd been married, had a three-year-old son, caught her husband cheating, ditched him, and ultimately decided that life was more fulfilling if she played for the other team."

"How old is she?" I asked.

"Ancient," Lizzie said. "Your age."

"Is this the real deal?"

"Who knows? But it's promising enough that I opened a frequent flier account with Air Canada."

As soon as we got to Lizzie's house, she opened a bottle of wine. "I haven't talked to you in days," she said as we headed for the living room. "What have you been up to?"

I'd braced myself for this moment, but I never managed to come up with the right words. So I broke the news in her language. I handed her the lab report Dr. Byrne had given me Monday morning.

She lowered herself to a chair and read it. Twice.

"Why didn't you call me as soon as you got this?" she said.

"If I thought you had a cure, I'd have called you immediately. But you're going to go through hell with me. I didn't want to rob you of these past few happy days."

"You didn't owe me that, Mags. I know I'm your sister, but I'm also the idiot doctor who told you you'd be fine. You could have at least called and slapped me with a lawsuit for malpractice."

She took a third look at the lab report. "Your numbers are off the charts. How do you feel?"

"Fine. I mean, I've been a little nauseous lately, but I kind of chalked that up as part of the general gastric distress that comes with being mayor. But for the most part, I don't feel all that bad."

"Neither did Mom at first."

"I know. Dr. Byrne said I have close to the same numbers as she did when she was first diagnosed."

"I'll call Dr. Honig at Memorial Sloan Kettering," Lizzie said. "I'm sure he'll do me a favor and be willing to see you immediately."

"Don't," I said.

"What are you talking about, Maggie? Honig is at the forefront of research in hematology."

"I know who he is. He was Mom's specialist when she tried that last Hail Mary. There was nothing he could do to save her, and there is nothing he can do to save me."

"And who made you an expert on medical science?" she said.

"Lizzie, how well do you know me? Do you think you're the only one who's been keeping up with the latest on this bad-blood shit? It's like pancreatic cancer. It was a death sentence when Mom had it, and it's a death sentence now. Early detection is too late. It means nothing."

"So, you're just giving up hope?"

"The only thing I'm giving up is chasing miracles. Did you forget about those last few weeks we spent with Mom? What was her biggest regret?"

She pursed her lips, refusing to say out loud what she already knew in her heart and her well-educated medical mind.

"Let me refresh your memory," I said. "She knew she had a short time left and a lot of things she wanted to do, and she was kicking herself for trading it all away. She let the chemo suck the last bit of life out of her. I'm not going to do that. I knew this day could come, and I have a lot to do before I shuffle off."

She picked up the bottle of wine and refilled our glasses. "So, are you planning to climb Mount Kilimanjaro or see the Taj Mahal?"

"No. That's a bucket list. I have a things-to-do list."

"Like what?"

"First, I want to spend all the time I can living like a normal human being and doing everything I can to enjoy my family while I'm still here."

Lizzie nodded. "If there's a 'first,' there's more to the list. What else?"

"I want to find the woman who's going to take my place."

"As mayor?"

"No, as Alex's wife. As Katie and Kevin's Mom."

"Are you . . . are you serious?"

"Yes. I've given it a lot of thought."

"You're gonna piss away the little time you have left to look for a girlfriend for your husband? Trust me, Maggie—he won't have any problem. He'll be surrounded by people willing to help lift him up, not to mention a hospital full of nurses happy to administer sympathy."

"Oh . . . you mean like Connie Gilchrist was there for Dad?"

"That was different, Maggie. Dad was a blubbering wreck. Alex is made of much tougher stuff. He deals with life and death every day."

"Other people's deaths, Lizzie. But if I die, he'll revert to that little boy who never got over the fact that his mother left him in a shopping basket and disappeared from his life forever. He'll put up a steely exterior, but inside he'll be as devastated as Dad was. The predators like Connie can smell that."

"Maggie, it's a noble goal, and I love you for it, but if you die, Alex will grieve, but he'll move on. You can't orchestrate what happens after you're gone."

"Lizzie, what do you think would have happened to our family if Connie had married Dad and took him for all he was worth?"

"Train wreck," Lizzie said.

"Right. Dad would have taken the brunt of it, but you and I would have been collateral damage. And we'd still be living with the guilt that we didn't do for Mom what she couldn't do for herself."

"Is Alex on board with all this?"

"No. I haven't even given him my diagnosis yet. I need a little time to get my head together before I deal with his."

"Okay, but what happens when you find . . . sorry, but I'm not calling her the next Mrs. Dunn. What happens when you find her? Do you bring her home one night, and say, 'Hey, Alex, I'd like you to meet Maggie two-point-oh'?"

"I haven't worked out the logistics, but I'm hoping to do what Mom did."

"Oh my God," Lizzie said. She knew exactly what I was talking about.

The night before Beth married our father, she sat down with the two of us and said, "I just want you to know that I have your mother's blessing to marry your father." Our mouths dropped.

"A few months before your mom died, she invited me to lunch. I'd been a widow for two years, and she asked me if I was ready to give it another go. I told her that I was ready for the *concept* of another relationship, but I couldn't deal with the thought of going back into the dating scene at the age of forty-two. She said, 'Maybe I can save you some time. I think you and Finn would be perfect for each other.'

"I was shocked, but intrigued. We talked. I guess technically you might say we conspired, and eventually I promised her I'd find a way to introduce myself, but I would wait at least a year after she was gone."

"You should have made it a week," Lizzie said. "Connie Gilchrist swooped in like a hawk on a field mouse."

"That's exactly what your mom was afraid of. But . . ." she said, tapping the modest gold engagement ring with the tiny marquise diamond in the center, "it all worked out in the end."

"Does Dad know that Mom—" I groped for the word.

"Set him up?" Lizzie said.

Beth laughed. "No. And he can't. That was part of my promise to your mother. But she never said anything about keeping it a secret from you, and I think that it's important that you know that when your father and I exchange our vows tomorrow, your mom will be the happiest woman in heaven."

For the next two glasses of wine, Lizzie and I reminisced about the remarkable Mary Katherine Donahue McCormick—state champion track star, fearless biker chick, devout Catholic, loving wife, devoted mother, and all-around kick-ass human being.

"So," Lizzie finally said, "have you come up with any candidates? Mom set the bar pretty damn high with Beth."

"I don't have anyone yet," I said. "I was waiting for you to get back. I have a delicate question to ask you."

"Ask me anything. Nothing is off-limits," she slurred. She looked at her watch. "It's only two a.m. in Donegal. The night is young, lassie."

"Okay. How hot are you for this Canadian doctor, because if you were straight, you'd solve all my problems in a heartbeat."

She practically spit out her wine laughing. "You're batshit crazy," she said.

"I know," I said. "It runs in my family."

She leaned over and hugged me. "I love you, Maggie," she said. "Whatever happens, we're in this together."

They were the exact same words she had said to me that unforgettable afternoon with Mom at Magic Pond.

CHAPTER 47

There was no way I could tear myself away from Lizzie. I called Alex.

"The kids are going to need sustenance," I said, "and you've been elected to pick up a pizza, feed them, and then be ignored."

"No problem," he said. "What are you going to be doing?"

"Lizzie is home, and the two of us are bonding."

He laughed.

"What's so funny?"

"I believe I detected a hint of dysarthria in your voice."

"What does that mean?"

"It means you're slurring your words. 'The kids are going to need shushtenance' was my first clue. My medical brain immediately started to wonder if you had a ministroke, but the party boy in me is guessing that you girls are well into your first bottle of wine."

"One of you is right on the money, Dr. Party Boy. You figure out which one. I'll see you later."

"Hold on, pal," he said. "I will either *pick* you up later, or I'll see you tomorrow. As good as I am at providing nourishment for their adolescent bodies, the kids still do better with two parents."

It was an innocent joke, but it was a total gut punch. *Two parents.* I couldn't speak.

"Did you hear me, Maggie? I don't care if you and Lizzie get shit-faced, but promise me that neither of you will be driving tonight."

"Promise," I said meekly. "See you tomorrow. I love you."

"What an incredible coincidence," he said. "I love me too."

It was a tired old line, but it always made me smile.

I hung up. "That clinches it," I said to my sister. "You're stuck with me for the rest of the night. Doctor's orders."

"Perfect," Lizzie said. "You can help me with the laundry."

I followed her into the laundry room and watched as she rooted four days' worth of dirty clothes out of her suitcase, threw them in the washing machine, and headed for the kitchen.

The first bottle of wine seemed to have evaporated, so we popped the cork on a second.

"We should make a list," Lizzie said, picking up a pad and pencil from the counter.

"Of what?" I said.

"Criteria," she said as we went back to the living room. "It's like online dating. You're the gold standard. If we're looking for your successor, we should write down all the special qualities you have that Alex adores."

She sat down and started to write. "Let's see . . . pushy, annoying, control freak, adequate boobs . . ."

"I see you've lost no time finding the humor in all this," I said.

"I don't know what you're talking about," she said innocently. "Now, how do you spell 'intransigent'?"

"You know what would be extra special?" I said, playing along. "It would be great if we could find a woman whose grandmother was the only female physician in a county of more than fifty thousand people. Dad loved that about Connie. And Alex is a doctor, so he's bound to love it even more."

We drank and laughed our way through the most serious conversation we'd ever had. Fifteen minutes and another half bottle of wine into the exercise Lizzie put the pencil down.

"I think we've got it," she said, looking at the pad. "This is solid."

"Read it back to me, Miss Moneypenny," I said.

"Wanted," Lizzie said. "New wife for successful doctor with two slightly annoying but incredibly adorable teenage children. Candidate should be incredibly intelligent, fun loving, moderately patient, really, really great with kids, have an amazing sense of humor, adore long walks on the beach, and be able to suck dick like a Park Avenue call girl."

"Wait a minute. I don't remember saying anything about dick sucking," I slurred, my dysarthria in full bloom.

"I thought you told me Alex said you give world-class blow jobs."

"I do. But that should be my legacy. When I die, that title is retired. Strike the dick-sucking part," I said.

She scribbled on the pad. "Okay. Did we leave anything out?"

"Duh . . . what about healthy? The first one broke down halfway through the race. The next one should have great genes and no family diseases coursing through her veins. The only things she should have inherited are a trust fund and the loyalty and devotion of a Labrador retriever."

"Damn it, Maggie, you're making her sound spectacular. Alex can't marry them all. Maybe if I'm lucky there'll be a dyke in that pile of applicants."

"What about Olivia?" I said.

"Oh my God," Lizzie said, laughing hysterically. "I completely forgot that I have a girlfriend."

By the time the clothes were ready to come out of the dryer, we were both too plastered to fold.

We staggered upstairs and crawled into the same bed for the first time since we were kids.

"Thank you," I said as I curled up next to her.

"For what?"

"For making me laugh."

"That's the thing about the McCormicks, Maggie," she said. "It's in our DNA. We know how to laugh through the pain."

"God knows," I mumbled as I drifted off, "we've had plenty of practice."

CHAPTER 48

Friday morning I woke up with a throbbing hangover and an iPhone full of emails, all of which reminded me that I was no longer Madam Mayor. At least temporarily.

It was the weekend of our twenty-fifth high school reunion, and for the next few days, I was once again Madam President.

Our lovable class clown, Duff Logan, was the reunion chairman, and together with his self-anointed Committee of Middle-Aged Dorks, Dweebs, and Misfits they planned three *"Spectacular Midlife-Crisis-Defying"* events.

Saturday night was the *Not-Too-Old-To-Party-But-I-May-Doze-Off-Before-Dessert Dinner Dance*. Sunday was the *See-You-In-Another-Twenty-Five-Years-If-I'm-Lucky Farewell Brunch*. But the highlight of the weekend promised to be Friday night's *Cracking of the Keg—The Great Reveal of the Heartstone High School Class of 1998 Time Capsule* to be held at McCormick's.

A few months earlier, Duff created a Facebook page dedicated to generating buzz for that long-anticipated event. There was a photo of the keg still gathering dust in the storeroom of our family pub. Below that he had added a caption in big craggy letters right out of a horror movie poster.

What Embarrassing Secrets Lie Within?

He posted a few of his own crazy thoughts, and within days people took it as a challenge and started adding comments that got the group hyped up for that long-awaited Saturday night.

I had been thinking about that night since high school, and I wondered what the forty-three-year-old me would be like. Who would I marry? How many kids would I have? Where would I be in my career?

Little could I ever have imagined that I would wake up that morning in my sister's bed, after spending the previous night doing her laundry, getting rip-roaring drunk, and playing a spirited round of a game we had dubbed *Matchmaker Noir*.

I put down my phone, got out of bed, threw on yesterday's clothes, and followed the smell of fresh-brewed coffee down the stairs.

"Give me five minutes, and I can make you a cup of chai tea," Lizzie said.

"My central nervous system can't wait five seconds for caffeine," I said. "I'll have whatever brown beverage is in that pot over there."

"It's reunion weekend," Lizzie said, pouring me a steaming mug of coffee. "How are you feeling about that?"

I added a splash of milk to cool the coffee down and took a long, gratifying swallow. "The same way I feel about everything these days," I said. "Remember what Grandma Caroline used to say?"

"Self-pity is a waste of precious time. Shut up and play the cards you're dealt."

"Exactly. I've been looking forward to this reunion for a long time. I'm going to dress to kill and have the time of my life."

"Good for you," Lizzie said. "By the way, I forgot to tell you. I'll be there too."

"The hell you will," I said. "Since when did the class of '99 get invited to the class of '98's reunion?"

"I'm not a guest. Did you forget that Dad and Grandpa are still in Ireland? Dotty asked if I'd come in and work the bar."

"That's ridiculous. You haven't worked the bar since you went off to med school. Tell Dotty to call someone else."

"Maggie, the poor woman was stressed out. This is the biggest private party she's ever had to handle on her own. I'm happy to help. Besides, I'm willing to come out of retirement just to see what's in that famous time capsule of yours."

"It could be great, or it could be a dud. Nobody knows," I said, taking another hit on the coffee. "But, hey, as long as you're going to be there, do me a favor and make yourself useful."

"Sure. Name it."

"There'll be at least a dozen age-appropriate single women at the reunion tonight. Check them out. My perspective may be a little jaded."

"Good idea. I'm your wingman," she said, and quickly turned around to get something out of the refrigerator.

It took a few more seconds before the fog lifted from my booze-addled brain. "You cunning runt," I said.

She didn't turn around.

"My *wingman*? Bullshit, Lizzie. You played me," I said.

She still didn't look back. Suspicion confirmed. Nothing in that fridge was more important than squaring off and dealing with my accusation.

"You're smirking, aren't you?" I said.

"I don't smirk," she said, her face still hidden, a hint of glee in her voice.

"Turn around and look me in the eye," I said.

She turned around. Her face was deadpan.

"You rigged this," I said.

"I have no idea what you're talking about," she said.

"Last night I told you I was looking for my replacement, and this morning you're suddenly working at the bar, happy to check out prospective candidates."

"Maggie, you just asked me to do that."

"I never would have asked you to come to my reunion. *Never*! I only decided to ask you to help because you were going to be there anyway."

"So, it all works out," she said. "Win-win."

"One last question then," I said. "And I want a totally honest answer."

She nodded, her expression as vacant as a tournament poker player.

"Exactly when did Dotty ask you to work the bar?" I said.

A wide grin spread across her face, and she shrugged. "About five minutes ago. Right after I called her."

CHAPTER 49

"Before we go in, I have a confession to make," I said to Alex, after we pulled into the parking lot at McCormick's.

He came around to my side of the car and put his hands together in mock prayer. "Please don't tell me you're thinking about running for Congress," he said. "Anything else I can handle."

"You know Duff Logan, don't you?"

"Sure. Funny guy. What about him?"

"When I was in high school, I thought he'd make the perfect boyfriend."

He laughed. "You were right. And he did. But for Warren, not for you. Why are you telling me this now?"

"Because we are going to be spending the next few days with eighty-seven people I went to high school with, most of whom you've never met, and I wanted to let you in on the only secret I've ever kept from you so that you are not tempted to ask them any questions about my questionable past. Got it?"

"Damn," he said. "I guess now I'll have to scrap the intro I worked on. Hi, my name is Alex. Just how big a slut was my wife in high school anyway?"

I put my arms around him. "I can't believe I'm dragging you through an entire weekend of this memory-lane mania," I said. "Thank you."

He pulled me close and kissed me.

"Hey—I have an idea," I said, trying to sound like it had just popped in my head and not something I had decided six hours ago. "We haven't had any alone time together in ages. Let's go away next weekend. Just the two of us."

"Fantastic," he said. "I put the boat in the water at the end of April, and we've only taken her out twice. Why don't we sail to Block Island for the—"

"Alex, that's a father-son weekend. As much as I love cramming my body into a bunk bed, squatting on a tiny toilet, and waking up at four in the morning because that's when the fish are biting, I'm talking about you and me going somewhere with a few more amenities—like a shower."

I grew up within spitting distance of the Hudson River, but for me, boats are confining. Alex, who was raised in the Great Plains of Kansas, swears he never feels freer than when he's cutting through the water with the wind in his sails.

"Why do we bother owning a sailboat if we're not going to use it?" he said.

"That's a good argument for selling the boat, not for getting me to be trapped on it for forty-eight hours. Why don't you and Kevin make a plan to spend some time smelling like real men on the high seas, and I'll think of something more romantic for the two of us this weekend."

"No problem," he said. "Have your people call my people with the details."

I didn't bother telling him that *my people* had already made a reservation at the Mohonk Mountain House, a hundred-and-fifty-year-old Victorian castle resort in the Hudson Valley. There's never a right time to tell the love of your life that you're dying, but this felt like the right place.

One more kiss, and we walked around to the front of the building, where someone wearing the Heartstone High School hawk mascot costume high-fived us and escorted us through the front door of the restaurant.

Duff Logan and his husband, Warren Tremaine, own a successful party-planning business, and I knew they'd give us a lot more than our meager budget could afford.

They did not disappoint. Somehow they'd managed to transform an Irish pub into an all-American high school gymnasium, circa 1998. The ceiling was festooned with lights, balloons, and miles and miles of crepe paper. The walls were covered with group pictures from our past—blowups taken right out of our yearbook. And the sound of Elton John singing "Can You Feel the Love Tonight?" filled the air.

Duff, hovering near the entrance, spotted me, hurried over, leaned in for a double cheek kiss, and shook Alex's hand. "So," he said, his arm sweeping across the space, "what do you guys think?"

"It's fantastic," I said. "It's like our senior prom on steroids."

"More like our senior prom on Metamucil," he said, "but I'll take the win."

"Maggie!" The shout came from across the room.

I looked up. "Brenda!" I yelled back.

"And so it begins," Alex said. "I'll get you a drink."

He headed toward the bar, and I braced myself as I watched Brenda and two other women come scurrying toward me. For better or for worse I was about to go back to high school.

I don't enter into any situation blindly, so I prepped for this weekend by scouring the web for blogs and posts about the ins, outs, ups, and downs of reunions. The war stories ranged from mortifying tales of embarrassment to sordid confessions about hooking up with old lovers, to pithy tweets that said, "Waste of time. These people were boring then, and they're even more boring now."

Alex brought me a glass of wine, and I worked the room, while he opted to sit at a table with the other good sports who never even heard of Heartstone High until they married one of its graduates.

I spent the next hour reliving old memories, sharing family photos, smiling for selfies, reconnecting, reuniting, and secretly searching for the Cinderella who could effortlessly fit into the glass slipper I'd be dropping when my biological clock struck midnight.

A high school reunion may be the single most judgmental place on earth, and I couldn't help but fall prey to the temptation. I made mental notes of who got fat, who was losing his hair, who was drinking too much, and who looked desperate to impress the people they couldn't impress twenty-five years ago.

I knew they'd be judging me too. Bring it on, I thought. I look damn good, I'd walked through the door with my dreamy, successful hunk of a husband, and I was mayor of Heartstone. As long as I didn't tell anyone I wouldn't be around for my twenty-sixth reunion, I was pretty sure I'd take first prize in the "Wish I Was Her" bake-off.

On a scale of one to ten, I quickly gave the party an eight, but as the evening wore on, I dropped it to a five. There was a reason I hadn't stayed in touch with most of these people. And the two I cared about the most—Johnny and Misty—weren't there.

When I asked Johnny if he was going to the reunion, he gave me a flat-out "no way." Except that he'd said it in three words to make sure I knew he was serious.

"Maggie, I hardly ever showed up in high school back when I was supposed to," he said. "Why should I show up now?"

"Because look how far you've come. You could be the biggest success story of the night."

"It doesn't matter. It still won't stop some asshole from introducing me to his old lady as the school drug dealer. I can't erase my past, but I don't have to go back and have people rub my face in it."

Misty, on the other hand, had promised me she'd be there. "Fashionably late," she said. "And with Carl on my arm."

Carl was Black, thirty-six years old, and six feet tall, with a smooth dome, neatly trimmed stubble, and a physique to be reckoned with. Together they made a stunning couple. What people never knew was that they weren't a couple. Carl was Misty's personal trainer, and from time to time she'd invite him to a party as her plus-one. This was one of those times.

"I kind of had the reputation in high school as being a bit of a slut," she said to me when we had lunch a few weeks before the reunion.

"*Kind of*?" I said. "The editors of our yearbook wanted to vote you 'Most Likely to Succeed in the Adult Film Industry,' but the faculty adviser nixed it."

"Whatever," she said. "All I know is that if I show up at that party alone, I'll be fighting off cockeyed Casanovas all night. But walk into a room with Carl, and men keep their distance."

She was right. The two of them arrived just as dinner started. Heads turned. They always do when Misty enters a room. But with a guy who looks like an action-movie hero at her side, there was no mad dash of men offering to get her a drink.

I waved at Misty, and she and Carl joined Alex and me on the buffet line. Then the four of us found a booth and had a nice relaxing dinner without any pressure to dredge up stories of the good old days.

At seven thirty Duff took center stage. He waited for the crowd to settle down, and then he said, "Ladies and gentlemen, the President of the Class of 1998."

I stood up, and much to my surprise, the room filled with the ruffles and flourishes of drums and bugles, and the United States Marine Band played "Hail to the Chief." Duff Logan thought of everything.

I walked to the front, and he handed me the mic. I stood there and stared at the crowd. I cocked my head from side to side and slowly scanned my classmates. The room grew silent as they waited, and it was a good fifteen seconds before I finally spoke.

"Jesus, you fuckers got old."

It brought the house down, just as Lizzie had promised me it would when she came up with the bit that morning. I flashed her a thumbs-up, and she waved at me from the bar.

I quickly thanked everyone for coming, and half a minute later I turned the show back over to Duff, returned to my seat, took Alex's hand, and sat back to watch the culmination of a crazy idea I'd had twenty-five years earlier.

CHAPTER 50

The time capsule was wheeled out, and Duff banged on the steel top with a hammer. "All these years," he said, "and it's still tighter than Principal Drucker's sphincter."

The TV monitors in the bar sprang to life, and the screens lit up with a live-stream video image of the keg. A man wearing a hard hat and safety goggles walked out, revved up a power tool, and the DJ blasted Metallica's "Seek and Destroy" to rev up the audience.

Sparks flew, and a minute later the top was off.

Duff pulled out a manila envelope, opened it, and the camera zoomed in on a photo of Mr. Conti, everyone's least favorite gym teacher. The anonymous donor had taken a Magic Marker, added the classic cock and balls graffiti, and scrawled Mr. Cunty on the man's forehead.

Duff invited the artist to stand up and take a bow, but there were no takers. "Well, that concludes the sophisticated portion of our program," he said, and the crowd hooted, thrilled to be transported back to our teenage worldview and our sophomoric sense of humor.

Not everything that emerged from the keg was inspired, but it didn't matter. Duff was a natural-born showman, keeping us laughing as he pulled out Randy Berman's three-sentence book report with a big red F at the top, a Wu-Tang Clan T-shirt, a petrified package of Fruit Stripe gum, a menu from the cafeteria, a hall pass, a faded copy of the school literary magazine, and the biggest laugh of the night, a lock of Joey Morgan's hair, which immediately got him to stand up, rub his bald pate, and yell, "I knew it was worth saving."

It took about half an hour to get to the bottom of the time capsule, and Duff was ready with a big finish. "Back then," he said, "I asked you each for a picture of the *one thing* that got you through your senior year." He paused, and then added, "I personally took a picture of my right hand."

The room roared.

"All the pictures were stored in a separate envelope, which I opened this morning. Here they are."

Waiters wheeled out four large standing bulletin boards and lined them up against one wall.

"Enjoy the show," Duff said and walked off to a standing ovation.

One by one, people stood up and headed for the display—some eagerly, some reluctantly. Lizzie joined Alex and me, and Misty and Carl were right behind us.

Everyone's yearbook photo was pinned to the board, along with the picture of what their teenage self credited as the one thing that got them through their senior year.

There were lots of pictures of *things*, some lighthearted, some touching, all telling—a bong, a Bible, a case of Budweiser, an Alanis Morissette album, a wad of cash, a basketball court, a Chevy pickup truck, a *Penthouse* magazine, a box of condoms, and the leg braces and metal crutches that had been getting Chris Trowbridge through school since the day he started kindergarten. But more than half of the pictures were pictures of family members—moms, dads, grandparents, siblings, dogs, cats, and Aubrey Crandall's horse, Spirit.

The display was organized alphabetically, and when I got to the *M*'s I stood there and smiled at what I had submitted. On one side was my yearbook photo—*Maggie McCormick, Class President. Voted Most Likely to Kill Somebody to Get What She Wants.* On the other side was a picture of me, Lizzie, my father, and my grandfather.

"Sweet," Alex said.

"Great minds think alike," Misty said.

I looked at her. "What do you mean?"

"I did exactly what you did."

I felt my stomach wrench. I couldn't believe after what her father had done, she could say that her family got her through her senior year. But who was I to judge? Maybe the memory of her mother and brother sustained her over that horrible period after their death.

We left *M* and made our way through *N*, *O*, *P*, *Q*, and *R* until we got to *S*. There next to the headshot of the young, beautiful Misty Sinclair was a picture of a happy family gathered around a Christmas tree.

But it wasn't her family. It was mine.

Lizzie poked me. She didn't say a word, but I knew by the intense look in her eyes and the quick head toss in Misty's direction exactly what she was thinking.

We found Cinderella. She's been right here among us the whole time.

CHAPTER 51

Misty? Was it that simple? I thought as I stepped into the shower that Monday morning after reunion weekend. Misty?

Since that bloody night on Crystal Avenue, she had practically become family. Somewhere over the years I dropped the word *practically*.

She was like a sister to me. She adored my kids. They called her Aunt Misty. And if I ever said something as straight-out dumb as, "When I die, will you marry my widowed husband and raise my children?" she might just say yes out of blind loyalty.

But what would I be doing to her? Misty's company had a multimillion-dollar contract designing and decorating the interior of the trauma center. How would it affect her job if I died, and she took up with the head of the hospital?

The reunion weekend had been a perfect distraction, but now it was time to get back to the task at hand. Do I ask Misty to—

I stopped myself midthought. I realized I'd skipped a step—a big one. Before I ask her anything, I should tell her that I'm dying.

"Details, details, details," I mumbled and turned the showerhead to pulsating massage, hoping that the hot water beating down on my head would jar my thinking into its fine-tuned micromanaging mode.

Driving to the office I made my first rock-hard decision. Misty could wait. First tell Alex. I wanted to tell him. I needed to tell him. But it was only Monday morning, and by now he was probably in the middle of juggling half a dozen emergencies, three or four calamities, and a major crisis or two. I couldn't exactly stop by his office and say, "Honey . . . you got a minute? As much as I love costarring in your life, I can't stick around for act two. How do you feel about Misty being my understudy?"

The clamor inside my head went on and on and on and on, my brain racing, my thoughts garbled, my heart aching to sit down with my husband and plan our final journey together. All I had to do was wait till the weekend.

Monday passed. By Tuesday I was scanning my email contacts, sizing up women to see how they stacked up against the current contender. The week dragged, but Friday finally came, and by seven that evening Alex and I were on the Thruway on our way to Mohonk.

The weekend was everything I hoped it would be. We slept late, hiked the trails, spent hours at the spa, ate when and what we wanted, and of course made love. By Saturday night, I had second thoughts. Why ruin a perfect weekend? But I had made a vow not to come home without telling him, even though I knew that as soon as I did, our life as we knew it would be over.

One more night, I thought. I'll tell him Sunday at breakfast.

It reminded me of my mother who withheld the worst news from my father for as long as possible, even to the point of having Nurse Demmick shoot her full of B-12 until there weren't any cover-ups left, and she could no longer keep it a secret.

After dinner, Alex and I strolled down to the dock and found a quiet place to sit where we could watch the sun set over Lake Mohonk.

"You want to tell me what's going on?" he said.

"What do you mean?" I asked, but in the pit of my stomach I knew. No matter how hard I tried to act normal, there's always someone who can see right through the smoke screen. Alex was a gifted diagnostician. He didn't need a lot of clues.

"Something's bothering you," he said. "All last week I got the feeling that your mind was someplace else."

"It was. The reunion."

He shook his head. "That was all on Duff. There was no reason for you to be preoccupied with the reunion. And you weren't much better this week. Is it me? I know I've been spending a lot of time at the hospital."

"No, it's not you," I said. "You're perfect."

He smiled. "Perfect? You talk like that, and I'm going to start worrying about your mental health." He took my hand. "Come on, babe, what's wrong?"

There was no putting it off another day. The time had come.

"How strong are you?" I said.

The words hung in the air, and his face went stone-cold. He knew the story of that last picnic at Magic Pond, and he knew the life-changing news my mother delivered after she said those four words.

"I'm the strongest person you know," he said. "Tell me. Everything."

"Noah Byrne called me into his office after he retested my blood. The lab didn't screw up the first test. Noah just needed to verify the results, so he sent it to an outside facility in St. Louis."

Alex nodded. "Kensington. They're the best in the business. What did they say?"

I opened my purse and handed him the lab report. "I was going to wait till the weekend was over before I told you, but . . ."

He wasn't listening. He was reading. Carefully. Slowly. And just like my sister, he flipped back to the first page and read it again.

"This is dated June eighth," he said. "Today is the twenty-fourth."

"I know. I'm sorry. I couldn't tell you."

"For two weeks?" he said, looking up at the sky in disbelief. "I'm a doctor, for Christ's sake. Did you not think I could handle it?"

"I didn't need a doctor. I needed a husband. I watched what happened to my father when my mother broke the news to him. I wanted to spare you—at least for a while."

"Well, thanks a lot, but right now I'm too angry to process the thoughtfulness of that decision."

"I'm sorry. Can you forgive me?"

"There's nothing to forgive. What's done is done. I don't want to waste time rehashing it. We should focus on fighting this disease, doing whatever we can to reverse these numbers. What does Byrne have you doing since you found out?"

"Nothing."

"*Nothing*? Has he lost his mind?" Alex said, pulling his phone out of his pocket. "I'm getting him on the phone right now."

"Alex, stop!" I put my hand on his. "Doing nothing was my call. Noah was ready to hook me up to a chemo drip on day one. I said no."

He slowly put his phone away. "Why?" he said, reeling from my decision to forgo treatment. "Why would you . . ."

"Alex, there hasn't been a single advancement in this disease since my mother had it, and I'll be damned if I'm going to subject my body, my soul, and my family to the same horrific journey she went through.

"What I have is incurable and will probably kill me in six months. You just reminded me that you're a doctor. You can accept a fatal diagnosis. You do every day. But this time it's your wife, so you're ready to go on a quest for a miracle cure. I don't want that. I want to spend my time doing exactly what I've been doing this weekend. Living my life and enjoying my family."

We'd been sitting on the dock. He stood, helped me up, and held me in his arms.

"I love you," he said. "I'm sorry I yelled at you, but do you know how I feel when I realize that I've been consumed with trivial things like how big the new parking lot should be, while you're doing your best to cope with a terminal illness? Maggie, we have to be in this together. Promise me you won't keep any more secrets from me."

"I promise," I said. "No more secrets."

Except for one. I couldn't tell him I was on a mission to keep him from becoming a victim of predators like Connie Gilchrist. Or that I was pretty sure that Misty was the one.

"Who else knows besides Lizzie?" he asked.

"How do you know I told Lizzie?"

"Maggie, there's no way you could live with this on your own for almost two weeks. Lizzie came back from Ireland a few days after you got the report. You picked her up at JFK, then you spent the night together talking and drinking. Now that I'm finally in the loop, it's not too difficult to figure out what you talked about and why you drank so much. Have you told your father yet?"

"No," I said. "I'm not ready to tell him, or Grandpa, and definitely not Katie and Kevin."

"I agree. They'll find out soon enough," he said. "Have you told anyone else besides your sister?"

Just Johnny Rollo that morning at Corky's Diner. And Van. I told Van.

"Nobody," I said, spinning another lie and burying another secret. "Nobody at all."

CHAPTER 52

Telling Alex was a huge sense of relief. But it only lightened part of the burden. I still hadn't told him everything.

In fact, when I thought about my closest confidants—Lizzie, Johnny, Misty, Alex, and yes, Van—each one of them was privy to some of the most intimate details of my life, but not one of them knew everything.

"You're as sick as your secrets," my mother told me when I was eleven years old and stopped going to confession.

"What is that supposed to mean?" I snipped back at her.

"It means that the things we try to hide from the world are often the very things we are most ashamed of. Shame is a powerful force that can sabotage you and make you feel worthless," she warned me. "But it only gets its power when it festers in the shadows of secrecy. Let it out into the light—and you'll be at peace."

It was an excellent parental homily, but it didn't take. Now, thirty years later, with each subsequent trip to the attic, my dead mother was still harping on the same message. Only now she was ladling on a heaping helping of fear by reminding me that it was imperative to seek forgiveness before I died, or I would face one of three possible outcomes.

If my sins were misdemeanors, God might give me a pass and let me into heaven. Fat chance, I thought and immediately took that one off the table. For minor transgressions He would sentence me to do time in purgatory. But the operative word here was *minor*, and with the shit-load of mortal sins I'd piled up, there was no question in my mind—or my dead mother's—that unless I confessed, I'd be damned to suffer in the eternal fire of hell.

But first I needed to share my trespasses with someone. Someone outside my tight inner circle. Someone who would listen without judgment. And no one fit that description better than Esther Gottleib, an eighty-four-year-old Jewish grandmother.

I first met Esther when I was seventeen. My mother had just died, Van called me from Korea to say he had fathered a baby with someone else, I'd revenge fucked my drug dealer, I was losing sleep at night worrying about being rejected by the college of my choice, and I'd gotten hammered with Misty the night she came home to a dead family and her bed peppered with buckshot.

Esther was the shrink who got me through that confluence of upheavals. Dr. Byrne had referred me back then. "She's in the city," he said. "But she's worth the trip."

My father drove me the first time. After that, I insisted on going on my own. Every other Thursday after school, he would drive me across the bridge to the Metro-North station. I'd catch the train to Grand Central, take the number six subway to Sixty-Eighth Street and Lexington, and then walk a block and a half to the tree-lined circular driveway in front of a thirty-three-story white-brick apartment building. And now, a lifetime later, I was retracing the breadcrumbs of my girlhood.

A few days after my weekend with Alex at Mohonk I dug out Esther's phone number. I hadn't needed her wisdom in a quarter of a century, and I wondered if she were still alive, still practicing, and of course, would she still remember me? The answer was a resounding yes on all three counts.

"Maggie," she sang, making the mere mention of my name sound joyful. "I am so thrilled to hear from you, but of course I'm upset because it can only mean you need my professional services. Big picture—what's bothering you?"

"I'm dying of the same thing that killed my mother."

"Oh no. I am so, so sorry."

"Can I see you?"

"Absolutely. My boyfriend and I are traveling through Europe by train. Right now, you caught me at a café in Bulgaria."

"I thought I called your landline."

"You did, but it forwards to my cell. I may be old, but I've got this techno shit by the balls. I'll be back July third. I'll see you the morning of July fourth. Promise me you'll hang tough till then."

I promised, but she gave me her email address just in case.

July fourth was the anniversary of my mother's death, and riding up in the elevator to Esther's eighteenth-floor apartment my head was flooded with memories.

She was standing in the doorway when I got out of the elevator. "Oh my God, look at you," she said, giving me a fierce hug. "Even more beautiful than I remembered."

"And you look fantastic," I said.

"I'm older, shorter, fatter, and grayer, but I'm still fogging the mirror, so technically I suppose that counts for fantastic. Come in, come in," she said, escorting me to her office.

I sat down in a familiar worn-leather wing chair. "How much time do I have?" I asked. I laughed. "Let me rephrase that. I'm tired of asking doctors how much time I have. I meant how much time do *you* have?"

"I'm semiretired. My next patient isn't till Thursday, so you can talk as long as you want."

"The last time I saw you I was in high school. A lot has happened since then. I'm not sure where to start."

"Maggie, you didn't call to catch me up on all the glorious things that have happened in your life over the past twenty-five years. Something is troubling you. Deeply. And since you're facing a terminal illness, it's something you need to get off your chest sooner rather than later. Start there."

That was Esther. Skip the bullshit and cut to the chase.

I took a deep breath. It was time to let go of the one shameful secret that had been haunting me. Time, as my mother said, to let it out into the light so I could find peace.

I just had to say four words. Not my mother's four words, but my own. Words I had never uttered once to a single other soul.

"I'm having an affair," I said.

CHAPTER 53

Esther didn't blink. "Okay," she said. "*Now* you can tell me about your life. What's been going on since high school?"

For the next hour I talked, while Esther did what she did best—interrupt. She cut me off with comments and observations, and occasionally she cut me off right at the knees.

"What in God's name were you thinking?" she exploded when I told her how I had risked disbarment to get Johnny Rollo's drug possession charged reduced from a felony to a misdemeanor.

"And then I called you," I said, when I got to the end of my monologue. "I accept that I'm dying, but I'm trying to clean up my life before I go."

"Clean up *your* life? Or control Alex's life from the grave?" she said. "Why are you so hell-bent on finding him another wife?"

"Because I don't want what happened to me and Lizzie to happen to my kids."

"And you don't trust Alex to do what's best for Katie and Kevin?"

"He'll mean well, but he'll be a basket case, which makes him easy pickings for the wrong woman. I saw it happen to my father."

"You mean with Connie Gilchrist?" she said.

"How the hell did you pull that name out of your hat after all these years?" I said.

"I'm terrible with phone numbers, but I'm like Rain Man with names."

"To answer your question, yes," I said. "The world is crawling with Connies. You remember her name, but do you remember that she didn't just stumble on my father? She was a career criminal who targeted him."

"Your father and Alex are not the same person."

"They're men. Men fall for the kind of lies women like Connie feed them."

"Ironic coming from someone who's lying to her husband."

"Jesus, Esther, whose side are you on, anyway?"

"I'm on the side of facing who you are honestly. I want you to leave this earth with as clear a conscience as you can."

"So, you're saying I should definitely tell Alex about the affair."

"I definitely did *not* say that. Whether or not you tell Alex is your decision, not mine. Who have you told so far?"

"Nobody," I said. "Not even Lizzie."

She smiled. "Not even me."

"What does *that* mean?"

"It means that when I asked you what was your most troubling problem, you admitted having an affair, but you've been spilling your guts for over an hour, and you never once mentioned the man's name."

"What difference does it make what his *name* is?"

"If you told me his name was Joe Blow, it wouldn't make any difference, because the name would mean nothing to me. So, I'm wondering if you didn't tell me his name because it's one I already know."

I sat back in my chair and folded my arms across my chest. "Go on," I said.

"I don't have to go on. Your body language is screaming that you're hiding something. Do you think I'm going to judge you if it's someone from your past? You schlepped a lot of baggage up in that elevator, Maggie. I'd like to help you leave some of it behind, but I can't do that if you clam up on me."

I unfolded my arms and told her his name. She recognized it immediately.

"Van was your first," she said. "But then he broke your heart. When did it rekindle?"

"I don't know that the flame ever went out. It's been a rocky, confusing relationship. And it's not just about the sex. I have great sex with Alex. It's just that . . . I . . . I love him. I love both of them."

"Does Van love you?"

"Yes," I said without a second's hesitation. "And the fact that he can't show his love for me in public will only make it worse for him when I die."

"Don't project," she said. "A lot of people are going to grieve. Nobody is going to suspect you were having an affair just because he's in mourning."

I sat quietly for about thirty seconds. Finally, I blurted out what had been burning in my mind for days. "I think Misty should take my place," I said. "She's my best friend, and my kids love her."

"From what you've told me she sounds like she's come a long way since high school. I can understand why you'd choose her. Are you going to ask her?"

"No. I thought about it, but I can't just come right out and say, 'Marry my husband.' She might run for the hills. I know I would. So, I decided to ask her to do what my mother asked me to do when she was dying."

"And what's that?"

"Keep an eye on my family. Protect Alex and my children from the vultures who are ready to swoop in and hijack their lives. Be there for them. Misty will be working with Alex. She'll see him every day. All I want is for her to be my eyes, my ears, and my foot if she has to kick some gold-digging bitch to the curb. After that I'm willing to let nature take its course. If they're lucky, maybe one day they'll be as happy as Beth and my father. That's my decision, and I'm at peace with it," I said. "What do you think?"

"I think it's an elegant solution—mature, intelligent, and grounded in reality," she said. "Brava."

It was the last thing I expected her to say, and I was floored. "Wow," I finally spluttered.

"I also think you've been deeply affected by the story of Alex being left in that basket at the fire station, and for you, with your nonstop, overactive rescue gene, he will always be that abandoned baby," she said. "You absolutely don't want to leave him, but if you must, you at least want to do the right thing by him—just like his mother did. I'm proud of you, Maggie. Very proud."

"Thanks. I guess it's never too late," I said, a big grin on my face.

"For what?" Esther said.

"After all these years I'm finally starting to show signs of mental health."

CHAPTER 54

Surprisingly, I wasn't afraid of dying. But I was supremely pissed off about the inevitable finality of it all. A hundred times a day, no matter where I was, no matter what I was doing, no matter who I was with, I found myself thinking, *How can these people go on without me?*

Maybe even more difficult than coming to grips with the death concept itself was agonizing over when to share the news with everyone else. Misty, of course, was at the top of the list, but once I'd decided she should be the one to wear the crown if I could not serve out my entire term as Mrs. Alex Dunn, I felt no pressure to give her the bad news/good news.

Then there was my father, Beth, my grandfather, my children, my friends, everyone I worked with, and that was just the inner circle. It had never dawned on me how many people might actually care. But it added up.

Some nights I would lie in bed wide-awake, Alex sweetly slumbering at my side, and instead of counting sheep, I'd make a mental list of *People I Really Should Tell One of These Days*. Even though I never came up with the same number twice, I'd always get past a hundred before I drifted off.

And yet I told none of them.

It eased my conscience to keep them in my thoughts, but I wasn't ready to spring it on them. I did, however, have some fun rehearsing for the moment.

Hey, guess what? I've got this terminal disease, and I've only got a few months to live. I know, I know, it really sucks. Anyway, I just wanted to say a quick goodbye forever and give you a heads-up, because I really, really, really want you to come to the wake and the funeral. Well, hell, I can't tell you exactly when. All I know is it's coming up so fast, I stopped buying green bananas. LOL.

And then I'd do a mental rim shot and laugh—to myself, of course. There was no sense sharing this batshit-crazy thinking with anyone else.

I realized that the longer I kept my illness under wraps the less time I would have for farewells. But there was an upside to keeping it all on the down-low. It kept the early birds from circling my husband.

Life, so to speak, went on. I worked, I spent as much time as I could with my family, I went to the city once a week to see my shrink, and like my mother before me, I started writing long letters to my two children.

In mid-July, a groundbreaking ceremony was held, and construction on the new trauma center began. As mayor of Heartstone I requested that Magic Pond not be dredged until after Labor Day. First, so that the people of my fair city could enjoy it over the summer, and second so that I could soak up its healing powers in my remaining days. The head of the hospital graciously obliged. It was an unofficial meeting, and since we were both naked at the time, there were no witnesses.

The days raced by, and we rolled into August. Alex's forty-fifth birthday was on the eleventh, a Friday. That morning the four of us climbed aboard our boat, regrettably christened the *Dunn Deal*, and set sail for Block Island.

Alex was euphoric. The kids—not so much, but they put on a good game face. Not because they cared about their father's birthday, but because I had secretly promised them that if they went along without bitching and moaning, we'd buy them each a car on their sixteenth birthday. I, of course, was thrilled to be going anywhere, and I figured four and a half months down the road, when they turned sixteen, the car thing would be Alex's problem, not mine.

I continued to ruminate over when to go public with my medical prognosis. One thing I knew for sure: I had to wait till after Labor Day. I loved the symbolism of telling people at a time when the engineers were draining the life out of Magic Pond, and it gave me an eerie sense of optimism knowing that when the dredging was done, Eleanor Majek's gift to Heartstone would have a new life and bring its restorative powers to believers for generations to come.

Monday, August 14, was a beautiful summer day, and I still felt well enough to tackle the task of running my city. I was driving to the office when Misty called.

"I need to talk," she said.

"What's going on?"

"Not on the phone. In person."

"Sure," I said. "Are you free for dinner tonight?"

"I'm free now," she said. "Can you meet me at Corky's for coffee? Please."

Ten minutes later I walked into the diner. Misty was sitting in a booth at the rear. "Thanks for coming," she said.

"You sounded upset. What's wrong?"

"Ever since we were kids, we've trusted each other like sisters. There are no secrets between us," she said. "Until now."

No secrets. Until now. She'd found out, and I held my breath, dreading what she'd say next.

"Remember Hunter Wilding?" she said. She didn't wait for an answer. "The hedge fund guy. Wilding Capital. I completely redid their offices when they moved to the Freedom Tower last year."

"Of course I remember."

"I've been dating him for the past year. I desperately wanted to tell you, but he was in the middle of an ugly divorce, and if his wife knew that he was having an affair while they were still legally married, she'd have taken him for a couple of hundred million more than she got. As much as I wanted to share it with you, I had to keep it private."

I breathed a silent sigh of relief. She was having an affair and keeping it hidden from her best friend. I completely understood.

"I'm sorry," she said. "I don't feel good about keeping secrets from you."

"Don't worry about it. I'm just curious—why are you telling me now?"

"Because his divorce finally came through, and now I can open up. You're the first person I had to tell about Hunter."

"Wow. What is he like?"

"Kind, gentle, funny, thoughtful, super nice."

And super rich. "How serious is it?" I asked.

"Very. That's the other thing I wanted you to be the first to know."

Her left hand had been on her lap, and she put it on the Formica tabletop.

"Jesus," I said, staring at the diamond ring on her finger. "That rock is as big as a Steinway."

"I know. It's obscene, but that's the way Hunter is. Generous to the max."

"So, you're . . . you're getting married."

"Yes. Next year this time," she said. "And I want you to be my maid of honor."

PART THREE
ALL GOOD THINGS
MUST COME TO AN END

CHAPTER 55

The next day I took the train to New York City to see Esther.

"I am so sorry," she said when I told her about my coffee date with Misty. "But she's still your best friend. There's no reason you can't ask her to look after your family when you're gone."

"I know, but it's not the same thing. My plan was for the caretaking to spark something bigger, but now that she's going to marry a zillionaire, I doubt if she'll jump at the chance to take over all my middle-class cash and prizes," I said. "So, it looks like I'm back to square one."

Esther gave me one of her signature Jewish grandmother shrugs. "Fine. If that's where you want to be."

"Oh God, Esther, I don't have the patience for that cryptic shit. What do you mean if that's where I want to be?"

"Square one for you means you're going back to looking for the perfect woman to replace you."

"And what's wrong with that?"

"There are other options."

"Like what?"

"Like stop tilting at windmills. Don't spend the rest of your days in search of the impossible dream. Give up the quest for what you don't have and enjoy the things that you do."

"I have never in my life admitted defeat. Why should I start now?"

"Because winning takes time, and that's the one luxury you don't have. You are an exceptional woman, Maggie, and you have had an exceptional life. An outstanding student, a successful lawyer, a wonderful marriage, a happy family, the mayor of your town, for God's sake—you've packed more into forty-three years than most people could accomplish in a dozen lifetimes.

"You will not depart this earth defeated. You'll be remembered as a winner, a leader, a champion. As for not being able to orchestrate what happens to your husband and children after you're no longer running the show, I have news for you. Nobody can. The world has a mind of its own. Alex and the kids will have a strong support team when you're gone—your father, your sister, your friends. The thing they need from you most is what you can give them now while you're still alive. To hell with square one. Better yet, redefine it. Go home, and be the best damn wife, mother, daughter, sister, friend, and mayor you can be. And by the way— if your mother were here, I bet she'd back me up every step of the way."

I sat in that ancient leather wing chair, my fists clenched, my heart stampeding in my chest, my breathing shallow, my eyes locked on hers. And then the clarity came.

"Good advice," I said.

She gave me a dubious look.

"No, I mean it," I said. "You're right. I gave it my best shot, and it didn't work out. All those not-so-subtle Don Quixote references made me realize that I've become the knight-errant of Heartstone, New York. Quixote was certifiably nuts. I'm just a control freak who got a little crazy when she knew she was losing control. But my quest is over. I'm done. I mean it. Thanks."

"You promise?"

"I swear on my life," I said, a shit-eating grin on my face.

She stood up, spread her arms, and I melted into her, sobbing. Not out of sadness, but out of relief. It was over. I was no longer CEO of my life, my family, or my world. Alex and the kids would go on, just like my father, Lizzie, and I had done years ago.

Esther and I talked for another two hours, mostly about how and when to tell Kevin and Katie. They were twins, but they were polar opposites, and Esther gave me her insight on how to deal with each of them, and what to expect once they found out they were losing their mother.

"And Maggie," she said when we were done. "They're going to need a good shrink."

I smiled. "You know any?" I said.

She got up, and we hugged. We both knew it might be our last, but neither of us said a word.

It had been a long session, and even though it was only 2:00 p.m., I was exhausted when I left her building.

It was a typically hot August afternoon in the city, and I found a Starbucks, bought an iced coffee, and flagged a cab down on Second Avenue.

I had just slid into the back seat and was about to close the door when it hit. A wave of nausea swept over me, the world started spinning, and the coffee cup tumbled out of my hand and splattered to the hot roadbed.

"Are you all right, lady?" the driver asked me.

"I may not be," I said.

"Hospital is right around the corner, about three blocks. New York Presbyterian. You want me to take you there? No charge."

"Yes," I mumbled. "Hospice . . . bad blood . . . no charge . . . take me."

I slumped to the back seat, consciousness slipping away. I heard the cab door shut, and then we were moving.

The driver was talking, but none of it registered. And then there were more voices, hands lifting me up, gently setting me down. I felt the strap go across my chest, and then I was rolling, first gazing up at the blue sky, then squinting at high ceilings with bright white lights, and I could hear a woman asking me my name, and I tried to say Maggie, but I don't know if she heard me.

I don't even know if I was able to say it.

CHAPTER 56

When I came to, I was in bed in a hospital gown.

Wrong hospital, I thought. I should be in Alex's hospital, not this one. I should tell him where I am.

"Nurse," I yelled out, not bothering to look for a call button.

"Can I help you?" a voice crackled back through the intercom.

"Can I have my phone please, and can I get out of here? I'm feeling better."

"I'll page your doctor," she said.

My doctor? Just what I needed—another damn doctor.

"What I really need is my phone," I said.

No response. The faceless helpful voice was apparently done helping.

I closed my eyes. When I opened them again, there was a man standing next to my bed. Dark hair, dark eyes, white coat, clipboard.

"Mrs. Dunn," he said. "I'm Dr. Brubaker."

He was in his late forties, too old to be a resident. At least my doctor was a real doctor.

"I feel better. Can I go?"

"Can we talk first?"

"There's not much to talk about," I said. "It's hot as hell in the city. I must have passed out."

"It's a lot more than the heat, Mrs. Dunn. I have your blood work here."

"Well, then I guess my little secret is out. Can I go home now?"

"I'd prefer you didn't." Brubaker looked at the chart on his clipboard. "I have to tell you, I've never seen numbers like these before. If they get any worse, you will be dead within a few weeks."

"I know that. I mean I didn't know about the few weeks, but I know about the dying part."

"You *know?*" he said, as if he'd checked my IQ and found that number more horrifying than my blood count. "And are you doing anything about it?"

I shook my head.

"Who's your doctor? I'd like to talk to him or her if I could."

"Don't call my doctor. He'll only agree with you. He wasn't happy about the fact that I turned down the opportunity to look for a medical miracle in a haystack, but it wasn't his decision. It was mine. Just let me see the blood test results. I'm tougher than I look."

He sat down on the bed so I could look at the chart.

It was a blur of codes, medical terms, acronyms, and numbers, and in my condition, I couldn't make sense of it. For the next ten minutes Brubaker patiently took me through it line by line, number by number.

When he was done, I began to cry.

He put his arm around me, and we talked in fits and starts until I finally pulled it together.

"I guess I lied," I said. "I'm not tougher than I look."

"You're doing fine," he said.

"You just told me I'll be dead in a few weeks. Make up your damn mind."

We both laughed. Graveyard humor.

"Can I go home now?" I said.

"I don't suppose I can convince you to stay the night so I can evaluate you in the morning," he said.

"That depends," I said. "Does the hospital have an extensive wine cellar and a world-class sommelier?"

He laughed again. "I'm guessing that's a no to staying the night."

"Dr. Brubaker, I appreciate everything you've done, but I really want to go home."

"Where do you live?"

"Heartstone. I took the train in."

"Well, I'm definitely not letting you take the train back. Is there someone you can call to pick you up?"

"Yes."

"In that case," he said, reaching into his coat pocket and pulling out my cell phone, "make the call."

I went to my favorites list and hit the speed dial.

"Hey," I said through the tears. "I need you."

"Was that your husband?" Brubaker said when I hung up.

"Yes. He's on his way. It'll probably be about two hours with traffic."

"Why don't you stay here and get some rest while you're waiting."

"I will, but can I ask you a few questions before you go?"

"Under one condition," Brubaker said. "I get to ask you a few questions in return."

"Fair enough," I said.

I picked his brain for about ten minutes, and then it was his turn. His questions to me were intelligent and insightful, and I answered every one of them with a lie.

When he left, I crawled into my hospital bed and waited for my ride home. But it wouldn't be my husband.

I had called Johnny. He was the only one I trusted to help me make sense of whatever life I had left.

CHAPTER 57

The ride from New York Presbyterian to Heartstone was the most sobering and unforgettable journey I ever took in my life, and I don't think I could have handled it with anyone else but Johnny Rollo.

How far the two of us had come since the day that Van called me from Korea, and I went running to Johnny's seedy apartment, where I shotgunned coma-inducing marijuana and had the most uncomplicated sex of my life.

Twenty-six years later I loved the man beyond words, and I trusted him beyond measure. He was the only person with whom I could share the devastating news I'd just heard from Dr. Brubaker. Once again, my need to sweep the ugly parts of my life under the rug kept me from telling even my closest confidants—including my husband.

But that afternoon, in a Dunkin' Donuts parking lot in the West Bronx, I told Johnny everything—every transgression, every secret, every fear. For over an hour Johnny helped me work out a plan for moving forward.

By the time we were done, I was sapped. The emotions of the day and the sugar high from the donuts left me exhausted. I curled up in the back seat and slept till we got to the Heartstone train station parking lot.

Johnny waited while I got into my car, then he followed me home, and kept me in his sight until the garage door shut behind me.

Alex was in the family room. "You look exhausted," he said, getting up and giving me a hug.

"If that's your subtle man-trick way of asking me if I'm too frazzled to fornicate, the answer is, sorry, sweetheart, but I'm toast."

"I wasn't even thinking about that, but I'm happy to hear that you at least entertained the possibilities. Why don't you turn in?"

"Not yet." I plopped down in a corner of the sofa. "I've got a couple of things on my mind that I need to talk to you about."

"The doctor is in," he said, giving me his best bedside-manner smile.

"Have you thought about life after I'm gone?"

The smile faded, and his face grew grim. "For God's sake, Maggie, what kind of question is that? Of course I have. Hell, ever since that night at Mohonk, I've been obsessing over it. The kids will need therapy. What will their lives be like to grow up without their mother? Parenting is difficult enough with two parents. What happens when there's only one? And am I good enough to be that one, especially when I'm trying to deal with my own grief?"

"When my mother died," I said, "my father was so busy taking care of everybody else that he stopped taking care of himself, and . . . well, you know what happened."

"How could I not know? You told me all about it on our first date. The story of how Finn got suckered in by a con artist is McCormick family folklore. The good news is, I'm not as nice a guy as your father, and I'm certainly not nearly as trusting as he is. Can I promise that the same thing won't happen to me? No. But between raising a pair of teenagers and running a hospital, I doubt if I'll have any time to think about a girlfriend, much less do anything about it."

"I'm sorry. I didn't mean for it to sound like the jealous wife who doesn't want her husband to have a life after she's gone. You're a hot ticket, Alex Dillon Dunn. You'll have to beat women off with a stick. But I can't sleep nights worrying about Kevin and Katie, and I guess I needed to hear you say what you just said."

"Did you have any doubt?"

"All women have doubts. You were on the rebound when I met you. I figure if *I* could seduce you . . ." I said, licking my lips seductively.

"True, but the rules of the game have changed. I've got two kids. No woman is going to come between me and them."

"Thanks. I'll sleep easier."

"You said you had a couple of things on your mind. What else?"

"I came to a decision today at my session with Esther. I can't keep this hidden forever. I'm going to go public with my prognosis on September eleventh."

"September eleventh," he repeated slowly. "You picked quite an auspicious day."

"I know. That's part of my logic. I figure that 9/11 is already a painful day for a lot of people, so why do it on the tenth or the twelfth and give them another bummer anniversary to remember? Plus, it's a Monday, which gives me one last glorious weekend with the kids before I get to break the news to them."

"The way your brain works never ceases to amaze me," he said.

"But you'll support my decision?"

"A thousand percent. Until the day you finally tell people, this family will just go on living our lives like normal."

And for the next seven days we did. In addition to his normal responsibilities, Alex was happily immersed in overseeing the construction of the new trauma center. I split my time between running the city and getting my kids ready to go back to school. On the weekend I did my best to plan something that my teenage son and daughter would tolerate doing with their parents, and for the most part, life was peaceful, relaxing, joyful, and above all, normal.

Until it wasn't.

It was August 22 when the world suddenly, brutally turned upside down, and life as I knew it ceased to exist.

CHAPTER 58

It was a Tuesday morning, and I was making my own tea, when I got a text alert. I checked my phone. It was from my son.

> Where's Dad?

Kevin was my early bird, usually up at dawn. Katie was just the opposite. It was a daily challenge to pry her out of bed on school mornings, but this was summer vacation, so most likely she'd sleep till noon.

I texted back.

> I refuse to text someone who
> is only 50 feet away.

Kevin, who may be the family's next lawyer, came back with a rebuttal.

> And yet you just texted me. Makes no sense.
> Try again. Where's Dad?

> Kitchen. Come down.

He came bounding down the stairs.

"Good morning," I said.

He looked around. "I thought you said Dad was in the kitchen."

"You misunderstood. It's one of the shortcomings of typing instead of talking. What I was trying to tell you was that the person who knows where to find your father is in the kitchen, and she's a big fan of verbal communication."

"Ohhh," he said, smacking his forehead. "No problem." He looked down at his phone and read what he had just texted. "Where's Dad?"

He smiled, and I melted. He was a complex kid. The complete package on the outside, but a snake pit of insecurities below the surface. Katie would charge through life the way I did. But Kevin was going to need a lot of help. Of all the people I would leave behind, I ached the most for abandoning my son.

"Your father is swamped at work. He didn't make it home last night, so my best guess is he crashed on the couch in his office."

"I texted him ten minutes ago. No answer."

"It's seven forty-five. He may be at the construction site. Watching them build this trauma center is his favorite part of the job. I think he's becoming addicted to men in boots."

He gave me another gorgeous smile.

"Tell me what you need," I said. "There's always the remote possibility that I can help."

"Zach and his father are going skeet shooting on Saturday. They want to know if Dad and I can come."

"You see that? I *can* help. I'll ask him when I call him."

"Go ahead, Mom," he said, not moving. "I'll wait while you help."

I called Alex's cell. No answer. I left a voicemail.

"When he calls you back, tell him to text me," Kevin said, grinning like he'd just proven his point.

I showered, dressed, and tried Alex again at eight fifteen. Still no answer. At eight forty-five, just as I was leaving for work, his assistant Regina called me.

"Maggie, is Alex there?"

"No. I thought he spent the night at the hospital."

"If he did, he didn't sleep in his office," Regina said. "I tried his cell, but no answer. Then I paged him. Nothing. I finally went out to the parking lot. His car is not in his space, so I thought maybe he's still at home with the ringer turned off."

"He hasn't been home all night."

"Maybe he went out to breakfast somewhere," she said. "He had an eight o'clock meeting scheduled in his office with Harold Scott and Joe Stuart, but he didn't show up, and he didn't text either of them to say he'd be late."

"That doesn't sound like Alex," I said. "Now I'm worried."

"I didn't mean to upset you. He's been so busy he could be looking at the wrong day on his calendar, and—"

"How long have you known him, Regina? Alex doesn't get his days confused, and he doesn't blow off meetings with his two top guys."

"Well, now *I'm* worried," Regina said. "What should I do?"

"I have no idea. Let me think about it and call you back."

I hung up. Normally, when someone goes missing you call the hospital, but that's the one place I knew he wasn't. I called Chief Vanderbergen.

"Chief, this is Maggie Dunn. I'm sure this is nothing, but my husband didn't come home last night, and his office doesn't know where he is, and I'm a little nervous—no, I'm a lot nervous. I know it's only been about twelve hours since I heard from him, but it's not like him, and I need your help."

"Give me his cell phone number," the chief said. "I'll call you right back."

Seven minutes later my phone rang.

"Madam Mayor, we pinged Dr. Dunn's phone, and we're picking up a signal from somewhere in the middle of the Hudson River."

"Chief, that doesn't make any sense."

"Well, maybe he just decided to take an early morning sail."

"Then why the hell doesn't he answer his fucking phone?" I screamed.

CHAPTER 59

"Try to stay calm," the chief said. "I'm heading out to the location where they picked up the cell signal."

"Where? I'll meet you."

"Absolutely not. I don't want you driving. I'll pick you up. Where are you?"

"Home."

"Five minutes," he said. "One more thing—where do you dock the boat, and what's the make and model of the car Dr. Dunn drives?"

I told him, hung up, and immediately called my sister. "Alex is missing," I said, my voice shrill, my panic on point.

"What do you mean *missing*?" she said, and I vomited out a semi-coherent, condensed version of the emergency, all my fears coming to the forefront.

"I'm sure there's an explanation," she said. "Pull yourself together. I'll be right over."

"No. The chief is on the way. Stay where you are. We'll pick you up."

"I'll be in front of the hospital. Are the kids okay?"

"They're fine. I'm not telling them anything. As far as they know, Alex and I are at work, and as long as I leave money on the table for food, they won't even miss us."

"Does Dad know?"

"God, no. If I tell him, he'll round up every biker in the county and organize a full-scale manhunt. Right now, nobody knows except you, me, Regina, and the chief."

I was wrong. I had grossly underestimated the resources of Chief Horace Vanderbergen Jr. By the time he got to my house, he had alerted police agencies across the state, and within minutes, a cadre of cops on land, air, and sea had been mobilized to find the missing husband of the mayor of Heartstone, New York.

We picked up Lizzie, and we were driving along Station Hill Road when the state police radioed that they had located the boat.

"What about Alex?" I said.

"Madam Mayor, they're still preparing to board," the chief said. "I promise you that finding Dr. Dunn is their top priority."

Ten minutes later, he took the squad car off-road and navigated along a winding bike path, the woods lush with trees on one side, a vast panoramic view of the Hudson on the other. Lizzie and I were in the back seat, hip to hip, shoulder to shoulder, my hands wrapped in hers, the squawk of the radio assailing us nonstop.

"Up ahead," the chief said, spotting a lone boat anchored in a secluded sun-drenched cove, one of many sheltered inlets along the riverbank. "State Police Marine Patrol boat."

He stopped the car, and we got out as a state trooper strode toward us.

"Madam Mayor, I'm Sergeant Dennis Collins. We found your husband's boat," he said, pointing to the *Dunn Deal* about a hundred yards offshore.

"Is my husband all right?"

"He's not on board, ma'am."

"What do you mean he's not on board? How did the boat get there?"

"I can't say, ma'am. We searched the vessel. We found a wallet with Dr. Dunn's ID on the captain's chair, along with his hospital badge hanging from the throttle."

"He's a creature of habit. That's where he always puts it."

"We also found a key fob to a Lexus and a cell phone, but we're waiting for Crime Scene before we touch it. Would you mind calling your husband's mobile number?"

I took out my cell, but my hands were trembling so violently that I hit the wrong name on my favorites list. "Shit, shit, shit," I bellowed. "I dialed Dad." I hung up.

"I'll do it," Lizzie said. She took out her phone and carefully tapped Alex's speed dial.

Seconds later the sergeant's radio came alive. "Subject's cell is ringing," the voice said. "Caller ID says Lizzie."

The sergeant gestured for Lizzie to hang up. "Mrs. Dunn," he said, "was your husband in the habit of taking the boat out for early-morning sails?"

"No. It was mostly a weekend thing. He was too busy during the week."

"When did you speak to him last?"

"He called me around seven last night and said he was slammed at work. When he wasn't at home this morning, I assumed he'd slept there. But his assistant said he didn't."

"Do you know what he wore to work yesterday?"

"What he wore?" I closed my eyes and pictured kissing Alex goodbye a day ago. "He had on a blue suit, white shirt . . . I think the tie was also blue with thin green stripes, and black leather shoes—Cole Haan."

"Madam Mayor, this is not always easy, but I have to ask. Was your husband depressed, or under any severe emotional strain or stress recently?"

"Emotional strain? He runs a major hospital. It's practically in his job description, for God's sake. Who isn't under stress these days?"

"I understand, but I'm talking about an unusual amount of mental duress."

"Sergeant, I'm a former prosecutor, so I know exactly what you're talking about. I'm quite familiar with the horrible places you have to go when you conduct your investigations, but let me stop you right now. My husband is not like that. He would never consider hurting himself because he knows how much it would hurt his family. He loves us. He's not going to suddenly choose to leave us."

"I completely understand, and please be assured that we are treating this as a search and rescue. The governor herself has authorized another two dozen troopers to join the investigation, and we have offers of help from agencies up and down the state. We are determined to find him."

"Thank you, Sergeant Collins."

"But I do have to ask you one more question," he said.

"Anything," I said.

"Can you think of any reason why at some time between last night and early this morning, instead of going home, your husband would go to the boat, pull away from the dock, leave his wallet and other identification neatly arranged in plain view, and then disappear completely dressed in a suit, tie, and good leather shoes?"

My lips began to quiver, and the tears welled up. I had no answers. And then I heard the helicopter approaching.

"Oh God," I said, grabbing my sister and wrapping my arms around her. "Please let them find him. Please, please, please. My kids can't lose two parents."

CHAPTER 60

TWO WEEKS BEFORE THE FUNERAL

Alex was dead.

The police didn't say it in so many words, but they didn't have to.

The search and rescue effort was massive. For three days and two nights police boats crisscrossed the Hudson, aircraft scoured the coastline, and divers searched the murky waters.

The governor kept her word. The state police were out in force. They were joined by local cops, the County Sheriff, an NYPD harbor launch, even the Coast Guard.

All to no avail.

On Friday evening Sergeant Collins broke the news to me.

"Madam Mayor, I'm confident that if your husband was out there in need of assistance, we would have found him by now," he said in perfect textbook cop-speak.

"So, you're saying he drowned," I said. "He's dead."

"Officially he is still missing, but realistically, he couldn't possibly have survived in the water these past sixty hours," Collins said. "We are transitioning from search and rescue to a recovery operation."

"My family needs closure," I said. "How long do you think it will be before the recovery team finds his body?"

"It's difficult to predict. The current moves fast, and the river doesn't always give up its victims right away. It could be days, weeks, even months."

He didn't have to add "or never."

"One more thing, ma'am. I'd like to send a unit to your house at your earliest convenience." He paused, and his eyes apologized for what he was about to say. "We'll need some of Dr. Dunn's personal items for DNA testing."

It was standard procedure for missing persons. I knew it well from my years at the DA's office. Strictly business. Until you're on the receiving end.

The finality of it was soul crushing. I could barely speak. I managed to choke out a few words. "Tomorrow morning."

"I'm deeply sorry for your loss," he said.

"Thank you, Sergeant Collins."

He turned, and I watched him walk away. He had told me over the course of our time together that he was married with three young children. I imagined that a few hours from now he'd be pulling into his driveway, his wife would call out, "Daddy's home," and as soon as he walked through the front door his kids would pounce on him and wrestle him to the ground.

It was just a fleeting notion. Maybe that's not the way things were at the Collins home. But it's the way they had been at ours.

Within hours all the resources that had been mounted to find Alex packed up, and by the weekend the only sign of police presence was a single harbor unit searching the shoreline in all the logical places where a body might float ashore.

But it wasn't over. I still had to deal with the press. They were relentless. I'm just a small-town mayor, and Alex was the head of a hospital most people never heard of, but despite our relative obscurity, his disappearance was big news. Not just in the New York area but around the country and across social media.

Early on, a forensics team had gone over every inch of the boat. They found no indication that anyone had attempted to hijack it, no signs of a struggle, and no evidence that a crime had been committed. Alex's car, which was found parked in the Heartstone Marina, was equally pristine. That left two possibilities, and the media jumped at the chance to let their audience ponder the options.

The *New York Post* was the cruelest of them all. When the search and rescue mission was finally called off, the headline in Saturday's paper read:

DUNN GONE. ACCIDENT OR SUICIDE?

My father had no question which one it was. As far as he was concerned, Alex took the coward's way out. Finn McCormick was a throwback to the days when men were men, and they did what they had to do to feed, clothe, shelter, and protect their families. He had no idea that Alex was living with a wife who'd been given months to live. But even if he had, he'd have decided that would give a real man even more of a reason to stick around.

Lizzie, who lived in a world of medical realities, was much more pragmatic. She dealt with Alex's death the same way she dealt with my diagnosis. We're born. We die. Life goes on.

Katie, like her aunt, accepted her father's death, but Kevin held out hope. Like a child who envisions his divorced parents magically reuniting on Christmas morning, he clung to the dream that somehow his father had miraculously been rescued by a passing boat, was suffering from temporary amnesia, but would one day remember who he was and come walking through the front door ready to pick up where he left off and go skeet shooting with his son.

It was Kevin's way of coping, and I did nothing to quash his fantasy. But after years of working in the criminal justice system I knew with absolute certainty that in today's world it is impossible for someone to completely disappear.

The police ran an ongoing check of Alex's financials, and his picture was distributed to multiple agencies. But from the moment of his disappearance no money was touched, no credit line was tapped, no surveillance cameras picked up his image. Even if the social media theorists were right, and he had faked his own death, I knew that he couldn't totally escape detection. No one can. We all leave electronic footprints. But Alex left none. He was gone.

No matter how hard Kevin refused to accept it, I knew for certain that Daddy wasn't coming home.

CHAPTER 61

The day after I told Alex that I had been diagnosed with a terminal disease we began to research how teenagers react to the death of a parent, and what he could do to help them get through it.

The prospect was daunting. On the plus side, he wouldn't have to explain the concept to them. Adolescents understand that dying is a part of life, and they grasp the finality of it. But how they deal with death is wildly unpredictable.

"How did you cope when your mother died?" he asked me. "Did your schoolwork suffer?"

"Not a bit," I said.

"Did you isolate, get headaches, wet the bed?" he asked, reading from a long list we had compiled from various websites.

"None of the above," I said.

"Oh, wait, here's a good one," he said. "Teenagers may put on a brave front and act out by displaying risk-taking escapist behavior, such as turning to drugs, alcohol, or more sexual contact."

"Bingo," I said. "That's me, the textbook teenage risk-taker."

"Swell," he said. "Let's hope it skips a generation."

"Hey, so far we've amassed thirty-six possible reactions," I said. "Maybe you'll get lucky, and they'll just wet the bed."

We worked hard getting Alex ready for his role as a single parent to two grieving teenagers. And suddenly, it all fell to me.

Luckily, I had help.

Lizzie was great with Katie. They were two pragmatists in a pod. If they formed a club, their motto would be, *I feel terrible. There's nothing I can do. I've got to get on with my life.*

My father, despite his outgoing charm and personal charisma, has never been one to dig down deep and get in touch with his feelings, but with Alex gone, Finn stepped up as the male role model in Kevin's life. They spent hours together, and to his credit Finn did more listening than talking.

And when he did talk, he didn't try to deconstruct or analyze Alex's death. He stuck to simple messages. *Your father did what he did—there is nothing that you did to cause it, and nothing you could have done to prevent it. He loved you, adored you, cherished you. Your family loves you, and we will always be there for you.*

Misty talked to both kids about what it's like to face the suicide of your father when you're a teenager, and she stressed the importance of reaching out and asking for help. Wisely, she left out the part about Arnold Sinclair murdering his wife and son before taking his own life.

I did my best to be a touchstone of normalcy in their lives. Even though they spent time getting support from their friends, we ate many of our meals together, and every evening after dinner we would talk.

Their questions were predictable—why did he do it, why didn't he leave a note, what's going to happen to our family now that he's gone?

Esther gave me a crash course in how to respond. "Be honest, acknowledge their feelings, share your own feelings, and reassure them that they are safe."

"Tell them they're safe," I repeated. "So, I guess this would not be the best time to let them know their mother is dying."

"Good call. It would be even better if you didn't die at all," she said, tossing out a typical throwaway Esther Gottlieb ad lib. "And hugs. Physical contact is important. Even if they try to shrug it off—"

I held up my hand. "Would you mind repeating that?" I said.

"I said hug them," she said."

"No, before that."

"I said, 'It would be even better if you didn't die at all.'"

"That's good advice, Esther."

"'Don't die' is brilliant advice, but it's not exactly something I can write a scrip for."

"What about 'Don't die so fast'? Could you write a scrip for that?"

"You lost me," she said.

"When Dr. Byrne gave me the bad news back in June, he tried to convince me to go for chemo, or stem cell, or sign up for a clinical trial, but I said no. All that would do is buy me some time, and having watched my mother I knew it was shit time, and I didn't want to go through what she went through. I've been so locked into my decision that I forgot I had other options."

Esther leaned forward in her chair. "You would consider chemo?"

"Not then, but now I would. If it could keep me alive for another six months or a year, I'd suffer the indignities of chemo. Kevin and Katie just had one parent taken from them without warning. I can't '*not die*,' but I think Dr. Byrne can help me postpone the inevitable. That would give the kids a chance to brace themselves and find some stability after losing Alex. What do you think?"

She shook her head. "I think it's a difficult choice, Maggie. But you know the rules—it's one you'll have to make on your own."

CHAPTER 62

It was an easy decision, and on the Friday morning of Labor Day weekend, when most people were gearing up for summer's last hurrah, I was sitting on a table in Noah Byrne's examining room talking about my own last roll of the dice.

"I'm glad you're doing this, Maggie," he said.

"It's a no-brainer," I said. "My kids need me. They're better off with a bald mom than no mom at all."

"We don't have time for lab error, so I've told Rachel to take two samples and FedEx one of them out to Kensington in St. Louis."

"How soon can I start treatment?"

"It's a holiday weekend. I won't have a definite answer until Tuesday morning. Both reports will be in my computer when I get in. Meet me here at seven thirty. We'll go over the numbers, and we'll outline an aggressive plan to give you more time with your family."

"I think I'd like to bring Lizzie."

"Don't think. Bring her. You can't have a bigger champion in your corner." He looked at my chart. "Your vitals are normal. How have you been feeling?"

"I had a little incident a few weeks ago. I was in the city, and I passed out and wound up in an ER. But right now, I'm feeling good enough to brave the crowds and go back-to-school shopping with the kids."

"One condition," he said. "Don't shop till you drop. You need all the strength you can muster to fight this disease."

Later that morning Katie, Kevin, and I made our annual trek to Woodbury Common, a sprawling complex of over two hundred high-end outlet stores in Central Valley.

Alex's death had completely altered our lives, but there was no getting around the fact that my growing teenagers needed clothes, shoes, school supplies, and most of all, an escape from the Heartstone fishbowl where we were bombarded by well-meaning well-wishers who made us relive events we were trying to put behind us.

Three hours later, having found everything on our list plus a few things that weren't, we were desperately in need of sustenance. According to the mall directory, we had twenty-two options, but for the third year in a row, the unanimous choice was the double burger, cheesy fries, frozen custard experience at Shake Shack.

"You know what I hate about this place?" Katie said, chomping down on a burger. "They ruin everything by posting how many calories I'm eating."

"It's the law," I said.

"Grandpa doesn't put calories on his menu."

"He will when McCormick's becomes a chain. All he needs is nineteen more stores."

"Do you think Grandpa would do that?" Kevin asked.

"What? Open a second restaurant? I doubt it," I said.

"Why not? McDonald's started with one store. KFC started with one store. We could sell franchises."

"What do you know about franchising?" Katie said.

"More than you. I was talking to Hunter, and he knows a ton of shit about how to make money."

"Language," I said.

"Sorry, Mom." He squared off with Katie. "For your information, Hunter Wilding, who is marrying Aunt Misty, so he's practically our uncle, has money up the wazoo, and I was talking to him, and he said I could intern at his company next summer."

"Doing what?" Katie said.

"Learning how to get rich," he said. "Currently I have zero money up my wazoo, but *Uncle* Hunter said he'd teach me how to make a bleep-load of it. What are *you* doing next summer?"

"Oh, I don't know," she said, taunting her brother. "I was thinking about writing a book. It's called *The Sad Tale of the Delusional Boy with the Empty Wazoo.*"

I cracked up, and Katie joined in. Kevin, doing his best to keep a straight face, came back with, "Laugh now, peasants, but one day I will be president of the First National Bank of Wazoo."

That opened the floodgates for a round of sibling insults, most of which made no sense, but which were deemed hysterically funny because they all had the word *wazoo* in them.

Our laughter was infectious, and people around us started smiling, probably wishing they knew what was so hilarious, and imagining we were the happiest family around.

And maybe for one brief moment we were. I felt like we'd broken the logjam of unhappiness we'd been trapped in, and I sat there beaming at my two children who had suddenly been hurled into adulthood.

Katie, who was born with the gift of laughter, knew how to use it to help people heal. And Kevin, who never thought twice about money, had this sudden desire to strike it rich, and I wondered if it was his way of shaking off his insecurities and assuming the mantle left behind by his father.

The two of them had a long road ahead of them, I thought. But somehow I knew they'd be fine. My only goal was to share the journey with them for as long as I could.

CHAPTER 63

It was the Tuesday morning after Labor Day, and Lizzie and I were standing outside Dr. Byrne's office waiting for someone to show up and unlock the door.

"Thanks for coming," I said.

"Are you kidding?" Lizzie said. "You have this adorable habit of hiding the details of your life in a box in your attic. How could I say no when you finally invited me to peek inside? I'm flattered."

"Don't be," I said. "I only picked you because you're a doctor. Also, I know you, and even if the prognosis is terrible, you won't say anything that sounds like a Hallmark card."

"In that case, I'm glad I decided to go to medical school instead of pursuing my dream to study the poetry of Elizabeth Barrett Browning."

"Good morning, ladies." It was Dr. Byrne. "Sorry to keep you waiting."

"That's okay," I said. "We were early."

"How was your weekend?" he said, unlocking the door.

"It was good," I said. "I got to spend some quality time with my kids."

"Well, let's take a look at your blood tests and see if we can buy you a lot more quality time. The reports from both labs should be in by now."

We followed him to his office, and he booted up his computer. "Here's the first one," he said, clicking the mouse.

He stared at the screen, scrolled, and finally frowned. "Shit," he muttered.

"That bad?" I said.

"No, no, it's just that our lab here at the hospital seems to be off their game. This is exactly why I went to Kensington for a second look. Give me a minute. I'm sure their report is in here somewhere . . . ah yes. Got it."

He clicked again, scrolled some more, leaned into the screen, and slowly rubbed his chin. He didn't say a thing, but I could sum up the look on his face in one word—dumbfounded.

"Lizzie," he said. "Take a look at this and tell me what you make of it."

Lizzie went behind his desk, took the mouse, and studied the screen. "It looks like a lab error," she said.

"Except . . ." he said, taking the mouse and clicking. "Here's our lab." He clicked again. "And here's Kensington."

"Same numbers," she said. "They couldn't both get it wrong."

"Guys," I said. "Would one of you please tell me what's going on? I'm dying here."

Lizzie threw her arms around me. "No, you're not dying." She kissed me repeatedly on the cheek. "You beat it, girl! Against all odds—you beat it."

I looked at Byrne. "I'm not sure what she's saying."

"She's saying your blood tests came back perfectly normal. You don't have any sign of the disease."

I let go of Lizzie, slumped in my chair, and held my hands to my chest. "Are you sure?"

"Positive," Byrne said. "If it were one lab, I'd retest you immediately. But this also went to Kensington, and their analysis is gospel."

"So I don't need chemo?"

"You don't need anything. According to these numbers, you don't show any indications of HLH."

"I don't understand. How . . . how did this happen? How is it even possible?" I said.

"I have no idea," he said.

I pointed at my chart on his desk. "So how do you document my case for the insurance company?" I asked, half laughing, half crying. "*Patient is fine now. Don't ask me how.*"

"Oh, heck, physicians are a much more devious lot than that. When someone with a life-threatening disease is suddenly cured with no medical explanation, we have a catchall phrase we use. Two words: spontaneous remission."

"Well, guess what?" I said. "I've got two better words: fucking miracle."

"Sorry, sweetie," Lizzie said. "The medical community doesn't believe in miracles. If doctors wrote the Bible, it would say, 'The Red Sea unexpectedly parted due to unusual atmospheric conditions.' Or, 'After three days Jesus's condition was reevaluated, and he was upgraded from dead to resurrected.'"

The three of us were laughing now. Giddy. Celebratory.

"Noah," I said, my adrenaline soaring, "do you remember when I asked if you ever buy lottery tickets, and you said only when the jackpot is ridiculously big. You know you won't win, but you buy a ticket because it's *possible*."

"Of course I remember."

"Well, I didn't do chemo, or transfusions, or any of the things my mother did to beat this disease, but yet I'm cured. It's like I won the lottery without even buying a ticket. In my book, that's a bona fide miracle," I said. "I only have one question: How long can it last?"

"There are no rules, no guidelines. It could be days, months, or the next fifty years."

I looked at Lizzie. "Is he telling me the truth?"

"A thousand percent," she said, her eyes watery. "And don't ask me any more questions, or I'm going to start sounding like a Hallmark card."

"Congratulations, Maggie," Dr. Byrne said. "I want to check your blood on a monthly basis for a while, but the good news is you've got your life back. I just can't tell you how."

He didn't have to tell me. I knew exactly how.

There were only three people on the planet who knew the truth behind my medical miracle.

And now one of them was dead.

CHAPTER 64

ONE MONTH BEFORE THE FUNERAL

It all began to unfold that afternoon in New York Presbyterian Hospital when Dr. Brubaker took me through my blood test results.

He'd barely gotten started when I cut him off. "That's the wrong chart," I said.

He looked at me carefully. "What do you mean?"

"That's not my blood."

He pointed to my name and date of birth at the top of the page.

"I understand," I said. "But I know what my test results should look like. These are wrong."

I'm sure I sounded arrogant as hell. Most docs would bristle. Brubaker laughed. "Okay, what's wrong with them?"

"For starters, my white blood cell count is way too high."

"It's not high at all," he said. "Six thousand is perfectly normal."

"I know. But I'm not normal. My last white blood cell count was twenty-two hundred. I've been diagnosed with HLH."

"HLH," he repeated.

"It's a rare blood disease," I said. "I realize that emergency room docs don't see many—"

"I'm not an ER doctor, Maggie. I'm a hematologist, and I've seen my share of patients with hemophagocytic lymphohistiocytosis."

"You're a . . . I don't understand. Since when does a hematologist cover the ER?"

"You told the intake doctor you had HLH. They had me check your test results, and I'm here to tell you that you absolutely do not."

"How is that possible? My doctor confirmed the diagnosis. He—"

"Is he a hematologist?"

"No, but my mother died from HLH, and he's been monitoring me and my sister for years."

"The only thing I can suggest is that he found what he was looking for, even though it wasn't there. I've been a board-certified hematologist for seventeen years, and I can assure you that you don't have HLH."

I snapped. "Make up your mind! Two minutes ago, you told me I was dying."

"You are."

"From what!?"

"Vitamin D poisoning."

I tried to speak, but I couldn't.

"A normal healthy level of vitamin D for a woman your age is forty nanograms per milliliter. Over a hundred is toxic. Look at yours," he said, pointing at a number on my chart. "Four hundred and thirty-nine. That's lethal, Maggie. I don't know who prescribed such massive doses to you, but if it's the same doctor who misdiagnosed you with HLH, I'm going to call—"

"No, no, no, please. It wasn't my doctor. It was me."

"You?" he said.

I could almost feel the change in his demeanor as his antennae went up.

"Maggie, are you thinking of hurting yourself?"

"Oh, no, no—nothing like that. I have a wonderful husband, two amazing kids, and a dream job. I've never been happier."

"Your blood work suggests otherwise. I'd like you to have a talk with one of our social workers."

Brubaker was now in full-throttle suicide-prevention mode. If he thought I was a danger to myself, he had a legal obligation to keep me there. I needed an out.

"It was that damn TikTok video," I said.

He had no idea what I was talking about. Neither did I, but at least I was one step ahead of him. "What TikTok video?" he said.

"Oh God," I said, scrambling for time as I crafted the lie. "This is so embarrassing."

"Whatever it is," he said, "I've heard worse."

"I watched this video on TikTok that said heavy doses of vitamin D will revitalize your skin."

"That's insane," he said.

"They said it's supposed to be like Botox working from the inside."

"It's more like arsenic working from the inside. Do you know how close you came to killing yourself?"

"I should have done more research, but, you know . . . vanity."

"Just promise me you will cut them out entirely. Your levels should be back to normal in eight to twelve weeks."

"I promise," I said.

We talked for another few minutes. I thanked him and spent the next two hours in bed trying to process the facts.

Like most people I get my vitamin D from sunshine or food sources. I had never taken a single supplement. And yet there were lethal levels of vitamin D in my body.

By the time Johnny arrived there was only one logical conclusion. Someone wanted me dead, and somehow they were slowly poisoning me.

CHAPTER 65

A few hours later Johnny arrived at the hospital to drive me back to Heartstone. I waited until we were on the Major Deegan Expressway before I gave him the good news.

"According to the experts at New York Presbyterian, I don't have a deadly blood disease."

He let out a hoot and banged on the steering wheel with the heels of his hands. "What made you go into remission?"

"I'm not in remission. I never had it."

"You never . . . how the hell could you be misdiagnosed? What kind of doctor would tell you you're dying without being a million percent positive? Are you gonna sue, or at least get Alex to fire this guy?"

"Don't ask any more questions," I said. "Just listen. There's a lot to take in."

I unraveled the details as best as I could, telling him what I knew and what I suspected, but I was still putting the puzzle pieces together, and my thinking was riddled with holes.

"I need alcohol," I said when I was done.

"I've been clean and sober for fifteen years," he said. "You'll have to settle for coffee."

He got off the highway at the next exit and pulled into a Dunkin' Donuts less than half a mile away. He went inside, and five minutes later returned to the car with two large coffees, which he put in the cup holders, and a box of donuts, which he set between us.

"Nothing makes sense," he said, turning in his seat and squaring off with me. "Why fake a terminal illness?"

"That's the one thing that makes total sense," I said. "At my age, if I were to suddenly drop dead out of the blue, what would happen?"

"An autopsy, an inquiry, a police investigation."

"Exactly. But what if it's been established for months that I'm slowly dying of hemophagocytic lymphohistiocytosis?"

"They would know what killed you, but they would still do an autopsy, and they'd find out you were poisoned."

"No, they wouldn't," I said. "All the law requires is that a doctor sign off that my death is from a preexisting condition."

"Are you sure?"

"Johnny, I was a prosecutor. Give me a little credit for knowing the law. My mother didn't want to be sliced and diced in the morgue, and I've already informed Dr. Byrne that neither do I."

"Holy shit," he said. "It sounds like the perfect crime."

I smiled. "And yet I'm still here."

"So is whoever wants to kill you, Maggie. We have to figure out who that is. How many people live in Heartstone?"

"Fifteen thousand six hundred and forty-two, as of the last census."

"And you're the mayor. All you have to do is figure out which one of them wants you dead."

Great minds think alike, I thought. Johnny was starting in the same spot I zeroed in on a few hours earlier. Somewhere out there was a disgruntled citizen hell-bent on killing the mayor.

"It would have to be someone with serious technical chops," he said. "Someone who could hack into the hospital computer and change your blood numbers."

"Impossible," I said. "Alex has spent millions of dollars to keep that from ever happening. But on the outside chance that someone could do it without getting caught, they still would have to change the data at the point of origin. Kensington Labs in St. Louis has the actual results in their system. If I died, and my insurance company asked them for a paper copy, the truth would come out in a hurry."

"Clearly you've had more time to think about this than I have. So how does somebody create a lab report that says you're dying?"

"My theory is that my blood was never tested. Someone swapped it out for blood that was already infected."

"Someone," he repeated. "Who?"

"Follow the trail," I said. "Rachel, the phlebotomist, draws my blood. The next person to handle it is the lab technician who is going to analyze it. Unless . . ."

"Unless someone with access to the lab replaces it with the blood of someone who actually has HLH," Johnny said.

"Exactly. Then the report comes back to Dr. Byrne, and he tells me I'm dying. When I die, he honors my request and signs the death certificate without an autopsy just like he did for my mother. And whoever is poisoning me gets away with murder."

Johnny's criminal mind wasted no time coming up with a plan. "Starting now, you don't eat or drink anything unless you've made it yourself."

"Good idea," I said and dropped a half-eaten glazed donut back into the box like it was a live grenade.

"Very funny," he said, picking up the donut and shoving it into his mouth. "Okay, I ate it. We've just eliminated one suspect."

"Don't worry," I said. "You were never a suspect. You don't fit the criteria."

"Are you telling me that you worked out a profile of the perp already?"

"Years of practice working at the DA's office," I said. "I've narrowed it down to this. First it has to be someone who can easily swap out my blood samples. It could be Rachel, or Dr. Byrne, or pretty much anyone at the hospital who has access to the lab.

"But since HLH is a rare condition, it would also have to be someone who can get their hands on infected blood. That would take more medical know-how than most people have. Especially Rachel.

"And finally, it would have to be someone who spends enough time with me that they can easily get the vitamin D into my tuna salad sandwich, my yogurt, my glass of wine after a tough day at the office."

Johnny held up his hands. "I know where you're going with this, Maggie. But don't say it. There's only one supersmart medical professional who has total access to every corner of the hospital and most of the meals that you eat. Alex."

"Feel free to tell me I'm wrong. But someone is trying to murder me, and right now Alex is the only one that fits the profile."

"You're wrong," he said. "Alex is crazy about you. You're his rock, Maggie. You're the best part of his life, and he'll be the first to say so. He'd be lost without you. Why in God's name would he want to kill you?"

It was a question I knew he'd ask, and lying there in that hospital bed, I decided that when he did, I would have to tell him the truth.

"Think about it, Johnny. Why do most men murder their wives? I'll give you a hint. It's the oldest motive in the book."

"Jesus H. Christ, Maggie. You're cheating on him."

I nodded.

"And he caught you."

"He hasn't confronted me, but I can't think of any other reason why he'd try to poison me."

"And I thought I knew everything about you."

"You know everything else. I'm sorry I didn't tell you, but I was selfish, and stupid, and I wasn't exactly proud of myself."

"And I'm guessing you also didn't tell me because I know the guy," Johnny said.

Another nod.

"You want to tell me now?" he said.

I stared down at the box of donuts, unable to look at him.

Johnny put two fingers under my chin and gently tilted my head till our eyes met.

"Someone is trying to murder you, Maggie, and it sounds like they came pretty close to pulling it off this afternoon. The more I know, the more I can help. But if you're too ashamed to tell me who you're sleeping with, then you just might wind up dying of embarrassment."

"He's a cop," I said. "In Heartstone."

"Which one?" he said.

"The chief," I said, my voice cracking. "Chief Vanderbergen."

Johnny slowly let his fingers slip away from my chin.

"Vanderbergen?" he snapped. "You mean Van, the golden boy who popped your cherry, swore he'd love you forever, joined the Marines, knocked up some girl in Korea, then dumped your ass over the phone?"

I didn't answer. It was the old Johnny talking, the one who would get abusive when he was angry. It had been years since I'd seen that side of him, but my confession had unleashed the demons. I let him vent.

"Are you out of your mind, Maggie? You've got the world by the balls, and you're throwing away your marriage, your career, and your reputation for your asshole high school boyfriend."

He gripped the steering wheel and unleashed a volley of f-bombs. Then he snapped around and looked at me, his eyes filled with heartbreak and disgust.

"I don't know how you could even work with that scumbag cop, much less fuck him. No wonder your husband wants to kill you."

CHAPTER 66

I'm not a crier, but within the space of a few hours I felt like I'd lost my husband and my closest confidant. And for the second time in a few hours, I started bawling. First with Dr. Brubaker, and now in a Dunkin' Donuts parking lot in the West Bronx.

I wanted to be back in Esther's cozy Upper East Side apartment, crying my eyes out, confessing everything, telling her how stupid I'd been, and waiting for her tough love and sharp tongue to give me hope that I could stop self-sabotaging and start fresh.

Johnny let me cry, scream, curse, and pound my hands on the dashboard. A few minutes into my breakdown he opened the car door, said, "Don't go anywhere," and went back into the donut store.

A few minutes after that he came back with a fistful of Dunkin' Donuts napkins. "Here," he said, handing them to me. "You're getting snot all over my goddam leather seats. Marisol will kill us both if she sees this."

I couldn't help myself. The sobs turned into peals of laughter. Johnny could do that to me.

"That's better," he said. "It's a lot easier for me to apologize to you when you're laughing than when you're batshit hysterical. Sorry about the husband-killing-you crack."

"Well, I'm sorry for keeping my affair with Van a secret, but I knew you'd hate me for it."

"Maggie, you know me. I could never hate you for being a sex-crazed hellcat. It's part of your charm. But now that I know, I'm curious. How the hell did you wind up going back to this guy after all he did to you?"

"Remember Maryana Fipps?" I said.

Johnny's expression sobered. Of course he would remember. He was the father of three daughters. Maryana was a sixth grader who was found strangled in a county park five years ago.

"Chief Vanderbergen—Van—was a detective with the sheriff's department back then," I said. "He questioned the parks worker who discovered the body—a young kid in his twenties. He kept contradicting himself and backpedaling on his story. Ten minutes into the interview Van tripped him up, and the kid fell apart. He broke down in tears and confessed right there at the crime scene.

"But there were no witnesses to the confession. No camera to record his statement. Van arrested him, the parkie lawyered up, and then he totally denied any connection to the crime. I was the prosecutor. That confession was all we had, and the defense tried to get it thrown out at the hearing.

"Van's testimony saved the day, and the judge ruled in our favor. Then came the trial. The defense attorney kept Van on the stand for two days, tearing his testimony apart, trying to convince the jury that he was a publicity-hungry cop out to advance his career by railroading a poor, unsuspecting, churchgoing father of three into taking the fall for a crime that he didn't commit. Then he pounded it home claiming that the sheriff's department never even bothered to investigate any further after they went public with the bogus confession."

"But the kid was found guilty," Johnny said.

"Thanks to Van. He was a war hero, a decorated cop, a father, and a churchgoer himself, and he was so . . . so . . . *noble* up there on the stand that the jury believed him. It was the most draining trial I've ever been part of, and knowing that we got justice for Maryana was an emotional high. The two of us cried with the family when it was over. That night, we all went out to celebrate, and . . ."

Johnny held up a hand. "Say no more. You had a few drinks, and one thing led to another. I'm familiar with the syndrome, Maggie. But that was five years ago. And the two of you are still at it?"

"Yes. I love him. He loves me. It goes deep, Johnny. He was nineteen when he got Sujin pregnant. He made a decision to marry her, because his nineteen-year-old brain told him that was the right thing to do. But it didn't last, and they were divorced before we—"

Johnny cut me off. "So the answer to my question is, 'Yes, Johnny. We're still at it.'"

"But we've been very careful," I said. "Very discreet. At least I thought we had."

"Discreet? The Maryana Fipps murder was a page-one case. Both your careers took off after the two of you landed that conviction. You're not some midlevel assistant DA banging some anonymous beat cop. You're the mayor, and Van is your goddam chief of police."

"I know, but we've kept it professional. He calls me Madam Mayor. I call him Chief Vanderbergen. It's completely under wraps. I kept it from you, from Misty, even from Lizzie. The only person who knows is my shrink."

"And whoever Van told," Johnny said.

"He wouldn't. You might not like him, but give him credit for being smart. If it ever came out, it would ruin both of our lives."

"Then how do you think Alex caught on?"

"I have no idea, but I'm sure that the minute he found out I was cheating, he was done with me forever."

"Done with you forever is one thing, but poisoning you seems a little over the top. Has the man ever heard of divorce? It's a lot less messy than murder."

"You're right. Anyone in his rational mind would take the legal way out of the marriage. But Alex can't think rationally when he feels like someone he loves is abandoning him. On the outside he seems to be the stable grown-up head of a hospital, but inside he's regressed to a little boy, asking himself the same question that has haunted him since childhood: *Why wasn't I loved enough?*"

"Okay, let's save the analysis for your shrink and cut to the chase. I'm still not buying your theory, but let's just say your husband is planning to kill you. You dodged a bullet this time, but that doesn't mean he's going to quit. This plan of his—a phony disease, a slow-acting poison, no autopsy—that's downright diabolical. You're living with a madman, and he's fixated on killing you. What the hell are we going to do about it?"

"I have no idea, Johnny!" I screamed. "That's what I was going to ask you."

"Hey, calm down," he said. "Breathe. We've got this."

"I'm sorry. I don't know what to do. I've tried to play it out in my head, but nothing makes sense. I can't confront him. He'll deny it. I can't call the police. Hi, this is Mayor Dunn. Would you mind swinging by the house and arresting my husband for attempted murder?"

"I get that. No cops. No divorce lawyers. That ship has sailed. But we better do something soon."

"Like what?"

"First things first. Don't eat or drink anything that anyone gives you. And I mean anyone—Alex, your assistant at work, your sister, your kids—"

"My sister? My kids? Are you out of your mind?"

"Sorry. I think like a criminal. Trust no one. Don't eat or drink anything you remotely think could have been tampered with. If you suspect anything, whatever you do, don't eat it. Just get a sample, and I'll take it to a lab."

"Oh God, Johnny. I can't believe this. I thought I was dying, and then I found out I'm not. And now I have to go home and wonder if my husband is going to murder me in my sleep."

"He won't. He's too smart. He still thinks that the vitamin D is going to do the job, so he's still going to keep on feeding it to you. You're okay for now, but if you don't die in a few weeks, he's going to know you figured it out, and he's going to come up with a whole new way of—"

He stopped cold. "Shit," he said.

"What?" I said. "What now?"

"I just had an ugly thought. It's the way my mind works."

"Tell me."

"I hate even thinking this," he said, "but are you sure that Alex is planning to kill just *you*?"

"Oh my God. What are you saying?"

"Maggie, you just told me the father of your children went off the deep end. He's homicidal, and he can't think rationally. Two words come to mind when I hear that. Arnold Sinclair."

As soon as he said it, I yanked open the car door, leaned over, and puked my guts out on the Dunkin' Donuts parking lot.

CHAPTER 67

The mere mention of Misty's father was the reality punch in the face that I needed. I had to stop thinking of Alex as the young medical student I fell in love with, the devoted father of my children, my soulmate for life.

One day Arnold Sinclair had also been that perfect package—the smiling would-you-like-starch-in-those-shirts neighborhood shopkeeper, surprising his daughter with a new car on her sixteenth birthday, and taking his family to Aspen for Christmas. And the next day he was a feral beast planning their execution.

Johnny drove me to the Heartstone train station parking lot. "Here's your assignment," he said, pulling his car alongside mine. "There are four things I want you to do. One—tell Alex you're almost ready to go public with your blood disease, and pick a day about three weeks out."

"What will that do?"

"He's smart enough to know that your death will go smoother for him if he holds off until after everyone is braced for it," he said. "If you set a reasonable date, he'll wait. That will buy us time to figure out what the hell we're doing next."

"Did anyone ever tell you that you think like a criminal?"

"Thanks, Counselor. I was breastfed by a woman who did three years at the Albion Correctional Facility. It definitely gave me the edge over the kids whose moms didn't rob, steal, or stab their boyfriends."

"She sounds enchanting."

"Here's the second thing I want you to do," he said. "We need rock-solid proof that Alex is the person pumping you full of vitamin D—something I can take to a lab. Can you do that?"

"It sounds easy enough."

"Great. Three—find out how Alex knows about you and the chief."

"Not so easy, but I'll do my best. What's the fourth one?"

"Don't die."

"That's what my shrink said, but did you have to put it *last* on your list?"

He grinned. "You're right. I probably should have said 'not necessarily in that order.'"

I drove home, and I entered the house a completely different person than when I'd left that morning. I was now sleeping with the enemy.

That night I told Alex I'd decided to tell friends, coworkers, and family about my illness on September 11. He didn't ask me to hurry up and do it sooner, so I figured he'd be willing to keep me around for a few more weeks.

The next morning Alex came bounding into the bedroom grinning like a kid who spent the night locked in a candy store. He had my morning cup of chai tea in his hand. "Room service," he chirped.

The tea! The fucking tea! How could I have been so stupid? It was all I could do to keep from screaming. But one of the things I learned from working with undercover cops when I was at the DA's office is how to preempt suspicion. If I had balked at the tea—even for a moment—Alex would go on alert.

I grabbed it like a junkie copping an eight ball. "Oh God, you're a life-saver," I said. I took a big gulp, hoping it wouldn't be the one that killed me.

Satisfied that I was enjoying his early morning offering, he kissed me goodbye and left for work.

As soon as he was out the door, I ran to the bathroom, stuck my finger down my throat, and vomited. I kept at it, dry heaving until my throat was sore. Then I transferred a few ounces of tea to one of the sterile containers Alex keeps in his home office.

Johnny took it to a lab in Jersey.

"It's gonna be three days, kid," he said. "Hang in there. Just keep acting like everything is normal. You know . . . happy, upbeat, loving your life."

"Normal," I repeated. "Happy, upbeat, loving my life—just like Arnold Sinclair's wife did for the three days before he murdered her and her son in their beds."

CHAPTER 68

I still had one more critical assignment on my middle-aged Nancy Drew things-to-do list.

"Find proof that Alex knows about you and the chief," Johnny had said.

"What am I looking for?" I asked.

"Beats me. It could be anything—pictures, videos, maybe he hired a private detective and there's a written report. But it also could be electronic, like a flash drive, a memory stick, or one of those cloud thingies. I don't know shit about computers, but you've got teenagers. Maybe they can explain it to you."

"Oh, sure," I said. "I'll just say, 'Hey, kids, Daddy is planning to kill Mommy. Can you help me hack into his cloud thingy so I can find out what he has on me?'"

"You love doing this, don't you?" Johnny said.

"Doing what?"

"You dig yourself a hole, and then you act like I'm the one with the shovel. All I know is that Alex is not going to murder his wife on a rumor. He needs hard evidence. Your job is to find it."

I spent the next three days looking. I searched the house from top to bottom and back again. When Alex was asleep, I went to the garage and combed through every inch of his car.

Everything on his computer was password protected. But he accumulated so many passwords that he had to install a password manager to keep track of them all. Then he realized that if anything happened to him, I wouldn't be able to access our bank accounts, credit cards, insurance policies, or any of the countless websites that secure our electronic secrets.

So he gave me his master password. "It's not an invitation to go through my stuff," he said to me, half joking, half serious. "It's just in case of emergency."

I'd never been interested in his *stuff*, but I decided that saving my life qualified as an emergency, and I scoured his home computer.

I found nothing. Three days later I met Johnny at the diner, prepared to give him the bad news. But as soon as I sat down, he handed me a lab report.

"You were right," he said. "The tea was laced with vitamin D—about twenty times the daily dose. Not enough to kill you, but over time, the toxicity builds up, and it leads to heart irregularities, kidney failure, and death."

I could barely breathe. A wave of powerful emotions flooded over me now that my worst fears were fact. Shock. Anger. Despair. Heartbreak. Betrayal. But most of all, I ached for the life Alex and I could have had.

"I'm sorry," Johnny said. "But at least now we know for sure."

I shrugged. It wasn't exactly the kind of consolation prize to get excited about.

"What did you find?" he asked.

"Nothing. I searched everywhere. The basement, the attic, his office, his car, his computer—I can't find a thing."

"Then keep looking."

"To what end?" I asked. "You just proved that he's trying to poison me. Who cares how he found out about me and Van?"

"Because in the words of the famous Chinese philosopher, 'The more you know, the better off you are.'"

"If you mean Aristotle, I believe the actual quote is 'The more you know, the more you know you don't know.' And he was Greek, not Chinese."

"Fine. He was Greek. But the restaurant where I read the quote was Chinese. Look, *Mayor* Dunn, if somebody tipped off Alex, that's one more person who knows about your affair. That person has the power to destroy your life. We have to find out who they are."

"You're right," I said. "But I've looked everywhere. There's nothing."

"There's got to be something, Maggie. Go through the house again. And if you can't find anything there, search his office at the hospital."

"He'd never put anything that private in his office," I said. "Too many prying eyes."

"What about the boat?"

The boat. Alex's private little retreat. Another simple but brilliant Johnny Rollo idea. As soon as he said it, I knew he was right. Johnny, of course, could read me in an instant.

"You look like Wile E. Coyote when the light bulb goes on over his head," he said.

"That's a laugh riot, Johnny," I said. "When I'm dead, see if you can work it into the eulogy."

I drove to the marina. When Alex bought the boat and gave me the first official tour, he proudly pointed out its cool secret storage compartments. One, which I made him promise he would never show the kids, was the gun case under the bunk beds.

I got down on my hands and knees and ran my fingers along the bottom of the teak bed frame until I finally found a seam. I pried at it gingerly, somehow irrationally reluctant to sacrifice a fingernail to save my own life. No luck. And then I remembered what Alex had said.

"Even if the kids do spot it, they might try to jimmy it, but it won't budge. You can't pull it open. You've got to tap the hidden switch."

Tap, don't pull. But tap where? I wish I'd paid more attention when he showed me. Starting at the head of the bed, I began hitting the wooden base with the heel of my hand. I worked my way along, and the more I tapped, the more I felt like an idiot. And then I heard the electronic click, and like the bottom of a cash register, a drawer slid out from the base of the bed.

The gun was still in there. I took it as a minor victory. At least Alex wasn't ready to shoot me in my sleep. There was also a wad of cash and an envelope marked private and confidential that had been mailed to Alex at the hospital.

I took out the contents. First a photo of Alex, me, and the kids that had run on the front page of the *Heartstone Gazette* the day after I was elected mayor. Someone had written the words "Perfect Family" across it in red Sharpie.

Next came a packet of about a dozen pages stapled together. On the cover the sender with the red Sharpie had scrawled "Not So Perfect Wife."

I turned the page. My stomach wrenched as I stared at the printed screenshot of me, naked, straddling Van, my back arched, my head tilted up, my mouth wide open as the surveillance camera captured my sexual frenzy in midscream. The date and time were digitally burned into the corner of the image lest Alex wonder where he was at the exact moment I was violating our marriage vows.

I was loath to look at the rest, but I flipped through the pages. More of the same. Different times, different days, different positions. Every one of them grounds for ending our marriage.

CHAPTER 69

"I'm terrified," I said to Johnny.

"I know what you're going through," he said.

"I don't think so," I said, "because if you really understood what I'm going through, you'd know that this is the last place on the planet I'd want to meet you."

"What are you talking about?" he said. "We're at an abandoned rock quarry. There's nobody around for miles. It's as private as private gets."

"Except this particular rock quarry kicks up a lot of ugly memories. The last time I was here was twenty-six years ago. I got drunk with Misty, and by the time we got home, her loving father had murdered her mother and her brother, and if she hadn't snuck out of the house, she'd be dead too."

"Ignore it. That's just your brain putting crazy-ass thoughts in your head."

"Johnny, my life is in danger. It's my brain's job to put thoughts in my head—crazy-ass or otherwise."

"Maggie, I promise, I'm not going to let anything happen to you. What did you find on the boat?"

I looked down at the ground, the same way I'd seen so many defendants do as they struggled to say, "Guilty, Your Honor."

"Pictures," I murmured. "Me and Van."

"So, Alex had a PI tailing you."

"No. Van and I were too careful for that."

"Then where'd the pictures come from?"

"Last year Van's friend Sean Kennedy landed a big job in the UK. He left the country, put his house up for sale, and he asked Van to keep an eye on things till it was sold. As soon as I saw the pictures, I recognized the three vintage Marine recruitment posters that Sean had hanging over the bed. That place was our safe hideaway from December until the broker sold the house in April."

"Let me guess," Johnny said. "The broker was Minna Schultz."

I nodded. "Minna's last hurrah was going to be building that townhouse complex with the spectacular view of Magic Pond. Once the hospital decided to block her view with the new trauma center, she became obsessed with stopping them. She lost in court; she lost her bid for mayor, so she tried blackmail. She told Alex to find a new location for the trauma center, or she'd go public with the pictures of his slut lawyer-politician wife."

"She had him by the balls," Johnny said.

"Right. And she celebrates the win by going home, making herself a couple of peanut butter and jelly sandwiches, washing them down with Chardonnay, and drowning in Magic Pond. Suicide, according to the coroner."

"Coroners are just doctors, Maggie. Some of them are smarter than others."

"And Alex is smarter than all of them," I said. "A few weeks ago, I couldn't have even conceived of the thought, but now, after seeing how he's orchestrated my death, I'm positive. Alex killed Minna Schultz."

"And he got away with it."

"I couldn't sleep last night," I said. "He's not the man I married. He's psychotic. He's Dr. Jekyll and Mr. Hyde. He's known about me and Van for months, but he still plays the loving husband. I can't imagine how much he must hate me, how much he wants to hurt me, and yet we laugh, we make love, we plan for the future, he kisses me playfully every time he brings me my morning mug of poison. But I don't know if he can wait for the tea to do the job. He has all that anger and the rage building up inside him, and I'm afraid that one night he'll snap—take a scalpel and slit our throats. All of us. Me . . . Kevin . . . Katie . . ."

And then the fear consumed me. The steely resolve that had served me well during my time as a prosecutor crumbled. Sobbing, I threw myself into Johnny's arms. I wiped my face on his shirt and went on through the tears. "I would die for my children, Johnny, but please don't let them die for me."

He held me, and I closed my eyes. I inhaled the thick, sultry air, felt the late-afternoon sun play on my skin, as my ears picked up the gentle warble of a distant wood thrush. Slowly my composure returned. But I couldn't let go.

Finally, Johnny put his lips to my ear and whispered four words.

"Do you trust me?"

I stepped back and looked at him. His face was stoic, his eyes determined, his expression grave.

"What kind of question is that?"

"It's the right question. A few weeks ago, you trusted Alex. Knowing what you know now, I would understand if you said you will never trust another soul for the rest of your life."

I tried to speak, but all I could do was pull him back to me and lose myself in the shelter of his arms.

"I love you, Maggie," he said softly in my ear. "You're not only part of my life; you gave me a life—Marisol, my kids, my career, my freedom. I would do anything to reciprocate, to remove the fear, to restore the joy, to give you *your* life back. All I need is the answer to one question.

"Do you trust me?"

CHAPTER 70

I was sitting at the kitchen table, pencil in hand, making notes on the latest draft of the eulogy I would be giving for my husband.

It was bullshit. But it was exactly what my audience wanted to hear.

For them, we were Heartstone royalty. A modern-day fairy tale. Smart. Attractive. Successful. The perfect couple. What they didn't know was that individually we were damaged goods, each in our own way dealing with the pain of abandonment.

Alex had been unwanted and unloved since birth. Growing up he never felt that his newfound parents adopted him for who he was. He was convinced that he was merely a convenient surrogate for two desperate people who were forever grieving the loss of the only son they ever really loved.

And then I came along and gave him what he'd been searching for. I loved him with all my heart. I was all he needed.

But I had my own issues. I, too, had been abandoned. First by my mother, and then in a two-minute phone call from Korea that left me broken and alone. From that day forward my sexual behavior became erratic, rarely based on sound judgment or informed choices. I was a textbook case of the girl looking for love in all the wrong places.

In hindsight, we should never have gotten married. Alex needed stability, security, unwavering devotion, and most of all, fidelity. And I was the teenage tramp who grew up to become the wayward wife.

Most husbands who catch their wives cheating want out. Alex wanted retribution. Divorce wasn't good enough. For Alex the only punishment for adultery was biblical.

But of course, not a word of that would ever be uttered. Instead, I would sing the praises of Alex Dunn—tireless physician, dedicated public servant, loving husband, adoring father.

Like I said, pure bullshit.

"Mom?"

I looked up. My son was standing in the doorway. My heart smiled. Kevin was more man than boy now. I wanted to tell him he looked every bit as handsome as his father, but, of course, I knew better than to spark his insecurities with high praise.

I kicked it down a notch. "Thanks for wearing a tie. Dad would like that."

I stood up and gave him a hug. He smelled of weed, but I didn't comment on that either. So much for sending my sister Lizzie to supervise the kids.

"The circus is in town," he said.

I have yet to master teen speak. "What circus?"

"The one that's following us to Dad's funeral. Cop cars, fire trucks, motorcycles, and a shitload of paparazzi. Why do they have to stalk us like that all the time?"

"I know how you feel, but today is not about *us*, Kevin. This is about Dad. He was a revered member of this community. People are grief-stricken by his loss," I said, parroting some of the hokum that would soon flow trippingly from my tongue to a packed house at St. Cecelia's.

"Mom, I know. But why are we having a *funeral*? There's no body."

"Sweetie, you don't need a body to have a funeral. It's a ceremony to honor the dead."

"Dad's not dead. He's missing."

"Excellent point," I said. "I stand corrected. A funeral is a ceremony to honor the departed."

"But, Mom . . ."

"No buts, Kev. He may not be dead, but you can't tell me he's not departed."

"Fine. You win. Again." An impish grin spread across his face the way it does every time he wants to make me laugh. "You realize, of course, that if I marry a lawyer, I stand a good chance of living out my entire life without ever winning an argument."

He got the laugh. And it was genuine.

"Kevin, you have to remember that we're not the only ones who are losing Dad. He had hundreds of friends, coworkers, and patients he helped over the years. This *funeral* will give them a chance to say goodbye as well."

He looked over at the pile of papers on the table. "Are you still writing the eulogy?"

"Rewriting, editing, tweaking, second-guessing. You know me. I want it to be perfect."

"When did you start writing it?"

"A couple of days ago."

He looked surprised. "Really? Even though it's been two weeks."

It referred to the night the police went from search and rescue to looking for Alex's body.

"Two weeks ago, I was still hoping for a miracle. I decided it would be bad juju to even think about a eulogy. So, I waited another ten days. I finally went to see Father Connelly, and he suggested that a funeral Mass would at least give us a sense of closure. So, I didn't start writing till a few days ago."

"If I tell you something about Katie, will you promise not to yell at her? Otherwise, she'll know I told you, and she'll come up with new ways to torture me."

Kevin and I had a running deal. He loved to rat on his sister, but only if I promised not to give him up.

"My lips are sealed," I said. "What did she do this time?"

"She hacked into Dad's computer and read the eulogy he wrote for you."

I'm a lawyer and a politician. I'm well trained in the art of never letting the other guy know how clueless you are.

"Really?" I said, pulling out my go-to neutral response.

"Did you ever read it?" Kevin asked.

Read it? I had no idea he even wrote it.

"Of course I didn't read it," I said. "Unlike your sister, I respect boundaries." My voice was calm, but inside I was seething.

"I don't get it," Kevin said. "You waited a long time after Dad was . . . after he was departed . . . before you wrote his eulogy. Why would he write one for you while you were still alive?"

Because that was typical Alex. So cocksure of himself that he wrote his acceptance speech before he even shot the movie.

But my son didn't need to hear the bitter truth. He needed something that would reinforce the image of the perfect father, the committed doctor who pledged to "first do no harm."

"You never met my mother," I said, spinning the yarn as I spoke.

"Grandma Kate," he said.

I smiled. "She'd have loved hearing you call her that. She was only forty-one when she died. The disease that took her is very rare, but it's hereditary. Which means Aunt Lizzie and I are at greater risk than most people. Even though your dad dealt with life and death every day, one night he confessed to me that he was afraid that if I died young—emphasis on the *if,* Kevin—he'd be too devastated to gather his thoughts and write a proper eulogy. So I jokingly said, 'Write it now while you still worship the ground I walk on.'"

"Good one," Kevin said, always happy to let me know when my mom humor meets with his approval.

"Anyway, he took me up on it. But I would never think of reading it in advance. I told him I wanted to be surprised at my funeral."

I reached out and gave him a fleeting suitable-for-self-conscious-teenagers hug. "Speaking of funerals, we should get out there and join the circus. Go get Aunt Lizzie and Katie and save me a seat in the limo."

He left, and I gathered up the pages of my eulogy from the table.

The words that had once been true were now hollow.

How do you go from loving a man with all your heart to feeling relieved by his death, I wondered.

How do you decide that your children will be safer, live longer, if their father is gone forever?

How do you think the unthinkable? Do the undoable?

I did what I've been doing all my life. I gathered the facts, weighed all the options until I was down to one, then I braced myself for the consequences.

I didn't kill Alex. But that afternoon at the rock quarry when Johnny said those four words—do you trust me—I could have stopped it from happening.

And I had made a calculated decision not to.

CHAPTER 71

THREE WEEKS BEFORE THE FUNERAL

Johnny never told me the plan. Despite his Chinese fortune-cookie philosophy that the more you know, the better off you are, he decided that the less I knew, the less likely I was to tip off Alex.

So his call came out of the blue that Monday evening after the kids and I had dinner. "Hey, Maggie. It's Johnny. I think I may have left my bandanna in your car," he said.

Johnny had set down a rule back in our high school days. Never call, text, or page him with a message that said I needed help. "Just say you left your bandanna in my car. When I ask what color, you can say green, yellow, or red, and I'll know how fast you need me to get there and bail you out."

We hadn't used that code to communicate for more than twenty-five years, but when he called that night, I didn't hesitate. "Your bandanna? What color was it?"

"Red."

"I'll look for it," I said.

"Thanks. I'm working the night shift."

Red. I jumped in the car and raced toward the hospital.

Alex had called me an hour ago and said he should be wrapping up work "soonish." But that didn't mean he'd come straight home. He never left without stopping at the construction site to check on the progress of the new trauma center. He was like a kid with a multimillion-dollar new toy and hundreds of hard-hatted friends to play with.

My phone rang as soon as I pulled into the hospital parking lot. Johnny had seen me arrive.

"Stay where you are," he said.

Two minutes later he slid into the passenger seat of my car. "Don't ask questions. Just do what I tell you, and hurry—we've got to do this fast."

He handed me a key fob. "I want you to drive Alex's car to the boat. I'll follow in your car. Go! Now! Don't let anyone see you and turn off your cell phone so you can't be tracked."

Alex's Lexus was in his reserved space. I scrambled in, and I drove off unnoticed. Fifteen minutes later, I pulled into the marina with Johnny right behind me. It was dark, and the place was quiet.

"Strip down to your bra and panties and put these on," he said, passing me a pair of latex gloves. "It's 8:21. I'm on a lunch break, and I've got to be back on the platform by nine."

I did as I was told, and he shoved my clothes into a plastic bag.

"Take these," he said, handing me Alex's hospital badge, his cell phone, and his wallet. "Now I'm going to give you a set of instructions. Listen carefully, repeat them, and then follow them to the letter. Can you do that?"

"Yes."

Within minutes, I had set sail, and the *Dunn Deal* was making its way upriver. Mindlessly I put Alex's keys, wallet, phone, and his hospital ID badge exactly where Johnny told me to put them. And then I stopped. Alex was a creature of habit, and nobody knew his quirks better than I did. I picked up his ID from the captain's chair and hung it from the throttle. I waited till we drifted about a hundred yards out, then I dove into the water and swam to shore.

Johnny was waiting for me with towels and my dry clothes. I got dressed, and as he drove us back to the hospital parking lot, he told me what to expect over the course of the next several days.

We got back to the hospital parking lot at 8:52 p.m.

"Go straight home," he said. "And get some sleep. It's over, Maggie. You never again have to worry about Alex hurting you or the kids."

"Johnny, I'm numb. I don't know what to say."

"You were numb the last time we did this shit," he said. "But you still managed to come up with a few choice words. Do you remember what you said?"

"I think it was probably thank you. I owe you one."

"You see that?" he said, a wide smile on his face. "You do remember."

How could I forget? It was November 27, 1997. I got a message to Johnny's pager and told him that I'd left my red bandanna in his car.

"This better be good," he said when he showed up to meet me an hour later. "I'm missing the end of the Jets-Bills game. What's your problem this time, little girl?"

"Connie Gilchrist is dead," I said. "I just killed her."

CHAPTER 72

I remember every detail of that day vividly. It was the Sunday of Thanksgiving weekend, and I was a senior at Heartstone High School. The previous day Johnny and I had broken into Connie's house, and we'd discovered the manila folder with my mother's obituary and the details of our family life that Connie had highlighted when she was looking for her next widower to victimize.

I was determined to stop her, but how does a seventeen-year-old girl go up against a career criminal?

Beth. Beth Webster. Saint Beth. The librarian who cared so deeply about my father's pain that she had sent him a book that he of course never bothered to open. I liked her, trusted her, never once dreaming that she'd one day become my surrogate mother, Grandma Beth to my kids, and one of my closest confidants.

Years later she told me how uncharacteristically reticent I was that day. "After you asked me how to get background information on someone, I knew that it wasn't a school project," she said. "I could see the troubled look on your face. And then you very meekly said, 'Her name is Connie . . . or maybe it's Constance . . . Gilchrist,' and I knew I was about to dive into treacherous waters."

Treacherous waters or not, Beth dove in headfirst. She drilled down into those LexisNexis files and gave me the ammunition I needed. Grand larceny. Three victims. Prison time. Genghis Connie was everything I'd feared she was and worse.

My father and Connie had taken the train to New York, and later that day he called to say they wouldn't be home until the following morning.

That night I had the dream. More like a vision. My mother and I were sitting on a blanket on the grass at Magic Pond. The red Mustang came out of nowhere, barreling toward us. Connie was behind the wheel. My mother stood up, but she was powerless to stop the stranger who had run off with both her car and her husband. Then she turned to me, her eyes pleading, "Don't let that woman take Daddy."

I woke up that Sunday morning determined to confront Connie, to throw her criminal past in her face, to threaten her, to bargain with her if I had to—I was ready to do anything to drive her out of our lives.

No, not anything. I hadn't planned on killing her.

That afternoon I taunted her with everything I'd unearthed about her, every crime she'd committed, every lie she'd told, every trust she'd violated, but she didn't go down easily. She laughed in my face, challenged me, and threatened to have me arrested for breaking and entering.

But I kept at it, exercising my budding litigation skills, my harangues beginning to sound less and less like toothless teenage tirades and more like serious threats of exposure that could result in dire consequences.

And in the end, she buckled under. I'd won. She agreed to leave town. But she couldn't go gently. She lashed out at me by prodding the rawest nerve in my body. She attacked my mother.

"Finn McCormick couldn't possibly have fathered a piece of shit like you," she said. "My best guess—you're the product of some lowlife dirtbag who fucked your worthless tramp of a mother. I hope she rots in hell."

Those were the last words she ever spoke. Tears streaming down my face I lunged at her, hurling her backward against the fireplace. I could hear the crack as her skull met stone. I think she was dead before she sank to the floor.

I knew in an instant that my life was over. College, a career, my entire future gone in a moment of blind rage. Unless . . .

I paged Johnny. He knew what to do. First, we wrapped the body in plastic bags and dragged it to the garage. Then we cleaned up the blood.

"Don't they have some kind of chemical that can tell you if blood was there even if it's wiped up?" I said.

"Luminol," he said. "You spray it, and if there's any trace of blood, it glows blue in the dark. Right now this place looks clean, but I guarantee you it would light up like a Christmas tree."

"Then we'll get caught."

"Only if they spray it, and they won't. Connie is a grifter, a con artist. She's going to steal a bunch of shit from your father, and then she's going to take off. The cops are going to have a warrant out for her arrest. They won't be coming around here spraying the place with Luminol. Any other questions?"

"Just one," I said. "What do we do with the body?"

"You're right!" he said, smacking his forehead like he'd forgotten one small detail. "We can't leave her wrapped up in the garage. Sooner or later, she's going to start to stink up the joint."

"It's not funny, Johnny. If they find her, I'm going to go to jail."

"Don't worry," he said. "You're not going to jail. Next year this time, you'll be in college."

"Are you sure?"

He flashed me a smile. "Trust me," he said. "I got it all worked out in my head."

"Thanks," I said. "I owe you one."

Ten years later, at a crime scene on East Shore Road, while the four-hundred-pound body of a drug dealer named Sammy Womack was being pried out of the wreckage of his Escalade, I broke every ethics code in the book and finally made good on my debt.

CHAPTER 73

Van was waiting for me at the Dragon Heart Restaurant. He was sitting at a booth when I arrived, a notepad in front of him, pen in hand. There was a glass of white wine waiting at my seat.

"Are you planning on taking notes?" I asked, pointing at the pad.

"It's a prop," he said. "I thought it would be better if this looked like a business meeting, instead of what it really is."

"What it *really* is?" I said, toying with him. "And what might that be, Chief Vanderbergen?"

"I have no idea, Mayor Dunn. You're the one who invited me to meet you here. But it did dawn on me that to the best of my recollection it's the first time you and I have had dinner in public together since high school."

"And whose fault is that? To the best of *my* recollection, you're the one who moved to Korea. Jot *that* down in your little notebook, Chief."

He began writing, narrating as he wrote. "Mayor Dunn . . . is busting . . . my balls. I wonder . . . what she . . . really . . . wants." He put the pen down. "Something is on your mind. Go ahead, I'm listening."

I took a hit on my wine and looked around. It was early. The restaurant was relatively empty—mostly older couples and families with kids. I leaned in and lowered my voice. "Remember all those times we were using your friend Sean's house? Minna Schultz had a camera planted in the bedroom."

He didn't blink. "I know."

"What do you mean you know?"

"When Minna went missing, Montgomery and I went to her house to make sure she hadn't died in her sleep. The place was empty, but I snooped around, opened a few drawers, and I found printed screenshots of the two of us."

"Why didn't you tell me?"

"What good would that have done? I'm a cop. First thing on my mind was finding Minna and talking to her—in private. How did you know about the camera?"

I knew he'd ask, and since I couldn't tell him the truth, I was ready with a credible answer. "A few days ago, I was cleaning up some of Alex's things, and I stumbled across the same pictures."

"Those were just the tip of the iceberg," he said. "After they found Minna's body, I got a warrant to search the place and look for a suicide note. I started with her computer and found the screenshots immediately. Ten minutes later I turned up a thumb drive with all the original footage. I spent the next three hours combing the place and destroyed everything I could find, but I knew she'd already sent some of the photos to Alex."

"She was trying to blackmail him into scrapping the plans for the new trauma center," I said.

"That was her plan. But according to the ME, she apparently had a change of heart and decided to kill herself instead."

"You never bought the suicide ruling, did you?"

"Not for a minute. It's not easy to fool the medical examiner, but Alex did it. And it's not easy to fool me, but he knew that even if I figured it out—which I did—I'd never charge him with anything. Those pictures would be Exhibit A at the trial. Your life, his life, and mine would be ruined in one shot."

"How long have you known?"

"I first suspected him when he told that story about Minna screaming she'd get even with the hospital if it were the last thing she did—emphasis on *last thing*. Remember he said she yelled, 'Mark my words. I will haunt you'?"

"Yes."

"After that interview I questioned Harold Scott and Joe Stuart, who were at that same meeting with Minna and Alex. They don't remember her saying it. I knew Alex was just laying pipe to make us think suicide."

"That doesn't prove a thing. It you brought that to the DA, he'd laugh."

"What if I could put Alex's Lexus at Minna's house the night she drowned, and then told you he drove from there to Magic Pond? Would the DA still be laughing?"

"How did you—"

"I've had a GPS tracker on his Lexus for over a year. It wasn't exactly police work. It was strictly personal."

"And unquestionably illegal."

"So is murder," Van said. "It doesn't matter. I never planned on going to the DA, and if you hadn't found those pictures, I never would have told you. I'm sorry, Maggie. I know you thought the world of Alex, but sometimes even the best of us can be guilty of the most unthinkable acts. You of all people should know that."

For a split second my stomach clenched, and then I realized he was talking about everything I had seen as a criminal prosecutor, not of the unthinkable acts I had committed myself.

"Thank you for telling me," I said. "This explains a lot."

"What do you mean?"

"The police still consider Alex a missing person, but I've accepted the fact that he's dead. My question has been why. He was too experienced a sailor for me to believe it was an accident, and I couldn't wrap my head around the suicide theory. But this—this changes everything. I'm sure if Alex did kill Minna, he thought he was doing it for the good of a lot of people. But it must have eaten him up inside, and he finally couldn't live with himself. It helps me understand why he didn't leave a note."

The words came off the top of my head, but they couldn't have been more effective if I'd scripted them.

"I'm sorry for your loss, Maggie. You and the kids. That might sound hollow coming from the guy who was . . ." He stopped and looked around the room. "Anyway, I'm sorry. If there's anything I can do . . ."

"Thank you," I said. "You can start by losing that soulful look on your face. You're not coming off like a police chief at a business meeting with the mayor."

"Gotcha," he said, snapping out of it. He picked up his pen, wrote on his pad with businesslike efficiency, and handed it to me.

I read the brief message and gave him my best mayoral nod of approval.

"What an incredible coincidence, Chief Vanderbergen," I said, borrowing one of Alex's favorite bits. "I love me too."

CHAPTER 74

FOUR DAYS AFTER THE FUNERAL

Monday, September 11, arrived blistering hot and summery, defiantly refusing to offer up even a hint of the fact that autumn was waiting in the wings.

It was, of course, a hallowed day in America, a time for reflection and resolve, prayer and tribute.

Coincidentally it was a significant day in the history of our little town, albeit not nearly as solemn. Magic Pond, the mystical elixir vitae in the heart of Heartstone, was about to be dredged. According to our official records, the last time it had its toxins treated, its sediments suctioned, and its eco balance restored was in 1952. And while some local residents applauded the fact that the water quality would be vastly improved, most of my constituency was curious about how many thousands of dollars in coins had accumulated on the bottom, and what would the town do with the loot.

September 11 was also what Alex called his other birthday. The forty-fifth anniversary of the day he was left in a Dillon's grocery store shopping basket at fire station 6 in Hutchinson, Kansas.

One day. An auspicious trinity of reasons to embrace it.

I arrived at Town Hall at 7:30 a.m. At 8:46 a.m., the exact time that American Airlines Flight 11 hit the North Tower, twenty people from my office, along with about a hundred locals, stood outside in silence as a group of men from the American Legion raised the flag, then lowered it to half-staff.

I spoke to the crowd briefly, then a man wearing a Vietnam Veteran's cap read the names of the seven Heartstone citizens who had been killed in the attack, the final name being his daughter. A bugler played Taps, and the ceremony was over.

I went back to the office and the growing pile of work that had taken a back seat to Alex's disappearance and his subsequent funeral. At 1:15 p.m., my landline rang, and Wanda, my secretary, picked it up.

"It's Chief Vanderbergen," she called out from her desk. "He says it's urgent."

I grabbed the phone. "Chief, what's going on?" I said.

"I tried to reach your father, but he didn't pick up, so I'm calling you."

"Is he all right?"

"Oh, I'm sure he is. It's lunchtime, so he's probably too busy at the restaurant to answer the phone. It's not an emergency, but it's so damn weird that I had to call you."

"You've got my undivided attention."

"On December 2, 1997, your father reported a car stolen. It was a 1996 red Mustang GT convertible that was registered to your mother, Katherine McCormick."

"It was a great car, Chief. But it wound up in the hands of a horrible woman."

"It might just still be in her hands," he said.

"I don't understand."

"A few hours ago I got a call from the engineers over at the hospital construction site. Your mom's car was just dredged up from the bottom of Magic Pond."

"My mom's car? The Mustang? Are you sure?"

"Positive. The VIN checks out. It's been underwater for a long time, so it's covered with silt, but the air hasn't touched it, so it's still in good shape."

"That's crazy . . . but wait—how did it wind up in the pond?"

"That may take a while to figure out, but there are human remains in the driver's seat. Female. I'm betting it's the same woman who stole it. There's a waterlogged purse on the front seat. We're going through it now. How soon can you get here?"

"Fifteen minutes."

I got through to my father, conferenced in my sister, and told them both the news. Finn was out the door of the restaurant and on his Harley before I hung up.

By the time I got there, Magic Pond looked like a war zone. The landscape was dotted with heavy equipment. A dam had been built in the middle of the pond so that water from one end could be temporarily stored on the opposite side while the excavators cleaned away a hundred years of sediment and debris, using a massive pump that sat atop a barge. They were only in the early stages of the operation, but they had already dredged the serenity, the tranquility, and the magic right out of it.

The north end of the pond had been lowered by twenty feet, and two wreckers had towed the muck-encrusted Mustang to the shore.

As I worked my way through the flash mob of onlookers, emergency vehicles, and media trucks, I could make out two men at the center of it all—Van and my father.

My mind flashed back to that night on Crystal Avenue when Misty and I drove home drunk from the midnight rave at the Pits, and we were confronted with the aftermath of Arnold Sinclair's insanity. And just as I did then, I called out to the one person I trusted to help me make sense of a world turned upside down.

"Daaa-aaaad," I yelled, running toward him.

"Maggie," he said, wrapping his arms around me. "This is insane. It's Mom's car. Connie . . . she just drove . . ." He stopped, unable to put a coherent sentence together.

"Is it Connie?" I asked Van.

"We went through the purse," Van said. "The driver's license and credit cards are still legible, and they're all in the name of Constance Gilchrist, but we won't be able to ID the remains until we get it to the lab."

"I don't need the lab to tell me who it is," my father said. "It's her."

There was a commotion in the crowd, and Van yelled out to his officers. "Hey, hey, move those people back. This is a crime scene."

I'd almost forgotten. I'd spent so much of my day anticipating the moment of discovery that I hadn't thought a lot about the investigation that would follow.

But Johnny and I had discussed it at length once we knew the pond would be dredged.

Eventually the medical examiner would conclude that the bones behind the wheel belonged to Connie. He'd see her cracked skull where she'd hit the stone fireplace, but there wouldn't be enough left of her to determine whether that happened before or after the car plunged into the water.

The crime scene team would find Connie's suitcases in the trunk, packed with as many of her clothes as I could jam in, and they'd conclude that she was planning to leave Heartstone permanently. They'd also find my mother's missing jewelry, carefully wrapped in plastic. It would be nice to get them back after all these years. I couldn't wait to show my daughter the pink-sapphire-and-diamond teardrop earrings that one day would be hers.

"Maggie! Dad!"

It was Lizzie. Van gave a wave, and the cops let her through.

"This is insane," she said, using the very words my father had used. And while I can't be positive, I suspect they were the same words I'd said when Johnny and I launched the Mustang into the pond on that frigid November night a quarter of a century ago.

Johnny. I scanned the crowd. He'd be there. Looking curious and blending in with all the other fascinated spectators.

And then I spotted him standing silently behind the barricade. Several hundred yards behind him was another set of bones—the steel skeleton of the new building that would one day become the Dr. Alex Dillon Dunn Trauma Center at Heartstone Medical Center.

Despite what was going on at the pond, the construction site was still a beehive of activity. The cement trucks were lined up, their drums rotating, as one by one they continued their round-the-clock pour, dumping thousands of tons of concrete into the vast cavities that were becoming the impenetrable foundation, walls, and subfloors of the building Alex had fought so hard to see completed.

Johnny saw what I was staring at, and he gave me a subtle smile. I smiled back, remembering the last words he had said to me as I climbed aboard the sailboat, my dead husband's wallet, cell phone, key fob, and ID badge in my gloved hand.

"Don't worry, Maggie. In another few weeks, they'll find Connie," he said, his rubber work boots splattered with cement. "But they'll never find Alex."

ACKNOWLEDGMENTS

Six years ago, Maggie Dunn took up residence in my brain and refused to vacate the premises until I agreed to turn her story into a book.

"I'm a man," I told her. "The limitations of my Y chromosome might make it difficult for me to tell your story."

"I've got two words for you," she said. "*Get help.*"

So, I got help. I reached out to dozens of women—friends, family, fans—and asked what they would do if faced with the same diagnosis as Maggie's.

Not one of them suggested a similar path to hers.

That was good news. I wanted Maggie to be flawed, even unlikeable at times. What I didn't want was a character who was just like everybody else.

The first draft took me a year. I sent it out to my beta readers, and it was clear to them that I didn't go through my teenage years as a girl. Back to Square One.

Over the course of six years, I wrote seven drafts. If you enjoyed this book, a lot of the credit goes to Gina Heiserman; Elizabeth A. White; Lauren Sholder; Marie Sutro; Liana Diamond; Sylvia Karman; Martha Norcia; Angela Watson; Annie Bevad; Selma Kaplan; Drew DeBiasse; Gerri Gomperts; Janet Cooke; Lisa Demberg; my daughter-in-law, Lauren Karp; and my daughter, Sarah Karp Charles. Thank you all for your insight, your feedback, and your brutal honesty.

I also want to acknowledge the author Bonnie Garmus. Somewhere between my fourth and fifth draft, I read *Lessons in Chemistry*, and it inspired me. I've thanked Bonnie, and now I'm making my appreciation public.

Special thanks to Ken Mekeel, NYPD (Ret.) and to Haywood Talcove, CEO of LexisNexis Special Services. Back when Maggie was in high school, there was no Google, and LexisNexis was at the forefront of connecting individuals to global computer databases. Ken and Woody helped me make sure that Maggie's deep dive into Connie's background was in line with 1997 technology.

Thanks also to Gabe Diamond, Bill Neill, Alan Mosoff, Neal Smoller, Dr. Douglas Heller, Neil Ginsberg, Steve Norcia, Gary Pearl, Dennis Diamond, and Bob Beatty for your input, expertise, and support.

Thanks, as always, to Josh Stanton, Anthony Goff, and the entire team at Blackstone Publishing, most especially Stephanie Stanton, Josie Woodbridge, Bryan Barney, Sean Thomas, Courtney Vatis, and Emi Battaglia.

Heartfelt thanks to January LaVoy, the gifted narrator who brought my characters to life on the *Don't Tell Me How to Die* audiobook. Her interpretation added layers to the characters that even I hadn't fully realized were there.

Thank you to my assistant, Bill Harrison; my go-to designer, Dennis Woloch; my web magicians, Maddee James and Riley Mack at Xuni.com; and at WME, the unflappable Cashen Conroy and the man who has guided me through fifteen books, Mel Berger.

There are five people who made major contributions to this book who deserve standalone credits:

Jeremy Perrott. Jeremy has an unparalleled talent for thinking outside the box. When this book was in its nascency, he pushed me to places I dared not go and single-handedly made it more challenging to write and much more gratifying to read. Thanks, mate.

Michael Carr. A skilled rock climber, martial arts master, and blues harmonica player, Michael is also the most insightful, most committed editor I've ever collaborated with. And, as you can see by the fact that he let me end that last sentence with a preposition, he knows how to be flexible when working with a writer who likes to break the rules.

Laura Russom. Tough, smart, and brilliantly innovative, Laura is at the top of the pyramid of those young book marketers who cut their teeth on technology and can navigate the ever-changing digital landscape. A force to be reckoned with, she can sum up her goals in two words: *author success*. So yes, she had me at hello.

Andy Langer. Back in the day, Andy and I worked together as a creative team hoping to make a name for ourselves in the advertising business. Twenty years into the journey, I had a midlife crisis and moved on to film, television, and murder. Andy stayed on, honed his marketing, strategic, design, and directorial skills, and worked his way up from art director to advertising legend. He is the one person I trust implicitly with everything from "Do you think this is a good idea for a book?" to "What color should I paint the kitchen?"

Danny Corcoran. A detective first grade working homicide out of Manhattan North, Danny retired from the NYPD after twenty-four years and turned to a life of crime. We work together every day. His insider knowledge of both police procedure and the criminal mind is one of the reasons so many law enforcement officers read my books and come back for more. Danny guided me through this project since it was little more than a handful of index cards. And thanks to his years of experience working on the NYPD's elite Hostage Negotiation Team, he was there to talk me down from every ledge of self-doubt I found myself climbing.

During the course of writing this book, my dog Kylie (who is the namesake for Detective Kylie MacDonald in my NYPD Red series) crossed the Rainbow Bridge. I write better when there's a warm body at my feet, snoring like a freight train, so I looked for a new canine muse/distraction/reason-to-get-out-of-my-chair-and-go-outside. I found Charlie in Texas. He's a middle-aged, scared-of-his-own-shadow Australian cattle dog mix, who loves his new situation but can't figure out why I'd rather tap on a keyboard than rub his belly.

And, of course, my family: Emily, Adam, Lauren, Zach, Sarah, and Jim. I've been blessed to have their support always, no matter where my what-should-I-do-next, Energizer Bunny writer's brain takes me.

Finally, a loving farewell to my aunt, Pearl Ziffer Diamond, who passed a few weeks shy of her ninety-eighth birthday. She read everything I ever wrote, tuned out the bad words, and called me every few chapters to tell me I was the best writer ever and that I should keep on writing because people need more great books.

Familial bias aside, it's the kind of inspiration that keeps guys like me looking forward to the next chapter. Thanks, Pearl. I love you, love you, love you, and miss you, miss you, miss you every day.

Marshall Karp
November 2024